Fab Confessions of Georgia Nicolson

Vol. 3

Find out more about Georgia at www.georgianicolson.com

'*... and that's when it fell off in my hand.*' was first published in Great Britain
in hardback by HarperCollins *Children's Books* in 2004
'*... and that's when it fell off in my hand.*' was first published in paperback in 2005
'*... then he ate my boy entrancers.*' was first published in Great Britain
in hardback by HarperCollins *Children's Books* in 2005
'*... then he ate my boy entrancers.*' was first published in paperback in 2006
Published in this two-in-one edition by HarperCollins *Children's Books* in 2011
HarperCollins *Children's Books* is a division of HarperCollins*Publishers* Ltd,
77-85 Fulham Palace Road, Hammersmith, London W6 8JB

1

ISBN 978-0-00-741202-0

Printed and bound in England by Clays Ltd, St Ives plc

'...and that's when it fell off in my hand.'

A Note from Georgia

Dear Chumettes,

Bonsoir!!! I am writing to you from my "imagination den" (or my bed as some people call it), just to say how much I hope you like "...and that's when it fell off in my hand." Interestingly, the Hamburger-a-gogo types (who I suspect may be a button short of a cardigan) called my book "Away Laughing on a Fast Camel". They said that "...and that's when it fell off in my hand." sounds too rude.

They are indeed weird, but what you have to take into account is that they don't really speak English as such. For instance "fag" only means homosexualist in their land. It doesn't mean cigarette. So when I wrote that "Alison Bummer lit up a fag", they said they thought that was "kind of cruel" because they thought she was setting fire to a gay person. I think that illustrates what I am up against.

Anyway, my little chums, I have spent many happy minutes... er... hours writing this and there were a lot of other things I could have been doing, believe me. Juan and Carlos – my imaginary maidservants – could have spent time amusing me, but I said (in my mind), "No, Juan and Carlos! Put down your guitars! Stop plucking! I must write another book for my lovely fans."

That is how much I love you all.

A LOT.

I do.

I am not exaggerating.

I LOVE YOU ALL.

Georgia xxxxxxx

p.s. But I am not on the turn.

This work of near geniosity is dedicated to my family: Mutti, Vati, Soshie, John, Eduardo delfonso, Hons, Libbs, Millie, Arrow, Jolly and the chickens. Especial love and sympathy to Kimbo and I am sorry about the enormous nunga-nunga gene. Gidday to the Kiwi-a-gogo branch, and greetings, earthlings, to the Isle of Wight mob. Big LUUUUURVE to my mates even though I sometimes feel they do not appreciate the genius wot I am. Philippa Mary Hop Pringle, Jools and the Mogul, Jimjams, Elton, Jeddbox, Jo Good(ish), Lozzer, Dear Geoff (but it's huge) Thompson, Alan D., Gypsy Dave, Kim and Sandy, Downietrousers and his lovely wife, Mrs H and partner, MizzMorgan, Phil (don't, well I won't) Knight and his fabby Viking bride, Ruth, The Cock and family, Rosie, Sheila, Barbara, Christine and all the Ace Crew from Parklands. Love to Chris (the organ) and to Dezzer the Vicar and young Phil and all of the merry band of St Nicolas. To Baggy Aggiss and Jenny and Simon and of course Candy, to the Hewlings with love. Love to Black Dog and a special plea: please can I have a go at the joystick. Please. Loads of love and gratitude to Clare and Gillon.

And a special thanks to HarperCollins, now my worldwide family, with big kisses to Gillie and Sally in the UK and an especial thank you to the remarkable Alix Reid. Thanks also to the very talented team in the US... Finally muchos thankus to the thousands of really groovy and fab (if somewhat insane) types who have written to me and told me how much they like my books. Goodbye. Oh no, just a minute, thank you to everyone who bought *Dancing in my Nuddy-Pants* and made it #1 on the *New York Times* bestseller list. How groovy is that? It means I can swank around with my award at parties and so on. Although I have to say it's not easy wearing a necklace that is a fourteen-pound pyramid on a chain. But hey, that is the price of fame. (Or you might say it's the price of stupidity as the award is meant to stand on a shelf and isn't really a necklace.)

Alone, all aloney, on my owney

Saturday March 5th

11:00 a.m. as the crow flies

Grey skies, grey cluds, grey knickers.

I can't believe my knickers are grey, but it is typico of my life. My mutti put my white lacy knickers in the wash with Vati's voluminous black shorts and now they are grey.

If there was a medal for craposity in the mutti department, she would win it hands down.

I am once again wandering lonely as a clud through this Vale of Tears.

I wish there was someone I could duff up but I have no one to blame. Except God, and although He is everywhere at once, He is also invisible. (Also, the last person who tried to duff God up was Satan, and he ended up standing on his head in poo with hot swords up his bum-oley.)

11:20 a.m.

This is my fabulous life: the Sex God left for Whakatane last month and he has taken my heart with him.

11:25 a.m.

Not literally, of course, otherwise there would be a big hole in my nunga-nungas.

11:28 a.m.

And also I would be dead. Which quite frankly would be a blessing in disguise.

12:00

It is soooo boring being brokenhearted. My eyes look like little piggie eyes from crying. Which makes my nose look ginormous.

Still, at least I am a lurker-free zone. Although with my luck there will be a lurker explosion any minute.

Alison Bummer once had a double yolker on her neck; she had a big spot and it had a baby spot growing on top of it.

I'll probably get that.

12:05 p.m.

Phoned my very bestest pally, Jas.

"Jas, it's me."

"What?"

"Jas, you don't sound very pleased to hear from me."

"Well... I would be, but it's only five minutes since you last phoned and Tom is just telling me about this thing you can do. You go off into the forest and—"

"This hasn't got anything to do with badgers, has it?"

"Well... no, not exactly, it's a wilderness course and you learn how to make fire and so on."

Oh great balls of *merde* here we go, off into the land of the terminally insane, i.e. Jasland. I said as patiently as I could because I am usually nice(ish) to the disadvantaged, "You are going off on a course to learn how to make fire?"

"Yes, exciting, eh?"

"Why do you have to go on a course to learn how to open a box of matches?"

"You can't use matches."

"Why not?"

"Because it's a wilderness course."

"No, wrong, Jas, it's a crap course where people are too mean to give you any matches."

She did that sighing business.

"Look, Georgia, I know you're upset about Robbie going off to Kiwi-a-gogo land."

"I am."

"And you not having a boyfriend or anything."

"Yes, well..."

"And, you know, being all lonely, with no one to really care about you."

"Yes, all right Jas, I know all th—"

"And the days stretching ahead of you without any meaning and—"

"Jas, shut up."

"I'm only trying to say that—"

"That is not shutting up, Jas. It is going on and on."

She got all huffy and Jasish.

"I must go now. Tom has got some knots to show me."

I was in the middle of saying, "Yes I bet he has..." in an ironic and *très amusant* way when she brutally put the phone down.

12:30 p.m.

Alone, all aloney.

On my owney.

The house is empty, too. Everyone is out at Grandad's for lunch.

I was nearly made to go until I pointed out that I am in mourning and unable to eat anything because of my heartbreak.

Mine is a pathetico tale that would make anyone who had a heart weep, but that does not include Vati. He said he would gladly leave me behind because talking to me made him realise the fun he had had when he accidentally fell into the open sewers in India.

1:15 p.m.

Looking out of my bedroom window. Entombed in my room for ever. Like in that book, *The Prisoner of Brenda,* or whatever it's called.

Except I could go out if I wanted.

But I don't want to.

I may never go out again.

Ever.

1:30 p.m.

This is boring. I've been cooped up for about a million years.

What time is it?

Phoned Jas.

"Jas?"

"Oh God."

"What time is it?"

"What?"

"Why are you saying 'what'? I merely asked you a civil question."

"Why don't you look at your own clock?"

"Jas, have you noticed I am very, very upset and that my life is over? Have you noticed that?"

"Yes I have, because you have been on the phone telling me every five minutes for a month."

"Well, I am soo sorry if it's too much trouble to tell your very bestest pal the time. Perhaps my eyes are too swollen from tears to see the clock."

"Well are they?"

"Yes."

"Well how come you could see to dial my number?"

Mrs Huffy Knickers was so unreasonable.

"Anyway, I'm not your bestest pal any more, Nauseating P. Green is your bestest pal now that you rescued her from the clutches of the Bummer twins."

I slammed down the phone.

Brilliant. Sex Godless and now friend to P. Green, that well-known human goldfish.

Sacré bloody *bleu* and triple *merde.*

And poo.

Oh Robbie, how could you leave me and go off to the other (incredibly crap) side of the world? What has Kiwi-a-gogo land got that I haven't? Besides forty million sheep.

I think I'll play the tape he gave me again. It's all I have left to remind me of him and our love. That will never die.

2:20 p.m.

Good grief, now I am really depressed. His song about Van Gogh, "Oh No, It's Me Again", has to be one of the most depressing songs ever written.

2:30 p.m.

Second only to track four, "Swim Free", about a dolphin that gets caught in a fishing net, and every time we eat a tuna sandwich we're eating Sammy the dolphin. Fortunately I never eat tuna, as Mum mostly stocks up on Jammy Dodgers and there is definitely nothing that was ever alive in them.

2:35 p.m.

If I am brutally honest, which I try to be, the only fly in the ointmosity of the Sex God was that he could be a bit on the serious side. Always raving on about the environment and so on. Actually, his whole family is obsessed with vegetables. Let's face it, his brother Tom (otherwise known as Hunky) has chosen one to be his girlfriend!

Hahahahahaha. That's a really good joke about Jas that I will never tell her but secretly think of when she flicks her fringe about or shows me her Rambler's badge.

I will never forget Robbie, though. The way he used to nibble my lips. He will always be Nip Libbler Extraordinaire.

2:50 p.m.

Oh no, hang on. The Sex God used to snog my ears. It was Dave the Laugh who enticed me into the ways of nip libbling. Which reminds me. I wonder why he hasn't phoned me?

Did I remember to tell him that I was thinking about letting him be my unserious boyfriend?

I should punish him, really. It was, after all, he who introduced me to the Cosmic Horn when I was happy just having the Particular Horn for the Sex God.

2:55 p.m.

Phoned Rosie.

"RoRo."

"*Bonsoir.*"

"I am having the cosmic droop."

"Well, fear not, my pally, because I have *le* plan *de la* genius."

"What is it, and does it involve the police?"

Rosie laughed in a not-very-reassuring way if you like the sound of sane laughter. She said, "I'm having a party for Sven's return from Swedenland next Saturday."

"What kind of party is it going to be?"

"Teenage werewolf."

"Oh no."

"Oh yes."

"Good grief."

"Bless you."

"Rosie, what has Sven been doing while he's been away, working for Santa Claus on a reindeer farm?"

"He hasn't been to Lapland."

"How can you be sure? Geoggers is not your best subject, is it?"

"Well, excuse me if I'm right, but it isn't yours either, Gee. You missed out the whole of Germany on your world map."

"Easily done."

"Not when you're copying from the atlas. Anyway, I must go. I have a costume to make. See you at Stalag 14 on Monday."

Bathroom

3:00 p.m.

Sometimes I amaze myself with my courageosity. Even though I have been through the mangle of love and beyond, I can still be bothered to cleanse and tone.

3:30 p.m.

But the effort of a high-quality beauty regime has made me exhausted. I am going to go to my room and read my

book on my inner dolphin or whatever it's called. Anyway it is to do with peace and so on. I may even make a little shrine to Robbie to celebrate our undying love. Even though he hasn't bothered to write to me since he went to Kiwi-a-gogo land.

3:45 p.m.

Hmm. I have covered all the cosmic options with my shrine: I've put a photo of Robbie in the middle of some shiny paper, it has a figure of Buddha on one side of the beloved Sex God, and one of Jesus and a little dish for offerings on the other. Also, when I was accidentally going through Mum's knicker drawer, I found some incense stuff. I don't like to think what she and Vati do with it: some horrific snogging ritual they learned in Katmandu or something.

3:50 p.m.

I had to BluTack Jesus on to my dressing table because Libby has been using him as a boyfriend for scuba-diving Barbie and one of his feet is missing.

4:00 p.m.

Phoned Rosie.

"RoRo, explain this if you can with your wisdomosity. I only had the Particular Horn for SG before I met Dave the Laugh and then Dave the Laugh lured me into the web of the General and Cosmic Horns."

RoRo said, "He's groovy, isn't he, Dave the Laugh?"

"Yeah... sort of."

"Shall I ask him on Saturday?"

"It doesn't matter to me, because I am eschewing him with a firm hand."

"A nod is as good as a wink to a blind badger."

What in the name of Miss Wilson's moustache is she talking about?

My bedroom, in my bed of pain (quite literally)

10:00 p.m.

Libby's bottom is bloody freezing. If I didn't know better, I'd say she'd been sitting in a bucket of frozen mackerel. Still, she has been round to Grandad's, so anything could have happened; he is, after all, the man who set fire to himself with his own pipe.

10:05 p.m.

She might have a cold botty and be mad as a snake, but she looks so lovely when she's asleep and she is my little sister. I really love her. I kissed her on her forehead and without opening her eyes she slapped me and said, "Cheeky monkey." I don't know what goes on in her head. (Thank God.)

10:15 p.m.

Do the Prat Poodles deliberately wait until I'm drifting off before they start their yowling fest? What is the matter with them? Have they been startled by a vole?

I looked out the window. Mr and Mrs Next Door have put a kennel outside in the garden for the Prat Poodles, but the poodley twits are too stupid and frightened to go into it. They are barking at it and running away from it. How pathetic is that? It's only a kennel, you fools. What kind of dog is frightened of a kennel?

10:20 p.m.

Oh, I get it!! Angus is in their kennel. I just saw his huge paw come out and biff one of the Prat Poodles on the snout. Supercat strikes again!!!

Hahahaha and ha di hahaha, he is a *très très amusant* cat. He has set up a little cat flatlet in the Prats' kennel. It's his pied-à-terre. Or his paw-de-terre.

10:25 p.m.

Uh-oh. Mr Next Door is on the warpath. Surely it must be against the laws of humanity to sell pyjamas like his. He looks like a striped hippopotamus, only not so attractive and svelte.

He's trying to poke Angus out with a stick. Good luck, Mr Hippo.

Angus thinks it's the stick game. He LIKES being prodded with a stick, it reminds him of his Scottish roots. Next thing is, he will get hold of it and start wrestling with Mr Next Door to try to get it away from him.

10:28 p.m.

Yes, yes, he's clamped on the end! Mr Next Door will never get him off by shaking it around. He will be there going round and round the garden for the rest of his life.

10:33 p.m.

Sometimes for a laugh Angus lets go of the stick and Mr Next Door crashes backwards. Then Angus strolls over and gets hold of the stick again. I could watch all night long... uh-oh, Mr Next Door has seen me. He is indicating that he would like me to step downstairs. Although I think shouting and saying "bugger" at this time of night is a bit unneighbourly.

Honestly, I am like a part-time game warden and careworker for the elderly mad. I should get a net and a badge.

Mr Next Door's garden

10:40 p.m.

Mr Next Door was sensationally red as he tried to shake Angus off the end of his stick.

He said, in between wheezing and coughing, "This thing is demented, it should be put down!!"

Oh yeah, fat chance – Angus nearly had the vet's arm off the last time he was in surgery. The vet has asked us to not come back again.

However, I used my natural talents of diplomosity with

Mr Mad. I spoke clearly and loudly. "You need another broom to beat him off with."

I said again, "YOU NEED ANOTHER BROOM TO BEAT HIM OFF WITH."

He said, "There's no need to shout, I'm not deaf."

And I said, "Pardon?"

Which is an excellent display of humourosity in anyone's book. Except Mr Mad's. In the end, I lassoed Angus with the clothesline and dragged him home and locked him in the airing cupboard. Dad's "smalls" (not) will be in tatters by morning, but you can't have everything.

Sunday March 6th

Dreamed about the Sex God and our marriage. It was really groovy and gorgey. I wore a long white veil, and when I was at the altar SG pushed it back and said, "Why... Georgia, you're beautiful." And I didn't go cross-eyed or speak in a stupid German accent. I even remembered to put my tongue at the back of my teeth to stop my nostrils flaring when I smiled. The church was packed with loads of friends, and everyone looked nice and relatively normal. Even Vati had shaved the tiny badger off his chin, and Uncle Eddie had a hat on so that he didn't look quite so much like a boiled egg in a suit.

The choir was singing "Isn't She Lovely?" and for some reason the choir was made up of chipmunks and Libby was in charge of them. It was sweet, even if the singing was a bit high-pitched.

And then the vicar said, "Is there anyone here who knows of any reason why these two should not be joined in matrimony?"

I was gazing into the dark blue of Sex God's eyes, dreamy dreamy. Then from the back, Jackie Bummer (smoking a fag) shouted, "I've got a reason: Georgia has got extreme red-bottomosity."

And Alison Bummer (smoking two fags) joined in, "Yeah, and the Cosmic Horn."

And I could feel myself getting hotter and hotter, and I couldn't breathe. I woke up crying out to find Libby sitting on my nungas with Charlie Horse and singing, "Smelly the elepan bagged her trunk and said goodguy to the circus."

8:15 a.m.

It's only 8:15 a.m. On Sunday. I want to sleep for ever and ever and never wake up to life as a red-bottomed spinster.

8:30 a.m.

Maybe if I make a special plea to Baby Jesus for clemency, he will hear me. If I promise to put my red bottom aside with a firm hand, he might send the SG back to me.

8:35 a.m.

I can't pray here – Baby Jesus won't be able to hear a thing above Libby's singing. Maybe I should make the supreme sacrifice and go to God's house. Call-me-Arnold the vicar would be beside himself with joy; he would probably prepare a fatted whatsit... pensioner.

9:05 a.m.

What should I wear for church? Keep it simple and reverential, I think.

9:36 a.m.

My false eyelashes are fab.

9:37 a.m.

Maybe I shouldn't wear them, though, because it might give the wrong impression. It might imply that I'm a bit superficial. I'll take them off.

9:38 a.m.

It has taken me ages to stick them on, though. Anyway, if God can read your every thought because of his impotence ability, He will know that I really want to wear my eyelashes and have only taken them off in case He didn't like them. They didn't have false eyelashes in ye olde Godde tymes so it is a moot point.

Perhaps He will think they are my real ones.

9:40 a.m.

But that would make Him not an impotent all-wise God, that would make Him a really dim God. Who can't even tell the difference between real and false eyelashes, even though He has been watching someone put them on for the last half an hour.

And I say that with all reverencosity.

Anyway, surely He is looking at the starving millions, not sneaking around in my bedroom.

In the loo

9:50 a.m.

Is He watching me now? Erlack.

In the street outside my house

10:10 a.m.

Quiet, apart from Mr and Mrs Across the Road's house. As I passed by, there was loads of shouting and yowling. I hope Mr Across the Road is not ill-treating Angus's children. He looks like a kittykat abuser to me. And he has a very volatile temperament. The least thing sets him off. He's like my vati. He appeared shouting and yelling at his kitchen door as I went by to God's house. At first I thought he was wearing a fur coat and hat until I realised the coat and hat were moving. He was completely covered in Angus's offspring.

Naomi as usual is not taking a blind bit of notice. She is a bit of a slutty mother: mostly she just lolls around in the kitchen window enticing Angus with her bottom antics.

Last week the kittykats, who are ADORABLE, if a bit on the bonkers side, burrowed their way under the fence and were larking around in Mr and Mrs Next Door's ornamental pond.

I said to Mutti, "I didn't know the Next Doors had flying fish in their pond."

And she said, "They haven't."

The flying fish turned out to be goldfish that the kittykats were biffing about in the air. When the mad old next-door loons noticed and came raging out of the house, the kittykats cleared off back under the fence. I don't know what the fuss is about: they got the boring old goldfish back into the pond. Even the one caught in the hedge. Anyway, as punishment, the kitties were caged up in the rabbit run. Not for long it seems.

Mr Across the Road was trying to get the kittykats off him, but they had dug their claws in. They are sooo clever.

He shouted at me, "They're going, you know. They are going."

Rave on, rave on. I bet he loves them really.

Church

Call-me-Arnold was alarmingly glad to see me. He kept calling me his child. Which I am clearly not. My vati is an embarrassment in the extreme, but he is not an albino. Call-me-Arnold is so blondy that his head is practically transparent.

I really gave up the will to carry on when Call-me-Arnold got his guitar out to sing some incredibly crap song about the seasons. Why can't we just sing something depressing like we do at school and get on with it? I even had to shake hands with people. But I must remember this is God's house and also that I am asking for a cosmic favour.

At the end, after most people had filed out, I noticed that some people were going to a side chapel and lighting a candle and then praying.

That must be the cosmic request shop. Fab! I would go light a candle and plead for mine and Robbie's love.

I went up and got my candle and lit it, ready for action, but an elderly lady was kneeling right in front of the display thing. I could hear her mumbling. She had a headscarf on. On and on she went, mumble mumble. Bit greedy, really. She must have had a whole list of stuff to ask for.

Ho hum, pig's bum.

I knelt down behind her because I was feeling a bit exhausted. I had, after all, been up since the crack of dawn. (Well, eight fifteen.)

I was holding my candle and thinking and thinking about the Sex God and our love that knew no bounds and stretched across the Pacific Ocean. Or was it the Australian Bite? Anyway, our love was stretching across some big watery thing.

I think I might actually have nodded off for a little zizz, because I came round to see a small inferno ablaze in front of me. Oh hell's teeth, I had accidentally set fire to an elderly pensioner! The end of her headscarf was blazing merrily and she hadn't even noticed.

I started beating the flames out with my handbag. I was trying to help, but she started hitting me back with her handbag. Before I knew it, I was in a handbag fight.

11:45 a.m.

I did try to point out that long dangly scarves on the very elderly could be considered a health hazard around naked flames. But Call-me-Arnold wasn't calling me his child any more and he didn't ask if he would see me next week.

Which he won't.

Lunchtime

I am exhausted by trying to get along with the Lord.

Monday March 7th
Back to Stalag 14

As a mark of my widowosity, I wore dark glasses and a black armband. Also I found a black feather from Mutti's sad feather boa that she wears if I don't spot her first. I stuck that in the side of my beret, which I pulled down right over my ears.

I was walking along with Jas and I said, "Even in the depths of my sadnosity I think I have a touch of the Jacqueline Onassis about me."

She said, "Why? Did she look like a prat as well?"

A quick duffing up showed her the error of her ways.

Oh God, oh Goddy God God, a whole day of Stalag 14.

Assembly

Our revered and amazingly porky Headmistress Slim rambled on about exams and achievement and said wisely, "Now, in conclusion, girls, I would say, it's not all about winning, it's how you play the game."

What game? What in the name of Ethelred the Unready's pantyhose is she talking about? As we filed off to the science block, Hawkeye was in a super-duper strop for some reason. She made me remove my armband and she was marching up and down looking at people like a Doberman, only much taller. And not a dog. She alarmed a first former so much that the first former fell into a holly bush and had to be fished out and sent to the nurse to calm down.

I said to Rosie, "I think widowhood has toughened me up. If Hawkeye gets on my case I am going to say to her, 'Hawkeye, sir, when you have suffered the torments of love like I have, you will not give a flying pig's bum about your Latin homework. Romulus and Remus could have been brought up by ostriches for all I care.'"

Rosie said, "Yeah right, well, let's see what happens when she gives you double detention."

"Do you know what I saw on TV the other night? Ostriches fall in love with human beings. On ostrich farms they go all gooey and even more dim when humans come to feed them. They try to snog them."

"Ostriches try to snog humans?"

"Yes."

"*Non.*"

"*Mais oui, mon petit idiot, c'est vrai.* It is very very *vrai.*"

"How can they snog when they have beaks?"

"You are being a bit beakist, Rosie."

Lunchtime

The Ace Gang are going on and on about the teenage werewolf party. Jas said, "Tom and I are going to wear matching false ears!" And then she had an uncontrollable laughing spaz.

I said, "Jas, when was the last time you saw a teenage werewolf with false ears?"

That made her stop snorting like a fool. She was all shuffily on the knicker toaster (radiator). "Well... it's, well... I mean..."

Rosie – who is in an alarmingly good mood now that Sven is winging his way home on his sleigh – slapped me on the back and said, "What do you get when you cross a mouse with an elephant?"

We all just looked at her and she put her glasses on sideways and said, "Massive holes in the skirting board!"

I feel like a bean in a bikini, tossed around on the sea of life. Set apart from my mates because of heartbreakosity. I love them but how childish they seem, chatting on about false eyebrows. I may never wear extra body hair ever again.

3:00 p.m.

We should be having Hawkeye for English but she is too busy torturing people, so Miss Wilson will be taking most of our lessons this term. She is a tremendous div, so English will be more or less a free period.

Oh, what larks! We are doing *Macbeth* as our set play. Although Miss Wilson says we are not allowed to say its name: we have to call it "The Scottish Play", because it's bad luck to say its name. As I said to Rosie and Jools, "Hurrah! A play about blokes in tights talking in Och Aye language for a thousand years."

We've all been dished out parts and, tragically, Jas is going to be Lady MacScottishplay. Rosie, Jools and Ellen are the three witches and I am some complete twit in tights called Macduff. Nauseating P. Green is my wife, Lady Macduff. She is thrilled and keeps mooning over at me.

I don't see how I am supposed to be a bloke, because they are – as we all know – a complete mystery.

4:15 p.m.

On the way home Jas was looking at her hand and going, "Out damn spot."

I said, "It's not the spot on your hand you have to worry about, Jas, it's the huge lurker lurking on your chin."

That shut her up and got her feeling about.

Actually, she hasn't got a lurker on her chin, but if she goes on fingering it long enough she will have.

Home (ha)

5:00 p.m.

Oh brilliant, Angus has gone into my wardrobe and found some of my knickers to attack. He was ambling out of my room with his head through one of the legs like some sort of Arab sheikh. I kicked at him but he dodged out of the way. He was purring really loudly; he loves it when you get rough with him. He is a good example of the benefits of rough love. I should really give him a good kicking every day.

Kitchen

5:30 p.m.

Oh yum yum and *quelle surprise*, we are having *les delicieuses* fish fingers and frozen peas for our tea! I am sure that I am developing rickets: my legs look distinctly bendy. Vati came

in in a hilariously good mood. He kissed me on the head even though I tried to dodge him. I said, "Father, I need my own space and frankly you are in it."

He just laughed and said, "I've just seen Colin and he and Sandy are having a *Lord of the Rings* party and we're all invited."

Mutti said, "What a hoot."

I said with great meaningosity, "Vati, I will never – and I repeat, never – be wearing an elf's outfit in this lifetime, and for the sake of any sensitive people on the planet – that is, me – I beg you not to consider green tights."

He just smiled and said, "I know you are secretly very thrilled, Georgia."

He and Mutti laughed. And Libby joined in with a very alarming sort of laughing. Like a mad Santa Claus and pig combined. "Hohohogoggyhoggyhog."

I don't know what they teach her at nursery school, but it's not how to be normal.

Only 6:30 p.m.

I wonder what time it is in Kiwi-a-gogo land? They are twenty-four hours ahead of us and it's Monday here, so it must be Tuesday there.

6:35 p.m.

Does that mean that SG knows what I will be wearing for the teenage werewolf party before I do?

Not that I will be going.

Will I?

I will be the last to know as usual.

Oh Baby Jesus and your cohorts, please make something really great happen. Otherwise I am going to bed. But I will wait for half an hour because I trust in your ultimate goodnosity.

7:35 p.m.

It's not much to ask, is it? But oh no, Baby Jesus is just too busy to make anything interesting happen. Maybe he is holding the pensioner inferno against me.

In the loo

Sitting in the loo of life contemplating my navel.

My navel sticks out a bit. Is it supposed to do that? I hope it's not unravelling. That would be the final straw.

Vati keeps books in the loo. How disgusting is that?

Pooing and reading. What is he reading? It's called *Live and Let Die*. How true.

8:30 p.m.

No one has bothered to ring me. I wonder why Dave the Laugh hasn't phoned me? I could phone him, but that would mean he might think I am keen on him.

Which I am not.

8:45 p.m.

Vati's book is about James Bond, who is a sort of special-agent-type thing. Vati probably thinks he is like James Bond. Which he would be, if James Bond was a porky bloke with a badger attachment.

9:00 p.m.

I am in the prime of my womanhood, nunga-nungas poised and trembling (attractively). Lips puckered up and in peak condition for a snogging fest.

And I am in bed.

At nine p.m.

9:05 p.m.

Not alone for long, because my sister is now in bed with me. She has got her bedtime book for me to read to her. *Heidi.* About some girl who goes up a mountain in Swisscheeseland to live with some elderly mad bloke in lederhosen, who sadly for her is her grandfather.

I know how she feels. At least my grandad doesn't wear leather shorts. Yet.

9:15 p.m.

So far Heidi and Old Mr Mad of the Mountains have herded up goats and eaten a lot of cheese. A LOT. They are constantly eating cheese.

9:20 p.m.

Even Libby was so bored by the cheese extravaganza that she nodded off to sleep, so I slipped downstairs to phone Jas. I did it quietly because there will only be the usual tutting explosion from Vati about me using the phone if he hears me.

I whispered, "Jas?"

"Oh, it's you."

"What do you mean?"

"Well, I've got my jimmyjams on and I was reading my book about the wilderness course that Tom and I are going to go on."

"Oh I am sooooooo sorry, Jas, soooo sorry to interrupt your twig work just because I am all on my own without the comfort of human company and my life is ebbing away."

There was silence at the other end of the phone.

"Jas, are you still there?"

Her voice sounded a bit distant. "Yes."

I said, "What is that cracking noise?"

"Er..."

"You are actually playing with twigs, aren't you?"

"Well... I..."

How pathetico.

She said all swottily, "Look, I have to go. I've got my German homework to do."

"Don't bother learning their language, they are obsessed with goats."

"What are you talking about?"

"Lederhosen-a-gogo-land people are obsessed with goats... and cheese."

"Who says so?"

"It's in a book I am reading about them."

"What book?"

"It's called *Heidi*. It is utterly crap."

"*Heidi?*"

"*Jah.*"

Mrs Picky Knickers sounded all swotty and know-it-all. "*Heidi* is a children's book about a girl who lives in the Alps in Switzerland."

"Yes, and your point is?"

"That's not Germany."

"It's very near."

"You might as well say that Italy and France are the same because they are very near."

"I do say that."

"Or Italy and Greece."

"I say that as well."

"You talk rubbish."

"Yeah but I don't play with twigs like a... like a fringey thrush."

She slammed the phone down on me.

Well. She is so annoying.

But on the other hand, no one else is around to talk to.

Phoned her back.

"Jas, I'm sorry, you always hurt the one you love."

"Don't start the love thing."

"OK, but night-night."

"Night."

10:00 p.m.

Oh, I am so restless and bored. I think my mouth may be sealing over because of lack of snogging. Or shrinking. I wonder if that can happen? They say "Use It or Lose It" on all those really scary posters in the doctor's surgery, mainly for very very old people who are too lazy to walk about, and then their legs shrink, possibly. But it may be the same for lips.

10:05 p.m.

No sign of any shrinkage on the basooma front.

In the loo

11:00 p.m.

In Dad's James Bond book it says, "Bond came and stood close against her. He put a hand over each breast. But still she looked away from him out of the window. 'Not now,' she said in a low voice."

Now I am completely baffled. What in the name of arse does that mean?

A hand over each nunga?

Like a human nunga-nunga holder.

Do boys do that?

Wednesday March 9th

No letters from the Sex God.

And I haven't heard anything from Dave the Laugh either.

Still, what do I care, I am full of glaciosity for him.

I wonder if he will go to the party on Saturday. Not that I am interested, as I will be at home embroidering toilet roll holders or whatever very sad spinsters do.

Bathroom

7:30 a.m.

Oh fabulous, I have a lurking lurker on my cheek. The painters are due in this week and that is probably why I am feeling so moody.

That and the fact that my life is utterly crap.

Still, a really heavy period should cheer me up.

Maybe if I disguise the lurker with some eye pencil it will look like a beauty spot.

Breakfast

Mutti said, "Georgia, why don't you just hang a sign on your head that says, 'Have you noticed I've got a spot, everybody?'"

I tried to think of something clever to say to her but I am too tired.

8:20 a.m.

I was dragging myself out the door to another day of unnatural torture (school) when the postman arrived. It takes him about a year to get up our driveway because he tries to dodge Angus. Angus loves him. He is his little postie pal. The postie, who is not what you would call blessed in the looks department, was furtively looking around and shuffling about. I said helpfully, "Angus is off on his morning constitutional, so I am afraid you can't play with him."

The postie said, "I know what I would like to do with him and it involves a sack and a river. Here you are."

And he shoved a letter at me. Not ideal behaviour from a servant of the people I don't think.

Then I noticed it was an aerogram-type letter. For me. From Kiwi-a-gogo land. From the Sex God.

Oh joy joy joy joyitty joy joy.

And also thrice joy.

I looked at the writing. So Sex-Goddy. And it said "Georgia Nicolson" on it.

That was me.

And on the back it said:

From Robbie Jennings

R.D. 4

Pookaka lane (honestly)

Whakatane

New Zealand

That was him. The Sex God. I started skipping down the street until unfortunately I saw Mark Big Gob and his lardy mates. He doesn't even bother to look at my face, he just talks to my nungas.

Mark was leery like a leering thing and he said, "Careful,

Georgia, you don't want to knock yourself out with your jugs." And they all laughed.

Thank goodness I had worn my special sports nunga holder, or my "over-the-shoulder-boulder-holder", as Rosie calls it. At least my basoomas were nicely encased. Anyway, ha di hahahaha to Mark Big Gob – nothing could upset me today because I was filled with the joyosity of young love.

I did stop skipping though, and walked off with a dignity-at-all-times sort of walk.

But Mark still hadn't had his day; he shouted after me, "I'll carry them to school for you if you like!"

He is disgusting. And a midget lover. I don't know how I could have ever snogged him.

8:35 a.m.

Jas was stamping around outside her house going, "Oh *brrrrr,* it is so nippy noodles, *brr*!"

She had a sort of furry bonnet over her beret. I said, "You look like a crap teddy bear."

She just went on shivering and said, "Do you think we will get let off hockey because of Antarctic conditions?"

"Jas, you live, as I have always said, in the land of the

terminally deluded and criminally insane. Nothing gets us off hockey. We are at the mercy of a Storm Trooper and part-time lesbian. Miss Stamp LOVES Antarctic conditions. You can see her moustache bristling with delight when it snows."

If Jas has to wear a furry bonnet in cold weather, I don't think much of her chances of survival on her survival-type course.

Still, that is life.

Or in her case, death.

She was still going "*Brrr brr,*" but I didn't let it spoil my peachy mood.

"Jas, guess what? Something *très très magnifique* has happened at last."

"*Brrr.*"

"Shut up *brrring*, Jas."

I got out my aerogram.

"Look, it's from SG."

"What does it say?"

"I don't know."

"Why not?"

"Because I haven't opened it yet, I am savouring it."

"It's not a pie."

"I know that, Jas. Please don't annoy me. I don't want to have to beat you within an inch of your life so early in the day."

I tucked the aerogram down the front of my shirt for safe keepies as we trudged up the hill to Stalag 14. But I had a song in my heart.

"Jas, I have a song in my heart, and do you know what it is?"

But she just ran off into the cloakroom to sit on the knicker toaster for a few minutes to thaw out.

Still, I did have a song in my heart called "I Have a Letter from a Sex God in my Over-the-shoulder-boulder-holder".

Assembly

Slim told us exciting news this morning. Elvis Attwood, the most bonkers man in Christendom and part-time caretaker, is retiring. We started cheering but had to change our cheering into a sort of "For He's a Jolly Good Fellow" thing because Hawkeye was giving us her ferret eye. Slim was rambling on in her jelloid way, chins shaking like billyo.

"So, as a special thank you for all the magnificent work Mr Attwood has put in over the years, we will be having a going-away party for him. We will have music and so on, and perhaps Mr Attwood will show us how to 'get with it', as you girls say."

She laughed like a ninny. Get with it? What in the name of her enormous undergarments is she raving on about? The last time Elvis did any dancing he had to be taken to the casualty department. So every cloud has a silver lining.

I said to the Ace Gang as we trailed out of Assembly to RE, "What started out as a scheissenhausen day has turned out to be a groovy gravy day."

I am looking forward to RE because while everyone has their little snooze I can read my letter from the beloved.

RE

We all snuggled down at the back. RoRo was knitting something for the teenage werewolf party. I think it might be a full-length beard. Jools was doing her cuticles and Jas was reading her wilderness manual. She loves it because it has lots of photos of girlie swots building incomprehensible things out of twigs. Anyway, time to read my letter. Miss Wilson was beginning to ramble on about "world peace" and

asking us for our views. I didn't want to have to answer anything, I just wanted her to soothingly write stuff on the board or rave on. So I put my hand up. That startled her. I said, "Miss Wilson, I have been very troubled in my mind."

That started Rosie off in uncontrollable sniggering. Miss Wilson looked at me through her owly glasses. She is the most strangely put together person I have ever come across. Where does she get her clothes from? Did you know that you could get dresses made out of red felt with matching booties for grown-ups? She has clearly been to the circus shop that Slim buys her wrinkly elephant-tights from.

Anyway, Miss Wilson was vair vair interested in my troubled mind.

"Is it something of a theological nature, Georgia?"

"Yes indeedy, Miss Wilson. This is what is troubling me. If God is, you know, impotent..."

Miss Wilson went sensationally red, so now her head matched her booties.

"Well... er... Georgia, erm, *impotent* means not being able to have any children... I rather think you mean *omnipotent*."

"Whatever. Well, if He is, does that mean that He is with you even when you are in the lavatory?"

Miss Wilson started rambling on about God not being really a bloke like other geezers but more of a spiritual whatsit. Hmmm. She has a very soothing manner. Jools had finished her cuticles and was having a little zizz on her pencil case.

I opened my letter with trembly hands. I wondered how long it would take me to fly to Kiwi-a-gogo land.

Dear Georgia,

Sorry it has taken me so long to write to you but it has been *full-on* since I got here. The countryside around here is *fantastic*, it's all *formed from* volcanic activity. There are volcanoes near here that are still live and there is a lot *of* geothermal activity.

Yesterday when we were eating our lunch outside, the table was heaving and lurching about. That's because the molten steam trapped beneath the Earth's crust makes the ground move and shake around. It was amazing! The sheep were going backwards and *forwards*, and the trees were going up and down. There *are bore fields around the whole area where they tap the steam and make electricity out of it. The lads took me to see a rogue bore called Old Faithful that explodes every fifteen minutes.*

Rogue bore? He could have stayed here and just sat still in our school for a few minutes; it's full of rogue bores. Sadly, they do not explode.

And that is all the letter was about, just loads and loads of stuff about vegetables and sheep and lurching tables. Not one thing about missing me.

I couldn't believe it.

At the end, it said,

Well, I must go, some of the guys are going down to the river. It has natural hot springs that run through it. We go down there at night and lie in it playing our guitars.

He was going down to a river and he was going to lie in it. That was the big nightspot.

I wrote a note to Jas.

Jas,

SG just talked about opossums and rogue bores and a river and then at the end he said, "I hope you are well and happy. You're a great girl. Gidday. Robbie x"

One measly kiss.

11:00 a.m.

After RE I was in a state of shock. I could hardly eat my cheesy snacks. We sat on the knicker toaster in the Blodge lab and the Ace Gang had a look at the letter.

Jas said, "Well, he said you were a great girl."

I just looked at her.

"And it's really interesting about the molten steam and the geothermal... stuff."

I just looked at her again.

Rosie said, "Forget him, he's obsessed with marsupials. When he comes back he'll be playing a didgeridoo and be like Rolf Harris. Move on."

4:15 p.m.

Walking home with Jas. I said to her, "I cannot believe my

life. I've kept reading SG's letter over and over but it still rambles on about steam and vegetables."

Jas looked thoughtful (crikey) and then she said something almost bordering on the very nearly not mad. She said, "Maybe it's in code."

"In code?"

"Yes, so that, erm, the customs people, or say it fell into the wrong hands, like your mum and dad... well, so that they couldn't tell what he had really written."

I gave her a hug. "Jas, I am sorry that I ever doubted your sanity. You are a genius of the first water."

In my room

4:45 p.m.

So let's see.

5:30 p.m.

If I underline every fourth word, that might work.

6:00 p.m.

I think I have got it! Phoned Jas.

"Jas, I think I've got it."

"Go on then."

"OK. It's sort of in shorthand even when it is decoded but... anyway... this is what it says:

'Dear Georgia. Me, you fantastic. When we were heaving and lurching about it was amazing. Me explodes every fifteen minutes. At night me in it playing you. You're great. Love Robbie.'"

There was a silence. Then Jas said, "Did you say, 'me explodes every fifteen minutes'?"

"Yes... keen, isn't he?"

In bed

7:00 p.m.

It wasn't in code. It was just a really, really crap letter.

Nothing can be worse than how I feel now.

7:30 p.m.

Wrong. I cannot believe my vati. He has sold our normal(ish) car and bought a Robin Reliant. You know, one of those really really sad cars that only the very mad buy? It has got three wheels. It is a three-wheeled car. I shouted down to Vati, "Why?"

He was all preened-up and dadish.

He shouted back up, "It's an antique."

I tried logic with him. "Vati, sometimes antiques are interesting – the crown jewels, for instance, they interest me – but this is just a really old crap car that only has three wheels."

He was polishing it. It's red and it has a racing strip.

Vati said, "Hop in and I'll take you for a spin."

As if.

Dad started rustling around in the boot and shouted to Mum, "Connie, come on, I'll take you and Libby for a ride in the Sexmobile."

He is so ludicrously pleased with himself.

And Mutti was as bad. All dillydollyish and also she had a tiny skirt on. At least she had on a skirt though, unlike Libby, who was in the nuddy-pants.

8:00 p.m.

In the end they all went off, including Angus, who I actually thought was driving the car at first. He had his paws on the steering wheel and was looking straight ahead. Even though I am on the rack of love, it did make me laugh. Then Vati's head popped up. Not content with the humiliatorosity of the Robin Reliant clown car, Vati also bought a Second World War flying helmet and goggles.

As they drove off, he wound down the window and shouted, "Chocks away!!!"

What does Mutti see in him? He must have been like this when she met him. Which means, in essence, that she likes porky blokes with badgers on their chins who are clearly mental.

At this rate I am going to spend the rest of my life with them, so I should get used to it, I suppose.

8:05 p.m.

I can't. I would rather plunge my head into a basket of whelks.

8:10 p.m.

What is it with boys?

I may do some research on them for my part in *MacUseless* or *The Och Aye Play*.

I may as well, as my so-called mates can't be bothered to ring me.

8:30 p.m.

Phone rang.

If it's Dave the Laugh, I am going to give him the full force of my glaciosity. I hate boys.

It was Rosie.

"Gee?"

"Oh hi, I'm glad you rang because I am sooo—"

"Did you hear about the dog who went into a pub and said to the barman, 'Can I have a pint and a bag of crisps please?'"

"Rosie, I don't—"

"The barman said, 'Blimey, that's brilliant. There's a circus in town. You should go and get a job.'"

"Rosie, I have—"

"And the dog said, 'Why? Do they need electricians?'"

And she slammed down the phone.

I am seriously worried about her dwindling sanity. I'd just got back upstairs to my bed of pain when the phone rang again. Why can't we have a portable fandango thing or, alternatively, a servant called Juan who answers it?

Is it so much to ask?

This time it was Ellen.

"Georgia, it's me. I was, you know... for the party. Well, do you... think I... well, if you were me, would you or would you just kind of, you know... or not?"

What in the name of Hitler's pants and matching bra set is she on about?

"Ellen, how can I put this? What in the name of arse are you talking about?"

"Dave the Laugh, should I, you know, well, would you?"

Oh marvellous, I have to be Wise Woman of the Forest for my mates. Also it reminded me that if Ellen found out about the Dave the Laugh snogging scenarios, there might well be fisticuffs at dawn.

Still, I am not God and also I am very very busy with my own problems. My lurking lurker has to be dealt with before it makes a surprise appearance. Not that I will ever be going out again anyway. My lurker could grow to the size of my head if it wanted to. Erlack, now I feel sick.

Ellen was rambling on and on about Dave the Laugh and how to entice him and so on. In the end, in sheer desperadoes, I said, "Look, do you know why Dave the Laugh is called, you know, Dave the Laugh?"

Ellen said, "Er. No, why is that?"

I am being pushed to the limits of my nicosity, but I tried, God knows I tried.

"He's called that because he likes a laugh, and well, to be frank, Ellen, you are a bit lacking *vis-à-vis* the laughometer scale."

9:00 p.m.

I wish when I am speaking complete and utter bollocks people would not take me seriously. It's not my fault that I have advised Ellen to develop an infectious laugh, is it? Oh, I am so tired.

9:30 p.m.

By the time the Circus Family came home, I was tucked up in my bed with the lights off. Not that it makes any difference whatsoever.

Sure enough, it was tramp, tramp up the stairs. Open door, blinding light as Mutti switched it on. Swiss Family Mad came and sat on my bed. Angus now had the goggles on and a scarf round his neck.

Mutti said, "Oh, it was really good fun, Georgie."

Libby got in bed with me and started prodding my lurker, going, "Spottie bottie boy."

Then Vati came in. Into my bedroom. He was looking at me and I was only wearing my pyjamas.

I said, "Did anyone notice that my light was off and that I was asleep? Did anyone get that?"

But they just went on chattering and giggling, and Vati was playing tickly bears with Libby and Mutti.

Please save me.

Thursday March 10th
Maths

I am going to have to kill Rosie – she is soo overexcited about the return of Sven. Every time Miss Stamp turns round she does mad disco dancing. Miss Stamp turned round a bit sharpish and caught Rosie nodding her head like a loon. She said, "Rosemary Mees, what are you doing?"

Rosie said, "I was agreeing with your excellent point on the roundness of circles."

She got a bad conduct mark for cheek, but she is still as mad as a hen.

She sent me a note: What swings round and round a cathedral wrapped in cellophane?

I tried to ignore her but she kept looking and raising her

eyebrows until I thought she would have a nervy spaz. So I mouthed back, "What?" and she sent another note: The lunchpack of Notre Dame.

Dear God, am I never to be free?

English

Oh rave on, rave on. Not content with boring us to death with *MacUseless*, we are also doing two more books. *Wuthering Heights*, or *Blithering Heights*, as we call it, and *Samuel Pepys' Diary*, about this horrifically boring bloke called Samuel Pepys. He quite literally, from what I can gather, peeps about. He just looks up ladies' skirts most of the time and says "prithee". Still, we all have to accept he is a genius. On the plus side, the dirty bits will make Miss Wilson go completely spazoid.

4:30 p.m.

Walking home with Jas and Rosie when we saw Dave the Laugh and Rollo and Tom. Jas went ludicrously girlish, even though she has been seeing Hunky for about a zillion years. I should know – I am like that bloke, Pepys's mate... Boswell, who had to write down all the boring stuff that Pepys did because he was his secretary or something.

I could write a diary about Jas: "Prithee it bee Thursdayee and Missee Jas gotte uppee this morning and puttee on her pantee forsooth and lack a day, her bottom I declareth groweth by the minutee."

I had a bit of a nervy spaz when I saw Dave. He was all cool. Rats. He said, "Easy girls, don't be selfish, there's more than enough of me to go round."

I gave him my glacial look but he just winked at me. I couldn't smile even if I wanted to because I had got so much lurker eradicator (cover-up) on that I couldn't move my face.

Rosie said, "Are you coming to Sven's teenage werewolf party on Saturday? There will be snacks."

Rollo said, "It's not fish fingers, is it?"

Rosie looked pityingly at him. "Rollo, keep up, this is a teenage werewolf party."

Dave the Laugh said, "Babies' tiny heads then, is it?"

Rosie said, "Now you are ignoring the sophisticosity of the occasion. It is of course sausages with lashings of tomato ketchup."

Dave said, "Of course it is. See you later, chicklets. And

Georgia, it is useless trying to ignore me – it just gives me the Mega Horn."

And he and the lads went off whistling the theme from *The Italian Job*.

4:45 p.m.

How annoying is that?

I could kill him.

He completely ignored my glaciosity.

Rosie and Jas were looking at me in a looking-at-me sort of way. Which I hate. Tom walked along with us. Jas was wittering on to him and holding his hand.

"I've found this stuff in the library about different kinds of fungi you can eat. You know, for our wilderness thing. Well, if we got lost away from the others in the group we could eat it and not starve."

I said, "Forgive me if I'm right, but are you talking about mushrooms?"

Jas got all huffy. "Well. All YOU are interested in is Dave the Laugh."

I tried to look as bewildered as a bee who finds itself in an egg-cup hat.

"I am not at all interested in Dave the Stupid Laugh – it's just that I am even less interested in grey shapeless things that lurk about the woods."

They were all looking at me still.

I tried again. "Oh come on, get real... Dave the Laugh, I – me – I mean..."

Tom said, "So you do like him then?"

Jas said meaningfully, "Yes, well, SOME people know SOMETHING about SOMETHING."

Oh good point, well made. Not.

I wanted to kill her and make her eat her fringe. And her knickers.

Rosie, who had been practising being blind and using me as her guide dog, said, "I've got an uncle in Yorkshire who eats cow udder as a treat."

That can't be true.

Can it?

5:00 p.m.

Walking home all alone.

I let myself in when I got to our house.

I opened the door and yelled out, "Hello Georgia darling,

take your coat off and come and warm yourself by this blazing fire! I've made a nourishing stew for you, and when your father comes home from being really masculine and rich we can talk about the four hundred pounds a week you need for a decent pad in London."

As if.

6:00 p.m.

Mum is out tossing herself around a room full of red-faced loons in leotards. Again. Who knows where Dad is. Out in his clown car causing havoc.

Brrr, it is so nippy noodles and dark.

Got into bed it was so chilly bananas.

Oh I am so cold and bored.

7:00 p.m.

Phone rang. It was Ellen.

"I heard you saw Dave on the way home and he's definitely coming on Saturday because he said he was and that means he is. Do you think?"

I said, "Put it this way, there will be snacks and Sven possibly in a Viking outfit, of course Dave the Laugh will be there."

And then Ellen started doing this thing. I thought she was having a fit at first. She was snorting and going "Hnnurknurkhhhhnuuuuuurkkk."

"Ellen, what are you doing?"

"I'm practising my infectious laugh."

Good grief.

Bedroom

I am so depressed and bored I may even have to do some homework.

In Mutti's bedroom

7:15 p.m.

I wonder if Mutti has got anything new I could wear to the party.

Ho hum.

I have squirted my lurker with her Opium. I think it might be retreating to where it came from. Although with my luck it will probably re-emerge on the end of my nose, giving me that two-nosed look that is so popular amongst the very very ugly.

7:30 p.m.

I haven't even got the heart to write to the Sex God, otherwise known as Marsupial Man. He'll probably be lying in a river somewhere anyway.

7:40 p.m.

My new address is:

Georgia Nicolson
Crap House
Crapton-on-sea
Crapshire
Crapland

7:45 p.m.

What is this book that Mutti has hidden in her knicker drawer?

How to Make Anyone Fall in Love with You.

8:00 p.m.

This is amazing.

8:30 p.m.

Phoned Rosie.

"Rosie."

"*Quoi?*"

"Do you know how to make anyone fall in love with you?"

"Well, in Sven's case I reel him in with snacks and snogging."

I've seen the two of them snogging and eating snacks at the same time, so I didn't really want to talk about it much.

I went on, "My mutti's got a secret book and it tells you how to make anyone fall in love with you, even normal boys, boys who are not Svens."

Friday March 11th

Odds bodkin, what is the matter with grown-ups? They are all mad as hens (madder). Usually when you do plays you just read them out in order and so on. Not at this hellhole. Miss Wilson decided we had to "get into" our parts by improvising. How crap is that? Very, very very and thrice very crap.

Off we all lolloped to the gym, where we had to "be" different colours to music. Rosie, who as we know is not entirely normal at the best of times, almost hung herself with one of the gym ropes when she was being purple.

All of the Ace Gang (apart from Swotty Knickers) got a bad conduct mark when Miss Wilson spotted that we were doing "Let's go down the disco" dance to every colour.

Nauseating P. Green is loving it, though. Tottering and blundering around. When we had to be "very very tiny", she crept round barging into benches and gym mats. Sadly, then we had to do "very big", and it was only quick thinking by Ellen that prevented P. Green from destroying the cassette player with her elephantine feet. If the safety inspector had popped in, the school would have been closed down.

But then the next worst thing happened – Mr Attwood came bonkering around. He came into the gym with his flat cap on and his ridiculous overalls that he only wears to keep his fags in. We were being items of food (I was being an egg and Rosie was being a sausage). Anyway, Elvis said, "This area is for the use of physical education as stated on the schedule."

Miss Wilson tried to explain, "We're improvising Shakespeare, Mr Attwood."

Mr Attwood was not impressed. He said, "That's as may be, Miss, but it's not on the timetable and the gym mats are in a state of disarray."

He went off harrumphing about, complaining and muttering and holding his back as he moved around.

Oh, how we will miss his jolly cheerful ways when he leaves. Not.

Still, he had got us out of being bits of food.

I patted him on the back as I went by.

He went sensationally ballistic, even for him.

"I've seen you, prancing around like a fool. I know what you're up to. I've locked my hut."

Quite, quite scarily mad. As we loped slowly back to the classroom, I said to Jas, "Mr Attwood is being unusually insane, isn't he? He will be going to the insane caretakers' home when he retires. Do you think he's got senile dyslexia like my grandad?"

Jas was a bit flustered and red because, sadly, she had enjoyed the workshop. Her hair was all stuck up on end. She said, "You mean senile dementia."

"Whatever, Jas, you are getting very picky, which is a shame because your fringe is all sticky-uppy."

She dashed off to the loos to wet it down, just in case she sees Hunky on the way home. She is very vain.

6:00 p.m.

I have decided that life has to go on and I have an obligation to the Ace Gang to force myself to go to the teenage werewolf party.

6:30 p.m.

Also I want to show Dave the Laugh that I am not remotely interested in him.

8:00 p.m.

What is it with parents?

Usually they don't take any notice of you, always saying "Be quiet!" or "Go to your room!", etc. But when you want to be quiet and go to your room with your mates, they won't leave you alone.

Ellen, Jools, Rosie, Mabs, Jas and me were trying out different make-up techniques and hairstyles and then it was *tap tap tap* on the door – a door which, by the way, had a clear notice attached to it that said, politely, "Go away, everyone, and that means you Mutti and Vati in particular, but also Libby and Angus." I know Libby and Angus can't read yet, so I had pinned a photo of Libby, looking particularly attractive in the nuddy-pants but wearing a pan on her head, and I had put a line through it, and for Angus I just did a big paw mark with a cross through it.

Vati barged in and we all started screaming.

He said, "Hi, girlies, do you want a little spin in my new car?"

I said to him, "Vati: a) you are banned from my room and b) do I look like the sort of person who is stupid and mad?"

Unfortunately we were all having egg masks at the time, so we did look like the stupid and mad.

8:30 p.m.

I put the chest of drawers against the door so that no one could get in.

I said, "I am going for the sophisticated werewolf look: black, black and just a hint of black, with black lipstick."

Ellen said, "Is there anyone going to the party that you fancy?"

Jas looked at me – she had her fringe in a roller, which made her look even more ridiculisimus than normal, but that didn't stop her from doing her looking thing.

I looked back with my very worst look. But it didn't stop her.

She went on and on in between mouthfuls of cheesy Wotsits. "Yes, Georgia, is there going to be anyone at the party that you might have a LAUGH with?"

I hate her. I hate her.

I said, "Well, you never know, do you? I have to try and have a life after SG. I've made a little shrine to him. Do you want to see it?"

I'd hidden the shrine under a cloth so that it was a very secret thing. Unfortunately, when I took the cloth off, Jesus had come unstuck and crashed over into Buddha, and they looked like they were snogging. The photo of Robbie is the one he gave me when I went round to his house for the first snogging extravaganza. It's one of him lying on his bed just looking into the camera. God, he's so gorgey and when he looks into the camera it's like he is looking right into my heart. I could feel tears welling up in my eyes.

The Ace Gang were really nice to me. Rosie put her arm round me and said, "Just think of him surrounded by marsupials."

To change the subject in case I did uncontrollable weeping I showed them Mutti's book, which I have sneaked into my room.

They all sat down on my bed and I started to read stuff out. They were ogling me like goosegogs.

I said, "OK, this is really cool, it tells you how to become a boy magnet *extraordinaire*. There's a list. Number one is, let me see, oh yes... 'Smile broadly'."

We practised smiling broadly. Good grief, how scary Jas is when she smiles broadly. Surely boys don't like this? Perhaps I read it wrong. Nope, it definitely says that boys like you to smile broadly. Still, there are limits.

I said to Jas, "Jas, if you don't mind me saying, your broad smile is a bit scary potatoes."

She went all huffy and red.

"Well, you've got some room to talk, Georgia. When you smile broadly your nose is about four feet wide."

Oh charming. That is the thanks you get for trying to be a good pal.

Ellen said, "OK, my face is aching a bit from the smiling thing. What's the next tip?"

I looked at the book. "'Throw him darting glances.'"

We practised throwing each other darting glances. Easy peasy.

Number three was "Dance alone to the music." I put on

a CD and we practised dancing alone to it. Do you know, my new taut and all-encompassing nunga-nunga holders really do keep my nungas under control. Even if I leap wildly in the air and jiggle my shoulders around to the music.

I shouted to Jas above the music, "Is there any evidence of nip nip emergence in this top?"

She began peering at my nungas really close up. I said, "Stop it, lezzie, I only asked you to glance for nip nip emergence. I didn't ask you to ogle my nungas."

She really got the megahump then and tried *ignorez-vous*ing me. She didn't storm off in a strop though, because she wanted to know what number four on the list was. I said, "Okey-dokey, number four is... 'Look straight at him and flip your hair.'"

We did excellent hair flipping. Which is what we mostly do all day anyway.

Number five was "Look at him, look away, toss your head and then look back." There was a lot of tossing and so on until I got a really bad neck cramp.

Number six was quite hilarious. "Lick your lips and parade close to him with exaggerated hip movements."

Rosie started doing it round the room. I said, "Surely boys don't like this. You look like you've got replacement hips."

The next one was a bit more sensible. It said you had to do "sticky eyes". You have to sort of look him in the eyes and then drag your eyes away from his as if they've been stuck with warm toffee.

In my house it is quite likely that you could wake up with toffee in your eyes, but I don't suppose that's what the author had in mind.

10:00 p.m.

The girls all crashed off home with plenty of things to think about and practise for tomorrow. I watched them out my window doing the hip thing down the street, like elderly hula dancers in overcoats.

I felt a bit cheered up.

Midnight

Only nineteen hours till the party.

12:05 a.m.

What do I care though? I have given up boys.

12:13 a.m.

How weird is this? There is a bit in the book about different cultural ways of entrancing boys. It says that in Mongolia when the woman is in the mood (i.e. full of red-bottomosity) she puts out a flag. Then when the man comes by, he sees the flag and races off to get his lasso and horse. Then she runs off and he chases her on his horse and lassos her.

12:20 a.m.

Night-night one and all.

Saturday March 12th

11:00 a.m.

Woken up at dawn, even though I should be getting lots of beauty sleep. Mutti was yelling and going ballisticisimus. She was shouting, "You horrible horrible brute!"

Well, she only has herself to blame, it was her who married him.

I hauled myself up to see what fresh hell was going on. At the kitchen door Mutti was hurling things at Angus, who was sitting in the flowerbed with a bat's ear in his mouth just out of her range.

Mutti was very very red and wearing her dressing gown, which isn't very nice for community relations, as it is practically transparent. She was going on and on. "This so-called bloody pet of yours is... is... It's like a graveyard for small rodents in our house. I wouldn't mind but he gets through about a ton of cat food a day. Big BRUTE!!!"

Shouting at Angus, in my humble opinion, is as useless as challenging a centipede to an arse-kicking contest. But I didn't say. Instead I tried the reasoned sensible approach for which I am famous.

"Mutti, you see the thing is, you are hurting Angus's feelings by yelling at him. I think he's crying."

"He will be crying when I get hold of him. If he lives long enough to cry."

She is so violent. I said, "In my cat book it explains things; you see, Angus brings you birds and bats' ears and stuff because he thinks you are a really useless cat in the nuddy-pants. He thinks you are too dim and stupid to catch your own snacks. The bat ear is his little gift to you. And you are yelling at him. He is very puzzled and upset."

By this stage Angus was lying on his back with the bat ear caught between his front paws, tossing it about. Not crying as such.

12:30 p.m.

Back in my bedroom to start preparations.

I've done the base coat of my nails, toes and fingers. Now then, what is next on my list in order? Ah yes, relax your mind.

I lay down on my bed with a cucumber slice over each eye. Ahhhhh. Let go of all tension.

Fat chance. Libby came barging in singing, "Sex bum, sex BUM, I'm a sex bum!" Which I think is unsuitable for a four year old.

I managed to get Libby out of my room and put her into the airing cupboard – she likes it up there. Vati was in the drive cleaning his clown car. I have asked him if he will wear a mask when he goes out in it. Actually I have asked him to wear a mask at all times, but you might as well ask for the moon. I opened my bedroom window and yelled down at him.

"Vati, my dear little sister doesn't sing 'Bar bar bag sheet' any more, nor does she sing 'Three blind lice'. Do you know what she does sing?"

He was too busy polishing the clown car to take any notice. In fact, if I had gone to Kiwi-a-gogo land and a very fat Eskimo called Carl had moved into my bedroom, he still wouldn't have noticed. I don't know why people bother having children if they are going to spend the whole time pretending they don't exist. I went on regardless, like Sherpa Tensing.

"As you ask, I will tell you what she sings. She sings 'Sex bum, sex bum, I'm a sex bum.'"

And he laughed.

I said, "I hope you find it as amusing when she turns out to be a child prostitute."

By the time I looked round from the window, Libby was back in my bed with her *Heidi* book.

"Heggo, Gingey, time to read."

I tried to explain to her that I am busy and have to get ready to go out, but she gave me a glancing blow with scuba-diving Barbie.

I have at least managed to keep Angus out of my room. I have closed the door. Libby thinks it's very funny because Angus knows we are in here and he keeps putting his paw under the door and groping around.

But he can stay out there. I don't want bat essence on my party things.

4:00 p.m.

No wonder small children are mad. Heidi, who is still living with her mad grandad in the mountains, is clearly a bit on the insane side from the beginning, because it says, "It was with a happy heart that Heidi lay down on her bed of hay."

Good Lord.

4:30 p.m.

Then this boy called Peter is jealous of Heidi's new friend (some soppy nitwit in a wheelchair). So he pushes the soppy nitwit's wheelchair off the edge of the mountain while the soppy nitwit is having some cheese in the house.

(I must make a note to myself to NEVER go to Swisscheese-a-gogo land.)

5:00 p.m.

Ah well, it all ends happily as the soppy nitwit learns to walk because she hasn't got a wheelchair any more.

So, in conclusion, this is the moral of *Heidi*: always push invalid chairs off the top of mountains when you get the opportunity. The end.

Excellent advice.

7:00 p.m.

Time to go. I think I look rather groovy and mysterious in my teenage werewolf outfit. I decided against the black lipstick in the end because it made me look a bit like those sad Goths who turn up at gigs in the summer in leather bondage stuff and then have to sit really still because they are too hot to live. And then they stick to the seats.

Also, I have some new and groovy lippy and lip gloss in different flavours.

Très très gorgey and *bon*.

Went downstairs for Vati's traditional lecture about the length of my skirt, make-up, curfew time, drinking, snogging or anything. I hate it when he talks to me like a so-called grown-up. It's very embarrassing in a clown car owner. He was slumped on the sofa as normal. Gosh, he is porkus bigus these days. I said, "Vati, I really think that you should get in shape."

He didn't even look round. He just said, "I am in shape. Round is a shape."

While he was laughing like a loon at his *très pathétique* joke I slipped quietly out the front door.

Escape!! Freedom!!! Party!!!!

Not that I am really cheered up.

Just brave.

7:45 p.m.

We all met up at the clock tower and walked to Rosie's together.

As we went through the gate I said to Jas, "Rosie's mutti and vati are always away; how sensible and reasonable they are. All my mutti and vati do is hang around the house asking me what I am doing and also why am I doing it and when am I going to stop doing it."

Jas, representative for the terminally annoying, said, "My olds have given me my own key... It's a sort of token of my passage into adulthood."

I said, "Are you sure it's the key to your house? Perhaps it's the key to someone else's house and is therefore not a token of adulthood, but just their way of saying goodbye."

Hunky laughed and Jas gave him a "look", but as I was giggling at my own deep amusingosity she shoved me really hard and I nearly fell off my heels. My shoes, in keeping with my new sophisticosity, are quite high. In fact they are so high I may even be able to look Sven in the eye, which will be scary.

I am a bit nervous about seeing Dave the Laugh.

8:15 p.m.

Tom rang the bell and the door was ripped open by Sven. Yeah!! Sven back again. Crikey, I had forgotten how alarming he can be. Even by his (high) standards he had gone a lot too far this time. He had a Viking helmet on over an Afro wig and he was drinking out of a horn. He picked me and Jas up and said, "Hey swingers!! Coming on in why dontcha, chicks and laddies."

What planet does he live on? And how do you not go there?

Nice to see him, though. I have never seen furry shorts before.

Then Rosie popped up – she was entirely covered in fur: eyebrows and sidies, furry hands and knees, and even fur poking out of her shoes.

I said to her, "There is the suggestion of the wildebeest about Sven in those shorts."

And she said, "I know, exciting isn't it? Help yourself to snacks and drinks."

The pink chipolatas in tomato sauce really did look like severed fingers. Yum yum.

9:00 p.m.

Quite a crowd at the party. All the usual suspects: Sam and his mates from sixth-form college, the Foxwood crowd, Damion Knightly (known as the Dame) and his mates from St John's, plus loads of girls we knew from gigs and Moorgrange School. Some of the boys were quite fit, but none had that *je ne sais quoi*, that Sex Goddy charm that brought out the red-bottomosity in me.

And no sign of Dave the Laugh.

Good.

At least I could relax.

Jas said, "Dave the Laugh's not here."

I said, "So?"

And she just looked at me.

She is turning quite literally into a staring person.

9:15 p.m.

I thought just for a laugh I would try out some of the tactics from Mutti's book.

The Dame came over and said, "Hi, Gee, come and dance about like a prat."

And he pulled me on to the dance floor (the bit in between the sofa and the dining table). The Dame was blundering around to some really loud rock music that Sven had put on. Sven was actually on the table thrusting his furry shorts around like a sort of Viking lap dancer. Rosie was doing the twist very very fast till she was a blur of fur.

Anyway, I thought for practice I would try "sticky eyes" on the Dame. So I looked him in the eyes. He looked a bit startled at first, like he was thinking, "Oy what are you looking at, mate?" But I did that dragging my eyes away from his thing and then looking back. And it worked!!! He was sort of mesmerised. In fact it was a bit like I had hypnotised him. I kept looking him in the eye and then I moved to the fireplace, still looking at him. And he followed me there like a boy zombie. I went behind the TV and he followed me there. I went and stood by the window and he followed me there. It was amazing.

Then Dave the Laugh walked in. Gadzooks and also crikey!

He was dressed all in black like me and he looked cool.

His hair was slicked back and he had false fangs. Which I am alarmed to say I found a bit attractive. You could do excellent lip nibbling with them.

I had stopped looking at the Dame but he still followed me as I went to the snacks and drinks table. I was sort of casually pretending that I hadn't even noticed Dave the Laugh. Which was a bit difficult to keep up, because he shouted, "OK all you chicks who find me irresistible, follow me. No pushing."

Oh vair vair *amusant*. He's so bloody confident. He went off into the kitchen and a few girls (including Ellen, who as we know has no pride to speak of) went after him. I was just looking at the kitchen door when Dave suddenly appeared back through it again. I was so shocked that I turned round really quickly and practically snogged the Dame, who was lurking behind me.

He said, looking all dreamy and hypnotised, "Do you fancy going outside?"

I said, "Er, it's minus a million degrees out there."

And he said, "I'll keep you warm."

Is there a crap book that useless boys read called *Tips for Being Useless*? If there is, the Dame has read it. I didn't even bother replying. Then Ellen came dithering over to me. She was all red and spazzy.

"He's – you know, well, he's... I... should I... well, you know?"

I said, "Ellen, look, don't have a nervy b. It's not attractive. Listen, why don't you try that dancing-on-your-own tactic?"

She thought that was a good idea and started dancing around looking all dreamy and moody, and slightly swishing her hair about. Within seconds one of Sam's mates started dancing with her.

Surely this how-to-make-anyone-fall-in-love-with-you thing can't be this easy?

Dave the Laugh was looking at me, but I wasn't going for it, fangs or no fangs. I could go up to him and say, "Hi, Dave. Bye, Dave. You are so yesterday, but fangs for the memory."

Shut up, brain!!!!!

He was looking at me but he didn't come over, so I thought I would go look at the CD collection in a sort of cool way because the tension was making me want to go to the piddly-diddly department.

I had to walk past him to get to the CDs so I flicked my hair a bit and did the hip-waggling thing. (Which is not as easy to coordinate as you might think.)

Yess!!! Result is he followed me. I was looking at the CDs and didn't realise until the last minute that they were all upside down and I couldn't see the titles. He said, "Georgia."

I didn't even turn round.

"Georgia, I know your hips are bad but do you fancy a quick snog? I've got healing hands."

He is appalling!!!

It sort of made me laugh, though. He is soooo full of himself.

I turned round to him and looked at him like it said in the book (the bit I hadn't told the Ace Gang yet). It said, "Number eight. Let your eyes slide down the nose to the lips, caress the lips with your eyes for a moment and then slowly venture south to the neck."

Dave took his fangs out and said, "So, Sex Kitty..."

It was really weird because I felt like I was melting into Dave. And we would have snogged right there in front of everyone. I knew Ellen was there and I knew everyone would see and it would be dreadful, but all the blood in my brain had gone off on a little holiday to my lips.

Just then a girl's voice came into my head from behind Dave. It said, "Hi, Dave, sorry I'm late, I couldn't park my scooter."

Through the haze of frustrated snoggosity, I looked at the voice. It belonged to Rachel, a girl I know vaguely from hockey and gigs.

Rachel said, "Oh hi, Georgia, how's Stalag 14?"

I just went a bit goldfishy, opening my mouth but not saying anything. Dave looked like a rabbit caught in car headlights. Dave the rabbit eventually managed to speak. "Oh. Hi, Rachel," and he gave her a kiss on her cheeks.

She kissed him on the lips and put her arms round his neck. Then she pulled him away and said, "Come on, big boy, let's groove."

I just stood there.

Dave looked back at me and shrugged his shoulders. Then they went off into the other room. Rachel still had her arms around him.

I couldn't believe it.

It was unbelievable, that is why.

I couldn't stay.

I slipped out and got my coat and crept out into the dark night.

I waited until I got to the gate and into the street but then I just couldn't help it, tears started pouring out of my eyes.

Even though I would look like a panda in a skirt I didn't care.

I heard footsteps behind me. If it was Dave coming to apologise, he could just forget it. Then I heard Jas's voice. "Georgia, it's me, I'll – I'll walk back with you. I saw what happened."

She might be a complete and utter fringey annoyance, but Jas was my bestest pal.

She put her arm around me and said, "This is just friendly, it's not, you know... I'm not... er..."

I said, "Oh this is awful. It wasn't just that I was displaying glaciosity to Dave... it's well, I thought he wasn't just a snoggee but also a mate. He taught me the secrets of the Horn and now he's gone off with another girl..."

Jas went, "I know."

"Just went off immediately with another girl."

"I know."

"I'm not even warm in my grave."

"I know."

"She's got slightly ginger hair."

"I know."

"My smile is much nicer than hers."

"I know... er... hang on, is it?"

"Yes."

"Right."

"I am abandoned on the ship of life."

"I know."

"Jas, you are not really cheering me up."

"Well, I know, and that's because there is really nothing to be cheerful about; I would hate to be you."

In bed

11:45 p.m.

Jas says she will never sympathise with me again after I pulled her stupid hat down over her stupid face and she fell over a paving stone. That is the good news, but otherwise life is absolutely beyond the Valley of Crap and entering the Universe of Totally Useless.

Midnight

I lit a candle at my altar to Robbie (after I had removed scuba-diving Barbie and some chewed-up moth).

Why oh why did this happen to me? I must have done something incredibly bad in a past life.

Perhaps I was that Roman bloke who played with his instrument while Rome burnt down – Tyrannosaurus rex. Oh no, I don't mean Tyrannosaurus, I mean Nero. If it was Tyrannosaurus rex, that would mean that a dinosaur played a violin, which is clearly not going to happen.

Maybe if I pray for forgiveness and promise to be a better person, Baby Jesus will let me have what I want.

Looking out of my window at the infinite sky, I prayed out, "Dear Baby Jesus, I am sorry for my sins, even though I do not know what they are, which seems a bit unfair if it is going to be held against me.

"But that is your way. And I am not questioning your wisdomosity.

"In future, however, would it be possible for my life to be not so entirely crap? Thank you."

Son of Angus, otherwise Known as Cross-eyed Gordy

Sunday March 13th

I have accidentally come on a nature ramble with my "family". That is how upset I am. And the nature ramble involved getting into the clown car in order to get into nature. This should give you some idea of my state of sheer desperadoes. Vati had his World War Two flying helmet on and his goggles. It was vair vair sad and tragic.

I slumped down in the back of the clown car. I even let Libby make me look "niiiiice". Her idea of looking nice is not the same as most other human beings' (apart from pygmies'). She tied my hair in little pigtails with bits of wool. But I don't care. My life is over and I am a mad toddler's playdough person.

Vati was in an appallingly good mood. When two women

were walking along (practically at the same speed as the clown car), he wound down the window and shouted, "Your big day is here, ladies, the Sex Bomb is officially in his car."

Oh God it was soo humiliating.

I said to Mutti, "I don't think Dad's medication is working, Mum."

2:00 p.m.

Eventually we arrived in "nature", which to some might look like a boring old field in the middle of nowhere. I'd only come to get away from the tension of not answering the telephone. If I had stayed at home and the phone rang, I wouldn't be able to answer it in case it was Dave the Laugh apologising. But then if it didn't ring, I would be indoors waiting all day knowing that he hadn't rung and I hadn't been able to ignore him.

2:20 p.m.

The only bright spot of the day was the sight of Vati jogging off into the fields like a fat mountain goat. I was just sitting in the back of the clown car waiting for my life to be over. Mum and Libby were eating a picnic, Libby in her attractive country costume of furry coat and rabbit hat. Unfortunately I am only too well aware that beneath the furry coat lurks her nuddy-pants outfit. Pray God there will be no poo business in the car.

Dad was cavorting around looking interested in nature, yelling, "Oh my word, there is some cuckoo spit," or "Voles!!" when suddenly he just disappeared from view. Completely gone. I thought about yelling, "Thank you Baby Jesus, it's a miracle!!" But I am still hoping for a bit of a result from the Lord, so I restrained my delight.

Mum got out of the car and tore off across the field shouting, "Bob, Bob, where are you, darling?"

I could hear a muffled yelling. I supposed I had better go and see what had happened to the Portly One. Libbs and I ambled over to where Mum was looking down. And there he was, up to his armpits in a hole.

Even though I am in the depths of despairiosity and so on, it did make me laugh. A LOT. Dad was all red and shouty. "It's a bloody badger hole!!"

That made me go uncontrollably spazoid.

As Mutti pulled him out, he was all grumpy, like the very psychotic get.

"They're a bloody menace, badgers. I am going to inform someone of this. I could have injured myself quite badly. It's not funny."

As Mutti helped him back to the clown car, I said, "I think you should write to someone, Vati, and have badgers banned. While you are at it get beavers banned because they may have been in cahoots with the badgers. They may have encouraged them to dig that hole for a laugh, and—"

"Shut up, Georgia."

Oh that's nice, isn't it. Mutti was inwardly laughing but restrained herself. On the way home she had to drive the clown car because Vati was incontinent. Or do I mean incompetent? Both I think.

At home she made him some tea while he lay groaning and moaning on the sofa.

5:00 p.m.

I was in the kitchen hanging around and Angus was doing his famous staring at the door trick. I'm not falling for it, though. He sits and looks all longingly at the door for ages. Just staring and staring at it. Eventually some poor fool gets up and goes to open it for him. Angus looks out and then he looks at you, then he looks back at the outside. And you can see him thinking, "Nah, I won't bother now."

It's very annoying.

Mum was cutting the crusts off toast for Dad. Which she never does for me. I said to her, "Hey, Mutti, if someone discovers that Vati just floods people's homes as a job, and he gets the sack from the Water Board, he could always get a job as a badger finder. Say you wanted to know where the badgers were in a field... well, you just set Vati off walking and when he disappears from view you know there's a badger there."

Still only 8:00 p.m.

It's so dark and gloomy. Like life. No phone calls.

I HATE Dave the Laugh.

Even though it is very nippy noodles, I can't bear being cooped up in the house. I thought I'd go sit on the garden wall and try to calm down.

I was just sitting there in my big coat and scarf and hat in the street light, looking at all the houses where other people were doing stuff – roasting chestnuts, snogging, etc., when Oscar, Mr and Mrs Across the Road's son, came out on to his driveway on his bike. He was doing wheelies and all that

pointless boy stuff that they do: making the bike hop along, braking really suddenly, sitting on the seat backwards and steering it behind his back. All boys are mad as snakes – which is why I must train myself up for lesbianism, even if it involves growing a moustache. If it involved growing a beard under each arm, I was practically home and dry. The orang-utan gene is not having a winter vacation.

Anyway, Oscar saw me watching him and he winked at me. I just looked at him. What is he winking for? Then he winked again. Is he in training for owldom? He shouted over, "Do you fancy it then?"

"Pardon?" I said, "What?"

What is he talking about?

He leant back against his bike and crossed one leg over the other in what I imagine he thinks is a casual way.

He said, "Me and you."

"Me and you what?"

"You know... getting it on."

"Pardon?"

"You know, letting the monster out of the bag, setting free the trouser snake."

I couldn't believe what I was hearing. I said, "Oscar,

forgive me if I'm right but you are twelve."

"I know, but I like older women."

Unbelievable. Now I am being propositioned by toddlers. Soon it will be Josh, Libby's little mate from nursery school.

Oscar was still winking at me while I was staring at him when Mark Big Gob came by on his way out. Oh brilliant! He said, "Clear off, Oscar! Bedtime." Oscar looked hard, but he cleared off all the same, saying, "Yeah, well, I was going to go in, I've got a chick phoning me. Dig you later."

Has he gone completely mad?

Mark Big Gob looked at me – or rather, he looked at my nungas.

"You're looking cool, Georgia. Why don't you come for a walk with me Tuesday? I'll be out by the back field at eight o'clock. See you then."

I was just going "What??? What???" in my mind, but nothing was coming out of my mouth.

As if!!! Meet him in the back field???? As if!!!!!

What had happened to his tiny girlfriend??

Anyway, it didn't matter what happened to her. As if I would meet him by the back field or anywhere!

Boys are truly unbelievable.

Monday March 14th
Break

All huddled up in our Antarctic weatherproof tepee behind the five's court. (The Ace Gang get all our coats and button them to each other around us, like a coat tepee.) Mmmm, nice and snug, but it does mean you can't use your arms. We put the snacks in the middle of us inside the coat tepee. You have to eat them blind, grabbing stuff from any bag you can feel and forcing two fingers with the snack in them through the communal neck hole. Tricky if you all try to do it at the same time.

Rosie said, "That was a vair vair good party. I didn't get to bed until eight a.m. and then I had to get up at ten because of my olds coming back."

Ellen said, "I thought your olds were, you know, cool with you having parties."

Rosie said, "Oh they are, it's just that there were a lot of rogue sausage snacks to round up after Sven did his famous 'Let's go down the disco' dance on the cocktail cabinet."

Jools said, "Leslie Andrews is covered in lovebites; she is six inches deep in foundation and she still looks like she has been attacked by lemmings. She tried to wear a polo-neck sweater in Games, but Miss Stamp made her take it off and then tutted for England when she saw the state of her neck."

Oh rave on, who cares about the stupid party? I don't want to talk about it. In a fit of subtlosity I said, "What shall we get as a thoughtful leaving gift for Elvis? Handcuffs? A straitjacket? A T-shirt with 'I am a complete and utter tosser' written on it?"

However, I was *ignorez-vous*ed and Jools said, "You left early, Gee. Why...? Did you have the painters in?"

Jas looked at me. She is still not officially talking to me since the hat over the stupid head scenario.

Everyone looked at me.

Stop looking at me in that lookingy way.

Ellen said, "I am soo upset about Dave the Laugh. I thought he might have got over the thingy, you know, Horn stuff, but then he... you know, brought that girl, you know... er..."

Rosie said, "Rachel."

Ellen said, "No, I'm, I mean I'm Ellen... I you..."

Rosie said, "Ellen, get a grip. The girl, Dave's Horn mate, she's called Rachel."

Ellen went dithering on, "Yes, I mean Rachel. I couldn't believe it when he turned up with her."

I said, "I know."

Ellen was rambling on for England (taking over from Jas, all-time world rambling champion). "I mean, you know, he's supposed to be like a great guy..."

I said, "Yeah... he's supposed to be a great guy but actually he's a snivelling wormy-type guy who leads people on and he... then he..."

Everyone was looking at me (a bit cross-eyed because our heads were so close together). Oh dear, I have slightly blown my glacial disinterest in Dave. I thought quickly. "I mean, it's not fair... on Ellen, is it?"

I said it like I was a great pal. Jas said in her mind, "You skunk girl." So I said telepathically back to her, "Shut up, Wilderness Woman."

Home

6:38 p.m.

The kittykats are going to be sent away!! Mr Across the Road came round, partly to talk about the *Lord of the Rings* party they are going to have. He said, "I'm going as Gandalf and Oscar is thinking about going as a hobbit." Hmm, that's attractive in a twelve-year-old nymphomaniac. I let a smile play around my lips at the thought of my dad in green tights. However, Mr Across the Road – who has taken an unfair dislike to me for some reason – said viciously, "I've found homes for six of those monstrous things, God help the people they are going to, but I can't find anyone stupid enough to have the seventh, so it'll have to go to the vets."

Go to the vets??? I knew what that meant. One of the kittykats was headed for the big cat basket in the sky... After he had lumbered off, Dad settled down on the sofa to read his newspaper. Angus was snoozing in front of the fire.

I said to Dad, "Dad, did you hear that??? Please, please can we save the kittykat: think how upset Angus will be. In fact, I think he understands every word we say and he knows what Mr Across the Road the kittykat abuser said. Look, look, Dad, I think he's crying."

Unfortunately at that moment Angus woke up and leapt straight through the newspaper Dad was reading, tearing it completely in half. Dad got hold of Angus, who also had surprised himself with his insane leap, and flung him across the room. Of course, old nimble paws landed on his feet and ambled off.

Dad was full of lividosity. He said, "Absolutely not in a million years, never, ever, not ever. Do you get it, Georgia, NO."

7:00 p.m.

In the kitchen Mutti was pretending to iron something. I said, "Mutti, that's an iron you know, they can get quite hot."

She said, "Shut up."

In my bedroom

7:15 p.m.

Libby was just doing a spot of housework – she has a handbrush and she brushes and mutters to herself. She was saying, "Bloody thing, bloody thing," as she worked. Obviously gaining her knowledge from my parents. When I lay down on my bed of pain she came and nuzzled me. "Georgia, Georgie Porgy... I LOBE you, kissy kiss kiss."

I wish she had more snot control. I told her, "Angus's kittykats have to go away."

She said, "NO."

I said, "Maybe Mummy will let you have one if you ask her."

Libby gave me a very very scary smile and toddled off with her brush.

I heard her clanking down the stairs singing, "Mummy, Muuuummmmmmeeeeee."

Ten minutes later

I can hear mumbling going on in the kitchen. Libby said, "Nice Muummmeee."

I couldn't hear what Mum was saying but I could tell she was using a reasoning sort of voice.

Then there was banging and shouting. Mutti yelled, "No Libby. Stop that!! No biting and not on my best... Oh hellfire!!"

10:00 p.m.

Our new kittykat is called Gordon. Libby LOBES Gordon very much. She has put him in his pyjamas and tucked him up with me and her other toys. He is very very gorgey but he is a bit on the cross-eyed side.

Gordy is happily sucking on Libby's dodie and all is quiet.

Tuesday March 15th

Gordy woke up at six a.m. and crawled under my chin like a little ginger beard. He is so adorable.

7:00 p.m.

Stalag 14 was indescribably boring today. We had *Blithering Heights* followed by double French. I told the Ace Gang about the absolute cheek of Oscar and Mark Big Gob.

Jas pretended to be giving me her icy shoulders, but even she got interested when I described Oscar looning around trying to get off with me. She said, "Were you wiggling your hips like in the book?"

"Jas, I was sitting down on the wall. Anyway, he's twelve."

She looked all wise-woman-of-the-forestish (i.e. stupid).

"Perhaps you were doing internal hip wiggling."

What is she raving on about?

Still, she is talking to me by mistake and so I win the glaciosity game hahahaha.

7:45 p.m.

I don't know why I have applied make-up to stay in my room.

Mutti and Vati have got Uncle Eddie here and a few of their crap mates. Uncle Eddie popped his head round my door, almost blinding me with the glare from his baldiness. I began to say, "Er, Uncle Eddie, this is a loon-free zone—"

But he said, "What has a hundred legs and can't walk?"

"Uncle Eddie, I am sixteen years old, I—"

"Fifty pairs of trousers... hahahahah it's the way I tell 'em!"

And he looned off to the loon gathering.

I cannot have any peace. I am forced out of my own home because of the high loon count.

7:59 p.m.

I crept out of the house into the back garden. I would just see if Mark Big Gob had the audacity to turn up for our "date". And I could tell him to bugger off.

8:00 p.m.

He's not there. God, even someone I was going to stand up has stood me up before I had a chance to stand them up.

8:02 p.m.

Mark Big Gob came out of the shadows smoking a fag. He

really has got the biggest gob known to humanity. He said, "You're keen."

How annoying is that. I was going to say, "Well, actually I was just here to tell you to bugger off", when he said, "Fancy a fag?"

Er...

I said, "No thanks, I only smoke cigars."

What am I talking about?

He held out his hand.

"Come on then."

I honestly have no control over any part of my body, because even though I had no intention of doing it, I took his hand. Which was a mistake in very many ways. Mostly because I had forgotten that I am taller than him and I have long arms, so I had to do the crouchy orang-utan thing to keep at the same height as him.

Anyway, we loped off up the hill. It was bloody dark and extremely nippy noodles. I had worn my big cardigan, but I still felt a bit chilly because it only buttoned up halfway. Mark is not a big talker and I couldn't think of a single thing to say to him. We got up to the bit at the top we call the bushes – it's really Snog Headquarters. There was no one there tonight, though. Mark let go of my hand and put his fag out. Then he alarmed me by putting his hand round the back of my neck and pulling me to him quite roughly. Blimey. Just as I was deciding what to do he shoved his tongue in my mouth. No warmsy upsies, not even "My your skin is looking nice," or "What a lovely blouse." Not even a nodding acquaintance with one two three four on the snogging scale.

It wasn't that nice actually. His tongue had more than a passing similarity to Angus's. Not that I have snogged Angus, but there has been the odd occasion when he has licked my face and the tongue has inadvertently slipped into my gob. I didn't quite know what to do with my tongue or my teeth. My tongue was sort of being forced back to keep out of the way of his. For one horrible moment I wondered if there was something called "tonsil snogging" that no one had told me about. Mark seemed to be enjoying it even if I wasn't. He was sort of groaning and holding me really close. I was just thinking I might try and get my hands free (they were sort of trapped in between us) when Mark did this thing: he stuck his hand (which was freezing) down the front of my T-shirt and into my nunga-nunga holder.

Number eight, upper-body fondling!! Actually it gave me such a shock that I jumped back and Mark was thrown off balance. He stumbled into the bushes. He came out a minute later covered in twigs. He didn't look pleased.

He said, "What did you do that for?"

I said, "Well. Er, it was all a bit... I don't know that I want you to..."

He lit a fag and said, "What did you come here for... a chat?"

I said, "Well... I..."

What did I come here for? Very good question. Excellent point, well made. Boredom mostly, I suppose. I didn't think I should say that. Mark seemed really angry. He said, "Do you go all the way or not?"

I said, "Well, no I..."

Mark started walking off. "Girls like you make me sick."

And he was gone. I was left at the top of the hill alone. What had I done now? I felt really weird. And lonely.

I walked back down the hill. When I went through our gate, Angus was lying in wait and pounced on my trousers round the ankle. With a heavy heart and even heavier trousers I dragged him indoors.

Midnight

What does Mark mean, “girls like me”?

Wednesday March 16th

Walking to school with Jas.

“Jas, what number have you got up to with Hunky?”

She went all red and girlish. “Er...”

“Come on, Jas, I tell you everything.”

Jas said, “I know and I wish you wouldn’t.”

“Jas.”

“Well. Er, when we went camping we, you know, had a bit of quality time together.”

“Snogging time you mean?”

“Well yes... we, er, got up to six and a half.”

“Ear snogging. Is that all?”

She got huffy then and started adjusting her knickers. “There is more to life than snogging, you know.”

I said, “Oh yeah, like what? Going off into the forest snuffling out truffles?”

“Pigs do that.”

“Yeah, and your point is?”

Jas said I am being all mean and moody because of Dave

the Laugh, but what she doesn't know is that it's not just Dave the Laugh, it's Oscar, and now Mark Big Gob as well. I feel all ashamed somehow. Like I am tainted love.

Break

Rosie and I managed to escape the Storm Troopers (Wet Lindsay and her pathetico prefect pals). Jas wants to read her book about twig houses, so she has gone off to the five's court with the other girlie swots. Hawkeye insists that we have windows open, even in Antarctic conditions. She says it's good for us but she also says reading absolute bollocks is good for us, so I don't trust her. It is, after all, she who thinks that *Blithering Heights*, as we call it, is a "classic". When in fact it's a load of Yorkshire people hurling themselves around a moor in the wind singing "Heathcliff, it's me Katheeee come home again." And so on. We've only read three pages and already I want to slit my wrists. Anyway, where was I before I so rudely interrupted myself? Oh yes, so because Hawkeye has windows open all over the school, we could get in through the science block window.

Once we got in, we lit a few Bunsen burners for warmth.

Voley is still here in his little pickling jar for ever, waving at us. I said, "Hello, Voley. My dad fell down a badger hole."

I thought he would like to know the news from the forest, even though he has been pickled for years.

Rosie was trying to toast a bit of banana over the naked flame of a Bunsen burner. I sensed a burning-down-the-science-block situation but I didn't want to spoil her girlish high spirits by saying anything. Also, I had just got myself all snuggled up in some science overalls. I decided to tell Rosie about Mark Big Gob.

She listened and said, "He is clearly a knob head, but you knew that. Forget it, we have more important things to think about. There's a lot of work to do at school, and this is a very important term."

I looked at her in amazement. "Rosie, please tell me you are not talking about exams and it's not the way you run the race but the winning that counts."

She gave me the famous cross-eyed look. "Do not be a twit and a fool and a prat. I'm talking about our plans for Mr Attwood's leaving do."

Hockey

I did actually cheer up in Games. There is nothing like socking a bit of concrete about a pitch and smacking shins with my hockey stick to get the juices flowing. Additionally, Nauseating P. Green was goalie, which is a guaranteed laugh. It is funny enough seeing her lumbering around in huge pads picking the ball out of the back of the net, but the *pièce de résistance* was when she fell over on her back and couldn't get up. Like a big tortoise waving her shin pads about. She finally managed to get up after about ten minutes, and just as she was on her feet a ball whizzed in and hit her in the tummy and down she went again.

Cruel, but funny.

Jas's place

5:00 p.m.

Jas and Hunky are going on this wilderness thing soon, so Jas made me go up to her room and look at the stuff she is taking with her. Good grief, the things I do for friendship.

Her room is ludicrously tidy, all her soft toys arranged in size order. Very sad. I said that as I looked around. "Very, very sad."

But Wild Woman of the Forest was too busy rooting around in her wardrobe. She was all enthusiastic. "Look at these. They are my special army-issue waterproof trousers. Even if I, like, accidentally fell into a swamp I would still have dry legs."

I looked at the hideous yellow things. "Are you sure those are not just massive incontinence knickers, Jas?"

She was just rambling on as if I wasn't there, which actually, in my mind, I wasn't.

On and on, completely gone off to Jasland.

"You should get yourself a hobby, Gee, and then you wouldn't end up throwing yourself at boys and losing your dignity."

How annoying is she?

Vair vair and thrice vair annoying.

6:00 p.m.

After about a million years of looking at really dull bits of Wellington boot etc., I slouched off home.

I am so sick of walking. Walk, walk, walk, that's all I ever do. I'll wear my legs out at this rate. To pass the time I did what I used to do as a kid – I pretended to be riding a horse. I galloped along tossing my head about, saying "Giddy-up"

and flicking a pretend whip. The bit between the bottom of Jas's road and my house was very quiet, so I really let my horse (Dark Star) have his head. I flicked at his haunches with my whip and felt the wind on my face and the freedom of the hills. "Yes, yes, ride on my beauty!" I pulled Dark Star to a halt so that we could cross the road, which was just as well, as across the road was Cad of the Universe, Dave the Laugh. Oh brilliant. Thank you, God. My head was practically dropping off from redness and I hadn't any lip gloss on because I had given up on boys.

I crossed the road and walked past him. I treated him with total glaciosity. He said, "Come on, Georgia, talk to me."

"What can you possibly have to say to me?"

I walked on. At least I haven't got ginger hair. Although with my luck, I probably have hair that is sticking out at right angles after my galloping fiasco. As usual, though, Dave kept on. He tends to ignore me ignoring him, which is annoying. He put his arm through mine.

"Georgia, look at me. Come on, Sex Kitty, don't get the megahump. We weren't going out officially, were we? You couldn't make your mind up, then I met Rachel and she was keen... well, she is after all only human—"

I looked at him with a "don't even bother" look. He smiled.

"Can't we be friends? We've always had a laugh together."

I felt my heart melting. He was right, really; we hadn't been officially a couple, and he was a laugh to have around. I found myself going for a coffee with him and telling him all about Mark Big Gob. Dave the Laugh said, "He really is an enormous twit of the first water."

It sort of made it better when he said it. I know that Rosie had said the same, but it seemed different when a boy-type person said it. As we left the coffee bar and walked along arm in arm, he stopped and took my chin in his hand. (I don't mean he snapped it off my face and held it.) He just sort of lifted my face up to his and gave me a little kiss really gently on the lips. I could feel the jelloid knees coming on. Damn!

As I walked off, he called back to me, "Don't worry about Mark Big Gob. I'll have a word."

Home

Oh joy unbounded, Cousin James is coming to stay overnight. I said to Mutti, "Why?"

And she said, "He's family."

I said reasonably, "Mutti, what does that mean? Does it mean that if Hitler was my cousin we would have to have him round?"

She got all parenty. "Now you are being ridiculous. Go and do your homework. Oh, and don't have a bath – Gordy has done a cat poo in there. I'll have to clean it up."

Gordy has done a cat poo in the bath??!! Why would he scramble all the way up the sides of the bath just to do a poo when he has his own personal cat-poo tray in the outhouse? Anyway, how could he get up the sides of the bath? Either Libby gave him a leg up, or Angus helped him. I bet it was Angus. When I went into my bedroom Angus was curled up on my cardigan cleaning himself. I wish he wouldn't do botty grooming on my things. I said to him, "You are quite literally a crap dad, Angus. You wait until Gordy starts staying out all night creating mayhem – you'll be sorry."

Angus fell into a light doze as I was telling him off. Anyway, why would he be worried about Gordy staying out all night creating mayhem? That's what he does himself. It's his job.

9:00 p.m.

Doorbell rang.

No one answered it, of course. Mum and Libby (and I think from the yowling, Angus and Gordy) are all in the bath. I don't know how they can bear to go in there. I personally will never be having another bath in this lifetime, not even if Mum has cleaned it with nitroglycerin.

Ring ring on the bell.

9:03 p.m.

I shouted out, "Don't worry, I'll get it. I've only got exams in two weeks, but you just lie around and relax."

Tramp tramp.

If I get all the way down and it's Cousin James and I have to speak to him I will have a nervy spaz.

9:05 p.m.

I opened the door and it was Mark Big Gob. Crikey. He looked a bit shifty and nervous.

"Georgia, I've got something to say about the other night."

He wasn't going to have another attempt at storming my nunga-nunga holders, was he?

I said warily, "Oh yes. What is it?"

"Well, I'm, I'm..."

I'm what? The Count of Monte Cristo? Stupid? Wearing false lips? What???

Mark said, "I'm sorry. I apologise."

Blimey O'Reilly's trousers. Then I noticed he had a swelling on his mouth and a split lip. Cripes, was his mouth expanding even more, like the Incredible Hulk?

He said, "Do you accept my apology?"

How weird was this? I felt like I was in a film. One of those really old-fashioned films where everyone wears pantaloons. Like *Gone with the Wind*. Maybe I should say, "Why sir, thank you kindly for apprising me of your feelings. I do declare I have never seen tighter pantaloons!!"

But I didn't get into the film thing because Mark is not the brightest button on the cardigan. I said, "Er... yes, well yes."

As he shuffled off, Mark turned round and said, "Will you let your mate know I've been round?"

"What mate?"

"You know, Dave."

Then he went off.

Wow!

And three times wow. In fact wowzee wowzee wow!!!

What had Dave the Laugh done?

9:15 p.m.

Phoned Rosie and told her.

She was very impressed – she loves the smack of violence.

She said, "Hmmm, my kind of guy. It's a good job Sven wasn't involved; a boy at a party I went to pushed into the loo line ahead of me and Sven threw his trousers into next door's garden."

"Why would Sven chuck his trousers into next door's garden? Was it a fit of pique?"

"Georgia, he threw the boy's trousers into next door's garden... and the boy was still wearing them."

"*Sacré bleu.*"

"*Mais oui.*"

9:35 p.m.

In theory, and especially given my special relationship with Jesus, I am against violence. However, there is a time and place for everything, and I think Dave biffing Mark is one of those exceptions that make the rule.

9:40 p.m.

It slightly gives me the Horn, actually.

Unlike Cousin James, who unfortunately has arrived. He is reading Tolkien's *The Hobbit* and goes on and on about it.

He said, "It's very interesting, but did you know that even now people go on a pilgrimage to Tolkien's grave and they speak in Elfin?"

James has a bit of trouble with the word "interesting". In fact, sad sacks chatting in Elfin over some dead bloke's grave is not "interesting", it is "stupid".

Still, at least he is reading rubbish and not trying to play tickly bears with me.

Midnight

What is it with boys and elves?

Thursday March 17th

Phoned Dave the Laugh and thanked him *vis-à-vis* the duffing-up incident. He said, "It's a pleasure, gorgeous."

But he didn't say "see you later" or anything.

Saturday March 19th

At one time I had boys snogging my ears and so on, and now I am alone for the rest of my life. How did that happen? How come I have peaked already?

11:00 p.m.

Started a letter to SG:

Dear Robbie,

It's raining here and we are doing a crap play about some Scottish fools who...

11:15 p.m.

I can't talk about school to him, otherwise he will remember that I am still at school.

Friday April 1st, All Fools Day

You are not kidding.

Friday April 8th

I have tried to write to Robbie so many times, but the sadness is that I don't have anything to say to him. He

doesn't want to be my boyfriend and I just have to accept it.

I am going to take down my shrine to him.

11:00 p.m.

Mum came in after I had taken down my shrine and she caught me crying.

She sat down on the edge of the bed and stroked my hair, which is normally a killing offence, but it was all scrubbled up and greasy anyway. She said, "I'm sorry, love, I'm sorry you're so upset, but you will have fun again and you will have nice boyfriends because you are lovely and funny and my darling daughter."

That made me cry more.

Then Libby toddled in and came up on the bed beside me.

"Look, Ginger, nice."

She had what I think was probably once a biscuit in one hand and Gordy by the neck in the other. She put him on my bed and he started attacking my knees under the bedclothes.

Midnight

Mum made me a milky pops drink like she did when I was little and ill. Which was nice. Except that I put it down on my bedside table and Gordy plunged his head in it. He has been having a sneezing attack for about ten minutes.

Snog factor 25 and a half

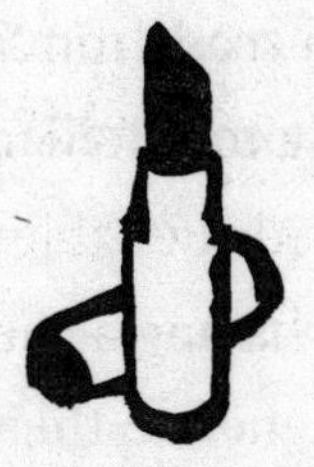

Monday April 11th
School

Hot news straight off the press: The Stiff Dylans have got a new lead singer to replace the Sex God. Ellen was full of it in the loos. We were all holed up there at break. If any Storm Troopers come in we have to stand on the loo seat so they can't see our feet. The trick is to leave the door a bit open and stand right to the other edge of the loo seat, so the cubicle looks empty. We are clearly geniuses, because it works.

Anyway, Ellen said, "He's half Italian and half American and he's called Masimo."

Jools said, "I'm going to learn how to speak American immediately."

"Mabs reckons he's dishy and fit as a flea."

"Angela Richards saw him arrive at the Phoenix. She lives just across from it and she said he turned up on one of those really cool Italian scooters."

11:00 a.m.

I listened to their girlish chatter with great sadnosity. It was all right for them; they could just replace one lead singer with another. They did not know the heartbreak I had gone through because the Sex God had chosen wombats and rogue bores instead of me.

Jools said, "Angela said he is the coolest, fittest-looking boy she has ever seen. When he drew up and was parking his scooter this group of girls sort of gathered around just looking. Ogling him. He said *ciao* to them."

I said, "How is he going to be able to be in the band if he can't speak English?"

Ellen said, "He can speak English, he's half American."

I said, "Oh yeah, and that's the same, is it? I'll just say this – Americans don't know who Rolf Harris is, and they call knickers 'panties'. That is not really speaking English, is it?"

Rosie said, "Yeah, you've got a point, Geegee, but perhaps

in the spirit of neighbourliness and red-bottomosity we could help him to speak properly."

Hmmm.

Swimming

Herr Kamyer was "in charge" this arvie because Miss Stamp was doing some certificate or other.

I said, "It's probably in advanced lesbianism."

It probably is, actually.

In the pool

I swam under Jas's legs and she squealed like a girl because I surprised her.

She was very grumpy because in her panic she had got her fringe wet.

My crawl style is quite stylish I think. Unlike Nauseating P. Green's style. She really is a fiasco waiting to happen. She wears armbands and she still sinks without a trace every few minutes.

Anyway, the funniest bit for me was when Herr Kamyer entered stage left. He came out in his swimming knickers and we all went, "Phwoaar," which made him have such a dither attack that he stepped off into the deep end by mistake. Without removing his glasses. He spent about a million years diving down to look for them. Herr Kamyer is the palest man known to humanity. His legs and arms are like a stick insect. He does a very amusing breaststroke (in my opinion) like a cross between a human being and a twit, with just a touch of blind beaver. I could watch him for ages.

We were all having splashy fun when the fire alarm went off. Oh *merde*! Now what? It couldn't be a real fire, and even if it was, wouldn't we be better off staying in forty-five million gallons of water, like where we already were?

But oh no, that would be too simple. The lifeguard was Mr Attwood. He came perving along with a whistle and started yelling at us to get out of the water and go to our mustering points. What mustering points? What are we, bucking broncos?

I said to RoRo as we dragged ourselves up the swimming pool steps, "I can't believe this!"

When we tried to go and get changed, Elvis had locked the doors to the changing rooms. He said, "Come on, come on, follow the exit signs pronto."

Rosie, who was practically hitting Mr Attwood in the spectacles with her nungas, said, "Yes, but where do the signs lead?"

And he said, "Outside to safety. Now get a move on."

"Outside??"

Minutes later we were outside, in early April, in the car park. In our semi-nuddy-pants.

We were shivering like mad when Mr Mad came round with some BacoFoil stuff. I said to him, "This is hardly the time to be roasting vegetables."

And he, in a rather surly way for someone who was supposed to be calming me down in the face of a towering inferno, said, "It's to wrap around you."

Marvellous.

Thank you.

3:00 p.m.

I will not easily forget standing in a car park wrapped in BacoFoil next to Herr Kamyer, also in BacoFoil.

He was still trying to be normal. Not that he has the slightest idea what that is, as he is German.

He said, "So girls, shall we sing a little song to practise

our German? I know, let us do the funny camping one of when the Koch family go away and they forget many things which we must list."

God save us all.

Saturday April 16th

Jas has gone off to the Forest of Fools with Hunky, so the rest of the Ace Gang went to Churchill Square for essential shopping items. It's incredibly nippy noodles and parky, but that didn't stop us casually sitting on a wall chatting and lad spotting. There were hordes of lads ladding about. There is an all-nighter at the Buddha Lounge tonight, but unfortunately since my report card I am virtually under house arrest. It's a lot of fuss over nothing. Slim said on the "remarks" part of my report card, "Georgia is an intelligent girl whose academic career is blighted by her immature japes."

"Immature japes". Lawks a mercy! I bet when Slim went to school they used to make their own fun with bits of old Weetabix packets. And a really great night out was going down the grocers and thinking about what you could make with dairy products. But tragically, life is not like that. We do not do "immature japes", we do really sophisticated japes.

1:15 p.m.

Just as we were reapplying lippy after our nutritious lunch of choc-ices, Dave the Laugh and Rollo came along. When they saw us, Dave said, "Be gentle with us."

What was he going on about? Ellen practically exploded with ditherosity. I, on the *au contraire*, was a visage of casualosity. I even remembered to smile with my tongue behind my back teeth. Dave winked at me. Shut up winking.

Rollo was looking all sheepish. I think he still likes Jools, even though he finished with her. Jools is keen but she's playing hard to get. Ellen has obviously taken my hints from our boy bible on "how to make any fool fall in love with you" seriously. She was flicking her hair around so much I thought she might snap her neck. And also she was combining it with darting glances. Dave said, "All right, Ellen?"

And she said, flickyflick, "Yes, I'm all right, Dave. Are... you... all right?" And she gave a very meaningful flick and darting glance. But no one got it.

As I was being a bit reddish, Dave's so-called girlfriend turned up. She is not pretending to be reddish, she IS reddish. Good grief she's friendly. She said, "Oh hi, everyone, great to see you again."

Was it? Why? Before I knew it we were all pretending to be really jolly and friendly for no reason. It was very very tiring. After they had gone, Jools and Rollo were talking to each other "privately", so Rosie and Ellen and me went to try out make-up in Boots. When Ellen went round the other side of the "Rich Chick" range, I said to Rosie, "Rachel's a bit like Jas, isn't she, only more ginger. It's all 'ooohhh look, some cuckoo spit' and 'ooooh have a nice day' and 'ooooh your hair is nice' and—"

Rosie said, "Yes I think I've got the picture, Gee, and I think you are being very bitter and twisted and that's why I *aime* you so much."

I thought Ellen was busy trying on flavoured eye shadow (a bit of a mystery that one, unless there is such a thing as eye snogging, which quite frankly wouldn't surprise me). Anyway, Ellen popped her head up really suddenly and said, "You are not very nice about Dave the Laugh, Georgia. I mean, I am, and I'm the one he... well, you know, I'm the dumpee. Not you. I mean, what has he ever done to you? You know that time when you were supposed to snog him at the fish party, well..."

I started blabbing about my mates being like part of me.

Fortunately at that point Jools came running over like an excitable elephant in a frock.

"He says he'd like to give it another go."

We spent the rest of the afternoon arguing about whether you should give a boy a second chance.

Who knows, the whole thing is a bloody mystery.

Home

I am under heavy manners this weekend, even to the extent that I am being forced to stay in and baby-sit whilst the so-called grown-ups go out and make fools of themselves. The rest of the Ace Gang are going to the funfair. I tried saying to Vati that we had been set "going to the funfair" as homework, but all he said was, "Georgia, let me put it this way... No."

Mutti said, "Anyway, you're baby-sitting for us. It's Uncle Eddie's birthday and we're going out."

They are going to some really sad karaoke bar. Uncle Eddie won first prize the last time singing "Like a Virgin", so that should give you some idea about how crap it must be.

Mutti was tarting herself up in the bathroom. She said, "Honestly, when he started singing 'Like a Virgin' it was like Madonna was there in his body."

Christ, what an image.

As a fabulous parting gift, Mum said, "Oh, by the way, I've made an appointment to see Dr Gilhooley. Put it in your diary."

I said, "Oh no. No, no, no, there is nothing wrong with me that having normal parents wouldn't fix. I will not show him my elbows again. They're fine, I'm living with them."

Mutti said, "It's not about your health. I just want to see him because he's so gorgeous."

She saw me looking sick and said, "No, not really. I want to fix up a work experience day for you there. I know how much you like biology."

"What???? What??? Just because I can do a fantastic impression of a lockjaw germ does not mean I want to be a doctor's receptionist."

"It'll be interesting. It will give you a taste of real life."

"Mum, you've been in his surgery, you know it's not a taste of real life, it's a taste of pensioner hell. I am not sitting around all day in a place full of people like Mr Next Door in incontinence trunks."

I may as well be invisible, because she just went out tutting.

7:50 p.m.

After Mutti and Vati had roared off in the clown car – or Robinmobile, as I call it – I went up to see what my little sister was up to. She is obsessed with Gordy and is trying to teach him to jump through her hula hoop. Good luck, mad toddler. It's not that Gordy can't leap, he can – in fact he leaps all the time for no apparent reason. But it is senseless leaping, not hoop leaping.

8:00 p.m.

Gordy is so alarmingly cross-eyed, it may be that he can't even see the hoop. I wonder if you can get cat glasses?

Angus is not in. He's on the wall with Naomi snogging and wrestling. It's a bit pervy snogging in front of your offspring. I should know – my olds are always fondling each other and it's disgusting. There is some manky big black cat from up the road hanging about. I see him around Naomi sometimes; he is a rival for her love.

Naomi is a dreadful minx; she seems to entice Manky, even in front of Angus. She is the furry-faced shame of womanhood.

8:25 p.m.

Oh *quel dommage*, Gordy is wrestling with his own tail and the tail is winning, so Libby has turned her attention to me. Oh dear.

"Gingey, let's go play outside now."

"Darling, it's nearly bedtime. I know... we could read *Heidi*."

That's when the *Heidi* book hit me quite hard on the head. Libby had apparently gone off cheese and lederhosen. She was stamping her little foot.

"Outside, naughty boy... OUTSIDE!"

Oh hell's biscuits.

And she wouldn't even get dressed. I had to put a blanket over her jimmyjams (at least she had the bottoms on, for once). She was leaping around, yelling, "Hickory dickory dot, the cow leapt over the SPOOOOON!!"

I opened the front door and she went leaping out into the dark night. Angus looked down at us from the wall and casually biffed me with his paw. Thanks for your help, furry pal. When we got to the gate I said to Libbs, "There, that was nice leaping, wasn't it? Let's go back to snuggly buggly bed and—"

But she had undone the gate and was leaping away down the street in her blanket. I went after her and tried to pick her up. She nearly had my eye out.

8:40 p.m.

Ten minutes later we were still leaping "over the spoon". My plan was to leap with her and sort of round her up and head her back to our house. But I'd just get her in the right direction and she would do some quick leaps and get round me again. By this stage we had got halfway down Baron's Street, and when I looked up from another failed attempt to head Libby off I saw Dom from The Stiff Dylans getting out of his van with his guitar. Probably turning up for a jamming session at the Phoenix. Libby was leaping in a circle, so I had a chance to smile at Dom.

He said, "Hey, hi, how are you, Georgia. And Libby."

Libby ignored him because she was busy leaping. But she still managed to tell him, "Gordon pooed in the bath."

Dom said, "I won't even ask. Have you heard from Robbie?"

I felt a bit tearful. "Yeah, he really likes it there."

Dom said, "Yeah. I heard. Pity. Ah well... erm, come to the gig on the eighth. We've re-formed and got a cool new singer, so it looks like the record deal might go ahead."

I said, "You've got a new singer. Yes, well, that's cool..."

I was thinking, *Yes, that is cool if you can replace a Sex God, which you can't, even if he is a bit obsessed with vegetables.* But I didn't say that.

A silver scooter tore round the corner and stopped outside the Phoenix.

Dom said, "This is him actually – Masimo."

So, at last, this was the so-called Italian-American pseudo Sex God. Huh. How interested was I out of ten? Minus twelve. Unfortunately Libby was interested in the noise of the scooter, and also because it had mirrors and stuff on it. She went leaping over to the scooter.

I yelled, "Libby, come back here now!"

One word from me and she does as she likes. I could hear her saying to the new singer, who was bending over taking off his helmet, "Heggo, I am a moo cow."

Oh bloody Blimey O'Reilly.

I went and got hold of her round the arms, pinning them down so that she couldn't hit me, and lifted her up. But with an alarming change of mood she started kissing me really wildy all over my hair and face. She was ruffling my hair up and messing up my lip gloss. Very very annoying and wet.

"I LOBE you, my Ginger."

I hadn't actually looked at the pretend Sex God as I was busy trying to wrestle with Libby, but then he spoke with an accent that was quite Italian.

"Hello, Ginger. And *ciao*, little moo cow."

I looked at him. Ohmygiddygodstrousers! He was absolutely gorgeous. Really really gorgey. Really gorgey! And I do mean gorgey. That's why I said it. He had very black wavy hair and a tan – a tan in England in April. And he had eyes and teeth and a mouth. He had a back, front, sides, arms, everything. His mouth wasn't as big as Mark Big Gob's (whose was?) but it was on the generous side. And he had really long eyelashes and AMBER eyes. In fact he had eyes like someone I knew, and then I realised he had eyes like Angus. How freaky deaky!! They were the same colour as Angus's! But they didn't have that casual madnosity that Angus's had. In fact they were smiley and soft and dreamy.

Then I realised that about two hundred years had passed since he had said hello.

I forced Libby's mouth off the back of my neck (in a loving and caring way). I thought, *Act natural and normal, do not under any circumstances have an uncontrollable laughing attack*. I took a deep breath. "Ah yes well, er *ciao* to you too. I'm not really ginger, it's just a trick of the light. Hahahahahahaha."

Oh brilliant, I was having an uncontrollable laughing attack.

Dom must have realised that my brain had dropped out because he said, "Masimo, this is Georgia. Georgia, this is Masimo, our new lead singer. Georgia was, erm, friendly with Robbie."

Masimo. Masimo. Whohoa Masimo! I must get a grip. Masimo was locking up his scooter. He looked up and looked me straight in the eye. I managed not to fall over. He said, "Well, Georgia, it was really nice to meet you. I hope we meet again. *Ciao*."

Then they walked off to go into the Phoenix.

I said, "Yes, *ciao*."

And Libby shouted, "Night-night, botty boy!"

I turned round and carried her off as fast as I could.

"Libby, why did you say that naughty thing? Don't say it again!"

Libby was singing, "Have you seen the botty boy, the botty boy, the botty boy..."

Where does she get all this stuff from?

God, she weighs a lot these days. I was exhausted when we finally got home. I tucked her up in her bed – she didn't want to come into my bed because she was cross with me for yelling at her. She wouldn't even give me a good-night kiss, although she did manage a quick whack round my ear with scuba-diving Barbie.

In bed

Good grief.

The Dreamboat has landed again.

Midnight

Now I've really got the Cosmic Horn. The only fly in the armpit is that he hasn't shown the slightest interest in me.

12:35 a.m.

Although he did say, " I hope we meet again."

But does it mean that he hopes we meet again, or, you know, like he hopes we meet again but not really?

Oh happy days, I am on the rack of love again.

Monday April 18th
Stalag 14

Had to try to apply make-up on the move because I woke up so late. So there was a mascara-brush-in-the-eye incident. Jas was all fresh faced by her gate. And ludicrously cheerful. And loud.

"Hi, Georgia, look, I've got my Wilderness badge. I've put it next to my Rambler's badge. Do you see? Great, isn't it?"

"Jas, something really—"

"Well, when we got there we had to construct a shelter out of branches and Tom—"

"Jas, I don't want to hear about your twig house. I want to tell you about Mr Gorgeous."

Jas said, "You know the Ace Gang rule."

"What Ace Gang rule?"

"She who starts first must be heard."

"Yes, but it was ages ago we made that rule... and anyway, you are just going to rave on about twigs whereas I want to tell you about this gorgey—"

But Jas had her hands over her ears and was humming. Oh my giddy aunt's brassiere.

I mouthed at her, "OK, you start."

She gave me a scary smile. "Are you sure you're interested?"

I felt like yelling, "Of COURSE I'm not interested, you complete twit!!" But I smiled back and said, "Of course I am, go on, tell me about making a nourishing stew out of bits of old turnip and badger poo."

She looked all stroppy.

"You're not really interested."

"I am."

"You're not, otherwise you would ask an intelligent question."

Oh dear God.

"Oh OK, er, did Tom's Swiss Army knife come in handy?"

"Ah well, it's funny you should say that because..."

8:50 a.m.

Three million years later she finished her ludicrously boring ravings on, by which time we had arrived at Stalag 14. Hawkeye – not world renowned for her deep love of me – was eyeing me like a mad beagle.

"Georgia Nicolson, you are covered in make-up, you look like a creature of the night. Go and take it off immediately, and also take a bad conduct mark."

I was grumbling to Jas as we slouched off. "Creature of the night, what is she going on about?"

As I came out of the loo to scamper off to assembly with that lovely red scrubbed look so beloved by the very sad, I bumped into Wet Lindsay.

"Georgia Nicolson, you are three minutes late for assembly. Take a bad conduct mark."

I said, "I tell you what, Lindsay, why don't you just boil me in oil and call it a day?"

But I said it after she had trolloped off on her extremely knobbly legs.

English

We are doing the life of the Bard of Avon, otherwise known as Billy Shakespeare or the Swan of Avon, as Rosie calls him, because she deliberately misheard "bard" as "bird". Miss Wilson was raving on about his doublet and how he invented language.

Oh I am sooo bored, and distracted by my new pash, Masimo. I can't stop thinking about him. He is by far the dreamiest boy in the universe and probably beyond.

I sent a note to Rosie and said to pass it on to all of the gang. I wrote it in Shakespearean-type language, because I can't help being artistic. And also I have a thirst for knowledge(ish).

I wrote: Odds bodkin I am boredeth. I feeleth a let us goeth down ye olde discotheque coming on.

Rosie wrote back: Forsooth and lack a day let us grooveth!!

So when Miss Wilson turned her back to write something dull on the blackboard, we had a quick burst of manic "Let's go down the disco" dancing to relieve our girlish tension.

Vair vair *amusant.*

Break

Miss Wilson will be very pleased with Billy's enduring effect on the culture of England. When Rosie sat on the knicker toasters in the Blodge labs, she leapt up and said, "Lawks a mercy, I burneth my bum-oley!"

Which made me laugh a LOT. I think I may be hysterical with love.

I don't know whether to tell the Ace Gang about Masimo. They might think wrongly that I am a superficial sort of person who leaps from Sex God to Sex God.

I decided to keep my love news extravaganza for the lugholes of my one and only bestest pal, Jas.

School gates

4:00 p.m.

I couldn't wait to tell her, but I had to because she was droning on and on to the rest of the gang at the gates about her slug-eating weekend. On and on. I may have dropped off for a minute, because she had to say, "Come on then, Georgia, don't you want to get away from this place?"

As we ambled along, I started telling Jas about Masimo.

"He is beyond gorgey, Jas – really really *bon* and also *formidable* in the extreme. He's got these eyes, you know, really fab, like Angus's eyes only, you know, great. Also he has got snog factor twenty-five and a half."

"I thought the snogging scale only went up to ten."

"Jas, pay attention. I said snog factor – that means like sex appeal."

"Why haven't I been told about the snog factor thing."

"Look, Jas, I just made it up and—"

"Well, why have a rule if you are just going to break it and make up your own stuff? It would be like if we were in the wilderness camp and it said to make your own fire and someone used matches."

Oh God, I couldn't believe we were back here again,

round the sodding campfire. I said, "Anyway, he is fabby beyond the dreams of avarice. I have got all of the Horns combined for him: Particular, General and Cosmic."

Jas looked very disapproving. "You said Robbie was your only one and only only one and now it's Masimo, who you've only seen for two minutes. You will end up a lonely person with a reputation for promiscuosity."

What is the matter with her? She is the Mother Teresa for a new generation, with a crap fringe. I was furious. I said, "Yes, but do you know what the good news is, Jas? I won't end up YOU, Mrs Slug Eater."

She got the megahump and we were walking along *ignorez-vous*ing each other when we came across Dave the Laugh AGAIN. Since he got a girlfriend I've seen him all the time; I wonder if he's stalking me. I was about to say that when he grinned and said, "Look, Georgia, stop following me around, you know I love it."

Damn!! By this time we had reached Jas's gate and she went into her drive and said, as a parting shot, "Georgia thinks Masimo is really cool. She likes him, if you know what I mean."

I couldn't believe it!! She had ratted on me and cheapened

my love by announcing it on Radio Jas. I could feel my ears going red. As we walked on, Dave was looking at me in a looking-at-me way. Which I hate.

"You just can't resist a lead singer, can you, Georgia? He's flash."

I said, "He's not flash, he's Italian, that's what they're like."

Dave said, "When I saw him, he was carrying a handbag."

"That's not a handbag, that's a... er... wallet thing."

"It's a bag he carries in his hand, known as a handbag."

I said quickly, not necessarily bothering to involve my brain in the process, "He keeps his revolver in it."

Dave looked right into my eyes. He said, "Excuse me – are you officially mad?"

I said, "No, are YOU mad?"

And he went, "No... are YOU mad?"

We'd got to my gate by then and we could have gone on with the "No, are YOU mad?" game for ever, but as I started my bit Dave stopped me by tickling me in the ribs. It made me splutter and I got spazoid and he kept doing it. Now I was playing tickly bears with Dave the Laugh. He'd probably start talking Elfin in a minute. What is the matter with boys? I said to Dave, "What in the name of arse is the matter with boys?"

And he looked at me and then just snogged me! How dare he!!! I tried to tell him off but I couldn't speak for the snogging. I don't like to admit this under the circumstances, but he really is a cool snogger and I forgot everything in the puckerosity of the moment. When we stopped for breath he said, "Phwoar – excellent snogging, Georgia."

I said, "Why did you do that? You're going out with someone else."

Dave said, "So?"

I said, "Well, it's not right."

"What isn't?"

"You enticing me and snogging me when you're going out with someone else."

"Georgia, you're repeating yourself, and anyway, there's an explanation."

Oh here we go. He'll tell me that it's really me he likes and that it's *moi* he wants, but I'll have to say, "I'm sorry, Dave, but I'm putting you aside with a firm hand – I am in love with another."

I looked at him sympathetically. "What is the explanation, Dave?"

"I like snogging you and I have got the General Horn."

"But..."

"It's my age. I'll grow out of it when I'm about forty-five."

"But I..."

"Don't you like snogging me?"

"Well, that's not the point, I mean, don't you like Rachel...?"

"Yeah, she's cool, but I like you as well, and come to think of it, I quite fancy your mum."

"You fancy my mum????"

I couldn't believe my earlugs! Actually, I think even Dave felt like he had gone that little bit too far. He said, "It's nothing personal, it's just my hormones. Tell them off."

I just looked at him.

He said, "Look, girls and boys are different. Girls like to be touched twenty times a day in a nonsexual way to feel good about themselves – that's why I tickle you and link arms with you – but boys think about sex, snogging and football, and also snogging whilst playing football. Simple."

Home

No one in.

I am completely and utterly living in a state of confusiosity.

Dave is clearly insane.

But what if he's right?

Actually, the way he describes it, it explains a lot of things – Oscar, Mark Big Gob, Cousin James, and those boys from Foxwood that run into our legs and say, "Any chance of a shag?"

5:00 p.m.

But on the other hand, what about Hunky with boring old Jas, and Sven and Rosie? Oh, I don't know.

5:05 p.m.

Also, I sometimes get the Cosmic Horn, so does that mean I'm half girl, half boy?

5:30 p.m.

Does that mean I will have periods and also be heavily bearded and good at reading maps?

Actually, looking at my legs, I suspect I do have a touch of the hermaphrodite about me. When does the hair do its growing? It wasn't there this morning and now it's about a foot long.

5:45 p.m.

Mutti came in from work. I looked at her. How could Dave the Laugh say he quite fancied her? I wonder if she fancies him. Probably – she has no moral backbone. Ohohohoh get out of my head!!!

6:00 p.m.

The phone rang and for once Mutti answered it. She started giggling. "So, it's like a sort of dance orgy thing?" Then I heard her going, "No!!" Then more silence... "No!!!... and he took off all his clothes... to the music??"

Good Lord.

Then Mum began again, "Uh-huh... no... no... no... No!!!"

I thought I would have to kill her to stop her, and then she started again, "So does everyone get naked? Oh I see... he just spontaneously took everything off because he'd got carried away by the music. Wow! What time does it start? OK, what are you wearing? OK, see you there."

Bedroom

The world, which once seemed a simple place, has gone mad. Mutti has gone off to dance with men in their nuddy-pants. She

says it's called "Five Rhythms". I bet. Dad is out with his ludicrous mates in the Robinmobile, probably marauding around harassing women. Libby is destroying some poor fool's house. She has taken Gordy round in his cat basket to "wisit" Josh. I don't think that Gordy was specifically invited. Even Angus is off in his luxury bachelor pad with Naomi; he's back in the Prat Poodles' kennel because Mr and Mrs Next Door are out.

6:30 p.m.

I will have to try to distract myself from thinking about Masimo and the whole Cosmic Horn thing. I'll try doing some homework. Another bad conduct mark and it's Detention City for me.

6:45 p.m.

How boring is *Blithering Heights*? Remind me never to read anything else by Emily Brontëchitis.

7:00 p.m.

I am soooo restless.

Phoned Jools and Ellen and they said they would meet me at "homework club", which is our code for the clock tower.

8:00 p.m.

It's incredibly nippy noodles but at least my face is snug. It should be – it has several layers of make-up on it. I've got so much mascara on I'm going to have to do eyelid exercises to keep my eyes open. We sat on the wall by the Co-op. Mark Big Gob came by with his unusually lardy mates, but to my absolute amazement he said, "All right?" to me. Which is the nearest thing to him saying, "Good morrow, Miss Nicolson."

Jools and Ellen were totally fazed. Jools said, "He acted almost like a human being."

We discussed the mystery that is boydom. Jools is still thinking about whether to go out with Rollo again. She said, "The last time, he finished with me because he wanted his freedom – so will he want it again in a week, when we start going out again?"

Hmmmmm.

I said, "I'm going to have to read more of my *How to Make Complete Fools Fall in Love with You* book.

Ellen said, "You said the book said that if I danced by myself, Dave the Laugh would come and get off with me. He got off, but not with me... so what the book says is rubbish."

I said, "The book didn't have a chapter called 'Dance by

Yourself, Ellen, and Dave the Laugh Will Get Off with You'. It just said that it was a way of enticing boys into your web. And someone did come and dance with you, just not the right someone."

Sometimes I amaze myself with my wisdomosity.

As we walked along, we happened to pass by the Phoenix. (Well, when I say "happened" to pass what I mean is that I deliberately wandered that way.) There was a light on and The Stiff Dylans' van was outside. Wow... trembly and jelloid knees.

I said, "I bet Masimo is in there. You know, the new singer with the Dylans. He is absolutely groovy and marvy and fab."

Jools said, "So you quite rate him then?"

I said, "There's a stage door sort of thing that you can get in, and we could have a look at him and the Dylans rehearsing. Come on, it'll be cool."

Ellen was having a dither attack and talking rubbish about private property and so on. But she followed me and Jools round the back in the dark to the stage door. It was open, so we quietly went in. We could hear the band playing. The door to the main club room was straight ahead, but to the right was a room that they used as a dressing room. I'd been in it for snogging extravaganzas with Robbie. Thinking of him made me feel a bit wobbly, but he had chosen furry freaks called wombats rather than me; I had to think of the future. We opened the door and I said to Jools and Ellen, "There's a gap at the top of the wall from where you can see right on to the stage. We could step up on this chair and then on to those boxes."

My skirt was so tight that I had to tuck it into my knickers to get up. Jools said, "Now I have quite literally seen everything."

Ellen wouldn't get up because she was a scaredy cat. Either that or she was wearing something alarming in the pants department. She has probably been studying at the Jas school of big knickers.

It was so exciting. When we got up there we could see right on to the stage and no one could see us – the boy stalkers.

Oh general jelloidosity... there they were, the lads. And one lad in particular. Masimo was wearing a groovy Italian shirt and jeans. He was singing "Play Cool" and it sounded marvy with a bit of an accent.

Jools whispered, "Phwoar."

And I said, "I know."

After a few minutes they stopped playing and Dom said, "Shall we pack it in for now? I'm starving."

Masimo said, "Yeah, I think it is... how you say... kicking? Do you like to come round to my house and I will fix us some pasta and vino?"

Dom said, "*Ciao bella, mon amigo.*"

And they all laughed and started packing up their gear. Masimo said, "Oh damn... *Scusi*, first I make a phone call."

Ben said, "Hot date, Masimo?"

Masimo smiled – good grief, he was sex on a dish when he smiled. "Well... it's just someone, she... I will tell her another night. It is cool."

He jumped off the stage. Oh God's shortie nightie, he might come into the dressing room... and although I was keen, I thought being found on a box practically in your nuddy-pants seemed just that little bit too keen.

We scrambled down, nearly killing Ellen, and rushed off to the door and outside.

11:00 p.m.

I had to run home to make sure I got back into Gestapo Headquarters before the olds returned. *Pant pant pant.*

Masimo was *pant pant* gorgey... but who was the girl on the phone *pant pant*?

Angus was just strolling home with a mouse tail, as a special present for Mutti. How pleased she will be. I raced upstairs and leapt into bed to dreamy dream how to entrance Masimo.

Perhaps I had better learn Italian.

I may suggest to Slim that I give up German because there's no chance I'll be going there ever since I learnt that snogging in German is *knutschen*. And as that would leave a gap in my school schedule, I could learn Italian instead because I have a deep interest in er... ancient Rome and so on.

Tuesday April 19th
Jas's house

Jas must be setting off at dawn to get to Stalag 14 because she was there before me. She is trying to *ignorez-vous* me, because I called her Mrs Slug Eater.

Maths

I gave Jas my most attractive smile but she pretended she was interested in quadratic equations.

Break

Absolutely typical of this bloody place. I went to see Slim about my Italian plan and I didn't even get to the ancient Rome bit. In fact, to be honest, I didn't even get to her office. Hawkeye asked me why I was hanging around waiting to see Slim, and I explained my interest and she said, "Don't annoy me any more than you do simply by turning up to school. Off you go."

That's nice and encouraging isn't it? I don't know why she's a teacher; she hates us. Oh no, I tell a lie – she likes all the useless girlie wet beaky swots like Wet Lindsay and Astonishingly Dim Monica and so on.

Lunchtime

I borrowed an Italian book from the library, *Parliamo Italiano*, and found a comfy loo, put my feet up and read.

Five minutes later

Constantly disturbed by ludicrously excited first formers chasing each other and saying, "Oh we did something really brilliant in Blodge – we looked at pond life under a microscope." Surely I wasn't like them at their age.

Christ, now they are playing tig. Well, they were until Wet Lindsay came in to torture them. Of course, she came rattling at my study door.

"Who's in there?"

"It's me."

"Who's me?"

"I am."

She completely and unreasonably lost her rag.

"Get out here now!"

Oh odds bodkin. I sloped out of the loo. She was remarkably red, and there is really no excuse for her knees.

"I might have known it would be you."

I said, "Lindsay, forgive me if I'm right, but there is no law against going to the piddly-diddly department, is there?"

She said, "Don't be so cheeky."

I didn't bother to reply. As I was leaving, she said, "Off you go and play with your silly playmates. Honestly, when will you lot grow up?"

I really hate her. She has never forgiven me for going out with Robbie, or for when she fell over into the sanitary dispenser when I was trying to help her in the school panto.

Outside

Brrrr. I found a little sheltered corner round the back of Elvis's hut. The old maniac was nowhere to be seen. So I snuggled under my coat to learn about the Pasta-a-gogo people.

Blodge

Rosie said, "Where in the name of Slim's chins have you been all lunchtime?"

I told her about my Italian studies. "The main nub and thrust of their gorgey language is that you add 'o' to everything."

She said, "Oh, OK, what is... er... 'desk' then?"

"Deskio."

She looked at me. "What is 'snog'?"

"Snoggio."

I think she was quite impressed.

4:15 p.m.

No sign of Jas. She must be running like the wind when the bell goes, or lurking around until she sees me going home. She is so childish.

Home

5:30 p.m.

Mutti insisted on taking me to Dr Clooney's surgery. She has made an appointment with him to talk about my work experience. The whole thing is a fiasco. Jas is going to work in the Jennings's fruit and veg shop, which means she will be snogging Tom, and Rosie says her work experience will be "having the flu", and so that means her work experience will be snogging Sven. I don't know why everyone is bothering with all this work business. I have set my sights far higher than having a job. I am going to be a pop star's girlfriend. It's hard work, but someone has to do it. Try telling that to my mum, though. I did try actually. I said, "Look, Mum, it's pointless going to find out about jobs and stuff, because I am going to be rich beyond the beyond of the Universe of Beyond."

She was trying to capture Gordy and Libby, and was getting quite bad-tempered.

"Oh yes, and how are you going to do that, exactly?"

"I have a plan."

"Does it involve hanging around with someone in a local band and them getting a record deal and then you

living in a luxurious flat in London and America and having anything you want, for ever and ever? Is that your plan?"

Wow, sometimes she is almost psychic. How did she know all this? Had she been tuning in to Radio Jas?

I said, "Wow, how did you know all that?"

She was stuffing Libby into a pair of dungarees, so she had to speak quite loudly over the growling. I think Gordy was in the dungarees somewhere too.

"I'll tell you how I know, Georgia, because sadly, I know what rubbish your brain is full of. Get your coat on."

Charming.

Gordy is being left behind in a secure unit (Libby's old playpen with the table on top of it). Libby wouldn't let go of the bars of the cat prison until Mum let her pop Pantalitzer doll in with Gordy to keep him company.

I've never really got Pantalitzer doll. It has a weird plastic face with a horrible fixed smile, and the rest of it is a sort of cloth bag with hard plastic hands on each side like steel forks. It says "Made in Eastern Europe", so that is another place I won't be visiting.

Vati has gone off on what he calls a "secret mission"

with Uncle Eddie. He said to Mum, "I'll be back for you later. Keep yourself warm for me."

And then he snogged her. How disgusting is that?

Dr Clooney's

Oh, how very embarrassing all this is. I want to be home dreaming up my plan for entrancing Masimo. And also it's only seven days to the gig, and I haven't even started my cleansing and toning routine, let alone thought about making my eyes as sticky as possible. I should buy some more false eyelashes, otherwise known as boy entrancers. You can get some with tiny little sparkly bits in them. Or is that going a bit too far? I don't want to blind him, merely mesmerise him.

But maybe I have gone completely mad, like Ellen. Maybe I am just delirious with red-bottomosity. He only said it was nice to meet me. To be fair, he didn't say, "I want you to be my girlfriend." Or even, "Do you want to come out for a cup of coffee?"

Oh Lord. Perhaps I am just being *le grand* idiot.

Speaking of idiots, when we walked into Dr Clooney's waiting room, Mr Across the Road was sitting there. He's

really cheered up since the kittykats were cruelly given away. He's especially cheerful that we have got Gordy. As he said, "Only a complete fool would take him in."

He said to Mum, "You're looking gorgeous as ever, Connie. Nothing wrong, I hope?"

Mum giggled in a horrible way. It's always like this when she's around men. Thank goodness I have a bit more dignitosity than her. I have certainly not learned my boy-entrancing skills from her. She said, "Oh no, I'm fine, thank you, we all are. It's just that Georgia is thinking of taking up a career in medicine, so we've come to talk to the doctor."

Mr Across the Road went, "Oh yeah, hahahahahaha... yeah, good one."

But then he realised that Mum was serious and crossed his legs. I don't know why.

Mum had her usual dithering attack when we went in to see Dr Clooney. He is very fit for a medical man. He said to me, "Any more elbow trouble, Georgia?"

"No."

"Lungs not making a peculiar wheezing noise?"

"No."

"So, what is it: eyebrows growing uncontrollably?"

I started to say, "Well, no, but if there's a cream that..."

But Mum was batting her eyelashes and speaking rubbish. "Well... hehehehhe, as you know, Georgia is very interested in science and medicine and so on... aren't you, Georgia?"

I said, "Well, I can do an impression of a lockjaw germ."

Mum glared at me, but Dr Clooney said, "Go on then."

And I did it.

Dr Clooney said, "That is very very lifelike."

I was quite flattered and said, "I can also do a hydra wafting plankton into its central vortex with its tentacles. Do you want to see it—"

But old Mrs Dancing-in-the-nuddy-pants-with-strange-men-and-calling-it-aerobics interrupted me. "So I was wondering, as she has to do work experience for school, if she could perhaps come into your surgery for the day."

Dr Clooney said, "Nothing would give me greater pleasure. I mean it. Nothing. The day that your family walked into my surgery, well... life hasn't been the same."

That's when we noticed that Libby had got a blood pressure bandage thing wrapped round her head like a turban.

In the clown car
7:00 p.m.

I crouched down in the back of the Robinmobile as Mum rambled on. "He is so nice, isn't he? You know, so nice, isn't he?"

I didn't say anything, but that didn't stop her.

"He said nothing would give him more pleasure..."

I said, "I bet he's got a proper grown-up's car and not a clown car."

Mum got all defensive. "Your father loves this car, and it is not a clown car, it's quite stylish."

"Mum, if you had your face painted white with a red wig on and a clown nose, nobody would notice. They would think, 'Oh look, there's a clown driving a clown car,' and they would be right."

"Your dad has to have hobbies."

"Yes, but why do they have to be so crap?"

She started to tell me off, when a terrible thing happened: Uncle Eddie came round the corner. Not on his usual very embarrassing prewar motorbike and sidecar, but in another Robinmobile! Oh my God they were breeding. And Dad was sitting next to him. They both had goggles on.

They drove along beside us. When we got to traffic lights, they would draw up next to us and then "accelerate" away when the lights changed. Pretending to be a racing car. Libby loved it, but I just kept my head right down. Mum was trying to laugh it off, but I know she was thinking, "How did I end up married to him?"

Home

I had no idea that Pantalitzer was stuffed with pigeon feathers. It was like a pigeon snowstorm in the front room when we got back. Gordy's head was just poking out of a pile of feathers.

Mum went ballisticisimus. "This house is a bloody madhouse. He's worse than Angus!!"

Angus seemed quite pleased. Then Vati came bounding in and tried to grapple with Mum. She shoved him off and said, "Oh get off, Bob! First it's bluebottles in the garage from your fishing, now it's clown cars. I just want—"

"Him to be more normal?" I said helpfully.

Mum shouted, "NO!!"

"More absent?" I tried.

She turned round at the door and yelled, "I just want to

be more... more... ME!!!!"

Crikey.

10:00 p.m.

Anyone who's seen the size of my mutti's basoomas (which is practically everyone, as she is always revealing them) will not join in with her wish to be more.

Dad was going, "What did I do?"

But I have no time to sort out their lives. In fact, I wish they would shut up about themselves. On and on they go. They've had their chance, and now it's my turn.

My bedroom

Midnight

There has been a lot of murmuring and crying downstairs. It's keeping me awake. Then Dad started singing to Mum a song called "That's Why the Lady is a Tramp". Which personally wouldn't have cheered me up.

It's disgusting. They are snogging. My parents are snogging. I can hear the lip smackingness from up here. I'm going to soundproof my room.

12:10 a.m.

I wonder how I can casually bump into Masimo. He's bound to be surrounded by girls at the gig.

Hmmm.

Thursday April 21st

Got up early so that I can brush up on my boy skills from Mum's book.

8:10 a.m.

Good Lord. Apparently girls like boys to say stuff like, "You are the most beautiful girl in the world," and boys like you to go "Uummm" or "Oooohhhh".

Well, that is useful, because whenever I think about Masimo, my brain goes away on a short holiday to Idiotland, but even I should be able to manage "Uummm". Is that a high-pitched "Uuummm", or more of a "Uuermmmm", lower down?

You could alternate high and low, just in case.

Midday

Jas is still giving me her cold shoulders. Pathetico.

Miss Wilson had the nervy spaz to end all nervy spazzes

today in English. We were doing *MacUseless* and she had already told Rosie and Jools and Ellen off for doing "Let's go down the disco" during the witches' dance. Then Banquo (otherwise known as Moira Sanderson) said to the witches, "You should be women yet your beards forbid me to interpret that you are so."

And Rosie had a complete and utter laughing attack. It set all of us off. We had just about calmed down when Jas as Lady MacUseless said, "Thou creamfaced loon," and that set us all off again. I think I may have pulled something.

8:00 p.m.

Vati came crashing back from football with the "lads". I could hear them laughing and cracking open beer. I hope they don't come up to talk to me. Oh, too late.

8:05 p.m.

Vati and Uncle Eddie came trooping up, laughing like loons. I said, "I would love to chat, but I'm doing my English homework."

Vati went, "And you are studying *How to Make Anyone Fall in Love with You*, that well-known novel?"

Oh *merde,* I hadn't hidden the book. Now he will definitely be on my case for the next million years. I snatched it away, but fortunately before he could go on, the other lads yelled up the stairs. "Bob, come and look at this: Dave can get two legs down one trouser leg." And they went raving off.

I don't think much of the Portly One's fitness regime, supposed to convince Mum that he's a good catch. Uncle Eddie told me that Dad was sent off tonight at football after twenty minutes for persistently calling the referee, Mr Lancaster, "Maureen". Then he comes home and drinks beer.

If I have "little sense of responsibility", as Hawkeye says, I know who to thank for it.

8:30 p.m.

Mutti came home with Libby, and for a minute I thought I could hear Jas's voice. I hope Libby isn't doing impressions now. There was a knock on my door and it really was Jas's voice.

"Georgia, it's me. Can I... can I come in, please?"

Blimey. Jas was forgetting that she had eschewed me with a firm hand. I said in a dignity-at-all-times way, "Come."

And she came in all in a ditherspaz, with the piggy eyes

that are all too familiar a sight to me. She said, "Tom's going off for six months to Kiwi-a-gogo land."

I said, "*Non!*"

Then she started blubbing, "Six whole months! How can he go?? And leave me behind?"

I started to say, "Ah well, you see, when the Sex God said—"

But she blubbered on and on, "I mean, how can he just go? How?"

"Yes, well, that is exactly what happened when I was dumped for marsupials. I said—"

"I mean, I wouldn't go and leave him... I wouldn't." And she started the uncontrollable blubbing again. I shoved Charlie Horse in her arms and went downstairs for first aid.

When I went into the kitchen to get the milky coffee and Jammy Dodgers emergency rations, Libby was styling Gordy's fur into a sort of Elvis quiff with hair gel. Mutti was making her costume for the *Lord of the Rings* party. I wasn't aware that there was a prostitute in *The Lord of the Rings*, but as I have never got beyond the first mention of hobbits, I will never know. I said to her, "Dad got sent off for calling the referee 'Maureen' and you wonder why I got a bad report. By the way, please forbid Vati to wear green tights for this party, whatever happens."

She said, "Your father's got rather shapely legs."

Is she truly insane?

Then she said, "What's the matter with Jas? She just said it was something awful about Tom."

I said, "Hunky is going off to snog sheep in Kiwi-a-gogo land for six months."

Mutti said, "Oh dear."

And Libby went, "Oh dear oh dear oh deary dear deary dear dear."

I'd like to think she was being sympathetic, that's what I would like to think, but I'm not stupid enough.

I said, "I know what it feels like to be dumped for a wombat."

At that point Vati came in for another beer and a big hunk of cheese. He winked at us all. "Hi chicks."

And went out.

I looked at Mum. "I know what it's like to be dumped for a wombat, but I don't know what it's like to be married to one."

Mutti said, "Don't be cheeky. You could have worse dads, you know."

There was a bit of a silence then, broken only by the sound of farting from the front room.

The milk was boiling and I went to make Jas's emergency milky pops drink. Mum followed me and said, "So, what about Dave the Laugh?"

I went, "Huh."

And she said, "Isn't there anyone you like?"

I was a bit distracted, and before I could stop myself I said, "Well, the new singer for The Stiff Dylans is cool. He's called Masimo and he's half Italian and actually gorgey and fabby."

I immediately regretted having told her. In principle I think parents should really only be like sort of human purses, but I sometimes forget.

I needn't have worried that Mutti would be at all interested in me; she was rambling on about herself.

"I had an Italian boyfriend once. I met him in Rimini on a school trip. It used to take him an hour to get his hair right. I was on the beach with him one time and this girl in bikini bottoms and with high heels got on a motorbike and rode off."

Even I had to ask, "Do you mean she had only her bikini bottoms on?"

Mum nodded.

I went on, "Do you mean she let her nunga-nungas flow free and wild on a motorbike?"

Mum said, "Yes, and they weren't small."

I said, "Isn't it a traffic hazard?"

Mum said, "Well, that's what I said. I said to my boyfriend, 'Isn't that a traffic hazard?' And do you know what he said?"

I said, "No, what?"

And Mum said, "I haven't the slightest idea. He didn't speak any English."

And then she had a laughing spasm that Libby joined in with.

Is that what it's like in Spaghetti-a-gogo land?

8:45 p.m.

A little voice from upstairs went, "Georgia, I'm all alone up here."

My bedroom

Back in Heartbreak Headquarters, Jas and I snuggled up in bed and drank our milky coffee.

In between snuffling and slurping, Jas said, "How can I stop Tom going away?"

I could feel a touch of wisdomosity coming on.

"Well, Jas, there are of course two ways of looking at this."

"Are there? You mean the right way and the wrong way?"

"No, I mean your way and the trouser way."

She slurped attentively.

I went on, "His trousers want to go and see his brother and ferret around with vegetables. And you... er... don't want them to."

Jas said, "So are you saying... I should be more understanding when I say he can't go?"

I shook my head sadly. If I had had a beard, I would have twirled it. I went on, "No. What I mean, Jas, is that never the twain shall meet. If you try to stop him, he will have, you know, frustrated trousers."

"Frustrated trousers?"

"Yes, you know, his trousers want to go off on an adventure and you want them to hang around in your wardrobe of life."

"They might like it in my wardrobe."

"Ah yes, they might at first, but then they might hang in

your wardrobe for ages and then be too moth-eaten to wander free."

Jas said, "So you think I should let the trousers go, set the trousers free?"

"Yes, I think you should."

She looked thoughtful, which is a bit unusual and scary.

"OK, but Tom doesn't have to go as well, does he?"

Good Lord. I am on the brink of exhaustiosity. What is the point of me thinking up philosophical analogies if Jas thinks we really ARE talking about trousers?

Midnight

Poor Jasy Spazzy has gone home to her bed of pain. On one hand, I am really sorry for her, but on the other foot, I can't help remembering how she didn't give a flying fig's pants when Sex God went to Kiwi-a-gogo.

12:05 a.m.

However, to be a jolly good pal (and I sincerely hope that Baby Jesus is not having the night off in Africa or something and is therefore noticing my goodness, and planning a reward in the shape of a gorgey half-Italian half-Hamburger-a-gogo

bloke). Anyway, what was I saying before I so rudely interrupted myself? Oh yes, to be a jolly good pal I may get her a Curly Wurly and wrap it up in special wrapping paper.

12:15 a.m.

Oh, I can't sleep. I wonder how I can get to Masimo and impress him with my whatsits. Feminine willies. If I wait until the gig, he will be quite literally covered in girls.

Dom told me he goes to St Budes art college. I could accidentally on purpose bump into him on my way home.

The fact that it's on the other side of town is a bit of a logistical problem. I may even have to bunk off school.

12:20 a.m.

Which might mean I would miss "gaseous interchange" in Blodge, which is a blow.

12:25 a.m.

However, as "gaseous interchange" is another term for breathing and farting, I can make up for lost time by being in the same room as my father.

"...and that's when it fell off in my hand."

Friday April 22nd
on the way to Stalag 14

Despite my very wise trouser speech to Jas, she has decided to punish Tom by not seeing him or speaking to him.

I said, "How long has this been going on?"

And she said, "Well, I didn't get home till quite late last night, so..."

"So... you haven't actually been able to ignore him yet?"

"No, but when I see him I will."

She is still very unstable and sniffly. I gave her my special Curly Wurly gift with its special Christmas gift wrapping. We were just walking up the hill when I handed it over. It didn't have a very good effect on Jas – she looked at it and then flung her arms around me and started really blubbing and wailing. She was saying, "Oh Gee, you are such a good pal and I've been horrid to you... I am sooooo sorry, I really love you. I know you are always asking me to say so and I never will, but I do. I do love you."

Crikey. She had gone bananas. I thought she would stop after a minute, but still she went on. I tried to walk on but I ended up sort of shuffling along with her hanging around my neck. I bet it looked like the lezzie version of *Blithering Heights*. All I needed now was for Masimo to come by. Or some notorious sadists like Wet Lindsay or Hawkeye. Then I thought of the worst-case scenario... Miss Stamp. If Miss Stamp came by now, she would be in Lesbian Heaven. She would ask us round to her place for "tea". She would offer me extra coaching... oh my giddy God...

I pushed Jas off me quite firmly and said sternly, "Jas, remember your Rambler's badge – don't let yourself down, remember the Country Code."

What on earth was I talking about?

It seemed to make some sort of sense to Jas, because she stopped sniffling and adjusted her beret.

I went on cheerily, "Six months isn't long... is it? It's only twenty-four weeks. You could do something really great in twenty-four weeks for when Tom comes back."

She said, "Could I... like what?"

I said, "Well... you could... grow your fringe out and that would be a good thing, wouldn't it? A new you, Jas, imagine it. A new fringeless you."

I could see I had got her attention, which is sad really.

Break

We have had an extraordinary meeting of the Ace Gang on the Blodge knickers toaster to discuss the Jastragedy. The nub and gist is that we have taken a sacred vow (you make the vow and then are given a Chinese burn by the person next to you). Anyway, the sacred vow that we will never break is: "We, the Ace Gang, will never let any boy come between us and the Ace Gang. We are all for one and one for all, once and for all." Or whatever it is that the Three Musketeers say.

I have to say in principle I agree, but in practice I crossed my fingers while I made the vow because, if I can snaffle Masimo, I'm afraid it is one for one.

English

I think everyone must have crossed their fingers, because our vow of sisterhood lasted about ten minutes. We'd just

settled down for an hour of complete misery and bollocks (*Blithering Heights*) when two window cleaners bobbed up at the windows. They were not what you would call very fit-looking boys, but they were boys. And none of us had seen a boy for... er... about an hour and a half, if you don't count Elvis Attwood, which we don't.

The whole class had a massive dither attack. Some girls dived under their desks and started applying lip gloss and some started flcking their hair around like loons.

Miss Wilson said, "Now, girls, settle down, it's just a couple of window cleaners. You're all acting as if you've never seen a member—"

She was interrupted there by Rosie saying "Oo-er."

Miss Wilson went fantastically beetroot but carried on, "As if you have never seen a... a... person of the male... gender. Please show a bit of grown-up behaviour and don't let yourselves down." Then she started tripping lightly in the Valley of the Prehistoric. "When I was a young lady, I—"

Jools said, "Did you meet the Swan of Avon, Miss?"

Miss Wilson rambled on, "No, Julia, I did not meet the Swan of... er, it's not the Swan, it's the Bard of Avon."

Jools went on, "Oh so you knew him quite well then, if you knew his real name."

By this time most of the class were pressing themselves up against the windows and Miss Wilson had to go for reinforcements. Hawkeye soon saw the lads off into a different part of the school.

Boo. Still, at least it had passed a pleasant half an hour, and we hadn't been forced to wander round blasted heaths and so on.

Lunchtime

Practically the whole school has been tracking the window cleaners like they're pop stars, chasing them about and screaming. It's mad.

Wet Lindsay and her henchwomen no sooner hand out reprimands and beatings (not really, but they would obviously like to) than another group of girls creeps up.

Even the little first formers were prancing about, singing stupid songs like, "Window cleaners, window cleaners, give us a wave, give us a wave."

In the end Captain Mad (Elvis Attwood) set up a sort of armed guard to keep us at bay. Although, to be frank, I don't think a garden hoe is going to frighten some of the Upper Fifth if they decided to have a go. Melanie Griffith could just send her nunga-nungas on a lone expedition and he would be on his back.

Even Jas is cheered up, and she's determined to come to the gig to show Tom how much she's ignoring him. As I left her at her gate, she said, "You have got to help me ignore him and make him jealous and so on."

"Jas, I am not going to snog you for anything."

1:00 a.m.

I have got everything ready for tomorrow night, even though I want to play it cool and just sort of remind Masimo who I am. I am not going to be throwing myself at him or anything. I am going to play the callous sophisticate.

The callous sophisticate with really groovy false eyelashes, or my boy entrancers, as I call them.

Saturday April 23rd

It's like a hobbit house. Vati has got himself and Uncle Eddie big false ears. You can imagine how attractive Uncle Eddie looks in his. Also, I didn't know there was a gay elf in

The Hobbit but there is, and it's my dad. He's leaping around in his green tights going, "Oooohhh hello, I am Legalet!!"

Libby and Gordy have gone round to Grandad's for the night. God help them one and all; the mad meet the very very mad.

The most appalling thing has happened. The woman in the next-door madhouse to Grandad thinks she's his girlfriend and keeps knitting things for him.

Double sadly, she can't knit. As a lovely gift, she knitted him a jumper. It was only after ten minutes of him nearly suffocating that we discovered that she hadn't knitted a neck hole.

11:30 a.m.

I have got my bedroom to myself as make-up headquarters. Even Angus is out. He is defending his love for Naomi against her new suitor, Manky. If Mr Across the Road thought that Angus was Naomi's bit of rough he should see Manky, who is definitely her bit of rougher. Manky and Angus have already had a duel at dawn – Angus came home with a bit of Manky's tail as a victory souvenir. I may frame it.

4:00 p.m.

Now then, I've written a list of hit points for my plan:

1. Steam, cleanse and tone. Apply primer coat of pale ivory base, paying special attention to any lurker incidents.
2. Coat eyelashes with talcum powder for maximum build-up of mascara. (This is a top model tip – along with putting a white spot in the middle of your lips to make them look bigger – actually, I won't be doing this bit. I don't want any suggestion of Coco the Clown to mar my evening of LUUUUURVE.)
3. Dust all over face with powder to avoid the shiny twit look.

OK, I've done all that, now to point four.

4. Inspect for any orang-utan outbreak.

As I was trying to see the back of my legs in my hand mirror, Legalet came prancing in. "Hello, I'm Legalet and... Bloody hell, Georgia, what in the name of your grandad's outsize cycling shorts have you done with yourself – you look like a ghost!"

I leapt into my wardrobe and said from in there, "DAD, how DARE you look at me, I've only got my foundation coat on. And this is my bedroom. I don't come snooping around in your room. In fact, I have the good manners to ignore you."

As he went out, Legalet said, "Oh the joy of fatherhood, it never fades... By the way, what time do you want me to pick you up?"

What?????? He was dressed as an elf. An elf picking me up in a Robinmobile. Noooooooo.

I said, "Hahahhhahah, er, don't you remember? Jas's dad is picking us up."

Fortunately he's too excited to question me closely about Jas's dad, who is in fact in Birmingham tonight.

7:00 p.m.

I don't ever remember being this jelloid before, not even when I had Terminal Horn syndrome for the Sex God. I can hardly move my eyelids for mascara and false eyelashes. I wonder if they look natural? I didn't get the ones with the false diamonds in them. I just got the thick long ones.

Oh I can't take them off now: it took me about a million years to put the glue on and stick them on. It isn't as easy as it sounds on the packet. What I go through for luuuurve.

Stiff Dylans gig

8:15 p.m.

We all got massive giggling gertie syndrome on the way to the gig. Even Jas joined in with the jollity; she is determined to let Tom know that she has a life of her own. I didn't point out the obvious fact that she hasn't, because I am full of sympatheticositisnosity. Which is not an easy thing to say.

Anyway, she's letting Tom know that he's not the only codpiece in the sea. Going along the High Street, clattering along on our high heels, we sang "The girls are back in town, the girls are back in town." We were doing the linking up thing. We all link arms and are not allowed to break the chain for any reason. It makes getting round corners or crossing roads practically impossible. God help any poor person coming the other way; they could be dragged along with us for hours. Strangely, people seemed to cross to the other side of the road when they saw us coming.

We were allowed to break armsies at the entrance to the Phoenix. I was soooo excited, and sort of frightened too. Ellen, Mabs, Rosie and Jas hadn't even seen Masimo yet.

In the tarting-up area (loos) we reapplied lip gloss for maximum snoggosity.

Rosie said, "What is your cunning plan, Georgia? Full frontal or glaciosity with just a hint of promise?"

I said, "Deffo glaciosity with a hint of p."

"Is that why you're wearing furry eyelashes?"

I gave her my special cross-eyed Klingon look. "These, Rosie, are not false eyelashes, they are boy entrancers. They hint at a sophisticosity beyond my years."

The Ace Gang went out into the club and I had one last check in the mirror. I practised my "sticky eye" technique. God, I was good – I practically got off with myself.

Out in the club it was really kicking, quite dark and groovy. In fact when I first came out of the tarting-up area, I couldn't see anything for a minute until my peepers got used to the lack of light. I don't think the boy entrancers helped.

The Ace Gang had formed a posse around Jas at a table near the front. Tom, the official ostracised leper, was at the bar with a couple of mates. I could see no one else of any interest apart from loads of lardy blokes and some girls from our school.

9:35 p.m.

My nerves are shot to pieces. I can't stand the tension of this. I have to go to the piddly-diddly department every five

minutes. Jas was making me worse. She was Ditherqueen and a half. Going on and on about Tom.

"Is Tom looking at me? Don't look."

"Jas, I can't see if I don't look. But don't worry, I'll be very casual. I'll startle you with my casualosity. I'll sip your drink and look through the bottom of the glass and see if he's looking."

I lifted up the glass and looked.

"He's not looking at the moment – oh yes, hang on, hang on... yes, he's looking now."

Jas said, "How does he look? Does he look upset?"

"Er. Hang on, there's a bit of ice cube in the way, I'll just eat it... er, he's talking to Matt... oh, oh now he's looking over here."

Jas said, "How is he looking? Is it just like looking looking, or is it like, you know, looking like he's made a big mistake wanting to go and snog sheep instead of staying with me?"

I said, "Jas, it's a bit difficult to tell looking through the bottom of a glass. Also, I'm getting neck spasm. Have I smeared my lip gloss?"

I am truly a bloody great pal.

10:00 p.m.

I hadn't even seen Masimo yet. I can hardly remember what he looks like. Maybe I had imagined he was groovy. I hadn't actually stood right next to him. Perhaps he was a bit of a shortarse, or maybe he had an irritating laugh. Or he'd grown a goatee. Or he liked elves... or—

Then the DJ said, "And now it's time for The... Stiff Dylans!!!"

And they came onstage. Everyone except Masimo. Dom said into his mike above the whooping and clapping, "Cheers, thanks a lot, we're back! And tonight we would like you to go wild for our new lead singer. He's not entirely an English person, but someone with a touch of Latin blood – calm down, girls – I give you... Masimo. *Ciao*, Masimo."

And Masimo came onstage. Oh crumbly knees *extraordinaire*. He is, as I may have mentioned before, the Cosmic Horn personified. The girls at the front were going bananas jumping up and down. (Which is not something I would try, even with my extra-firm nunga-nunga holders.)

I said to Jools, "How very little pridosity they've got."

Jools said, "I know, the next thing you know they'll be

creeping around backstage getting up on boxes and stalking him."

I said kindly, "Quiet now, Jools. I'm concentrating."

The hard thing to do is to be noticed but not to be noticed being noticed, if you know what I mean, and I think you do.

He was so gorgey and a fantasadosy singer and soooooo sexy. When he was singing you felt like he was really looking at you. He would have had a hard time, though, because I was practically under the table – I didn't want to reveal myself too soon... oo-er.

The joint was really rocking and we had to dance. It was like being at the sheepdog trials and dancing, because Jas was so paranoid about Tom getting to her we had to circle round her, dancing. When any one of us wanted to go to the piddly-diddly department, we all had to shuffle and dance off together and then shuffle and dance back to our place.

I was exhausted and managed to have a bit of a breather by the stairs, and it was there that Tom got me.

"Georgia, why were you looking at me through a glass for ages?"

"I... er... well..."

"Did Jas tell you to? Does she want to, you know, sort of

make up? I mean, it's only six months and it's such a great opportunity. Can't you make her see?"

"Tom, I have to tell you this: I'm Jas's friend and we are officially *ignorez-vous*ing you. You are a mirage to me, I can't even see you actually."

He said, "And nothing would make you help me?"

"*Non,* and also we have taken an oath involving torture."

He just looked at me.

"What if I could help you really casually bump into Masimo?"

"Pardon?"

"I met him the other night at snooker."

"You met him... he met you... you he..."

"Yes. And he'll come and say hello to me in the break and I could be casually talking to you."

I said with all the dignosity I could, given that my skirt was so tight, "And you think that I'd betray my bestest pal Jas just for some bloke I hardly know? When I've taken a solemn vow with Chinese burns and everything?"

Tom looked at me. "If you don't mind me saying so, you are quite literally criminally insane."

11:00 p.m.

In the loos, Jas was sitting on the sink going on and on about her heartbreakosity. "He's a cad and a... user. He went out with me to fill in time until he could go and snog sheep."

Rosie, Ellen, Jools and Mabs were going, "Yeah, you're so right. Creep."

And, "Yeah, never have anything to do with him again."

Then they lost interest. Who wouldn't? And they all went back in to do mad dancing. It was just Jas and me. My little upset pally and me.

And only two minutes until the band had a break.

Jas was raving on and fiddling around with her fringe. I resisted slapping her hand because of her condition. Tempting, though.

She said, "I just can't believe him: all those weekends trailing badgers and mushroom hunting, I can't believe they just meant nothing to him. It's as if we never found that skylarks' nest..."

"Jas."

"Or that vole nest in the banks of the river..."

"Jas."

"I may as well never have learnt how to make a fire without matches."

I got hold of her.

"Jas, I think you should speak to him."

"What??"

"I think you should, you know, talk it over with him."

She stood in front of me, really red-faced. Bit scary actually.

"Georgia, are you saying that after all this, after all I've been through, I should TALK IT OVER with him?"

I said, "Er... yes."

And she said, "Oh, OK then."

She is unbelievably weedy, but I didn't say so because I wanted to check my boy entrancers before I went outside.

I said, "I'll go and talk to Tom first so that you don't lose your pridosity. I'll go and tell him that you might think about letting him explain himself. Then I'll come back to you, and you can look like you're shaking your head and so on and I'm trying to persuade you. Then eventually I'll tell him that he has four minutes and thirty seconds of your time. And I'll stand behind you with a watch."

11:07 p.m.

The band had left the stage by the time I went over to Tom. I said to him, "Mission accomplished. She will talk to you,

but I have to go over and try to persuade her, but you'll know that we're acting."

Tom gave me a hug. As he was hugging me (and I have to say that even though I blame him for being the brother of a Sex God who left me for wombats, I do like him)... Anyway, as he was hugging me, Masimo came over from the dressing room. As he walked through the crowd it sort of parted before him. There was an awful lot of flicking of hair and smiling going on. And that was just the boys!!! No, really it was the girls, especially that trollopy Sharon Davies. She's had blonde streaks put in her hair. I don't think they look very natural. Not like my boy entrancers. I put an extra slurp of glue on them when I was in the loo just now, so there is no chance of them coming off. I was just watching Masimo. Not directly – I was looking over Tom's shoulder. As I was being Miss Cool I saw Wet Lindsay walk in with her sad mates. She had a ludicrously short skirt on. If I had legs as thin as hers I'd wear big inflatable trousers so that I didn't startle anyone. But she is too selfish to bother.

Ohmygiddygod, Masimo was coming our way. Tom winked at me. Then he called over to Masimo, "Hey, Masimo, *ciao*."

Masimo heard him and smiled and came over. Oh please please don't let me go to the piddly-diddly department in the middle of the dance floor. When he reached us I could feel the heat of him being near me. Good grief and jelloid knickers akimbo. He said, "Hey, Tom, *ciao* – and it's you. Let me see... the lovely Ginger."

I went, "Hahahahahahahahahahahaha" until Tom hit me on the back.

Tom said, "No, this is Georgia."

I said – even though I knew I should shut up, but you know when you should shut up but you go on and on, well I had that – "Ah well, you see, Libby thinks I'm half cat, half sister, and she... er... calls me Ginger sometimes."

Tom went on trying to rescue me. "Georgia went out with Robbie for a bit before he went to Whakatane."

Masimo looked me right in the eyes. "Robbie is, how you say in English... not in his right brains to leave you behind." And he smiled again. Phwoar! I had to look down because I couldn't trust myself not to leap on him.

I looked down and then I was intending to look up and do that looking up and looking away thing, and also possibly a bit of flicky hair. Unfortunately, when I tried to look up again, I couldn't because my boy entrancers had stuck to my bottom lashes. So my eyes stayed shut. They were glued together. I kept trying to open my eyes, but I couldn't. In sheer desperadoes I said, "Oh I love this one." And started wobbling my head around to the music.

The tune was Rolf Harris's "Two Little Boys", the naffest record known to humanity.

Ohmygiddygod, what should I do? I kept up the head waggling and I was raising my eyebrows up and down to pull my eyelashes apart. I bet that looked attractive. I thought I'd better do some humming. I started humming along to the tune.

Masimo said, "Would you like to have a drink?"

"Hummmmmmm hummmmmmmm... No thanks, *non grazie,* I must groove to this one."

I must get away. I turned and head-wobbled off. I couldn't see a thing, obviously, so to stop myself from crashing into anything I put my hands out in front of me. But then I thought that would look odd so I tried to fit it into my dancing. I put one hand out in front and waved the other above my head like disco dancing. I knew the loos were sort of to my right and if I could just get there I could rip my boy entrancers off.

My "grooving" arm banged into something soft and someone said, "Oy, mind my basoomas, you cream-faced loon!"

It was Rosie, thank God. I said to her, "Rosie, lead me to the loos."

She said, "Clear off, you lezzie."

I was still madly flinging my arms around. Hopefully Masimo would think it was the eccentric English way of having a good time. Either that or he'd be phoning for the emergency services.

I said to Rosie, "My boy entrancers have stuck together. I can't open my eyes. Do something!"

She said, "Quick, put your hands on my shoulders and we'll conga dance over to the loos."

"Rosie, I don't think that's a very good—"

Before I knew it, she had forced my hands on to her shoulders and we were doing the conga.

Fifty-five million years later I broke free from the conga line – once we'd started doing it, the whole club had joined in. I yelled at Rosie to stop and take me to the loos, but she was having too much of a laugh. I got my hand to my eyes and tried to pry the lashes apart, and that's when it fell off in my hand – the boy entrancer I mean, not my eye.

I could see! I could see! I ran into the loos and ripped off the other one.

11:30 p.m.

I took a big breath and went into the club again. He had said I was lovely, and that Robbie had lost his brains to have left me. Which I think is a plus.

Tom and Jas were snuggled up in a corner talking and the rest of the so-called sheepdogs were all smooching with lads. That's when I saw Masimo. He was talking to Wet Lindsay; she had her stupid head really close to his.

In bed

1:00 a.m.

Raining.

Thundering.

Lightning.

Triple *merde*.

And a half.

1:05 a.m.

This is my unbelievable life: I am home in bed on Saturday. And my parents aren't even in yet.

How cruel is life?

If I had a Yorkshire accent and ate cow nipples, I would be an exact facsimile of Emily Brontë. I've probably contracted consumption by being out in the wind and rain.

Good.

1:30 a.m.

Ohhhh. What a crap night.

I didn't see Masimo again except on stage and he ignored me. I looked at him and I'm sure he saw me but he didn't smile or anything. Jas and Tom left early – so much for the strict four minutes and thirty seconds rule. At the end of the gig it was pouring down. Fabulous. Rosie, Jools, Ellen and I hovered about near the door waiting for the rain to ease off a bit. For once in my entire life I would have been glad to see Legalet drive up in the Robinmobile.

In fact, as an Ace Gang, we were quite literally hoisted by our own petards (which can be quite painful). Every single one of us had said that someone else's dad was definitely going to pick us up.

In the end we made a mad dash for a big tree across from the Phoenix, and we were planning what our next shelter would be when we saw Dom and the rest of the band come out and load up the van. It was raining so hard it was splashing up from the ground. Masimo wasn't anywhere around.

Then Wet Lindsay came out in her stupid leather coat with a stupid umbrella. All by herself, even deserted by her saddo mates. Teehee. I said to the gang, "Oh how thrice pathetico! She has to wait for her vati!!! Hahahaha."

Ellen said, "Still, she hasn't got two gallons of water down her neck like I have."

I said, "Look, she's all shuffly. I bet her thong is killing her. I hope so."

I was just thinking that we could button our coats together and make a sort of tent over our heads when I heard a scooter revving up. And Masimo appeared on his cool scooter with his parka on. I had a heart lurch. Then he pulled up to say good night to the rest of the lads. And then – and I can hardly bring myself to think about this – Wet

Lindsay got on the back of his scooter. I thought he'd kind of shove her off, but he didn't. He took her umbrella and held it over her while she put on a spare helmet, then he tucked the umbrella away and they motored off.

Rosie said, "Bugger me."

I got absolutely soaked on the way home but I didn't even notice. I was wet inside.

1:40 a.m.

Mutti and Vati are back, going "ShhhhhhSSSSSHHHHH" really loudly. They've brought Libby and Gordy with them.

1:45 a.m.

At last they are quiet and have gone into their bedroom.

1:48 a.m.

Vati has just farted "God save our gracious queen" and Mutti and he are apoplectic with laughter. Mutti stopped for a bit and then Vati said, "Now for verse two." And they started laughing again.

They are sad.

But at least they have each other. I haven't even got

my little sister in bed with me. I have no one who loves me.

And I never will have.

I really like him.

Once more in my bed of pain, crying.

2:01 a.m.

I think I must have cried myself to sleep, because the next thing I knew I had a big soggy cat bottom in my face. I opened my eyes to find four eyes staring back at me. Well, three eyes looking at me actually, and one was looking at the wardrobe. Angus and Gordy were absolutely soaking. They were doing shivering and cat sneezing. I said, "Go away into your baskets AT ONCE!"

Angus rolled over and started rubbing himself dry on my duvet. At first Gordy attacked Angus, in between sneezing, and then he started wiggling and diving into my duvet and burrowing under it near me. Urgh! I fished him out and lifted him up until we were eyeballs to eyeball and said, "Gordon, you are a very very bad kittykat – go into your kittykat basket!"

And he did that halfwit cat thing; he just let the tip of his tongue loll out of his mouth and left it there. Looking at me with the tip of his tongue sticking out.

Why do they do that?

Once they had both got nice and dry, they started scampering and crashing around in the dark in my room.

I put my head under the pillow.

Sunday April 24th

I went for a long moody walk across the fields. I didn't want to be in to answer questions about last night. I didn't even want to talk to my mates.

That is really it for me now, I've endured too much heartbreakosity for one lifetime. I'm going to concentrate on getting good exam results and then maybe going off to the Congo (wherever that is) as a doctor to help sick people. Even though sick people get on my nerves. I am at Dr Clooney's on Tuesday, so I may pick up a few hints about not letting moaning minnies get on my nerves. Surely there are no Mr Next Doors in the Congo?

I am sooooo depressed.

4:30 p.m.
About eighty messages from Jas. I suppose I should phone her.

5:00 p.m.
"Jas, it's me."

"Hi, Georgia. Tom told me how weird you were with Masimo. I thought you really rated him."

"I do."

"Well, why did you just go off waggling your head to a Rolf Harris song?"

Before I could explain, she started her famous rambling.

"Tom and I have come to an agreement. We're going to swap rings. When Tom goes off to Kiwi-a-gogo, our rings will mean that we'll stay true to each other until he comes back."

I didn't have the energy to stop her raving on.

"Also, as he says, it's a great opportunity to collect loads of data and stuff that he can bring back and that we could, you know... look at."

Old Rambley Knickers is back then. I think I preferred her when she was all upset and clinging round my neck.

Still, at least someone's happy.

I said to her, "You know, after you left, Masimo took Wet Lindsay home on his scooter."

Even Jas paid attention then.

"*Non.*"

"*Oui.*"

"Georgia, that is *très très merde*. Why did he do that?"

"I really don't know. Boys are a bloody mystery to me."

Jas said, "Shall I ask Tom to find out? He's a boy."

"I don't know, Jas, I don't want any more pain and—"

"Well, if I just casually ask him and don't make a big deal about it."

"Well, I suppose if it was a little secret—"

Then I heard her going, "TOM!! TOM!! GEORGIA WANTS TO KNOW WHY MASIMO WENT OFF WITH WET LINDSAY LAST NIGHT."

I couldn't believe this was happening. I tried to get her to shut up. Then I heard her mum shouting from somewhere, "Jas? I thought you said that Georgia liked Masimo. Why's he gone off with Lindsay?"

Jas said, "I don't know. That's why I asked Tom."

Jas's mum shouted, "What do you think, Tom?"

When Jas's dad joined in the conversation I put the phone down.

9:30 p.m.

Ring on the doorbell. Oh now what? Everyone is at Grandad's. It might be kitty trouble because I don't know where the furry psychopath twins are (Angus and Gordy).

I could just ignore the bell. No one would know anyone was in.

Except all the lights are on.

Oh God, if it's the cat vigilante group bringing the lads home on an assault charge, I'll go ballisticisimus, if I have the energy.

It can't be anything to do with the furry hooligans, because they're in the lavatory drinking out of the lavatory bowl. Erlack.

Opened the door in my jimmyjams, which I put on for comfort. They're a bit like Jas's knickers – on the large and shapeless front – but who cares, nobody is going to see me in them.

Crikey!!! Dave the Laugh. He leant against the door. "Hi gorgeous. Blimey, HUGE pyjamas!"

I went into the goldfish routine. "I... well... I..."

He said, "Can I come in? I bring you tidings of great joy, and it's not even Christmas."

I said, "Er, well... come in and er put the kettle on..."

"Do you think it'll suit me?"

I dashed upstairs when Dave went into the kitchen and did a rapid lip gloss, blusher, mascara fandango, and pulled on my jeans and a T-shirt. No time for nunga-nunga holders, I would just have to move very slowly with my arms crossed. *Pant pant.* I went into the kitchen.

Dave was wrestling with Gordy on the kitchen floor, and when he stood up Gordy was attached to his sleeve and just dangled there like a tiny ginger loon, which he is.

"Speaking as your Horn adviser, I've come to tell you I've just seen Masimo."

I went even more lurgified. Gordy crashed to the floor.

I managed to stutter, "Did, he say... was he, did he, was I... you know."

"I still say he's flash, but anyway, what in the name of arse made you walk off on Saturday? He thought you were very up yourself."

I said, "My boy entrancers got stuck together and then one fell off."

Dave said, "Your boy entrancers stuck together and then one fell off?!" And he was looking at my nungas to see if I still had two.

I said, "No, no, I mean my false eyelashes. First of all, I looked down and they got glued together and I was blind. So I sort of shuffled off to the music to try and unglue them, and then one fell off, so I had to go to the tarts' wardrobe."

Dave said, "Tarts' wardrobe?"

"Loos."

Dave said with sort of admirationosity in his voice, "Outstanding!"

Midnight

As my official Horn adviser, Dave says I must be friendly and smiley but play hard to get and not give up if I really like Masimo. Dave also said that because Masimo is so flash and Italian, even if he does quite rate me – despite the Rolf Harris fiasco – that will not stop him falling for flattery from other girls. Even Wet Lindsay. Dave also said that Masimo doesn't know anyone in town or any history, so he wouldn't know that Lindsay was wet and a worm and a thong wearer.

12:10 a.m.

Anyone would know that Lindsay was wet and a worm; just look at her legs for God's sake.

Anyway, if he falls for old knobbly knees, why should I want him? Mind you, the ex-Sex God went out with her for a bit. Hmmm.

Dave says that boys fall for that useless obvious stuff because they have boy insecuriosity – different from girl insecuriosity. It's because they are knob-centered, allegedly. Although I think that Dave just likes to talk dirty.

1:00 a.m.

Dave says you can't drop hints with boys because they don't get it.

1:10 a.m.

In my *How to Make Any Twit Fall in Love with You* it says:

1. You can never flatter boys too much; they will never know you are being ironic.
2. Never use hints with boys, because they don't get it. You have to ask for what you want.

It is vair vair tiring, this boy bananas.

2:00 a.m.

Also why does my Horn adviser always snog me?

2:05 a.m.

More to the point, why do I always snog him?

I suppose in the land of Cosmic Horn everything is fair.

Monday April 25th
German

Tried out my flattery technique on the dithering champion for the German nation. Herr Kamyer was wearing a pair of tartan socks, clearly visible beneath his shin-length leisure slacks. He was telling us about his riveting childhood in the Bavarian Alps. His childhood mostly consisted of camping and clapping games, interspersed with two tons of sausages. And the *Volk* of Lederhosen land wonder why they have a reputation for total crapness.

At the end of the lesson I went up to Herr Kamyer as he was packing up his books. I startled him a bit by coming up quietly behind him, and there was a minor ditherspaz incident. As he was picking his books up from the floor, I said, "That was really *sehr* interestink, Herr Kamyer, and may I compliment you on your attractive socks."

To my absolute amazement, he said, "Ach, thank you very much, Georgia. Der socks are from my mother and are a personal favourite of mine. I also have a matching tie."

I said, "Oh, I'd love to see that."

Herr Kamyer adjusted his glasses. "Vell, I vill vear it to show you."

I said, "That would be marv."

He went off all smiley and twitchy. Surely it can't be this easy. It must be because I've chosen quite literally a soft option.

Break, Knicker Toaster Headquarters

I told Rosie and Jools my news and the advice from Horn Headquarters (Dave the Laugh).

Rosie said, "I believe Dave, but Herr Kamyer's not really a bloke, is he? He's a German teacher. I bet you can't make it work on Elvis."

Lunchtime

The ultimate test. Elvis Attwood, the grumpiest bonkerist man in the universe.

Rosie and Jools insisted on being witnesses to what they

said would be an abysmal failure. They hid behind the science block loos.

Elvis was as usual prodding around (oo-er) pretending to do gardening. It is, as we all know, just a perving tactic so that he can try and see girls in their sports knickers. He should become a gym mistress, he easily could. If he grew his hair and wore a gym skirt, he would be Miss Stamp's double.

I approached Elvis casually.

"Afternoon, Mr Attwood. I'm sorry to hear that you will be leaving us." I could hear Rosie practically exploding behind the loos.

Mr Attwood looked up with that incredibly attractive grimace he keeps especially for me. I gave him a beaming smile, letting my nostrils flow free and wild for once.

He said, "What do you want? Have you been messing around in the science block? I found a drawing that was supposed to be me on the blackboard."

I said, "Oh, that's nice."

He said, "No it's not bloody nice, it was disgusting."

I said, "Was it the one of you in the nuddy-pants with an enormous pipe?"

He said, "Yes, that's it."

I said, "No, I haven't seen that one."

He grumbled on, "It's a scandal the way you lot carry on. Call yourselves young ladies? In my day you would've had your ears boxed."

I said, "Well, I agree with you, Mr Attwood. I think discipline has gone right out of the window. I mentioned it to Miss Heaton in detention but she wasn't interested. Do you know that in the Isle of Man they still beat people with twigs if they do wrong?"

He drew himself up to his full height (two and a half feet). "Yes, well, it would make you think twice if you got some twigs across your derrière instead of all this talking."

I said, "Yes, I do so agree talking is crap, Mr Attwood, 'scuse my language. I've often said in RE I would rather be beaten by twigs, but you can't tell people, can you?"

Mr Attwood looked a bit puzzled at the turn of events.

I said, "I don't know if you know this, but us girls all sort of look to you for a firm lead, Mr Attwood. I know you think we mess about, but actually we have a deep respect for you. You're a sort of father figure and naturally we rebel a bit, but at the end of the day we respect you."

You could see Mr Attwood squaring his shoulders. "When I was a lad we were given a decent set of rules. I was in bed by eight thirty and up by six thirty to do my chores."

I said, "Actually, my parents are much the same with me: early to bed, early to rise and so on."

There was a crash from behind the loos, as if someone had fallen over.

I said, "Well, thank you very much for your time, Mr Attwood. It's very good to have someone who's like a father figure."

Mr Attwood lit his pipe. "Well... yes, well, anytime. Do you know you've made me go back a bit to when we had simple pleasures: for instance, I've got a train set I had as a lad, in perfect condition, still in its box—"

"Gosh is that the bell? I must get along to English, we're doing *Blithering Heights*."

When I got behind the loos Rosie had her coat buttoned over her head to stop her laughing.

on the way home

4:15 p.m.

Lolloping along with Jas, I said, "It can't be this easy. It just can't be."

Jas said, "I know, it just can't be."

Four boys from Foxwood came by doing their usual orang-utan walk and shouting rubbish at us.

"Come on, girls, get them out for the lads."

I said to the one with terminal acne, "Hey, you're really nice-looking, would you like to see my nunga-nungas?"

He stopped doing his orang-utan impression. They all stopped.

He said, "Er... yes."

And I said, "Well, I wouldn't just for anyone, but, well, I've noticed you before... Meet me by the park loos at seven thirty."

And he straightened his tie and said, "Oh yeah, I think I can make that."

Unbelievable.

Absolutely unbloodybelievable!

Me and Jas just looked at each other.

Tuesday April 26th

Today is my work experience day at Dr Clooney's, so up at the crack of nine.

Quite groovy to put on make-up and ordinary clothes on a school day.

Mmmm, I wonder what's suitable wear for a doctor's surgery.

Black?

Yes, I think so.

Boy entrancers?

Oh yes, I think so. Even though there will most definitely be no boys to entrance, apart from Dr Gorgeous. It means I can get my staying-on technique right in the safety of the Valley of the Unwell.

5:10 p.m.

Good grief. Said goodbye to Dr Gorgeous. God bless him and all who sail in him, but I will never, ever, be returning to his surgery except on a stretcher and unconscious. It's hell on wheels in there.

Just a load of sick people moaning and sneezing. If I haven't got scarlet fever or Old Person's Lurgy, I'll be amazed.

Moaning and moaning on for hours. How can Dr Gorgeous stand it? And such a terrible pingy pongoes smell. It's the old men, mostly. I wonder if they get mixed up with their aftershave and mothball liquid. Or Bovril.

Perhaps there's a perfume called "Old Bloke" that's a big hit with the elderly and sends all the older ladies wild, knitting neckless jumpers and so on.

Anyway, that's it, there's a career I will never be having. I will not be going to the Congo. Which is just as well, as I haven't been able to find it on the map.

5:40 p.m.

Oh I was soooo happy to be alive and free. Free, free. I felt like scampering and skipping down the road. Plus my boy entrancers had stayed on all day with no suggestion of glue-eye.

I was singing a song in my head and moving my hips in time to the music. Like it said in the book. A car honked its horn as it went by and some boys shouted out to me. Probably moron boys, but it's a start. Now, if I could just add the flicky hair I would be laughing.

So let's see... hip, hip, flickyflick, hip, hip, flickyflick. Excellent!!! Now for the *pièce de* whatsit – downy eyes and upsy eyes.

Hip, hip, flickyflick, uppy, downy, hip, hip.

Yessssss!!!! Got it. I am a Sex Kitty.

Once more, with feeling.

Hip, hip, flickyflick, upsy, downsy eyes—

"*Ciao*."

Ohgreatballsof*ordure*: Masimo!!!! On his scooter. Saying *ciao*.

I looked up. Yes, there he was.

I said, "Oh, *ciao*."

How cool was that? Very very cool. Cooler than that, it was vair vair vair... shut up brain, shut up!

Masimo was still looking at me, like he thought that at any time I would start closing my eyes and dance off. I said, "How are you?"

Excellent. Normal as Norman Normal. Normaler.

He looked at me with his fab eyes. It would have been weird if he'd looked at me with anything else, with his ears for instance. Hahahahahahahaha. Oh God, I was doing out of control laughing in my head!!! This was a new and scary development on the nincompoop scale.

Masimo said, "I am cool."

I thought, *You can say that again, mister.*

Masimo revved up his engine. "Can I give you a lift anywhere?"

Blimey.

"I am going to rehearsal. Maybe I could drop you at your home."

Oh yes, that would be groovy, him dropping me at my house and seeing the Robinmobile, and maybe my mum in her aerobics outfit... or Libby in no outfit...

I said, "Well, I'm going to my mate's house. We're hanging out before we go clubbing."

What am I talking about??? Clubbing? I will be going clubbing – clubbing myself to death if I keep talking absolute arse-blithering rubbish. Then Masimo smiled at me and I got chocolate body syndrome, which is jelloid knickers with knobs. He gave me his spare helmet – great news, I would have pancake hair when I got to Jas's and took it off. But I didn't really care.

I climbed on the back of the seat. It felt really groovy, but I would have to think of a good way to get off that didn't involve a knickers extravaganza. I wasn't exactly dressed for bike work as I had my very very short black kilt on. Maybe if I shuffled over and put one foot on the floor and then bent the other knee up and sort of slid... Masimo said, "Hold on to me." And accelerated off quite fast. I put my hands on his waist. He had his parka on and everything, but it was like I got an electric shock touching him. The wind was blowing in my face and making my eyes water. Please don't let my boy entrancers blow off.

We sped along. It was really fab and I was feeling full of happiosity and bliss. I couldn't believe I was actually on the back of a scooter holding on to the Sex Meister.

Masimo shouted to me, "Please, tell me how to get to your friend's house."

Actually, Jas's house was about five minutes away, but I directed Masimo to go down the High Street even though that wasn't on the way. When we stopped at the lights I saw Dave the Laugh's Rachel and a few of the Upper Sixth going to Luigi's. They all waved like mad when they saw Masimo, even Rachel... Masimo just raised a gloved hand and we whirled off. I hope everyone recognised me under my helmet.

I could have stayed holding on to Masimo and riding round for ever: round and round, like that bloke on that doomed phantom boat, *The Flying Dutchman*. Of course, there are differences – he was not on a scooter, and I don't have a beard and am not Dutch.

Eventually I had to point out Jas's house to Masimo and

we pulled up outside. I got off without a police incident but Masimo didn't turn his engine off. I didn't think that was a good sign. It meant he wasn't going to hang around and chat.

I tried to remember some Italian and said, "Well thanks, er *gracias* a lot. Thank you a lottio. Thank youio a lottio."

Masimo smiled. "I am glad for doing of it. I am, how you say... full of sorrows for my English."

I said, "Oh don't worry, I hardly speakio any myselfio."

He laughed and said, "You are funny."

Oh brilliant, he thinks I'm funny. Not groovy or a Sex Kitty that he must spend the rest of his life worshipping and adoring, but funny.

Then he said, "I must go to my rehearsal."

And he revved up. I said, "Oh yeah, well *ciao*." Then I remembered my Horn teacher's advice so I put on my biggest smile. "It's really nice that you've come to town and... I... thought you sang *très bon*."

He smiled again. "Good. Thank you. I will see you. *Ciao*."

And he went off. I turned to go into Jas's gate feeling a bit flat and in the Valley of the Terminally Confused again. Had he just given me a lift out of politeness? Oh damn, damn and damnity damn damn. I hate all this.

I looked at him as he reached the end of Jas's street. He could be going to see Wet Lindsay after rehearsals for all I knew. How did she get boys to like her...? It was a bloody mystery. Maybe she slipped horse tranquiliser into their Coke?

As I was watching him indicating right, he did a big wheelie and curved back up the street very fast towards me. He slowed down in front of me and shouted, "Georgia, do you want to come with me to the cinema?"

I did my world-famous impression of a cod in a kilt. He turned the bike round again and said, "If you do, I will see you at seven thirty on Friday at the clock tower. *Ciao, va bene.*"

Then he sped off.

I rang on Jas's bell and eventually she answered it.

"Have you come to test me on my Froggy assignment?"

Is she really truly mad? I said, "Jas, be sensible. Let me in and give me something."

"Like what?"

"Sugar. I've had a shock. Get your secret chocolate stash out and I'll tell you."

As we were munching away in her bedroom, I told her all about it.

She said, "Blimey. So he's actually sort of asked you out."

"I know, fab isn't it?"

"But is he seeing Wet Lindsay as well? Maybe it's a double date thing and she'll come to the cinema as well, and you'll have one of those French things."

"What French things?"

"You know, *ménage à trois.*"

"Jas, he's Italian."

"Oh well, menagio à trios."

8:00 p.m.

I had to leave because sometimes Jas is so sensationally mad that I feel violence coming on.

But nothing can alter this fact: Masimo, the best-looking bloke in the universe, a Dream God, has asked me – Georgia Nicolson – to go out to the cinema with him.

8:30 p.m.

I might have known there would be a couple of flies in the ointment, one of them quite porky. Mutti and Vati were in a real strop and a half when I got in. Vati started, "Where have you been? And before you start, don't give me any

nonsense about homework club. I wasn't born yesterday, you know."

I felt like saying, "Not unless yesterday was eighty-five years ago."

But I didn't because I love everyone.

Then Mutti joined in. "You have got be straight with us, Georgia. If you want to be treated like a grown-up, then you have to show us you deserve to be."

Vati was still grumbling on, "It's not like we've never been young, but I at least treated my parents with respect and told them the truth."

I said to him, "Are you suggesting you want me to tell you the truth at all times?"

Mutti said, "Of course, my darling, we're your parents."

I said reasonably, just to clear things up, "Ah yes, but when I said how crap the Robinmobile was and why did we have to have a clown car, Vati went ballisticisimus."

They both just looked at me in that sighing, looking-at-me way. Still, I was in Cloud Nine land and maybe I would make a point of telling the truth from now on.

I took a deep breath and said, "OK then, I'll tell you. I was walking home from Dr Clooney's after a hard day with the elderly mad when the new singer from The Stiff Dylans came along and gave me a lift to Jas's on his scooter."

Vati was already a bit huffy. "How old is this 'lead singer'?"

I said patiently, "He's Italian."

Vati said, "What?"

I said, "He's Italian, isn't he, Mum?"

Vati looked at Mum. "So you know all about this then, Connie? What is it with you two? I'm always the last to know anything in this house. I slave away all day and then when I come back..."

I slipped out while he was raving on and went to my room. It doesn't matter what happens – divorce, orphanosity – it doesn't mean anything when you have a Sex Meister as your plaything.

9:00 p.m.

Libby has made Gordy a pair of cardboard glasses at nursery school. And a hat to hold them on.

Actually it's not a hat, it's a rubber glove, but it holds them on nicely.

11:00 p.m.

I haven't got long to plan my outfit for Friday.

Should I try to get Mum to buy me something new? Knowing her, she'll probably count the new kitten-heeled boots and two skirts and trousers she bought me on Saturday as new.

I wonder if I should consult with Dave the Laugh before I go on my date? No, because I don't want any chance of rogue snogging.

I'm so excited I am never going to go to sleep again.

Zzzzzzzzzzzzz.

Wednesday April 27th

Breakfast

Vati gave me a squeeze on the shoulder as I was eating my Frosties. And he and Mum seemed to be speaking. What fresh hell?

He said, "Georgia, thank you for telling us the truth Here's a fiver to get yourself something. Remember, it's always worth telling the truth to people."

I said, "Oh, well, if fivers are involved, I should tell you that I'm going to the cinema with Masimo on Friday night."

I thought Vati might explode, but sadly he didn't. He tried

to go on being reasonable, which was scary to witness He was mumbling as he got his flying helmet on, "Right. Good. Right. That's the sort of thing we mean. Good, right."

And then he went off to Flood Headquarters.

Honesty is definitely going to be my policy from now on.

Break, on the knickers toaster

I had been going through with the Ace Gang what I could wear on my date. And also showing them a new celebration dance I'd made up for the occasion. There was, I must admit, quite a lot of finger pointing and hip waggling in it, but that's the way with celebration dances.

Rosie said, "Georgia, you know that you're one of my bestest pals and that the Ace Gang is all for one and all the way to Tipperary and so on."

I said, "*Oui.*"

"However, if you go on being such a prat and a fool for much longer, I'm afraid I'm going to have to kill you."

Games

The Upper Sixth were getting changed when we came into the changing rooms. We are being forced to do a cross-country

run by Adolfa. But I don't mind because it means I will be in tip-top physical condition for my love date on Friday. (Of course, it will also mean that tonight I will be in bed by five thirty with severe exhaustion and bottom strain, but *c'est la vie.*)

Then I saw Wet Lindsay eyeing me like a Seeing Eye dog and also talking to her astonishingly dim and limp mates about me. I wonder if she knows anything about me and Masimo. Why should she? Still, it gives me the creeps. I feel that we have shared past lives together, and they have all been crap.

Detention

4:20 p.m.

Oh God and *Gott in Himmel* and also *Mon Dieu*. What is the matter with Hawkeye? She is so unreasonably surly. I went to the loos before Latin and I was just sort of dollydaydreaming about Masimo, so I was a tiny bit late for class. Herr Oberführer Grupmeister of the Universe (Hawkeye) said, "You should have been here at three p.m."

And I in a fit of spontaneous combustion and honestosity said, "Why, did something really good happen?"

I have to write out eight hundred times, "Rudeness is a poor substitute for wit."

Which is quite literally a pain in the arse. I mean it. I can hardly sit down after our cross-country run. At least I can walk, which is more than can be said for Nauseating P. Green. She should never have attempted the water jump in her condition (i.e. very fat).

4:25 p.m.

Hurrah, I have perfected a way of doing lines quickly. I've Sellotaped five pens to a ruler so I can do five lines at once.

The fifth line looks like a mad woman's knitting, but you can't have everything.

Thursday evening, April 28th

Jas is staying behind after school. Hard to believe that a human being can be interested in going around the sports field with the Blodge teacher looking for vole droppings, but that's old Jazzy Knickers for you. The most interesting person since... er... Quasimodo.

I must say, though, I am relatively impressed *vis-à-vis* her

glaciosity and independentology towards Tom. I think he's definitely very puzzled about how calm she's being, and he's not talking so keenly about going any more.

once more into the oven of love

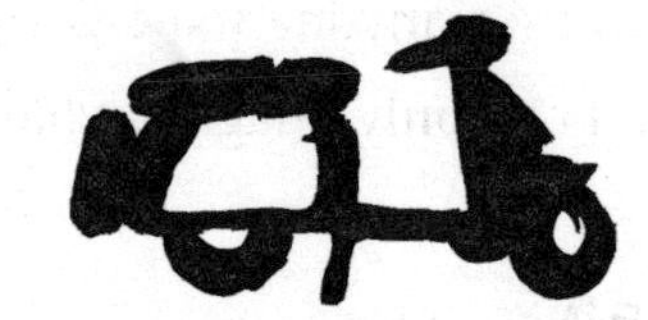

Friday April 29th
Lunchtime

Time is going so slowly.

I said to RoRo, "Do you think I should risk the boy entrancers?"

She said, in between mouthfuls of cold rice pudding, "What if there's a snogging incident? I mean, you know, they might get entangled in something."

"Like what?"

"His moustache."

"He hasn't got a moustache."

"I know, but if he had one. I'm just saying you can't be too careful."

Please don't let me emigrate to Madland just before the best evening of my life.

I don't think I will risk the boy entrancers, though.

4:30 p.m.

I ran home with gay nunga-nunga abandon. I ran and ran with a devil-take-the-hindmost attitude and hoped I wouldn't see anyone I knew. Thank the Lord for once that I didn't. I can only imagine what I looked like.

5:35 p.m.

Bathed and moisturised to within an inch of my life. Face pack on.

Should I make a list of conversational topics so that I don't accidentally say anything abnormal?

6:00 p.m.

The trouble is, I don't have anything normal to say. I can't talk about my family life when my vati has a clown car and my mutti has no moral code. I can't even begin to go into Libby, or Angus and Gordy. Or Grandad.

What about school and my mates?

Am I mad????

Hmm, well, what about books I've read?

Surely no one really wants to know about *Blithering Heights*, and somehow I don't think I should mention

How to Make Any Twit Fall in Love with You.

So that leaves make-up.

Oh God.

7:15 p.m.

I'm taking tiny tiny steps so that I am not early or hot. I honestly don't think I'm going to be able to speak: my throat feels like something has nested in it. Maybe I should just not turn up. He's bound not to like me. He probably won't turn up. He's Italian and fab beyond marvydom and older. He's got girls hurling themselves at him. I should just stick to my own league. That's what it says in my book. I just read it before I came out. It says you should choose someone in your own sort of area physically. If you are an eight you can choose a seven or another eight. But how do you know what you are? When Jas, Rosie, Jools, Ellen and I did that points out of ten for features, I got a nine for my hair but minus zero for my nose. Does that mean I'm an average seven? Because if it does, I'm definitely buggered because Masimo is beyond a shadow of a doubt a ten.

7:40 p.m.

I'm going to go home. He's not going to come anyway, and I can't hide in this shop doorway for much longer pretending to be looking at kitchen implements.

7:42 p.m.

Oh blimey, here he comes now. He's just ridden up on his scooter. Right. Casualosity at all times is called for.

Masimo had his back to me, so fortunately he didn't see me nearly fall over when I didn't see the wheelchair ramp thing on the pavement. He was locking up his scooter and then he turned to look around. God he is gorgey. He had a cool blue and grey Italian zip top on and a suit. Honestly, I don't think I've ever seen any of my boy mates in a suit. It looked really groovy gravy. But it did make him look like a grown-up. Still, I was being a grown-up myself(ish). He saw me and looked at me for what seemed like ages. I felt like doing some Irish dancing to fill in the time, but I didn't.

Then he sat down on the seat of his scooter and watched me come across to him. He said, "*Ciao*, Georgia, you look very gorgeous. Forgive me for being late."

Hell's biscuits, I don't think I can stand this. I managed to croak out those immortal and sophisticated words, "Oh hello."

He left his bike on the pavement at the clock tower, which I don't think is altogether legal.

We walked along to the Odeon. He was walking along quite close to but not touching me, although when we got to the door he opened it for me and sort of put his hand gently in the small of my back to guide me through. He only had to brush against me for my entire insides to start doing morris dancing. He paid for our tickets and we went into the dark and sat at the back in the official snogging seats. That must mean something, mustn't it? Or didn't he know they were the snogging seats? Oh dear *Gott in Himmel*. I kept thinking I must say something interesting, but what would be safe?

Before the film started, Masimo got us Cokes and he said, "So, Miss Georgia, you are quiet."

I said, "Oh yes, well, I'm just relaxing because it's been mad lately."

Masimo said, "Oh yes, what have you been up to?"

"Yes, well, I had to... er... do a cross-country run and—"

Fortunately he interrupted me. He said, "So do you like

sport? I am big sport fan. I like the football and I run, every day I run."

I said, "Oh yes, so do I. Nothing stops me running. If the weather is too bad I run around my room."

He laughed for quite a long time. So I laughed as well. But actually I do run around my room, and who can blame me?

We watched the film, but I can't remember a thing about it because of the extreme tensionosity. My shoulder was right next to his, and when he gave me some popcorn his hand brushed across mine. It gave me such heebie-jeebies that I nearly had a spasm and chucked the popcorn everywhere. I definitely was on the road to Spazzyville.

8:45 p.m.

Halfway through the film and still no sign of snogging. He's brushed my hand, our shoulders and knees occasionally touch, and that is it. Perhaps he found he didn't fancy me when he saw me and now he's just sitting politely through the film.

Perhaps he never even thought of me in that way.

Maybe I am like a chum.

Oh GOD.

10:00 p.m.

We went out into the night and Masimo said, "I will give you a lift home."

No suggestion of coffee or anything. So he definitely thinks I'm a mate. I am so depressed. But I cannot be a sad sack. I have to pretend to be perky and that I like being a mate to a Sex Meister who I just want to leap on and snog to within an inch of his life.

The Sex Meister seemed to know everyone we saw. He'd only been here for a week or two and all the girls in town seemed to know who he was. It was all "Oh *ciao*, Masimo," fluttery, fluttery, flickyflick. Pathetic.

I said with a really nice smile, "You seem to have got to know a lot of people."

He said, "Yes, they are nice. I don't know... the girls, they are very friendly here."

Hmmm, "friendly" was one word for it. He seemed to be a bit sad somehow. As we got near the clock tower, he said, "It's nice, it's just that, well, in Italy I had a girl, you know, a serious thing and it ended. She was sad, I was sad. So now I, how do you say... I have burned my hands in the fire of love."

One minute it's Dave the Laugh the Horn Master telling

me it's all to do with the Cosmic Horn and hormones, and then the Sex Meister goes all poetic and burns his hands on the oven of love.

Masimo smiled at me. "So now, I don't want to be sad any more. I want to be happy, have fun. Do you want to have fun, Georgia?"

I said, "Er... oh yes, Fun City is where I live usually. I'm a bit like you, really. When Robbie went off to Kiwi-a-gogo I moved from Love City to Fun City. Obviously stopping off in Sad City."

He laughed. "I understand. I think. So this is good, it is all fun."

"Oh yes, absobloodylutely fun as two short... fun things."

We got back to his scooter and got on it. He helped me into my helmet and as he fastened it he looked straight in my eyes and said, "Ah *caro*... you are sweet."

Then he hopped on and revved up and we scooted away. I loved being on the back holding on to him as we whizzed through the dark streets. It was like being in an exciting movie, except I didn't know whether it was a romance or a comedy.

We got to my house and I got off the scooter sharpish in

case of knicker display, took off my helmet and juujed my hair. He switched off the engine. Ahahhahahaha. Then he said, "Georgia, what do you know of Lindsay? Is she one of your mates?"

Er, what exactly was the correct answer to that? I would rather eat my own poo than be her mate, she's a slimy twit with the smallest forehead known to humanity. Or just a simple "I hate her to hell and back"? But then I remembered that I was "funny and sweet", not "a massive bitch", so I said, "Er... Lindsay, well, yeah, she's, you know... well, yeah..."

And left it at that.

Masimo said, "She has got for me a ticket to 'Late and Live', which would be groovy to go to, do you think?"

I smiled and nodded. I hope the smile came out right because as my mouth was smiling, my brain was going "Kill her, kill her, strangle her with her thong, stick her in a bucket of whelks..." Now I knew what it felt like to be Angus.

Then I saw Vati peering through the curtains. Oh God, now he was waving in a cheery casual way. He went away, and then Mum appeared waving and smiling. Stopwavingandsmiling!!! The only plus was that the Robinmobile was in the garage. Sadly, Angus and Gordy weren't. Gordon is not even officially supposed to be out at night. He's still wearing the glasses Libby made for him, although they are now on sideways. Angus and Gordy were wrestling with each other on the wall. I said, just for something to say, "That's Angus and Gordy."

Masimo went over to the wall; he was smiling. "Hey, they are great."

When Masimo got near, Angus stopped wrestling and sat up staring straight at him. Oh God, I hoped he hadn't got anything against Italians. Gordon came and sat next to him and they were both staring at Masimo. Then they both did the letting the tips of their tongues loll out of their mouths. Like idiot cats.

Why did they do that??

I couldn't think of a single normal or even "fun" thing to say after all the shocks I had had, so I said, "Well, I suppose I should go in now, it's a bit nippy noodles. Thank you for a fab night."

And Masimo said, "Ah yes, *ciao*." And he got on his scooter and started it up. Then he looked at me and kicked the scooter back up on its stand but left it running. He climbed off and came over to me. "Yes, thank you, Georgia."

And he put his face near mine and I thought, "Yes, yes, and thrice yes, he is going to snog me. At last, at last!!!"

And then he did kiss me. But just a tiny baby kiss. It was over in a second and really gentle, like brushing my lips with his. No suggestion of tongues or any handsies. Just a sort of peck.

And that was it.

He said, "See you later."

And roared off into the night.

Midnight

I am exhausted. What in the name of Sir Richard Attenborough's baby-doll nightie was all that about?

Saturday April 30th

10:00 a.m.

I can't believe this. Two more of Vati's sad mates have bought Robin Reliants. There's a clown car convention in our driveway. Vati and his incredibly sad mates are standing around discussing wheels or their new red noses or something. I'm hiding in my bedroom until they all go. They're all off to a rally, thank the Lord, which means at least I can be on my own with my miserablosity.

10:30 a.m.

Mutti came up to say goodbye and give me a kiss, even though I buried my head under my pillow. She said, "I am kissing the pillow where your head is and you can't stop me."

I went, "Hmmmfff."

She said, "We'll be back about eight. Eat something sensible, and that doesn't mean a jam and chip sandwich. By the way, that Italian boy is quite literally gorgeous."

Oh oh!!! Nooo, she was talking about him. No no. Shutupshutup.

11:00 a.m.

Peeking out of my curtained window as the Clown Rally departs.

I really can see why the youth of today are so ashamed of the older generation. You should see what Mum and Dad are wearing. They are all in leather. Vati has a leather jacket and trousers on, as well as his flying helmet and goggles, and Mutti has a leather minisuit on and thigh-length leather boots. She looks like a prostitute. And Dad looks like a brothel madam.

Libby, Angus and Gordon all have their own flying goggles now. There was a lot of late-night fighting, but in the end Libby persuaded Mum and Dad that Angus and Gordy had to go to the rally and needed goggles.

So there they are, sitting in the back window of the Robinmobile with their gogs on. Don't ask me why Libby wields such power over them. Angus is supposed to be my furry pal. It was quite nice last night having him purring away on my nungas when I was so upset. I thought he would hang about with me today to keep me company. Especially as I got up so early to feed him – I was out in the garden in the freezing cold at eight thirty.

I have a method for giving him his food that prevents any accidents (like me having my hand gnawed off). The method is, I lock him out of the kitchen and then I put his pussycat snacks in his kittykat dish (Gordon has his own eatery in the downstairs loo – it's handy because then he can have a thirst-quenching drink from the lavatory bowl... erlack). Anyway, I put Angus's food in his dish whilst he amuses himself by hurling himself at the door, like a furry battering ram. Then I let myself out through the kitchen door into the garden, and go to the front door and into the hall where Angus is headbutting the kitchen door. Protecting myself with the broom, I open the door and he dives in. Then I shut the kitchen door. So I'm never at any time in the same room as Angus and food. That's why I have two hands.

But this means nothing to him. One word from Libby and he's got his goggles on and is in the back of the Robinmobile. I'm surprised that he's not driving. He will be on the way back.

12:00 p.m.

Phoned Jasyissimus, my bestest pal.

"Jas?"

"Oh hello. What happened then? What number did you get to?"

"Oh, Jas, I am so full of confusiosity."

I told her what had happened. She sounded as if she was thinking – you could quite literally hear the cogs in her brain going round. Then she said, "So what you are saying is that officially you didn't even get on the snogging scale with Masimo."

"Well... no, we didn't... I mean, he handed me my Coke and touched my hand."

"But he didn't hold it?"

"No."

"Well, it's not number one then, is it? Unless you've added 'handing over a Coke' to the snogging scale without telling me. And what number would 'handing over a Coke' be, anyway? You might as well have a number for 'saying hello' or..."

She was beginning to annoy me quite badly. She's the opposite of telepathic – she's tele-pathetic, because she just goes on and on no matter how much she should just shut up. On and on she rambled...

"So, he didn't put his arm around you, so that's nil points so far. What kind of good-night kiss was it?"

"Well, you know, he put his lips on mine and—"

"For how long?"

"Er... about er two seconds."

"Two seconds??"

"Yes."

"Two seconds??"

"Yes yes, how many more times?"

"He put his lips on yours for two seconds?"

"YES, JAS!!"

"Well, that's not a kiss, is it? My aunties do that."

Then I finally snapped. "Well, that is because you have lezzie aunties – my aunties don't put their lips on mine."

"I have not got lezzie aunties!!"

It deteriorated after that and we both did stereo phone banging down.

1:00 p.m.

I tried to eat but it's no use, my tummy's all knotted up.

Jas is right, actually. I got nil points on the snogging scale because Masimo didn't want to snog me.

He wants to snog Wet Lindsay, but not me.

What's so wrong with me?

2:30 p.m.

Looked in the mirror.

There is the spready-nose thing. Could that be it? But Robbie and Dave the Laugh didn't seem to mind it.

My eyes are OK. I got mostly eights for them.

And my hair's OK. It's a bit of a boring brown, but since the snapping-off incident I haven't wanted to mess about too much.

My eyebrows are more or less under control.

Oh, I don't know.

Perhaps it's my nose. Someone did give me zero for it.

And that was its highest mark.

3:30 p.m.

Phone rang. It was Rosie.

"Gee, why haven't you rung me with all the goss?"

"Because there isn't any. Masimo gave me a sort of peck on the lips and said I was sweet and that he was going to 'Late and Live' with Lindsay."

Rosie went quiet and then she said, "OK, my little pally, I think we need to call an extraordinary meeting of the Ace Gang. Be round at my house at four p.m. for snacks."

I love Rosie.

But not in a Jas's auntie way.

4:10 p.m.

Rosie had made jam sandwiches with the crusts cut off as a special invalid dish for me.

She said, "Everything's going to be all right. I've got oven chips for later."

God, I think I'm becoming a lezzie. It would be a damn

sight easier than living in Heartbreak Hotel all the time.

Jools, Ellen and Mabs arrived, and Jools said, "To open our official Ace Gang meeting and as a tribute to Billy Shakespeare, Miss Wilson's boyfriend, I say, 'Let us indeed goeth downeth the disco!!'"

And we did our special disco inferno routine. Which I did have to say cheered me up.

We were all lolling and panting on the sofa when the doorbell rang.

Rosie came back in with Jas. We looked at each other and she said, "I am preparing myself to forgive you."

Which is tosh and a facsimile of a sham, as it is her who is in the wrong. It's not my fault she has lesbian aunties. But I didn't say that because frankly I need all the friend support I can get.

I told them my Masimo story and they all nodded wisely and fed me jam sandwiches.

At the end I said, "So what do you think?"

Rosie looked very very wise and owly and said, "Well, after hearing everything... this is what I think: number one, he's Italian."

We all nodded.

"Number two, he's a boy."

We all nodded again. It was like a nodding-dog convention. Rosie was just looking at me, nodding her head. I said after about twenty-five years of nodding, "Yes, and so?"

She said, "So... frankly, I haven't got a clue what it means."

The rest of them all went, "No, me neither..."

Qu'est-ce que c'est le point????

Sunday May 1st

I am going quite literally bonkers. I hardly slept last night. Masimo was going to go to "Late and Live" with Lindsay, so from about seven p.m. that was all I could think about.

How could he like her?

I suppose she is older than me.

But so is Slim, our revered headmistress, and Masimo doesn't fancy her.

I don't think.

Although anything could happen in a life full of people with no foreheads and lesbian aunties.

Now I really feel sick. I've just had an image of Slim in a short skirt with her massive elephantine legs jellying around on the back of Masimo's scooter going off to some gig.

9:30 a.m.

Not that it would drive off if she were on the back of it.

In fact, if she sat on the back of it, Masimo would probably shoot up into the air. Which would be a good thing.

9:40 a.m.

No it wouldn't. I really like him. It's not his fault he wants to have fun after a serious relationship. I cannot point the finger of shame at anyone with the General Horn. I too have heard the call of the Horn.

10:00 a.m.

But I really do like him.

It's just not fair that he doesn't like me.

1:00 p.m.

I've got big bags under my eyes. And I think I might have lost weight. I've only had jam sandwiches and oven chips for the last twenty-four hours. And cornies and toast that Mum brought me this morning, but that's all.

2:00 p.m.

All alone again, the Mad have gone to Grandad's. Yesterday was the Clown Convention and now today is the Mad Convention.

Angus, Gordy and Naomi are all in their bachelor pad, the Prat Poodles' kennel. Mr and Mrs Next Door have gone out and left the Prat Poodles to the mercy of the kittykats. Angus, Gordy and Naomi have finished the nice doggie dinner they found in the kennel and are now having an after-lunch game of Chuck the Squeaking Bone About. It's driving the Prat Poodles insane but they daren't come out from behind the dustbins.

3:00 p.m.

I've tried everything to take my mind off Masimo – played really loud music, yoga, chanting, praying to Baby Jesus, plucking my eyebrows. In the end I was so sheer desperadoes I even did my German homework.

4:00 p.m.

Rang Dave the Laugh. He answered the phone.

"Dave, it's me, Georgia."

"Aha, hello, Sex Kitty, just couldn't help yourself then. I know what you mean. I may have to get bodyguards soon, I'm so gorgeous. Sometimes I want to snog myself."

"Dave, I... want... well..."

Oh God I was going to blub.

He said, "What is it?"

I said, "I'm really really upset."

He sounded serious. "Are you, pet? Why? Tell me, or shall I come round?"

I said, "Well, I suppose you're... well... busy."

"Do you mean am I with Rachel? You know what I told you about boys, Georgia, you have to spell it out, you can't be subtle."

"Yes, OK, are you with Rachel?"

"No, I'm not, we went to 'Late and Live' and it was a late one, so she's with her family... Anyway, whatever, shall I come over?"

5:00 p.m.

Dave and I walked over the back fields, even though it was extremely nippy noodles. I told him what had happened. He said, "Yeah, I saw Lindsay and Masimo last night. He's incredibly flash, Georgia, he had a suit on – although I must say I didn't see his handbag."

I knew I should have been expecting it, but I still just wanted to blub. Dave put his arm around me. "Listen, I'll tell you the truth from a Horn Master's point of view. I think Masimo is playing the field. He can have anyone he wants so he's bound to be tempted. You said that he had a serious thing in Italy – and he wants to get over that and have fun. But I do think he likes you, because, well, despite being certifiably insane you are a lovely, funny Sex Kitty. And actually you are quite a sweet person."

I couldn't help it, I gave him a really big hug and tears came out of my eyes. Dave got out his hankie and dabbed them away. Thank God I'd thought better of wearing my boy entrancers. Who knows what would have happened when Dave dabbed my eyes. I could have ended up with a false moustache.

10:00 p.m.

Dave's advice is to not give up and be cheerful, but to be realistic. He says I should believe in myself and think I am the bees knees and then other people (boys) and maybe even Masimo will think I am too.

I don't know why, but I sort of believe him.

He's actually a great mate.

And Horn advisor.

He's a proper boy mate.

Who's like a mate.

And not a boyfriend.

It's relaxing just to talk to a boy and not have snogging on the menu of life.

Midnight

So how come we got to number six??

Tuesday May 3rd

Pelting down.

I said to Jas as we trudged along under our umbies, "My heartbreak has given me a new dignitosity."

Jas said, "Is that why you're walking funny?"

I gave her my special biffing on the arm that makes your arm go paralysed. It was her umbie-holding arm and she nearly speared a couple of first formers walking in front of us. That perked them up.

Assembly

Uh-oh, it's the fainting season again. We usually have an outbreak just before exams. Kathy Smith and Rosemary Duvall keeled over during "All Things Bright and Beautiful" and had to be carried out. Lucky swine. Slim said, "Settle, girls, settle, they will be quite all right."

Just then Isabella King crashed to the ground. They were falling like flies. I might try it myself: we've got double Physics next. Unfortunately Hawkeye was on the warpath. I could see her giving Isabella the third degree.

Slim was still aquiver. "You must all make sure you have a good breakfast; not eating causes fainting."

I said out of the side of my mouth, "No danger of her keeling over then. Do you reckon she stores extra supplies in her chins?"

Rosie started uncontrollable laughing. I can feel hysteria coming on.

As we left the hall, Wet Lindsay was beaking about. I looked at her and she had a really smug look on her face. She is so thin and useless, what can Masimo see in her?

Physics

We liberated the anatomy skeleton from the Blodge lab and put "Fatty", as we call him, in science overalls. We sat him at the back in between me and Rosie. Herr Kamyer is so duff that he didn't even notice until the skeleton put his hand up to answer a question.

Lunchtime

Ace Gang meeting in the science block lavs. I told them what my Horn advisor had said – well, I didn't actually say that Dave had told me, I let them think it was my own wisdomosity – and they all started nodding.

I said, "Please don't start the nodding fiasco again."

Jools said, "So what's your plan? Are you going to kill Lindsay?"

I said, "No, that would be childish. And I am displaying maturiosity these days. So I'm not going to kill her; we are all going to start a staring campaign."

The plan is that we all stare at a part of Lindsay every time we see her. Like her nose. Or her lack of forehead. Or her stick legs. And so on. She will get paranoid that she has a bogey hanging out of her nose, or her skirt is tucked in her knickers and so on.

The second part of my mistress plan is to get in tip-top physical condition by going running every day. Then when I'm fit as a frog I will casually find out where Masimo goes running and turn up. Like a fabulous running Sex Kitty. And he will be bowled over by my charms, although hopefully not by my nunga-nungas.

I will wear my new sports bra to keep them under control.

Simple pimple.

3:00 p.m.

Excellent progress in the staring campaign. I gazed at Lindsay's chin when she was talking to her stupid tragic pals in the corridor. She got all shuffly and then I noticed she went off to the loos. Obviously thinks that she's got a lurker. Hahahahaha. *Excellente!!*

3:45 p.m.

Jools, Ellen and Jas all gazed at the top of her head and they said she went off to the loos again.

She'll be practically living in there by the time we've finished.

4:30 p.m

Rightio. Part two of my luuuurve plan. Running begins.

4:32 p.m.

It has stopped raining but Gordon Bennet it's nippy noodles, I can see my breath freezing. What kind of stupid weather is this for May? No chance of nip nip emergence, though, because I have got my nungas safely strapped in.

5:00 p.m.

Phew, I'm boiling and out of breath. I thought I would be quite fit after hockey and everything but I'm not.

5:10 p.m.

I might not be able to breathe but at least I'm not being knocked out by my basoomas.

5:15 p.m.

Right, I'm going to just cut across the top of the field and then come down the hill and go home.

Can heads explode? Because I think mine is going to.

5:16 p.m.

There is some other fool out running. I can hear pounding along behind me but I haven't got the strength to look round. When I get home I'm going to get in the fridge, I'm so hot and red.

"*Ciao*, Georgia."

Ohmygiddygodspyjamas, Masimo!!!

Noooooooooooooooooooo.

He caught up with me and was running alongside me. I just kept running and turned and gave him what I hoped was an attractive smile. Attractive if you like a smiling tomato in a jogging outfit. He looked sooo cool, and not even sweating. Also he seemed to be able to breathe. And talk.

He said, "You know, I didn't get your phone number. Would it be possible that you tell me?"

I gave him another smile. It might be the last living thing I did. Then I saw the hill path and my brain was so starved of oxygen it had no control over any part of my body. My legs started stumbling down the hill path. They were just merrily careering down the path, carrying my head and body along with them. Thank God Masimo didn't follow me. As he continued along the top path he shouted, "OK, Miss Hard to Get, I will see you later when I get back from America, *ciao caro.*"

At that point the hill path curved round and I crashed into a bush and fell over.

In bed

9:30 p.m.

Oh ow ow. Ouch and ow.

He wanted my telephone number and I couldn't speak. I could only be very very red.

I can't stand this.

I hobbled downstairs and phoned Dave the Laugh.

"Dave, he asked me for my phone number tonight but I couldn't give it to him because I was too red. He called me 'Miss Hard to Get'."

Dave said, "Excellent work. You are of course studying at the feet of the Horn Master."

11:00 p.m.

Boys truly are weird. Dave says that I have accidentally done the right thing, I have become the mystery woman.

11:10 p.m.

He said, "See you later when I get back from America."

That's far beyond the usual "see you later" fandango.

Wednesday May 4th

Evening

Today was fifty million hours long. I have made Jas find out from Tom who can find out from Dom what is going on with Masimo.

8:30 p.m.

Jas said, "Masimo has gone to London for a week and then he's off to Hamburger-a-gogo to visit his olds."

11:00 p.m.

Hamburger-a-gogo land.

11:10 p.m.

Merde.

11:15 p.m.

Vati roared up in the Robinmobile. Bang bang clatter clatter. Shout shout. He is so shouty and trousery.

Then Mutti started going, "Wow!! Oh Wow. Fantastic!"

Pray God he's not got some new even more embarrassing trousers.

Oh dear *Gott in Himmel* and Donner and Blitzen, now they're tramping up the stairs to my room. They burst in and I pulled the blanket over my head.

Mutti said, "Go on, tell her the news. Tell her!"

Now what?

Vati said, "We're off to America at half term!"

I shot up in bed.

Midnight

I hugged my own father.

12:05 p.m.

We are off to Hamburger-a-gogo land. I can track down Masimo.

12:10 p.m.

I don't know exactly where he is, but how big can America be??

Georgia's Glossary

airing cupboard · This is a cupboard over the top of the hot-water heater in a house. It is used for keeping towels and sheets warm on cold winter nights. Er, at least that's what it's used for in normal people's homes. In my home it is Libby's play den or Angus and Gordy's winter headquarters. It is therefore far from hygienic. In fact, you would be a fool to put anything in there.

arvie · Afternoon. From the Latin "arvo". Possibly. As in the famous Latin invitation: "Lettus meetus this arvo."

BacoFoil · Aluminium foil for cooking things in the oven. By the way, did you know that Hamburger-a-gogo types leave out the second "i" in aluminium. If they can't be arsed to have vowels later on in words, where would we be? Do they say plutonum? Or titanum? No, they don't. Otherwise the whole thing would just become a sham and very very tedus. Not to menton confusng.

Blimey O'Reilly · (As in "Blimey O'Reilly's trousers".) This is an Irish expression of disbelief and shock. Maybe Blimey O'Reilly was a famous Irish bloke who had extravagantly big trousers; we may never know the truth. The fact is, whoever he is, what you need to know is that: a) it's Irish and b) it is Irish. I rest my case.

Blodge · Biology. Like Geoggers – Geography, or Froggie – French.

BluTack · Blue plasticine stuff that you stick stuff to other stuff with. It is very useful for sticking stuff to other stuff. Tiptop sticking stuff actually. I don't know why it's called BluTack when it clearly should be called Blue Sticking Stuff. Also, blue is spelt wrong, but that's life for you.

Bovril · A disgusting drink that is supposed to be good for you. It's made out of cows' feet. It is. Well, I think it is.

boy entrancers · False eyelashes. Boys are ALWAYS entranced when you wear them. This is a FACT... unless of course they get stuck together and then boys think you are mad and blind and not entrancing at all.

clud · This is short for cloud. Lots of really long boring poems and so on can be made much snappier by abbreviating words. So Tennyson's poem called *Daffodils* (or "Daffs") has the immortal line, "I wandered lonely as a clud." Ditto, Rom and Jul. Or Ham. Or Merc of Ven.

Curly Wurly · A choccy woccy doodah bar that is all curly and whirly. See milky pops.

div · Short for "dithering prat", i.e. Jas.

do · A "do" is any sort of occasion. A celebration. Say it was your birthday, I would say, "It's your birthday, let's have a bit of a do." Or, as in Elvis Atwood's case, I would say, "Let's not have a leaving do, can't he just go?" Or perhaps I'm being a bit harsh. No, I am not.

dodie · Dummy or pacifier.

duffing up · Duffing up is the female equivalent of beating up. It's not so violent and usually involves a lot of pushing with the occasional pinch.

Ethelred the Unready · Ah, I am glad that you asked me this because once more I am able to display my huge talent for historiosity. Most English kings and queens get nicknames like "Richard the Lionheart" (because he was brave and so on) or "Good Queen Bess". Ethelred (who lived a long long time ago, even before Slim was a young boy) is famous for being "unready". The Vikings came to

England to pillage and shake their big red legs at the English folk. They sneaked into his castle and caught Ethelred in the loo, and took over the castle. Hence his name – Ethelred the Unready. He's lucky that is all he's called. Things could be much worse: he could be called Ethelred the Pooey, or Ethelred on the Looey.

five's court · This is a typical Stalag 14 idea. It's minus forty-five degrees outside, so what should we do to entertain the schoolgirls? Let them stay inside in the cozy warmth and read? No. Let's build a concrete wall outside with a red line at waist height, and let's make them go and hit a hard ball at the red line with their little freezing hands. What larks!

fringe · Goofy short bit of hair that comes down to your eyebrows. Someone told me that American-type people call them "bangs", but this is so ridiculously strange that it's not worth thinking about. Some people can look very stylish with a fringe (me) while others look goofy (Jas). The Beatles started it apparently. One of them had a German girlfriend who cut their hair with a pudding bowl, and the rest is history.

gorgey · Gorgeous. Like fabby (fabulous) and marvy (marvellous).

half-term · Oh, of course you must all know what this is, you are toying with my emotions, you naughty minxes. A term is when you have to go to school, i.e. spring term, summer term, autumn term, etc. Half-term is halfway through the term when you get time off the sentence for good behaviour. Not really – you get time off because otherwise all the teachers would have a nervy b.

heavy manners · This is Jamaican patois and means keeping you under surveillance and possibly house arrest. I had a Jamaican mate and instead of saying "hi", or "hello", he would say "iry". But I thought he was saying "highway", so I would say "highway" back. He thought I was obsessed with motorways. It can be very difficult to get on with other nations if they will insist on speaking their own languages.

hobbit · Do we really have to do this? Oh God, are we never to be free? A hobbit is one of those little creatures in *The Lord of the Rings* with really big ears. They're bloody lucky to get away with just the ears compared to a lot of the other horrible things in the books – orks and so on. Is there anyone in *The Lord of the Rings* who is normal? Answer: no. The whole thing is a nightmare of beards.

japes · Enid Blyton wrote children's books about the Famous Five in the 1950s. These five complete wets and weeds had lots of "japes" and "jolly wheezes". If, for instance, they hid behind the door and then leapt out to surprise their parents, that would be a "wizard jape".

I think you get the picture of what extraordinarily crap books they were.

Kiwi-a-gogo land · New Zealand. "-a-gogo land" can be used to liven up the otherwise really boring names of other countries. America, for instance, is Hamburger-a-gogo land. Mexico is Mariachi-a-gogo land and France is Frogs'-legs-a-gogo land.

Late and Live · A late-night gig that has live bands on.

loo · Lavatory. In America (land of the free and criminally insane) they say "rest room", which is funny, as I never feel like having a rest when I go to the lavatory.

lurgified · This is an extension of the word "lurgy". To have the lurgy is to either have a physical or mental illness; so you could have the flu, but you could also have "stupid brain", which is what happens when you see a gorgey bloke and become "lurgified" – touched by the lurgy.

milky pops · A soothing hot milk drink for when you are a little person. (No, not an elf, I mean a child.) Anyway, what was I saying? Oh yes, when you are a child people give words endings to make them more cozy. Chocolate is therefore obviously choccy woccy doo dah. Blanket is blankin. Tooth is tushy peg. Easy is easy peasy lemon squeezy. If grown-ups ever talk like this, do not hesitate to kill them.

nervy spaz · Nervous spasm. Nearly the same as a nervy b. (nervous breakdown) or an F.T. (funny turn), only more spectacular on the physical side.

nippy noodles · Instead of saying, "Good heavens, it's quite cold this morning," you say, "Cor – nippy noodles!!" English is an exciting and growing language. It is. Believe me. Just leave it at that. Accept it.

nub · The heart of the matter. You can also say gist and thrust. This is from the name for the centre of a wheel where the spokes come out. Or do I mean hub? Who cares. I feel a dance coming on.

nunga-nungas · Basoomas. Girls' breasty business. Ellen's brother calls them nunga-nungas because he says that if you get hold of a girl's breast and pull it out and then let it go, it goes *nunga-nunga-nunga.* As I have said many, many times with great wisdomosity, there is something really wrong with boys.

Pantalitzer · A terrifying Czech-made doll that sadistic parents (my vati) buy for their children, presumably to teach them early on about the horror of life. I don't know if I have mentioned this before, but I am not sure that Eastern Europeans really know how to have a laugh.

parky · Another jaunty word for nippy noodles.

pash · Passion. As in, "I had a real pash on him until I saw his collection of vole droppings." Or, in Masimo's case, "He is my one and only super-duper pash." That is official.

pingy pongoes · A very bad smell. Usually to do with farting.

polo neck · I am not pointing the finger of shame anywhere, but did you know that in Hamburger-a-gogo land they call polo necks "turtle necks". Having a neck like a turtle has never been a big selling point for me... but let them have it their own way if the Hamburgese LUUURVE turtles so much.

rate · To fancy someone.

Robin Reliant · Oh, please, please don't ask me about this. Oh very well. You know how old blokes keep inventing things? For no reason? Well, they do. There's always some complete twit from a village called Little Beddingham or Middle Wallop – anyway, somewhere where there are no shops or television (or a decent lunatic asylum), and the complete twit is called Nigel or Terence and he invents things like a tiny shower for sparrows, an ostrich-egg cup, or a nose picker. You get the idea. Anyway, one of these types called Robin invented a car that only has three wheels. A three-wheeled car. Er – that's it. That was his brilliant invention. No reason for it. It's a bit like that bloke who invented the unicycle. All they do is encourage clowns. They should be stopped really, but I am vair vair tired.

scheissenhausen · Quite literally (if you happen to be a Lederhosen-type person) a house that you poo in (*scheiss* is poo and *haus* is house). Poo house. Lavatory. Or rest room as Hamburger-a-gogo types say. No one knows why they say that. Oh no, hang on, I think I do know. When they all lived in the Wild West in wooden shacks, one room was both their bedroom and their lavatory. Cowboys didn't mind that sort of thing. In fact they loved it. But I don't.

Sellotape · As you know, this is usually used for sticking bits of paper to other bits of paper. But it can be used for sticking hair down to make it flat. (Once I used it for sticking Jas's mouth shut when she had hiccups. I thought it might cure them. It didn't, but it was quite funny anyway.)

Sherpa Tensing · When English people were stopped from conquering places by spoilsports who said, "Clear off, this is our land," we had to have Plan B. Plan B was to conquer other things, like mountains. English blokes began hurling themselves up Everest like knobbly-kneed lemmings. The Everest folk got sick of them falling off or wandering around saying, "Where am I?" and blundering into their villages day and night in unnecessary anoraks. So they (the local folk – called Sherpas) decided to lead them up Everest just to get rid of them. And the head Sherpa-type bloke was called Sherpa Tensing.

smalls · An ironic term for underpants. Well, ironic in my vati's case: if his underpants were called "massives", that would make more sense.

tig · Apparently Hamburger-a-gogo people call this "tag". I won't ask why because I am full of exhausterosity and also want to go to the piddly-diddly department.

wet · A drippy, useless, nerdy idiot – Lindsay.

whelk boy · A whelk is a horrible shellfish thing that only the truly mad eat. It is slimy and mucus-like. A "whelk boy" is a boy who kisses like a whelk, i.e. a slimy mucussy kisser. Erlack-a-pongoes.

work experience · I include this because I am speaking on behalf of the youth of Britain. He can't speak for himself because he is too stupid. Anyway, whose idea was this? My vati's probably. Teenagers who are innocently filling in time at school, you know, painting their nails, chatting and snoozing, etc. are forced to go to a shop or hospital ward or office or science lab and spend a day there, so that they know what it is like to work. As I have said many times to my mutti, I am far, far too busy to work. And anyway, I know what work is like: it is crap.

'...then
he ate
my
boy
entrancers.'

A Note from Georgia

Dear Chumettes and Chums,

I hope you are all righty as two all righty things. I am, though ONCE AGAIN I am full of exhaustiosity. I have been as busy as a bee (two bees) finishing my latest oeuvre. Oh yes, AND I have been to Hamburger-a-gogo land to see for myself the nation that cannot be bothered to put the "i" in the second half of words... like aluminium, for instance, which those lazy cats spell alUminum. Where would we be if none of us could be bothered to finish off our words properly? I'll tell you where we would be, we would be up shi cree without a padd... that's where.

As you will see, I have reached new heights of sophisticosity in this latest of my oeuvres... boys, lipstick, snogging, snogging, red-bottomosity, jokes about sausages and pants - the list is endless.

I do this only because I love you.

Georgia

p.s. You don't know what oeuvre means, do you?

p.p.s. You think it is french for eggs, don't you? Like oeuf.

p.p.p.s. You think I have been saying that I have just finished writing my new egg.

p.p.p.p.s. Look it up in the glossary, you lazy minxes, I am far too tired to explain. I have to go and have a lie down on my snogging emporium (bean bag)... zzzzzzzzzzzz.

In memory and love for the boys, Oscar Kakoschka and Arthur Hewlings. God bless.

Luuurve to the fabbest family a girl could have: Mutti, Vati, Soshie, Johnboy, Eduardo, Hons, Bibbity, Kimbo, Jolly, Arrow, Millie and the three remaining chickens. Oh, and welcome to the new diggy dog, Billy. Big luuurve to the Kiwi-a-gogo and Isle of Wight branches of mayhem. And of course to the Ace mates: Salty Dog 'of course you haven't broken it you fool otherwise you couldn't speak' Pringle, Mizz Morgan, Elton, Jimjams, Guildford calling, Phil and Ruth in Froggland, Jeddbox, Big Fat Bobbins, Kim 'you can have that one mate' and Sandy, Jools and the Mogul, Lozzer or Mrs Bridges as I know you, Ian the computer, Jenks, the Hewlings and the Willans (yes that means you, Candy), Baggy Aggiss and Jo, B and J, Mrs H and Dan, Alan 'it's not a perm' Davies, Jo Good(ish). And of course to Stewpot and Sue (please no more jokes about snot). Ay up to the Northern branch: The Cock, Ann-marie, Katy and Patrick; to the Ace Gang from Parklands: Rosie, Barbara, Christine C, Linda, Ali and everyone. To Chris the Organ. Love to the Captain and thank you for letting me use your togglestick thing. To the St Nicks crew for everything, and in particular to Dezza the vicar for joy and love and the APPALLING jokes about farting. (And also to young Phil and family… just love, nothing to do with farting.) Also a big kiss to the new cruise mates: Bungalow Steve, Dancing Steve, Simon the Rock God and Adéle, Ironing Tony and Marg. Big luuurve to Mirella, Dave and the very gorgey Mattea. Thank you to Karen Cunningham for the lovely frocks and to that Eve the Minx. Finally thank you to everyone at my work family at HarperCollins: the divine Gillie, fabby Sally Martin and groovy Sally Gritten; to Caroline and all in the publicity and design departments – what a beyond marvy job you have all done. Thank you to Emma at Midas. Bye bye Dom. And as always best love to the Empress. The end. P.S. Hahahaha you thought I had finally shut up, didn't you? But finally, thank you to all the fabby readers of my books and all of you who have sent me such lovely letters (and now and again inscribed thongs...). I luuuurve you all. I do. I think this is everything... hopefully! Luuurve Lou xxxxxxx.

Jas, your spaceship has arrived. Please get in.

Saturday May 7th

Sun shining like a big yellow shining... er... warmey planet on fire thing.

Yessssssss!

10:05 a.m.

I am quite literally not wandering lonely as a clud, in fact I am treading lightly in the Universe of the Very Nearly Quite Happy.

10:10 a.m.

Something full of miraculosity has happened. My vati, world renowned fool and paid-up member of the Big Twit club, has for once in his entire life accidentally done something good. We are going to Hamburger-a-gogo land! Honestly.

And guess who is there already? Besides a lot of people in huge psychedelic shorts and that bloke who is half-chicken half-colonel. I'll tell you who is there, the Luuurve God is there! Masimo, the Italian Stallion, has gone to visit his olds, leaving me – his new, lurker-free-nearly almost girlfriend – back here in Billy Shakespeare land. So he thinks! Imagine how thrilled he will be when I pop up and say "Howdy!", or whatever it is they say over there.

Let the overseas Snog Fest begin!

10:15 a.m.

The only fly in the ointmosity of life is that Vati is making us go to some crap clown-car convention.

10:20 a.m.

And Uncle Eddie, the baldest man on the planet, is coming with us.

10:25 a.m.

Still, with a bit of luck they will both be arrested for indecent

exposure when they don their leather motoring trousers.

10:30 a.m.

Filled with the *joie de vivre* that is so much a part of my attractive but modest personality, I phoned my bestest pally.

"Jas, it is *mich,* your *sehr guttest* pally. I am calling you *mit wunderbar* news!"

"Oh God. Look, it's only a week till Tom leaves and we were just sorting out my—"

"Jas, I cannot waste time discussing your knicker collection; that is between you and Tom... quite literally... hahahahaha. Do you get it? Do you get it? Knickers... between you and Hunky... do you...?"

But as I should have known from long and tiring experience, it is useless to waste my wit on Jazzy. So I cut to my nub and gist.

"I am going to Hamburger-a-gogo land to meet Masimo the Luuurve God of the universe and beyond. And back."

"No you're not."

"I am."

"How?"

I explained to Jas about the trip and the "Howdy!"

business and everything, but as usual she displayed cold waterosity.

"Where is Masimo going to be in Hamburger-a-gogo land?"

"Ahaha!!!"

"You don't know, do you?"

"Well, not yet, but—"

"He could be anywhere."

"I know, but how big can America be?"

"It's huge."

I laughed. Nothing was going to spoil my peachy mood, let alone swotty nit-picking from Mrs Big Pantaloonies.

I said, "Is it as huge as your gym knickers?"

There was silence.

"Jas, come on, be happy for me."

"It's all very well for you, you can just fancy anyone, but it's different with Tom and me – he's off to Kiwi-a-gogo and I will be left here all on my owney."

Oh good grief.

Hunky is only going to the Land of the Big White Clots for a couple of weeks, but I am still going to have to listen to her moaning and rambling on about the twig-collecting

years. However, before she could start raving on about molluscs and cuckoo spit I had a flash of inspirationosity.

"Jas, listen, I have a plan of such geniosity that I have even surprised myself, and might give myself some sort of award."

She didn't even say "What is it?" There was just silence.

I said, "Aren't you even going to ask me what it is, Jas?"

"It's bound to be stupid."

"Oh, cheers, thanks a lot. Well I won't bother you with it then. Even though it involves you and your happiness and is *très bon* and also vair vair *gut. Au revoir. Bonne chance.*"

And I put the phone down. Even Jas cannot spoil my mood. Lalalalalalala.

11:00 a.m.

Better start planning my wardrobe for the Luuurve Trail. What do the Hamburgese wear? Cowboy hats, I suppose.

11:10 a.m.

From what I hear, the Hamburgese are a bit strict hygiene-wise. They're always in the shower and so on. It is to be hoped the customs man doesn't glance inside Libby's bag and find her night-time blankie, otherwise we will all be buggered.

Oh, so many things to worry about. I think I will have a little zizz to relax myself and then plan my cosmetic routine.

11:11 a.m.

Fat chance.

"Gingey! Gingey, it's meeeeeeee!!! I have just been to the lavatreeeeeee!"

My darling sister has kicked open my bedroom door. Hurrah.

11:13 a.m.

Oh good, and she has her "fwends" with her – scuba-diving Barbie, Charlie Horse, a parsnip and Cross-eyed Gordy. Gordy is under house arrest because he has not had the immunisation injections he needs before he is set loose into the wild jungle world of our street. I'd like to see the germ hard enough to take him on.

As they all snuggled comfortably into my bed, the phone rang downstairs and Dad answered it. Vati yelled up, "Georgia, quickly, one of your mates wants to talk rubbish with you for an hour or two on her father's phone."

He has not got the flare of charm, my vati; but on the other hand, what he has got are my tickets to paradise. I must remember that, however ludicrous he is, he has bought me a passage to the Luuurve Machine.

Masimo-a-gogo!!!

I shouted down, "Thank you, Papa, I'll be down immediately, and perhaps later I will entertain you with my piano playing."

We haven't got a piano, but it's the thought that counts.

11:15 a.m.

It was Jazzy Spazzy... tee-hee. I knew she would crumble and want to know my plan.

I said, "So, now do you want to know what my plan is?"

"If you like."

"No Jas, you are still not showing enthusiosity. Try harder."

"I can't."

"Yes, you can. Gird your loins and so on; laugh and the world laughs at you. Come on, you do really want to know my plan, especially as it concerns you, my little hairy pally."

"I'm not hairy."

"Have it your own way, just don't go near any circuses."

"Shut up. Go on then, tell me your plan. Although, unless you are going to give me the money to go to Kiwi-a-gogo with Tom, I don't—"

"Jas, forget about Hunky. He will be too busy lying around in streams with Robbie and hugging marsupials to get up to anything. This is about you and me on the road."

"What road?"

"OK, this is it: when I go to Hamburger-a-gogo... you come with me! Do you see? Driving across America, you and me. We will be like Thelma and Louise!"

"We're not called Thelma and Louise."

"I know that, I am just saying we will be LIKE THEM."

"And we're not American."

"I know that, but I—"

"And neither of us can drive."

Oh dear God.

I said, "Jas, your spaceship has arrived. Please get in."

12:00 p.m.

Ahahaha, Jazzy Spazzy has finally come to her senses (ish).

She has got the scent of funosity in her nostrils and wants to come to Hamburger-a-gogo land. A LOT. So now all we have to do is get our parents to let us. We have a two-pronged plan.

Prong One is a charm offensive on our muttis and vatis to persuade them to let Jas come to America with me. (And also to give her sqillions of squids for spenderoonies.) We are going to be really nice and sweet and listen to them ramble on about the Beatles. I've been practising my pleading and they would have to be made of stone not to give me the entire contents of their wallets.

However, if that fails and they say no, we launch Prong Two: relentless moaning. You know the kind of thing – "All my other friends are allowed to take a mate on holiday with them. How come I am the ONLY person in the universe who is not allowed to take a mate on holiday? Why is it just me? Why? Why oh why oh why?"

"Why?"

"It is sooo unfair."

"Why?"

Outside the front-room door
9:10 p.m.

Right, this is it. I've got my old Teletubbies jimjams on for maximosity on the loveablenosity front.

Front room

Mutti and Vati were on the sofa, curled round each other. I could clearly see Mum's knickers. Erlack. And the curtains were open; anyone could see in. A fat bloke passing by might think it was a brothel for the porkier gentleman. I was going to say that but then I remembered my prongs. So I said, "Good evening, Mother, Father."

Vati said, "How much?" without even looking at me. I laughed attractively.

"Oh, Papa, this is not a material matter, it's to do with friendship and love and—"

Mum said, "I don't care how many of your friends have had their navels pierced. You are not."

"But I—"

But she was still rambling on. "Ditto tattoos."

"But I—"

Vati joined in. "And no, you cannot have a flat in Paris

and a manservant to help with your homework."

Oh, how I nearly laughed. Not. I thought about telling Dad that Rosie said he looked like a brothel madam in his flying helmet and leather jacket, but then I remembered my charm prong and forced a little grin to play around my mouth.

"You two!!! Always kidding about you cheeky minxes! Anyway, all it is really is that, well... you know... Jas is all miz because of Tom going to Kiwi-a-gogo and, well... You know she's my pal, and... well... it would be nice for me if you know... anyway, can she?"

Vati said, "Can she what? Move in? Levitate? What?"

I bit the whatsit. "Can she come with us to Hamburger-a-gogo land?"

10:00 p.m.

Both of our parents have said yes. Unbelievable. Actually, I am not that amazed that Jas's parents said yes because they are, on the whole, not entirely mad. But my parents?

Weird.

It is a miracle for which I would normally thank Jesus. He does seem to be coming up trumps lately. I left Robbie to the snogging possums but then Jesus sent me a replacement Luuurve God. Hurray! As I say, I would normally thank him personally by laying gifts at his feet (or foot, actually, because one of his feet snapped off), however there is a bit of a problem. Libby has been rifling around in my room and she has nicked my statue of him. I'm afraid Jesus has not quite been himself since. The last time I saw him he had a frock on and Libby was calling him "Sandra", Barbie's new bestest pal.

I don't think God will hold it against us, as he is, after all, a merciful God.

10:10 p.m.

Unless you happen to be that snake in the Garden of Eden. Snakey only asked, "Anyone fancy a bit of apple?" and then God made him crawl around on his belly for eternity. Seems a bit harsh. (Although, as I pointed out to Miss Wilson in our interesting talks in RE, if you were a snake in the first place, being made to crawl around on your belly for the rest of your days doesn't actually seem that bad. Almost like being a snake in fact. I mean this with all reverencosity. I just have a lively mind.)

Oooohhhhh, I am so excited. I can't wait to tell the Ace Gang.

I even kissed my own father AGAIN. This is twice in two days. I must be a bit feverish.

In my bedroom

Libby, Gordy, Sandra and Barbie are all snoozing. They look so lovely and cosy. Our Lord, now heavily rouged, is next to Libby's feet. I don't know why she likes to sleep upside down. Perhaps because it is very scary waking up to see Gordy looking cross-eyed at you.

I looked out the window as I did my alternate nostril breathing. It is vair vair calming. You pinch one nostril closed and then breathe in through the other one, and then hold your breath and let the pinched-up one go and breathe out of that. And then you... well, anyway... all I can say is that the Lord Buddha did it, and he didn't just do it for nothing.

One minute later

I hope it's not like body building. I don't want to be really calm and have massive nostrils.

Two minutes later

For once Mr Next Door has done something nice. He has built a sort of anti-cat fence on the top of his wall made out of barbed wire. Angus will really like it. He gets a bit bored with leaping down on to the Prat Poodles and riding them round. He is the sort of cat who needs a bit of a challenge.

Five minutes later

Oh, here comes Supercat with Naomi. With his head up her bottom as ususal.

One minute later

Aha! He has removed his head and he has seen the new fencey. He luuurves the fencey.

Four minutes later

Old Nimble Paws did this beyond-fabby thing. He did a vertical jump! From standing on the wall he just shot straight up in the air and over the fence.

Five minutes later

Angus is really getting into it now. He leaps over the anti-cat

fence and then comes back into our garden by hurling himself through Mr Next Door's rhododendron bush. Excellent! He has made it into a track-and-field event. It is quite literally the Cat Olympics.

Five minutes later

I would prefer it if Naomi stuck to the usual giving of medals ceremony rather than licking Angus's trouser-snake area, but there you are – that is appalling furry tarts for you.

Monday May 9th

The crack of 8:00 a.m.

Crikey. I'd better not get carried away with happiness, otherwise I will be on time for school, or Stalag 14 as I so amusingly call it.

8:25 a.m.

Lolloping along to Jas's place, I had to pass by Mark Big Gob smoking on the corner with his lardy mates. He is quite literally a mouth on legs. Sadly he seems to have recovered his former (crap) self after the minor duffing-up incident with Dave the Laugh.

He just can't help himself, especially when, like now, he has the backup lardy lads with him. As I walked by in a dignified manner, trying not to let anything jiggle about, BG and the lard arses were just ogling my nungas like ogling oglers (if you can imagine the horror of that, and I think you can). Then he licked his lips! Erlack, he was licking his lips at me!

He is so *très* pathetico.

I may have to ask Dave to repeat the duffing-up incident.

Five minutes later

Jas was on her wall. I don't know what she had for breakfast but she has put on about twelve stone. Either that or her knickers have reached elephantine size.

When she jumped down, I saw it was because she had her skirt rolled over so much that she looked like a melon with a head and an annoying fringe in a school uniform.

She said, "My mum and dad want to come round to yours to talk about the arrangements."

"I must rush home and make them normal. Your mum and dad will never let you come with us if Dad happens to be wearing his masonic apron... or his velvet loons that he wears for 'grooving' in. No one in their right

mind would let a child of theirs anywhere near him."

Stalag 14

Hawkeye was on glaring duty at the school gates, so Jas had to do a quick dive behind me to let her skirt down. She was fiddling away as we walked along, so to distract Hawkeye with my youth and exuberance I started singing, "Oh, what a beautiful mornin', oh what a—"

"Why are you shuffling along like idiots? Put a spring in your step!"

I started doing a bit of springing for a laugh, but then she said, "Georgia, I have been glancing at your report card and it seems to me a bit of extra tuition wouldn't come amiss."

Bloody *sacré bleu*! I scuttled off to the loos as fast as I could.

Jas was pouting at herself in the mirror as I grumbled on. "'Glancing at your report card'. What kind of life is that? You might as well have a life 'glancing at paint drying' or 'glancing at a cactus not doing anything', or... anyway, it is no kind of a life for a human being. Which is why Hawkeye is so vair vair good at it."

Jas was now upside down under the hand dryer getting

maximum voluminosity into her fringe for the day ahead, but she nodded her head wisely, in an upside-down way.

Assembly

Usual routine: Klingon salute to the Ace Gang, a quick burst of "The Lord is my shepherd" and then some incomprehensible lecture from Slim, our huge headmistress. What is she rambling on about now? She has certainly excelled herself on the fashion front this morning. Polka-dot suit in a lovely subtle orange and black, and sling-back shoes. Parts of her feet have made a desperate bid for freedom out of the sling-back bit. I've never known anyone with fat feet. It's fascinating watching her. When she loses her rag (i.e. every time she speaks to us) every bit of her quivers in a tip-top jelloid way.

"So to my point, girls: achievement. What does it mean today in the modern world? I want you all to consider what achievement really means."

Then she stood there and looked at us. For ages. We stood looking back. She just stood there; we just stood there. Like a staring competition. Good Lord. It went on for ages and ages – you could practically see Miss Stamp's beard growing.

Two centuries later, Slim said, "How many of us could put our hands on our hearts and say 'I have achieved something really worthwhile this term.'?"

Me and Rosie put our hands on our hearts.

Corridor

9:30 a.m.

Oh bloody marvy. Wet Lindsay, who was stick-insecting around on snitcher duty, saw us with our hands on our hearts and is gave us her world famous 'How childish you are' lecture. Ho hum, pig's bum. Another fabulous opportunity to look at Mrs No Forehead.

9:36 a.m.

Hahahahaha! While Wet Lindsay was telling us off, me and Rosie kept our eyes fixed on her forehead. She couldn't say we were doing anything wrong, but afterwards she scuttled off to the loos for forehead inspection.

The staring campaign continues!

And she doesn't know I am off to America to a Snog Fest with the Luuurve God.

I said to Rosie as we ambled off to the Science block, "He

probably only took her to Late and Live because he is in the European Union for the preservation of rare species."

Rosie said, "What? The 'No Forehead Stick-insect Fighting Fund'?"

"Absolutemento *mon* pally."

We are indeed vair vair *amusant.*

Blodge

Miss Baldwin has got gigantic basoomas. Even bigger than my mutti's, and that is saying something. I was very much afraid that she would set fire to them with the Bunsen burner. Sadly there was no basooma incendiary action, so I couldn't use the foam extinguisher, which would have topped the lesson off in my humble opinion.

On the knicker toaster

Break

I told the Ace Gang about Operation Go to Hamburger-a-gogo Land. They were, as usual, agog as two gogs. Three gogs in Ellen's case. Thank the Lord she seems to have dropped her infectious laugh. I was going to have to kill her if she kept it up.

As we crunched through our nutritious snacks of cheesy Wotsits and chuddie, I said, "It is going to be marv, as I said to Jas – even though she didn't get it – we will be like the Thelma and Louise of England."

Rosie said, "But you won't have a gun."

"I might do."

"No, you won't. Your dad won't let you go to an all-nighter, so he is definitely not going to get you a gun."

"He is. He said I could have one when I got there."

Rosie just looked at me.

"Just a small one for emergency shooting."

They all just looked at me.

Ellen said (annoyingly), "Where... er... where is Masimo? I mean where is he going to be in America?"

I said, "Well, you know, near where we are going to be."

She went on in her vague, dumped-by-Dave-the-Laugh way. "Yes, but I mean, well... where are you going to be?"

I said, "At the clown-car convention in America."

Rosie blew a big gob-stopper bubble and then sucked it back in again. Then she put her face right up close to mine and said slowly, "Yes, but Georgia, where is the clown-car convention?"

"Memphis."

"And where is that?"

I laughed and said, "Good grief, I thought I was bad at geoggers. Don't you know?"

"YOU don't know, do you?"

"Of course I do. It's... down... a... bit from New York."

"Down a bit from New York?"

"Yes."

"Like you thought Hamburg was famous for its hamburgers?"

What had Rosie turned into? Memo the Memory Man? Honestly, just because I had been secretly exfoliating my legs under the desk in geoggers when we were doing the Rhine, and Miss Simpson sprang a surprise question on me...

I changed the subject. "So, what do you think I should pack for my trip?"

Jools said, "Well, not knickers, because they don't wear them there."

I said, "Wow, saucy minxes! You mean they go round in the nuddy-pants? They don't mention that in geoggers, do they? It's all boring stuff about wheat belts and the Atlantic drift."

Jools said, "Panties."

I said, "Oy, clear off with your panties talk. You are a nice-looking girl and everything, but I am just not interested."

Jools said, "No, that's what the Hamburgese wear."

The bell went.

Donner and Blitzen! How am I supposed to discuss my wardrobe if we keep having to go to lessons?

Oh, hang on though, it's German next, so that's OK. We can discuss it then without being disturbed.

German

Herr Kamyer was, as usual, rambling on about the Koch family going on one of their endless camping trips.

Keeping in mind that Koch is pronounced 'cock', and keeping in mind that they are the family that star in our German textbooks, you have to ask yourself this: what sadist decided to feature a family called Koch in our textbooks? They know that they are going to be read out by the naff and the sad (German teachers) to a load of giggling and hysterical girls obsessed with boys and rudey-dudeyness. The family could have been called anything, couldn't they? Schwartz or Schmidt, for instance, but oh no, it had to be the Kochs and their spangleferkels. How many sausages can one family eat? In the Kochs' case, the answer is A LOT.

I put my hand up because I am *sehr* interested in the Kochs.

Herr Kamyer said, "*Ja*, Georgia?"

I said, "Herr Kamyer, did all the Kochs go camping, or was it just the little Kochs and the big Kochs stayed behind? Or was it a mixture of little and big Kochs that came out?"

The whole class was in uproar. Herr Kamyer was, as usual, completely bewildered. He said, "Vat is zo funny about the Kochs? Do you not haf the Kochs in England?"

Happy days.

As we lolloped off I said, "German is such a restful and amusing language, isn't it? Incomprehensible, obviously. As, indeed, are the *lederhosen* that the Germans go yodelling in."

Jas was in Jasland and said, "You think *The Sound of Music* is what Germany is like, don't you? That's why you always rave on about singing nuns and yodelling."

"Well, *The Sound of Music* is, of course, a documentary-

style film. You can't argue with facts, and I do know what I'm talking about because Libby has made me watch it twelve times."

"It was set in Austria."

"Yes… and?"

"Last term you said that Germans were obsessed with goats and cheese."

"Yes… and?"

"That was because you had read *Heidi*, and that was set in Switzerland."

"Jas, what in the name of Beelzebub's stamp collection are you going on about?"

"You are crap at geoggers."

Oh, rave on, fringey nitwit. (I didn't say that bit aloud because I am grooming her to be my sidekick on the Road to Romance.)

Still, in the interests of world peace I might be forced to get the old atlas out and look at where Memphis is and so on.

Work work work, I'm so vair tired. And I still have to walk all the way home.

I wonder if Jazzy will give me a piggyback?

4:30 p.m.

No.

5:00 p.m.

I'll be bloody glad when Gordy is allowed out. When I arrived home he had the rubber plant on his head. I've put the stump back in the plant pot and superglued some of the leaves back on. With a bit of luck it will be all right till we go away, and then I can blame it on whatever fool cat-sits for us.

In my bedroom

How can I find out exactly where Masimo is?

Five minutes later

I can't trust Radio Jas to ask Tom to find out where Masimo has gone in Hamburger-a-gogo land. Anytime I ask her anything private it's usually on the Radio Jas airwaves in about two and a half minutes. Her idea of being subtle and finding out things is that she goes out into the street and shouts, "Anyone know anything about this secret thing I am never going to mention?"

Hmmmmmmmm.

I hate to admit it, but I need the assistance of Dave the Laugh.

Donner and Blitzen!

If I could just accidentally bump into him on the way home then I wouldn't have to phone him.

Ten minutes later

Because if I phone him and Rachel is there I will feel like a facsimile of a sham. I mean he is officially (ish) going out with her.

Five minutes later

Even though he keeps snogging me.

Ten minutes later

Anyway, how can I trust anything he says – it was him, after all, who said he fancied my mum!

But then he is also my mate and official Hornmeister.

Also, he said that I have accidentally done the right thing and become Mystery Girl with Masimo.

Tuesday May 10th
on the way home

Jas and me were ambushed by four Foxwood lads. Two of them deliberately ran into my legs on their bikes, fell off, got back on backwards and started circling us really fast yelling, "You slags!!"

Why?

We were just looking at them and then they fell off their bikes again, this time down a ditch. While they were climbing out we set off walking. After a couple of minutes we noticed they were lurking along behind us, pretending not to follow us. Then Dave the Laugh and his mates appeared round the corner. Dave smiled. He has a great smile and he looked as if he was really glad to see me. He has grown his hair a bit since I last saw him and it looked very cool. Oh shutupshutup, voice of the Horn.

He said, "Hello, Sex Kitty and pal."

Then he saw the boy bloodhounds following us.

"Well, if it isn't Tosser Thompson and his band of trainee tossers. On your way kids."

Dave really is quite well built and he was just standing looking at them.

One of the trainee tossers said, "Come on, it's not worth it." and they shuffled off, shoving each other and making pretend farting noises.

Wow! It was a bit like *Gladiator*. But not set in Roman times, and Dave was wearing his school trousers and not a goatskin... More's the pity. Shutupshutup.

Dave put his arm around me.

"You entice them, you know, with your sparkling personality and magnificent nungas."

He is soooo annoying. And rude. I tried to have a strop, but he is notoriously difficult to do that with.

As we walked along Jas said, "S'later" and went off home. Dave's mates all said "S'later" until it was just me and Dave.

I don't know if it's because I'm surpressing my red bottom, but he does seem to be getting better-looking all the time. But no, no, he is not the only one and only. He is yesterday's news. Last week's snog. Anyway, I said to him, "Aren't you rushing to meet your GIRLFRIEND? Won't your GIRLFRIEND be upset if she sees you with me?"

And he started that, "Are you mad?" thing. I managed to stop myself joining in, otherwise it would have developed into tickly bears and then possibly number six. Who knows?

Who knows what goes on in my mind? I will be the last to know. Even when I am totally and without doubtosity in luuurve, absolutely wouldn't dream of being with anyone else, etc. etc., still the Cosmic Horn rears its ugly head. And there is something about Dave and his special lip-nibbling technique. In fact he is one of the best snoggers I have come across, and I haven't even snogged Masimo yet. What if Italian boys are useless in the snoggosity department? What if Masimo looks cool but is a nunga-pouncer like Mark Big Gob? Or kisses all wet and sucky like Whelk Boy?

Dave interrupted my brain, thank the Lord.

"So, how are you, chicklet?

I said, "Fab fanks. I'm going to Hamburger-a-gogo land for a clown-car convention."

Dave looked at me.

"YOU are going to a clown-car convention? Mad as a hen."

I got quite huffy.

"I am very interested in old cars, as you know, and—"

Dave said, "You would rather snog Spotty Norman than go to a clown-car convention."

Fair point well made.

I said, "Well, there is another reason..."

Dave raised one of his eyebrows. Which was quite amusing.

We were passing Luigi's and Dave said, "Come on, let's do coffee, man."

And we went in.

Oh, buggering bums buggering bum. Sitting down at one of the tables were Wet Lindsay and Astonishingly Dim Monica. *Sacré* bloody *bleu.*

Perhaps they were doing reverse stalking.

Wet Lindsay almost threw up when she saw me with Dave. But she covered it quickly and was all dillydollyish with him. He said "Hi" and she batted her eyelashes and flicked her hair. She must have read that book, *How to Make Any Twit Fall in Love with You.* If she tried toffee eyes on Dave, I would have to kill her.

Even though Dave was slightly behind me, she looked straight through me and said to him, "Oh, Dave, it was really groovy at Late and Live, wasn't it? Mas and me had a great time. Did you and Rachel?"

I hate her double with knobs on.

Dave was coolosity personified. "Yeah, it was cool."

And then he deliberately pulled a chair out for me at a table not too near the grotesque twins. As I sat down he said loudly enough for them to hear, “Now then, even though you treat me bad, what would you like, Ms Gorgeous?”

He is soooo nice. I really like the way he is… you know… so nice to me.

Five minutes later

As Lindsay and ADM went out, Lindsay gave Dave what she probably thinks (wrongly) is her attractive smile. She said, “Bye, Dave, maybe see you when Mas gets back.” Then she stick-insected out of the door, without leaving a slimy trail on the floor, surprisingly.

I said to Dave, “I hate her, I hate her. She called him ‘Mas’. How crap is that?”

Dave looked at me.

“You don’t like her, then?”

As we drank our coffee (me trying to avoid the foam moustache fandango) I wanted to ask Dave if he could find out where Masimo was. But I didn’t think I could just launch in, so I thought I would ask some limbering-up questions first.

"Dave, you know those boys... well, just before you got there, they ran into my legs on their bikes, then they rode off backwards. Then they called us slags."

Dave said, "Ah, the old running into your legs, riding off backwards and calling you slags thing. Ah hum. Well, it's obvious, isn't it?"

"What is?"

"They fancy you."

"Pardon me?"

"Uh-huh. Clear as daylight."

"But why don't they say 'I fancy you'?"

"Because you might reject them in front of their mates."

"So they think running into my legs on their bikes is better?"

"Yep."

"And calling us slags?"

"Yep."

"And they think that after they've done that, I will say, 'Gosh, yes, I would love to go out with you and be your slag. Once my legs heal up.'"

"Yep."

"But that is mad. Boys are mad."

Dave looked all wise and did his eyebrow thing again.

We slurped a bit more, then I said, "But, why? How does it work? You know at break at school, when you talk about personal stuff, well..."

Dave said, "Let me interrupt you there, Kittykat. Lads don't talk about 'stuff' at break. They play footie or that other well-known game, 'Do you know any good dentists?'"

I said, "What?"

"You know: 'Do you know any good dentists? Because you're going to need one in a minute when I have to deck you.'"

Blimey.

Dave went on. "Of course, lads have the same feelings, we just communicate in a different way. Sometimes it does get personal though."

I looked at him. This was better.

"Yeah, for instance, yesterday one of the fifth form hung his girlfriend's knickers out of the science-block window."

5:30 p.m.

Walked home after my session with the Hornmeister still in a bit of a daze. When we said s'later, he gave me a kiss

on the cheek and didn't attempt tickly bears or anything. Perhaps he is going straight. Who knows? But, on the plus side, he has said he'll find out all he can about Masimo for me. He is such a good boy-type pal. He didn't mention Rachel, which is a bit odd as she's supposed to be his girlfriend.

5:35 p.m.

Crossing the High Street I bumped into Tom. I like Tom, even though I think he's mad to go to Kiwi-a-gogo land. And go out with Jas. And go on camping fiascos. And go on about food produce. Other than that, I like him.

He seemed to have a touch of sadnosity about him when he said, "All right, Gee?"

"Yes, fanks all right as an... all-right thing. And you?"

He was unusually silent for him and eventually just said, "You'll look after Jas for me, won't you?"

I said, "You bet your goddamn bottom dollar, mister. I've got a gun and I'm not afraid to use it."

He just looked at me. Like I was talking complete rubbish or something.

6:00 p.m.

Home in my room, covered in unguents for tip-top beautosity.

I will say this: mashed banana is vair vair good for the luuurve complexion, which is not easy to say when you have a face full of mashed banana.

I wish I had a photo of Masimo. I hope I don't forget what he looks like. I'll just lie down in my (unusually empty) bed and have a mental snog with him.

6:25 p.m.

Oh, buggering God's bum. Angus and Gordy have come in and started playing the mouse-disguised-as-a-foot game. They attack my feet for a bit really viciously until I pull my feet up under my bum, then they lie down and go to sleep. But they are not really asleep, they are just doing pretend asleep. As soon as I snuggle down to snooze off into Masimo land, they leap on my foot underneath the blankets and wrestle it. Then they "go to sleep" again. They don't really think my foot is a mouse and that it will creep out when it sees they are asleep, do they?

6:40 p.m.

How did Ms Furry Tart, aka Naomi, get past the armed warden (Vati) and into my bed?

Blimey, I am quite literally lying in a cat basket.

6:45 p.m.

I wish she wouldn't do that lying-on-her-back-with-her-legs-spread-open thing on my bed.

6:50 p.m.

Gordy is sniffing her bottom. This is disgusting!! In front of his dad. This is kitty-porn – surely there must be some sort of helpline for this. A kittykat helpline.

It could be called Paws for Thought.

7:30 p.m.

Oh, Masimo, soon we will be together and you can tell me all about Pizza-a-gogo land. The music. The art. The snogging. I wonder if they have special techniques that go with their passionate Latin temperament? I hope he doesn't get carried away and nibble my lips off.

7:35 p.m.

No, I hope he does! Nibble away, Luuurve God!!

Wednesday May 11th

In my bedroom

7:07 p.m.

How many hours is it till we go to Hamburger-a-gogo? Jas will know. I'm not phoning her though.

Doorbell rang.

I went quietly to the top of the stairs and looked down. Crikey! Loon Alert! It was my grandad, and he was wearing shorts! Not his huge, all-encompassing grandad shorts that he wore during the Boer War, but cycling shorts. In Lycra. Good grief.

Please, please tell me he has not taken up cycling. Please.

I went back to my room quietly.

Maybe if I hide behind the door they will think I am out and JUST GO AWAY.

One minute later

Oh, yeah. Dream on.

Mutti called up, "Georgie, Grandad's here!"

I kept silent behind the door. Naomi, Angus and Gordy were all in my bed – again – doing their idiot-cat-staring-at-me thing. They had better not give my position away. It would be all right if it was just Gordon – then I might have a one in two chance of not being caught; because although one of his eyes is fixed on me, the other is glancing out the window.

The advance loon party came clanking up the stairs.

"Gingey, Gingey, it's meeeeeeee, Libbbbeeeeee... Where is you?"

I heard her huffing and puffing outside my door and doing her alarming laugh. "Hoggyhoggy. Here I come, reggy or nut."

Then she kicked my door and it burst open, very nearly flattening my nose.

"Owwwwww."

She put her mad little face around the door and smiled at me. When, and how, did she lose her front teeth? And why did she think it was attractive to push her tongue through the gap?

"Gingey, there you is! Cheeky monkey."

She threw all the cats off the bed and started tucking

scuba-diving Barbie and Jesus/Sandra up nice and comfy under the duvet. I tried to reason with her.

"Bibsy, that's not really Barbie and... er... Sandra's bed, is it? It's my bed, and there's no room for—"

She put her arms up to me and said, "Kiss."

Oh, blimey. She is cute, though. I picked her up to give her a little cuddle, and she put her hand on my nose and was sort of squeezing it and twirling it around. It was quite painful, actually. Dear God I hope it doesn't swell up.

Grandad was the next to arrive at the open-bedroom loon party.

He popped his head around the door and said, "Hello, love, I've just been to the doctor because I've got a steering wheel down my shorts. I said to him, 'Doctor, will you do something about this steering wheel down my shorts? It's driving me nuts!' Do you see? 'Steering wheel, driving me nuts!' Do you get it? Do you?"

How DISGUSTING!!

He's an octogenarian.

My ears feel like prostitutes.

8:00 p.m.

Thank the Lord, Grandad has gone. Unfortunately not before giving me a present from his "girlfriend" Maisie. I am sorry I ever suggested that Grandad was mad. His girlfriend has reached new and giddy heights of bonkerosity. Have you ever been given knitted toeless socks? In green, yellow and purple?

No, I thought not.

Grandad is going to house-sit the kittykats for the week we are away.

I said to Mutti, "Let's just burn the house to the ground before we go. Because that's what it will be like when we get back. Face it."

Mum said, "You are so rude, Georgia. You'll be old one day yourself."

I was going to go put my toeless socks on to give her the gist of what I was saying about the elderly insane, but then I realised I was on a charm mission. Also, Jas's parents were coming round in half an hour. So I said, "Shall I make some snacks for when Jas's M and D come round?"

She looked at me as if I had turned into a talking egg.

Even Gordy stopped eating Mum's mules and looked at me with one eye.

9:30 p.m.

Phew. Jas and I did secret thumbsie-upsies as she and her mutti and vati left. Yessssss! And thrice yesss! We are off to Hamburger-a-gogo land!!

Jas has got one hundred squids for spendies.

How far can Memphis be from where Masimo is? Wherever that is.

11:00 p.m.

All's well that ends well. Libby is in her own bed with Barbie and Our Lord Sandra, and the big cats have been thrown outside to lay waste to the vole population. Gordy is in his basket in the kitchen. So I can get some well-earned beauty sleep. My nose doesn't seem any more swollen than normal.

11:15 p.m.

Dad says that Elvis Presley lived in Memphis and he was a musician (not that you would know that from the crap songs

that Dad sings). Anyway, he was a musician and Masimo is a musician, ergo Memphis must be somewhere that musicians hang out.

Midnight

Pray God that Dad doesn't take his Elvis Presley quiff with him. Sometimes for a "joke" he sticks the quiff on and starts shaking his hips about. It's disgusting – and also probably very dangerous hipwise for a man of his years.

He and his lardy mates, the "lads" think it's hilarious.

It isn't.

12:05 a.m.

Anyway, what do I care, I am on Cloud Nine in Luuurve Heaven.

We go on 22nd May, which is eleven days away. I am sooooo excited.

12:10 a.m.

Hawkeye called me a ninny and said that I "had the attention span of a pea" but what she doesn't know is that I have powers of discipline that would surprise a lot of people who accuse me of laziosity. When I put my mind to it I can do stuff. For instance, even though I'm tired now and it's midnight, it is imperative that I get up and go to the bathroom and cleanse and tone my... zzzzzz zzzzzzzzzzzzz.

Thursday May 12th
Ten days to Hamburger-a-gogo land
on the way to school

"Jas, I am so vair vair full to the brim with excitementosity. Aren't you?"

"Hmmm."

"Yes, so am I. Let's sing 'New York, New York' to get us in the mood."

"No."

"That's the spirit. You see, that is why coming to Hamburger-a-gogo is sooo good for you – it will broaden what there is of your mind."

I started to sing, "I want to be a part of it, New York, New YORK!!!!!"

I stopped because of intense pensioner-glaring when we passed the post office.

Jas was slouching along by my side like a trusty… badger.

"Jas, why do they call it that? New York, New York? We don't say London, London, do we?"

"Hmmmm."

"Perhaps it's because Hamburgese people are a bit on the slow side and don't get it immediately, so they have to say it twice."

9:30 p.m.

Vati made us watch a really old film tonight with John Wayne in it.

Midnight

I was right to be worried about them being a bit on the slow side. Crikey, John Waaaaaaayne speaks slowly. If all Americans speak so slowly, I'll be there all day queueing up behind people as they ask for a cup of "caaaaaawwwwwfffeeeee". (And I won't even know why I am in the queue, as I don't even like caawwfffee.)

Also, if Dad doesn't stop singing Elvis songs I may go insane.

Friday May 13th

Nine days to Hamburger-a-gogo land

Dawn

Dad burst into my room in his pyjamas and Elvis quiff, singing "Heartbreak Hotel".

Still, now that I'm up, I'll make a list of stuff to take to Hamburger-a-gogo.

7:25 a.m.

This is my packing list:

1. Make-up essentials
2. Really gorgey clothes

I've gathered my make-up essentials together and they fill a suitcase.

I wonder if I can get Jazzy to put some of my make-up in her bag. Mind you, knowing her, she's already filled her bag with her ginormous knickers – or big "panties", as we must learn to call them now.

Although "big panties" reminds me of incontinent knickers.

Still, let the Americans have it their way. I love them all. And I mean that most sincerely. Even though I have never met them.

Chaos headquarters

8:00 a.m.

Mutti was dragging Gordy out of Libby's rucksack, and Libby was hitting Mum on the head with her spoon.

"Bad Mummy, bad."

Libby had hidden Gordy in her rucky because she wanted to take him to nursery school with her. But even Mum noticed the rucksack walking around by itself.

Then the phone rang.

Mutti yelled at me, "Get that, Georgia, it's bound to be one of your daft friends."

Oh, that is nice, isn't it? It's much more likely to be one of her daft friends.

I answered it and said, "Yes, hello. Reception speaking, Hotel Insane."

It was Dave the Laugh. Oh my giddy God, and I hadn't even got any lip gloss on.

He said, "Hi, Sex Kitty, Hornmeister here. I'm in a hurry, but thought you would like to know that the extremely flash Masimo, who I personally feel might be on the gay side handbagwise—"

"Dave..."

"OK, OK. All I can find out is that he is staying in Manhattan and his surname is Scarlotti."

I said, "Oh, thank you thank you, Dave."

"It's cool. I'm sure we can think of some way you can repay me – it may involve heavy snogging. Bye."

And he put the phone down.

Yipppppeeeee!!!

Manhattan, here I come!

8:30 a.m.

Ran to meet Jas.

She was all flustered like a fringey loon.

I said, "Howdy."

"Come on, Georgia, we'll be late."

As we galloped along, I said, "I am going to speak American all day today."

Jas went, pant pant, "They speak English."

I said, "Don't be mad," pant pant.

We arrived on time, but only just. Wet Lindsay was on sadist duty. She looked at us as we panted by her like we were a couple of turds in uniform.

"Can't you two grow up and be on time for once?"

I gave her a big smile while gazing at her ear, and said, "Howdy. Now you all have a nice day. You hear?"

She stomped off to terrorise some first formers, but she was fingering her lugholes. Hahahahahaha. And also *hasta la vista*, baby.

Maths

God, maths is boring. And complete bollocks.

When I marry Masimo, I will have manservants to do my adding up for me.

And my quadratic equations, which I will never use.

Lunchtime
Operation Track Down the Luuurve God

Made Jas come to the library with me.

Miss Wilson almost fell off her stool when we came in.

I calmed her by saying, "Alrighty? Now you all have a nice day."

We lugged the big atlas to a table, and I leafed through the maps until I got to America and found New York, New York.

I said to Jas, "Now, where is Memphis, Memphis?"

Jas found it and said, "It looks a bit far down."

For once she is not wrong. On the plus side, Manhattan is only about an eighth of an inch long.

But it is about two feet from Memphis.

Still, there must be buses. Surely?

4:30 p.m.

On the way home I was singing "Home, home on the range, where the deer and the antelope play" to Jazzy. She loves a bit of a singsong.

I said that. I said, "You love a bit of a singsong, don't you, Jazzy?"

"No."

"See, I knew you did. You do a little dance while I sing the chorus. You could do a dance based on a deer. Go on, do the little deer dance, make your feet like—"

And that is when she kicked me. She can be very violent.

She said, "I haven't told him yet."

"What? Who?"

"Hunk— er, I mean Tom, about Hamburger-a-gogo land."

I looked at her in amazednosity. Radio Jas, the voice of the nation, had not told Hunky something?

She said, "I can be just as independent and adventurous as him."

I didn't laugh, even though I have seen the amount of knickers that Jas thinks she will need for seven days.

I MUST sort out my clothes this weekend.

Le Weekend

11:00 a.m.

Now then, I am going to take a "capsule" wardrobe. It's what Naomi Campbell and all the top models do. They just take the absolute essentials with them when they travel.

12:00 p.m.

I'm exhausted, but I have managed to whittle my capsule wardrobe down to six cases.

12:01 p.m.

And a rucksack.

12:03 p.m.

Apart from my shoes, which I can't get in, but Mum will probably put them in her case.

12:30 p.m.

Nobody has yet told Libby that Angus and Gordy are not coming with us on our holidays.

12:35 p.m.

When someone does tell her, I'll tell you one thing for free – it will not be me. I need all my limbs for my Luuurve Quest.

12:40 p.m.

Libby has made Gordy a paper bikini for his holidays, which might come in handy if he were coming on holiday.

And cats wore bikinis.

And if he hadn't immediately destroyed it and then buried it in the rubber plant.

Sunday May 15th

Seven days to Hamburger-a-gogo land

Midday

I hate my dad. He is so unreasonable. It's like dealing with a spoiled child.

I asked Mum if she would be so kind as to slip my shoes in her case, and all hell broke loose.

Dad said, "Why don't you put them in your case?"

And I said, "Because, Father, all of my cases are full."

Vati came stropping into my bedroom, saw my cases, and said, "Don't be ridiculous! You can take one case. That is it."

I said, "Excuse me if I'm right, Dad, but do you want me to look like a poor person in front of the Hamburgese? I am representing the English nation abroad."

But you might as well be talking to yourself.

2:00 p.m.

I've repacked, but there are still three cases of essentials. *Sacré* bloody *bleu.*

Jas phoned to tell me that she told Hunky about her trip and he has had the boy version of a nervy spaz. He phoned her eighteen times in two hours.

"He was so upset."

"Yes, you said."

"Really really upset. He phoned me eighteen times in two hours."

"Er... I know."

"Eighteen times."

"Wow... How many times did you say he phoned?"

I said it ironically, but Jas didn't get it. She just went on and on. "Eighteen times, and then he came round this morning really early and posted a love-poem-song-type thing through my door."

Oh no. Not a love poem.

"Do you want to hear it?"

"No."

"It's called, 'You are the only fish in my sea'.

Good Lord. Tom's whole family is obsessed with livestock.

To cheer her up and to get me out of my packing nightmare scenario I called a gang meeting.

The park, sitting on the swings
4:30 p.m.

Jas has read her poem to everyone, so I hope she's got it out of her system now. It is truly crap. That is a fact. But I didn't say so; I wanted Jas to perk up for our big adventure. I was soooo excited, and I was standing up swinging on a swing, singing "I want to be in America! Everything's free in America!!!"

Then Ellen said, "Georgia, have you actually snogged Masimo yet?"

I laughed in a sultry way. "Have I snogged Masimo? Have I—"

Jas said, "No, she hasn't. Well, not unless you count two seconds, which I don't, and anyway it's not on the snogging scale, so it's not... on the... snogging scale."

Oh, thanks, bestest pally NOT. I wish I had told her what I thought about Fish Boy's poem now.

Jools said, "Do you think Wet Lindsay has snogged him? You know, when they went to Late and Live. She must have, you know... wanted to."

Ohhhnooo. Get out of my head.

I said, "Who in their right mind would snog Wet Lindsay?"

Jools said, "Well, actually, Robbie must have snogged her because they went out together and—"

I started humming in my head so I didn't have to listen to this; it was making me feel quite sick.

Jas said, "Perhaps some kinds of boys like tiny foreheads. Tom said that he knows a boy who's mad for girls who wear really thick glasses."

Good grief. Still, at least, there was a chance for Nauseating P. Green.

Ellen was obviously in her own dream world. "That mate of Tom's – Speedy – asked me out when I was down the square, but... oh... I don't know, it's just there is something. I mean, he's nice but I still... you know... have feelings for... well, you know... Do you think?"

I said, "Can I ask you something, Ellen? What are you raving on about?"

I wished I hadn't asked.

"I mean Dave the Laugh. Is he going out with Rachel still... or ... er... what?"

Jas said, "He wasn't with her when we saw him the other day, was he, Gee? Did he mention her when you went for a coffee?"

Oh shutupshutup about Dave the sodding Laugh.

Ellen was just about to start the "I didn't know that you saw Dave the Laugh, what did you talk about, did he mention me, how come you went for a coffee with him?" scenario when Mabs saved my bacon (ish).

She said, "How do you know that Masimo wants to see you?"

"Well, he asked me for my telephone number and I couldn't give it to him because my head was about to drop

off from redness. So he said, "OK, Miss Hard to Get, I will see you later, when I get back from America."

Ellen was looking at me. "So he said 'See you later' then?"

I said, "No, not just 'see you later' like in 's'later' but more—"

But Ellen was locked into her own ramblosity. "Dave the Laugh said 'see you later' to me and I did the flicky hair and everything and dancing by myself and so on... and then he went off with Rachel."

The gang started nodding wisely (not).

I said, "Yes, but Masimo said 'see you later' after I had become Mystery Woman."

Rosie said, "Mystery Woman?"

"Yes, after I had accidentally treated him to my glaciosity."

Rosie had her face really close to mine.

"You are Mystery Woman?"

All the gang looked at me.

Jools said, "You are MYSTERY Woman?"

Then Mabs said, "YOU are Mystery Woman?"

What is this, a parrots' convention?

Rosie said, "Mystery Woman. You are Mystery Woman.

Not as you used to be – 'Oooooooh my boy entrancers have stuck together' Woman?"

Home

5:30 p.m.

Oh boo. Now I've got the screaming heebie-jeebies and doubtosity all rolled into one. Perhaps Masimo says "See you when I get back, Miss Hard to Get" to everyone.

5:45 p.m.

Just when you think things couldn't get any worse, they take a turn for the worserer.

Grandad has cancelled his cat duties because he's going on a bicycling tour to the Lake District. He says he has heard the call of the wild and is setting out tonight with his backpack.

I cannot believe the utter selfishosity of the elderly.

5:50 p.m.

Family "conference" (aka Dad shouting a lot).

We can't think of anyone stupid... er... kind enough to look after Angus and Gordy.

6:15 p.m.

Mum has tried all her so-called aerobics friends and none of them will come over.

I said to her, "Did you tell them about the mice cream incident?"

Of course she has, so she has only herself to blame.

6:30 p.m.

Sadly I have also shown off about Angus and Gordy's "adventures" and alluring little habits *vis à vis* woodland animals, pooing, etc. So none of my friends will have anything to do with them. Rosie said that Sven said he'd look after Angus and Gordy in a cave he has found. But the whole idea of that is far, far too weird.

Vati said, "What about a cattery, then?"

That's when Angus came in with a spade. We all just looked at one another.

Vati said, "Well, there is only one thing for it. I'm going to have to ask for a bit of neighbourly support."

7:15 p.m.

Dad went to Mr Next Door first. As he went through the

door he said, "Alfred and I have always had a bit of an understanding, although I know we've had our differences *vis à vis* the damage Angus has done to his rhododendrons—"

I said, "And when he rounded the Prat Poodles up and trapped them in the greenhouse."

"Yes, well..."

"And then rode them round like little horsies."

"Yes, well..."

"And the dog psychiatrist having to come in."

Dad took his coat off.

7:25 p.m.

Dad said, "I'll just pop across the road to Colin and, you know, see if maybe he could just keep an eye on feeding them."

7:28 p.m.

Dad's back.

He said, "He laughed."

Dad has slammed off to the pub to talk to Uncle Eddie and see if he knows any fools who might help us out.

7:33 p.m.

Doorbell rang. I looked down the stairs from the safety of my bedroom.

Mutti answered. Uh-oh. It was one of our beloved boys in blue. And as policemen go, he didn't look pleased. Now what?

I scampered down the stairs to give my mutti moral support. Although, as it happens, basooma support would have been more appropriate. Hasn't she got one single piece of clothing that doesn't reveal far too much flesh?

I put an interested look on my face. It's the one I use when Hawkeye asks me where my homework is. It usually results in double detention, but you can't have everything. The constable looked at me, and it wasn't his guardian-of-the-community-and-servant-of-the-people look.

He said to Mum, "Good evening, madam, can you tell me if you know this person?" And he held up Grandad's O.A.P. card, the one with the photo of him with the earring in.

Don't ask.

Mum said, "Yes, it's my father... Oh My God, is he all right?"

The officer said, "Yes, he is, madam, but he is a danger to himself and others."

I said, "You can say that again, officer. I don't need a helmet and truncheon to figure that out."

Mum said, "Shut up, Georgia."

Which I think is probably abusive behaviour, but I let it go.

It turns out that, for once, the officer was the bearer of glad tidings. Grandad had set out on his six-hundred-mile bike ride to the Lake District and fell off at the end of his street. But not before he knocked the policeman off his new community bike.

"I'd only had it for a week, madam."

I tried to look concerned.

The policeman opened his notebook. "The gentleman we have now positively identified as your father was wearing Lycra shorts and kept falling off his bike. I asked him to walk a straight line."

Mutti said, "Oh my goodness, had he been drinking?"

The officer said, "I don't know, madam, but he refused to walk the line on account of an old war wound. Then he said..." The officer looked down at his notes again. "...'Do

you want to come back to my place, constable, and have one for the road?'"

You have to give Grandad full marks on the lunacy scale.

8:00 p.m.

The policeman radioed into his station and Grandad was released from chokey after being charged with careless biking and not having a bell. Apparently the budgie bell he had Sellotaped on to the handlebar doesn't count.

He now has a criminal record.

Mum was all flustered and kept apologising to the policeman as he went off. "I am so sorry, officer. I hope you can mend your bike and you haven't been hurt at all."

The policeman said, "No, well, I'm quite tough, madam."

"Yes, well you do seem very fit. I do a bit of aerobics myself; it's awfully good for keeping in shape."

The policeman winked at her (honestly!) and he said, "Yes, I can see that. Anyway, madam, I'd better be on my way."

And then he said that classic thing that you think you'd only see on TV. He said, "Mind how you go, it's a jungle out there."

Mum practically wet herself with laughing. She is so so

sad and embarrassing. After the policeman had gone I just looked at her, and she said, "What? What?"

I said, "You know what. You were practically slavering over him."

"Well, he was a nice young man – of course, far too young for me."

Unbelievable!!!

In my bedroom

How very embarrassing my family is.

Midnight

Still, on the plus side, Grandad's cycling days are over and he can now be on house-burning-down duties for when we go to Hamburger-a-gogo land. Hurrah! And also zippety doo dah!!

Tuesday May 17th

Five days to Hamburger-a-gogo land

Evening

Oh, I just can't stand this hanging around waiting to go on the Luuurve Plane.

Come on come on!!!

I've been trying out arrival outfits. Boots or shoes? It's hard to know what to do weatherwise. Also, I may have to go from day wear to evening wear, depending on the time-zone business.

I am practising speaking Hamburgese, even in my own head. The key seems to be to add stuff, so instead of weather you say weatherwise. Timewise. Daywise. Luuurvewise, etc.

But on a more seriouswise note, this time business is v.v. aggravating fashionwise.

I said to Jas on the phone (she is opting for sensible sports casual for travelling)... I said to her (Mistress of the Time Lords), "Are we flying backwards in time, or what?"

"Yeah, they are six hours behind us."

"Why are they? Why can't they just keep up with us? Didn't we invent time?"

"What?"

"You know, Greenwich Mean Time – didn't we invent it? So why can't they just be the same as us?"

"Because they would be getting up in the middle of the night."

"So?"

But you can't reason with Jas.

Wednesday May 18th

Four days to Hamburger-a-gogo land

Evening

Grandad has come round for instructions about looking after the house and cats.

I am still in a ditherspaz about what to wear. I've been through all of my clothes about a million times.

Still, on the plus side, I have definitely decided what to wear nailwise. I've chosen Pouting Pink.

I am absolutely full of exhaustiosity.

8:15 p.m.

Dragged myself downstairs for a reviving snack.

In the front room

Grandad started fiddling about in his pockets.

"I've got something for you."

Oh, joy unbounded. A boiled sweet.

I love him and everything, but why does he have to

be so, you know... so... grandadish?

The TV was on, with my extremely unfit vati lolling around in front of it. As I sat down to try and get my tights away from Gordy, Vati said, "Now then, Georgia, why don't you tell me how much spending money you expect for the holiday. Then we'll have a good laugh and go from there."

Vair vair amusing. Sadly though, I have to humour him. I said, "Well, it's only for a week, isn't it? And we've got the hotel rooms and food and so on, so actually, all in all, I think a thousand quid would just about cover it if I don't buy anything extravagant."

Mum said, "Don't be silly, Georgia."

Grandad said, "Do you remember when you took Georgia to the doctor's surgery when she was a couple of weeks old?"

Mum ruffled my hair (very annoying) and looked all nostalgic. "I remember every single thing about your life, darling girl. You've been a pleasure and joy to me from the moment you were born."

Dad said, "Bloody hell, Connie! Calm down."

But Mum had gone off into Mumland, "Do you know

you had no hair when you were born – all baldy, like Uncle Eddie. So sweet."

Oh God.

Grandad was still rambling on like Rambling Sid Rumpo. "Yes, and there was that woman in the waiting room."

Mum went, "Oooh, yes, I'd forgotten her."

Grandad said, "And she was looking in all the prams and going 'oooh what a lovely baby' and then she looked in at Georgia and said 'Christ look at the conk on this baldy one! Come and look!'"

What?

All the 'grown-ups' were laughing.

Mum said, "Well that's why I always used to stroke your nose every time I fed you, so that I could sort of squeeze it into shape a bit."

I left the room and went into the hall. I looked in the mirror. My nose had been fondled from birth and it was still like it was?

Phoned Jas, "Jas, do you think I have grown into my nose?"

Jas went, "Hahahahahha... er... yes."

"But do you think it's still quite big?"

Jas was chewing something. "Well, let's put it this way... it's a generous nose."

10:00 p.m.

Generous.

2:00 a.m.

Woke up from a dream where a customs official at the airport charged me excess baggage for my nose.

Thursday May 19th

Three days to Hamburger-a-gogo land

In bed

11:00 p.m.

I am sleeping on my back and I've made a sort of splint for my nose out of elastoplasts and matchsticks, so at least it can't grow any more.

Friday May 20th

Two days to Hamburger-a-gogo land

8:00 a.m.

Tore off the elastoplasts. Ow bugger and ow and buggery

ow! I hope Masimo appreciates what a lot of trouble I'm going to beautywise, although unless my brain drops out, I will not be telling him that I sleep in a nose splint.

Went down to the kitchen for brekky. Yip yip and three times yip, in fact yipyipyip!! Last day at Stalag 14 and then I set off on the *grand* adventure *de* LUUURVE.

Bathroom
8:10 a.m.

I've been keeping up a daily plucking plan to keep the orang-utan gene at bay. However, I may get Jas to do an impartial inspection of the backs of my legs, as it's useless being smoothy smooth on the front if you're chimpish at the back.

Lalala. Massage in exfoliating products (Mum's) and make small circles to slough off naughty old cells and leave skin like baby's botty (without the poo).

The flight is eight hours, so I should have just about enough time to apply my make-up, do my nails and then be ready to bump into Masimo in a casual and natural way.

Lunchtime

As it is raining quite hard, for once we're allowed to loll around in the canteen. Sadly that means we have spectacular sad sacks as company. The rest of the Ace Gang went to the loo to redo their hair – they are so vain, they're like a bunch of Chelsea footballers. I bagsied a table by putting all my things on five chairs and then pretended to be learning my part as Macduff in *MacUseless* just in case Nauseating P. Green saw me by myself and came to tell me about her hamsters. Or her new enormous glasses. Her being cast as Lady Macduff is the worst thing that has happened. I think she thinks we are actually man and wife.

I was so busy pretending to read that I didn't notice the whiff of tiny foreheadedness until it was too late. I looked up to see Wet Lindsay sitting down with her skungy mates at the table next to me.

She said, "Georgia, normal people only need one chair to sit on. Clear those bags up."

I looked at her, and I was going to say something like, "Normal people have a bit of skull between their eyebrows and their fringe," but she was quite likely to give me detention, even on the last day of term. So I let a small smile play around my lips and imagined her in her thong crashing into the sanitary towel dispenser, like she did last term. Happy memories.

As I didn't respond, she went back to talking absolute bollocks to her sad mates. I don't know what was keeping the Ace Gang, unless Ellen had had another dither attack and fallen down in the lavatory. Or maybe Jas was chatting about her fringe.

I was unwrapping my lunchtime Jammy Dodger when I nearly fell off my chair. I could hear Lindsay whining on, whiney whine, and then she said, "Mas is having a great time in the States, he's been gigging with a group in New York an—"

What? What??

I was interrupted by the gang arriving. They were all singing "My gosh I'm fit, but don't I know it!" so loudly that I couldn't hear anything else Wet Lindsay said.

on the way home

4:30 p.m.

"Jas, HOW could he be in touch with her? Did he phone her? Why? Why?"

"Well, I don't know, but he's not... he's not, like, your boyfriend, is he? And..."

"Jas, I hope you are not going to try and be reasonable, because then I really will have to kill you."

Bedroom

Oh, no. I am once more on the rack of love.

I must speak to the Hornmeister.

Even if I show no pridenosity, I must know what he thinks.

I can't phone him now, though, in front of Mum. Why can't I have a mobile phone?

Oh Goddy God God.

5:00 p.m.

Libby has got her "boyfwen" Josh with her. Even my little sister has got a boyfriend. She and Joshy went off into her room and I could hear them murmuring and singing together.

Oh, I am so fed up.

5:15 p.m.

Mum is still pratting about; for once when I wish she was out she is in. Typico. She said, "Why are you mooning around? What are you up to?"

Honestly.

5:20 p.m.

I can't bear this tensionosity.

Libby came into my room to sing me a new song that she learned at nursery. I noticed that Josh had quite a lot of lipstick on. She cleared her throat and then began singing in her little but very piercing voice. The tune is the same one as for "Sex Bum". Quite quite delightful.

She sang, "Bum oley, bum oley, arsey arsey bum bum. Poo poo and bummy bum bum arse!!"

Yes, that is what my little sister is learning at her nursery school.

Songs about bottoms.

5:30 p.m.

I must speak to Dave.

Libby's back in for another round of "Sex Bum".

Oh good, Josh knows the words, too.

6:00 p.m.

Mum had to quickly scrub Josh so that his mummy will let him play with Libby again. I don't think Josh's mum suspected anything when she collected him. But she hasn't heard his lovely song yet.

7:00 p.m.

I HAVE to speak to Dave.

Crept downstairs, Mutti and Vati and Uncle Eddie are in the front room discussing the clown-car convention. When I listened at the door, I could hear them raving on.

Vati was saying, "Apparently there's a Robin Reliant from the sixties that has its original wheel hubs."

And Uncle Eddie said, "I've packed my special comedy underpants."

Good grief.

I girded up my loins and dialled Dave's number. What if he was with Rachel? That would be the *coup de* poo.

Oh, it was ringing. Maybe... I should just... Then he answered the phone.

"Dave?"

"*Bonsoir*, it is he."

"I must ask you something."

"Is that you, Georgia? I'm afraid I never do phone sex; I think it cheapens things."

"Dave, please..."

Later

Feel a bit better. Dave can be really nice in an annoying way. He's off to a club night tonight and Dom from the Stiff Dylans will be there, so he's going to find out what he can about Masimo and Wet Lindsay.

In my bedroom of pain
9:30 p.m.

Why can't my life be simple?

And happy.

Tell me that, Jesus.

I have rescued Jesus from Libby and replaced him on my dressing table. I've taken off the frock that Libby put on, but I can't get the rouge off. He looks like he has a bit of a holiday tan.

When was the last time I had fun?

Never, that's when.

I don't think I will ever laugh again.

In bed looking at the moon

11:00 p.m.

I wonder if Masimo is looking at the same moon as I am. He's probably too busy thinking about Wet Lindsay to look at the moon.

I read one of the many many books that Mum buys to try and make herself a better person – I think it was called "I'm OK, you're OK, but what if we only think we're OK but we're not really OK." – anyway, whatever it was called, it said in the book that men like blonde girls with sort of baby faces because they think they are babies and want to look after them.

Have I got a baby face?

Looking in the mirror.

Even when I was officially a baby and I did have a baby face, you wouldn't have known because my nose covered most of it.

I pushed the tip of it back with my finger.

Would boys like me better if I looked like a small pig with a bob?

Who knows?

Who cares?

I'm not even going to bother putting my nose splint on.

11:20 p.m.

The fact is that Wet Lindsay has heard from Masimo and I haven't.

And not one single person on the planet cares. That is the point, really – who does care? If I just disappeared from the planet, who would really care?

11:25 p.m.

I bet if I committed suicide no one would notice for days. And then, when I did get found, they'd all be going, "Why did she do such a stupid thing? She was always so happy and cheerful and brave. She never complained."

They would never suspect the deep sadnosity that had tainted my life.

11:30 p.m.

They might if I wrote a note spelling it out even for the very very dim.

I got a piece of paper and started a suicide note.

Dear Mum and Dad,

I can't go on any longer. Some people just cannot see beyond the superficial.

Maybe noses shouldn't count, but they do. It is tragic that you cannot pick your own nose. (Hang on a minute, that sounds a bit wrong, I'll cross that out.) People may say I am a crazy mixed-up confused teenager. Maybe they are right. Maybe they are wrong.

Who are they, anyway?

I realise I am an embarrassment to you all. Grandad in particular has said this many times. But the fact is I am too sensitive for this life.

Goodbye. I love you all.

Georgia

p.s. Don't blame yourself, Dad. You have learned to live with your nose. I can't.

I could imagine them all at my funeral. People crying,

looking at the photos I had enclosed in the suicide-note envelope. In particular, that really nice one that Jas took of me in my groovy leather skirt and boots. My mum gazing at the photo and crying and saying, "But she was BEAUTIFUL. So beautiful. Why didn't she realise it?" A woman coming up and saying, "I am from a modelling agency. Why, oh why did no one tell me about this girl? She is the most photogenic girl I have come across in all my long years of talent hunting." Them gazing at me in my coffin and crying... as they tried to force the coffin lid down over my nose!

Merde.

Saturday May 21st

One day to Hamburger-a-gogo land

9:30 a.m.

Re-reading my suicide note. I could kill myself now so as not to waste the note.

I can't really be bothered, though. I'd have to get out of bed.

What is the point of going to Hamburger-a-gogo land, or even *thinking* about Masimo, if he isn't interested in me and likes Old Thongy?

Anyway, what could I commit suicide with? There aren't any pills lying around the place because Mum and Dad are just too cheerful to bother getting any. And I'm not trying anything else, because it might hurt.

10:30 a.m.

Anyway, there's so much noise coming from the bathroom, how I am supposed to concentrate on being depressed?

Vati is giving Angus a bath in preparation for our holidays. I can hear him yelling, "Right, that's it, it's no use struggling. Angus, my friend, you are going in that bath for a good scrub. You smell like a dustbin."

The phone rang, but no one answered it, of course, so I dragged myself downstairs.

It was Dave. Ohmygiddygod.

He said, "OK, this is the deal."

At which point there was an enormous splash from the bathroom and my vati started shouting and swearing like the lunatic he is. "Buggering bastard bollocking bloody... SHIIIITE!!!"

Dave said, "What in the name of arse is going on?"

I was just about to apologise for my father, when

he appeared at the bathroom door absolutely soaking. He had obviously fallen in the bath.

He looked at me and said, "Don't say a bloody word."

It was vair and thrice times vair *amusant.* I didn't laugh, though, because a) I might be heartbroken, and b) if I'm not, I might still want to go to Hamburger-a-gogo.

I whispered to Dave, "My vati has just been bathing Angus with a firm hand, but sadly he has fallen in the bath himself."

Dave said, "I love your house. Anyway, this is the deal: Masimo, the well-known Italian homosexualist—"

"Dave..."

"Anyway, he sent a postcard to Dom and a couple to the other lads in the Stiff Dylans, and they all seem to have the same theme – you know, like, 'I am a flash Italian git on my holidays' type scenarios. Dom told Lindsay about the gigging in New York and so on. In my Hornmeister opinion, you are in exactly the same position as you were yesterday."

Thank you, thank you, God.

I said to Dave, "Oh, fanks, Dave. You are indeedy a pal of the first water."

"And sexy beyond words."

"And... sexy beyond words."

11:15 a.m.

Phoned Jas.

"Jas, he didn't get in touch with Thongy, he just sent a postcard to Dom, and Wet Lindsay pretended that he had got in touch with her! Hahahahaha. How pathetico she is. *Hasta la vista*, baby!!"

I slammed down the phone so that Jas couldn't spoil my mood by rambling on about Hunky.

Oh, I luuurve life!

And the Italian Stallion.

And I quite like Dave the Laugh.

In a laughy way.

If I have time in between snogging, I may send him a postcard.

11:20 a.m.

He actually asked for an American cheerleader or a ranch, but he was just being silly.

12:10 p.m.

Ditherspaz attack on the clothes front.

I said to Mum as she came in to hand me some clean "panties", "I have not got one single thing to wear."

She didn't even bother to reply, she just looked meaningfully at my two cases, one of which I was sitting on to try and make it shut.

12:20 p.m.

Maybe one set of boy entrancers will be enough to last me the week? That would save a bit of space.

12:24 p.m.

Nope, I still can't shut the lid of one of my suitcases.

Vati has relented and let me take two cases, but he will have a nervy b if I ask for another one.

Maybe I can make do with just eight pairs of shoes.

Oh, the tension, the tension.

12:30 p.m.

There was a horrible scratching and banging against my bedroom door. Angus was doing his paws-under-the-door thing. Oh God.

I said, "Go away, Angus, this is a cat-free zone."

I'm not having him in here dropping his bat ears and so on on my clean things.

12:45 p.m.

He will not go away. If I didn't know better, I would say that he sensed we're going away. This is driving me insane. Now Gordy is putting his paws under the door as well.

I got up and opened the door. Gordy was on his back wriggling around with his pretend mouse pal, but Angus was just sitting there looking at me with his tongue lolling out. And foam coming out of his mouth.

Honestly.

The foam was frothing all over his face and dripping on to the carpet.

My God, he's got rabies!

1:00 p.m.

It turns out that Angus has eaten his bath-time soap.

2:00 p.m.

Hurrah hurrah and total result! Grandvati has given me twenty squids for my holidays.

Vati said, "Oh well, that is a score less than I have to give you."

Is he mad?

I said to Mutti, "Mum, that's not fair, is it? I mean... it means that Grandvati hasn't really given me twenty squids. No, what it means is this: Grandvati HAS given me twenty squids out of his little tiny tiny pension-type money and Dad has STOLEN it from him. And another thing..."

2:15 p.m.

Relentless moaning strikes again!

Vati yelled at me, "Go on, then. Go and waste the money, just don't give a second thought to the hours it takes me to make the damn stuff."

I said, "Okey-dokey, I won't."

As I went out of the door to go and spendies my squids, I said, "S'later, Mum. I don't know whether to get another mood ring or a piercing."

I slammed the door before my father could explode.

6:30 p.m.

Two new lippies and a flavoured lip gloss. I wonder if Masimo likes strawberry flavour. I've got raspberry as well.

Maybe I should mix them for that fruit-cocktail-type snogging experience. Perhaps I should have got some custard flavour lip gloss, too. Shutup brain.

7:00 p.m.

Loon village round at my house.

Jas has come round to stay overnight. Her eyes are like little piggie eyes because of the bye-bye Hunky scenario. What a great laugh (NOT) she is going to be. I'm sure she'll perk up, though, when we're driving through Hamburger-a-gogo and she gets the smell of bucking broncos and beans in her nostrils.

Jas's dad actually SAID something when he dropped her off! He said, "Take care, my little love. Have a great time."

And then he said this really really touching thing to Jas that nearly made me weep. He said, "Here's a bit of extra cash; get something nice."

7:10 p.m.

It was Hug City when Mr and Mrs Jas left. Unfortunately it started Jas on an uncontrollable crying jag AGAIN. She is going to have to be more rufty tufty if she wants to survive this Vale of Tears we call life.

7:30 p.m.

Mutti has made us an unusually normal and nutritious meal, and Jas managed to stop sniffling enough to stuff down forty-five pounds of shepherd's pie.

My bedroom

8:30 p.m.

We are doing our last-minute emergency packing check. It's not made very easy by Gordy pouncing on my hand every time I move it. I will be damn glad when Gordy can run free and wild. He will be allowed out when we get back, and he can get rid of his pent-up kittykat aggression on the Prat Poodles and voles and so on.

As I predicted, Jas has got an insane amount of "panties" with her. I said, "Are you expecting a worldwide famine on the botty-hugger front?"

But she was rambling on about Hunky again. "What if he meets someone else in Kiwi-a-gogo land? A Maori or something?"

Before I could join in she went raving on. "He's given me a love token. Do you want to see it?"

"Jas, if it's some sort of secret tattoo thing like last time, I

don't really want to see—"

I might just as well have been speaking to myself.

"It's a sort of secret tattoo thing. Like last time. Look."

Is it normal to have a secret tattoo of two voles kissing? No, is the answer you are looking for. Jas has one though.

On her bottom.

Suddenly the enormous botty huggers make all kinds of sense to me.

"Tom made the tracing in technical drawing and then he inked it in. He's got a similar one on his—"

"Jas, Jas... please leave it out. I am trying to make sure I haven't forgotten anything essential – like something to kill you with."

But secretly I am vair vair happy because I am almost on the LUUURVE Trail and nothing Jas does can upset me.

I said, "Stop thinking about Hunky now. We must have a plan. As soon as we land we'll get a bus timetable to see what bus we must catch for Manhattan."

"You have to catch a Greyhound."

"Jas, I am not riding a dog all the way to New York."

"It's an American bus-type thingy, and anyway, I am not going to Manhattan."

"Yes you are, Jazzy Spazzy."

"No I'm not."

"Yes you are."

"No I'm not."

"Jas, if you go on being so vair vair silly, I will have to confiscate some of your botty huggers."

She got the megahump then and wouldn't even cheer up when I made an amusing hat out of her pink-spotted panties.

8:45 p.m.

There was a mad ringing at the door.

It was Grandvati and his "girlfriend" Maisie. I said hello to the elderly loons, and when they went off into the front room to talk to Dad about their cat duties, I followed Mum into her bedroom.

She said, "I'm really looking forward to this trip, aren't you? I wonder if we will bump into George Clooney. I hope we do! He's so... woof woof."

I said, "Mum, excuse me if I'm right, but did you just bark like a dog?"

She laughed. "Well, you know, he's gorgeous isn't he?

And he might really like English women."

"Mum, do you really think it's likely that George Clooney is going to be at a clown-car convention?"

Mum said, "Well, he's got lots of hobbies; he's got a pet pig."

I despair for her sanity.

To bring her back down to real life I asked her something that had been bothering me a lot. "I hope that you'll tell Grandad that Maisie can't stay overnight. We don't want our reputation tarnished."

Mum laughed, but not in an amused way.

I said, "Well, at least hide the matches."

She ignored me as she zipped up her suitcase, singing the theme to *ER*. She clearly is dreaming about driving around with George in a clown car. Possibly with his pet pig as chauffeur. Like a porky Parker.

9:00 p.m.

Next to arrive was Uncle Eddie. Joy unbounded. Uncle Eddie has a Hawaiian shirt like Dad's. Hurrah! I'm going on holiday with two porky surfers.

Uncle Eddie gave Dad a high five and said, "Hello hello hello, big up for the lads."

Oh Lordy Lordy.

I went to the loo, and when I came back into the room, Dad, Uncle Eddie and Grandad were wearing blond Afro wigs.

Why?

It all became hideously clear when Dad said, "Let the 'Hello America' Abba tribute begin!"

Oh nooo.

9:15 p.m.

Jas and me are holed up in my room while the grown-ups are singing "Waterloo". I said to her, "This is a good opportunity for you to nip downstairs and start ringing people in New York, New York called Scarlotti."

She didn't even bother to stop straightening her fringe.

9:28 p.m.

Another ring of the doorbell.

Sound out the bells of England, it was the Ace Gang. Yesssss!!! Even Jas forgot she was having a grumpathon.

Jools, Rosie, Mabs and Ellen all gave the time-honoured Klingon salute.

Rosie said, "We're not staying because we're going to the Catfish for a bop, but we have come with a message of wisdomosity."

Ooooohhh, how sweet.

They said all together, "Have a good time ALL of the time."

And then Rosie said, "*Bon voyage* and also Bon Jovi. See you in the next life; don't be late."

One farewell burst of disco inferno dancing and they were gone.

In the hall

9:30 p.m.

Jas went back to her fringe-straightening duties in my bedroom, but as the olds were singing along to "Dancing Queen" I quickly phoned international directory enquiries. The lady operator had clearly not been facilitated into the mystery of helpfulnosity, because when I politely said, "Good evening, would you connect me to anyone in New York, New York who has the surname Scarlotti?" she said, "Don't be so bloody silly." and put the phone down.

This is what the British Empire has come to.

In bed
11:05 p.m.

Jas needn't have gone to all the trouble of making a lesbian barrier of pillows, because Libby has got into bed between us. She is looking from one to the other of us, smiling, with no front teeth.

I don't trust this smiling business.

Libby was turning her head from side to side looking at Jas and then looking at me. I must make her go to sleep.

I said, "Night-night then, Bibsy, time for Boboland. Shall I sing you a little night-time song?"

"No."

Ten minutes later

She won't stop turning her head from side to side, saying, "Naaaiiice, naaiiice." It's very unnerving.

Thirty seconds later

She's just suddenly fallen asleep. Just kajonk. Asleep. No yawning, just unconscious. How strange is that? How do they do that, the toddly-type people – the instant-falling-asleep thing?

Jas whispered to me, "I will never get to sleep. I'm just thinking and thinking about Tom."

Twenty seconds later

And now she's just fallen asleep! She is vair vair superficial.

Oh God. Anyway, I am never going to get to sleep either as I'm so excited beyond the Valley of the Excited and into the Universe... zzzzzzzzzzzzzzzz.

Howdy, Hamburger-a-gogo land! Brace yourselves for a knicker invasion!!!

Sunday May 22nd

8:30 a.m.

Cor, we are quite literally up at the crack of dawn.

I had no sooner slumped into a dream about my lips turning into hamburgers and Masimo spreading some tomato sauce on them than Mum was shaking me awake.

She was dressed in some new jeans, which I have never seen before and never want to see again.

"Mum, do they like the prostitute look in Hamburger-a-gogo?"

Mum said, "Don't start."

But I am not wrong.

9:00 a.m.

Up and dressed in my travelling outfit. Finally decided on my pale-blue ribbed T-shirt, cool jeans and pearl-buckle leather belt, with my highest-heeled shoes. (The highest heels allowed by the fascist fashion *kommandant*, aka, my dad.) I have some ballet slippers to put on later so that I don't get deep vein whatsit, as Vati is too mean to spend an extra thousand pounds so that I can have a chair that turns into a little bed on the plane. As I said to Mum, "A thousand pounds is just TOO much to spend to ensure his daughter will walk again, but there you are."

I left Jas trying to decide which botty huggers to wear for comfortabilitynessnosity on the plane, and went to say goodbye to the kittykats.

We have managed to convince Libby that they are not flying with us because they are coming on the special cat plane, which has little cat baskets instead of seats. And, I must say, it was my bit about them having their own little video sets by their baskets showing films of dogs being chased by cats that did the trick. It amused Libby so much, I thought she was going to have a fit.

9:15 a.m.

Gordon should be under strict house arrest, but he has done a dash for freedom and is on the wall with his father. I notice that the anti-cat fence has been partially eaten.

Angus playfully biffed me around the head when I went over to them. Gordy rolled over on to his back and looked at me upside down. I tickled his little tummy – sooooo cute. Then he locked all his paws round my hand and stuck his claws into me. Owwwww! I tried to get him off, but he is very strong for a little kittykat. He wouldn't even let go when I lifted him off the wall and he just hung there on the end of my hand. I shook him off at last, and he spun round in the air and landed on all of his little paws. Excellent tail work on the landing.

Angus was looking sleepily down at his offspring, probably thinking, *I have taught that boy everything he knows.*

As I got eye-level with the big furry loony, he looked straight at me. He has the most yellow mad eyes you have ever seen, but in his own way I think he loves me. That is what I think. It was like he was looking deep down into my soul, thinking, *Yes, we are different creatures, but we have a bond deep down inside. You are a baldy fool who cannot even catch her own snacks, but we both have hearts and appendixes. And neither of us have trouser-snake addendas."*

A touching telepathic speech from him because usually he is not very talkative.

I said, "Bye-bye, Angus. I love you and I will be back."

He put his paw out and just patted at my nose really gently.

I think he understands every word I say and this is his way of saying "s'later".

9:25 a.m.

As we drove out of our driveway in Dad's friend's white van, Grandad yelled out to us, "Have a lovely time, and Georgia, try and get on with people!"

That's nice, isn't it?

I said to everyone, "That's a bit rich coming from a convicted convict, isn't it?" But no one heard me above the singing.

Even Libby was joining in with "Get off of my blue suede shoes". Or in her case, "Get offer my blue snail shoes".

9:30 a.m.

On our way to the airport of luuurve dreams. I am sooooo excited. I said to Jas, "I am going to call all the people who have the same surname as Masimo as soon as we get to whatsitsname."

Jas said, "Memphis."

"Yes, that."

In the departure lounge

11:00 a.m.

I said to Jas, "Hamburger-a-gogo land, here we come! Brace yourselves for a knicker invasion!!!"

12:00 p.m.

Mutti was sooo nervy about taking off. She is still holding my hand and she has only just let go of the bloke across the aisle's hand. He looks a bit apprehensive, and not entirely sane. Mutti, me, Jas, Libby, scuba-diving Barbie and Sandra are all sitting next to each other, and Uncle Eddie and Vati have seats in front of us. The man across the aisle offered to change seats with Dad so he could sit across from Mum but Dad said, "You wouldn't be safe next to my friend. We call him The Prince of Darkness at home. He needs very careful managing." Then Uncle Eddie looked back at the man, with two plastic spoons stuck up his nose. Why?

The Prince of Darkness and his porky pal, my vati, have already embarrassed themselves by ordering ridiculous cocktails with umbrellas in them. And flirting with the air hostesses. It is vair vair sad. If they start singing and putting on their Elvis quiffs, I will go mad. I suppose Dad imagines his leather trousers make him look like a groover. I said to Mum, "Was Vati meaning to look like a transvestite?" But she was fiddling about with her seat-belt.

She said, "Do you think I could get an extra one? This doesn't look very sturdy, does it?"

"I wouldn't bother about your belt, Mum, this aeroplane must weigh about a million tons, and that little belt is not going to save you when we nose-dive two miles into the Atlantic."

She said, "Shut up," which I don't think is very caring. However, live and let live. And also let the spirit of holidaynosity and Luuurvegoddosity run rife through the aisles of life, is what I say.

Jas, who is wearing her "travelling outfit", i.e., some

enormous joggers and pigtails, said, "Do you remember the captain on the boat when we went on the school trip to Froggyland?"

"Jas, how could I ever forget Captain Mad? We were lucky to crash into France, otherwise we would be still there going round and—"

Then the plane's captain came on the tannoy.

"Gud evening, ladies and gents, we're awae on our trip to Memphis, and hoots a clear nacht the noo."

Dear God. He was from Och Aye land.

I clutched Mum and said, "We're all doomed. Doomed, I tell you."

Which I thought was quite funny. Mum didn't.

Two hours later

Rollers in for bouceability hairwise. We checked first that there were no fit boys on the flight. Not, as I said to Jas, that I am remotely interested. I said, "I am eschewing the General Horn and red-bottomosity with a firm hand, but you never know."

Dad turned round when he smelled the nail polish (I decided to change Pouting Pink for Go Baby) and saw us in

our rollers. After he had stopped laughing, he and Uncle Eddie amused themselves by pretending we were space creatures. Dad kept showing us things and saying, "Spoon, do not be afraid. This is a SPOON." Then they'd go back to talking rubbish, and a few minutes later Dad would turn round with a fork to show us.

Vair vair amusing.

How we laughed.

Not.

Libby is in Libbyland making scuba-diving Barbie and Sandra do "snoggling". If Sandra wasn't in fact our Lord in a dress, it would be lezzie snogging. I blame my parents because of their lack of moral code.

Mum has relaxed enough to start her usual flirting with anything in trousers. She almost wet herself when the bloke across the aisle (Randy) asked her if she had been a child bride. (I told you he was mad.)

When she nipped off to apply yet more make-up, I leaned over her seat to talk to Randy. "Er, howdy. Do you know anyone called Masimo Scarlotti in Manhattan?"

Randy looked as if he was a rabbit caught in a car's headlights. He was vair vair nervous for no reason.

Eventually he said, "Well, er, Manhattan is a big place and..."

I smiled. "I don't think an eighth of an inch mapwise is that big really."

He just looked at me.

I said to Jas quietly, "I don't think that Randy has all the buttons on his cardigan, if you know what I mean."

But I gave him the benefit of the doubtosity. I smiled at him and he took a big glug of his vodka.

An hour later

Still on this sodding plane somewhere in the Atlantic.

The captain keeps telling us to put our watches back an hour; it's more like having a clock driving than a person.

Fifteen thousand hours, or something

Or is that our height?

I said to Jas, "Have we crossed the International Date Line yet? Are we going backwards or forwards through time? It could be 1066 for all we know."

Jas is reading her ludicrous fungi book so she didn't even bother to answer.

Half an hour later

Or perhaps half an hour sooner. Who knows?

The captain came and walked down the aisle saying hello to people. He was not what I would call a confidence-inducing sight, although at least he wasn't wearing a kilt. He looked close to eighty-five. Also, he bumped into an air hostess, so maybe he has failing eyesight. Or at the least, very bad spatial awareness.

As the captain passed by us, Mum said, "Is everything all right, Captain?"

And he winked. Honestly. A million miles up in the air with no visible means of support and you have a winker in charge. He said, "Aye, madam, it's gud weather for flying."

Libby looked at him and smiled her tongue-through-the-teeth smile.

"Heggo mister man, give me and my fwends naaaiice sweeties."

Mum said, "Libby, naughty girl, the captain is too busy to—"

But the captain had clearly never had any experience of the bonkers toddly folk because he said, "Come on, then, little lassie, let's see what we can find for ye."

Two minutes later

Libby lobes the captain. She is sitting on his knee at the back of the plane, singing him her poo song. He's joining in.

Mum was looking back and smiling and saying to me, "Aaaahh, that's sweet, isn't it?"

There was a bit of a pause and then she yelled, "Oh my God, who is driving the plane?!!!"

Touchdown

Miraculously we have landed safely. After making such a fuss about everything, Mum fell asleep. In fact all of the grown-ups were unconscious when we landed in Memphis.

Jas was checking her watch as we took our rollers out. She said, "Isn't it weird that it's more or less the same time as when we took off, and that we landed yesterday as far as Hunky is concerned?"

Good grief, I needn't have bothered about day to evening wear.

However, I have got maximus voluminosity and bounceability on the hair front.

I may write a book on international beauty tips.

Memphis airport

Howdy, Hamburger-a-gogo land! Let the Luuurve Trail commence!!!

Jas and I did a tribute disco inferno dance when we got off the plane.

Twenty minutes later

Waiting for our luggage.

I haven't seen anyone who hasn't got a moustache yet.

And, frankly, that is not attractive in a woman.

Customs

I was singing "Head 'em up, round 'em up, head 'em out, rawhide. Head 'em up, round 'em up head 'em out, rawhide rawhiiiiiiiiide" in an amusing and entertaining way as we got our stuff and trundled along to customs, but it was, I have to say, not going down very well. In fact it was like being in Hawkeye City.

The customs man asked me if I was bringing in any livestock. I thought he was having a laugh, so I said, "Only, as you see, my father and his mate."

He wasn't having a laugh.

Not at all.

In our rental car

A willing-but-dim Hamburger-a-gogo chap (with a moustache) showed us to a massive black limo-type scenario. It was called a "Mustang" or "Arsekicker" or something. Anyway, it was big as a big thing. Dad and Uncle Eddie were ecstatic, kicking the tyres and so on – it is vair vair sad. The W-but-D chap said, "This is your vee-hick-el, sir. Now, you all drive safely, you hear?"

What was he going on about?

What is a vee-hick-el?

Jas said, "Does he mean a vehicle?"

I said, "Get loose, Jazzy Spazzy. Who cares as long as the vee-hick-el is a Luuurve vee-hick-el. Prepare to enter the vee-hick-el. Adjust your knickers; we are on our way!!"

After a million years of Dad fiddling with keys, we got into one of the eighty-five million seats inside and snuggled down while Vati and Uncle Eddie twiddled with their knobs.

I hugged Jazzy. And amazingly she hugged me back.

I said, "Jas, I am sooo excited, aren't you?"

She said, "Ooh look, there's a little TV on the back of the seat!"

As the Thunderbird-a-gogo or whatever it was took off at one mile an hour, driven by Dad, I said to Jas, "I can almost smell Masimo."

She said, "Oo-er."

And then we both fell about laughing. I think I have got hysterical jet lag.

Dad and Uncle Eddie were singing "I left my heart in San Franciso" and have already started yelling "howdy" out of the window at anyone we pass.

It's only a matter of time before they are taken to jail. So things are looking up.

4:00 p.m. timewise

I think someone forgot to mention something to me. It's HUGE here! The buildings, the signs, the shorts. Everything is HUGE here. And bloody hot. I'd ask Dad to turn on the air conditioning if I didn't know what a waste of time that would be; he's already opened the sun roof ten times when he was trying to change gears. And more to the point, there ISN'T a gear stick; this is an automatic car.

4:30 p.m.

Fifty million years of swaying about in the back of a vee-hick-el driven by someone who doesn't know what side of the road is the right one (and that's when we are in England). It was only when we passed the same group of people for the fifth time and they started waving and cheering that Dad let Uncle Eddie drive.

Hotel

5:00 p.m.

This is more like it. A huge driveway lined with hibiscus and palm trees and a fountain and then a hotel with about fifty-six floors. Tip-top hotel life. As soon as we screeched to a halt a millimetre away from the fountain, some chap in a uniform opened the car doors. He seemed vair vair cheerful, like someone had told him a really good joke. Perhaps he had heard about the clown-car convention, or seen Uncle Eddie trying to park. He smiled and clapped his hands and said, "Well, how are you all doing? Come on in, come on in! Welcome to Memphis, folks. The home of Elvis. But this is not Heartbreak Hotel, no siree – this is YOUR hotel!"

Good Lord. I said to Uncle Eddie really quietly, "Put your

foot down and drive like the wind."

But Mr Smiley Mad Pants had already taken all our bags inside. Still grinning like he was really pleased to see us.

The receptionist (Candi) practically split her mouth in half, she was smiling and saying "alrighty" so much.

While Dad and Uncle Eddie sorted out the rooms, Mum said, "Aren't they all just, you know..."

I said, "Bonkers?"

Mum got all mumish. "No, aren't they all so nice? Let's have a little look at the pool."

Poolsidewise

Wowzee wow and also yee-hah!! Fabby pool all surrounded by palm trees and with miniature waterfalls and stuff. We tried out the sun lounger things. Libby gave Sandy and scuba-diving Barbie a bit of privacy by putting them on their own special lounger.

As soon as we sat down a waitress dashed over. Blimey. Sometimes *days* can go by in English restaurants before some complete fool comes ambling over to take your order, and then tells you they haven't got it.

Our waitress (Loreen) was beside herself with joy at

seeing us and said, "Well, howdy to you all, thank you for coming to Memphis. Can I get you ladies anything?"

Mum said, "Could I have tea for four, and perhaps a couple of ham sandwiches if that's not too much trouble?"

Loreen slapped her thigh, laughed for about a year and said, "With that cute accent you can have anything you want, ma'am."

Mum said to Libby, "Bibs, would you like a little ham sandwich?"

Libby looked at the waitress and started snorting and grunting and pretending to be a mad piglet. "Hoggy hoggy, piggy sandwich!"

And Loreen chuckled and said, "Now aren't you the cutest?"

Cutest?

Libby?

Good Lord.

Ten minutes later

Jas is writing a postcard to Hunky. We've only been here a minute. She has no pridenosity.

Mum started taking her jacket off. I said, "I beg you,

Mum, do not alarm anyone with your nungas."

She is in such a good mood, and obviously expecting to see George Clooney any minute, that she just smiled at me and lay back in her chair.

Jas said, "I wonder what time it is in Kiwi-a-gogo. If we are six hours back from England and New Zealand is twelve hours ahead of England, that means... erm... let me see."

I said, "Jas please work it out in your head and don't start talking about minutes to me. It makes my brain go jelloid."

Once I have had a snack, I will have the strength to get on the phone to the Luuurve God.

Fifteen minutes later

Loreen has arrived with our "snack". My sandwich is made out of two loaves of bread, chips, a huge gherkin and a piglet.

Loreen said to Libby, who was gnawing her way through forty pounds of ham, "Is that alrighty for you, Miss Beautiful?"

Pardon?

Then, attracted by the gnawing, Cindi, a waitress with eight-foot hair came over and said, "Now you leave her alone, Loreen; she is mine." Then they had a bit of a mock mini fight over Libby, shouting, "Now you give her here, she is miiiiine."

Quite quite weird.

We sat there chewing as Loreen and Cindi sort of pushed each other around. Finally Loreen won and she picked up Libby and gave her a cuddle.

Libby didn't hit her.

I was amazed.

We were all amazed.

It was amazing, that's why.

She was cuddling my sister; my sister wasn't biffing her.

Now Loreen was kissing Sandra. Blimey.

Then some bloke passing by with twenty-five pounds of sausages on his plate stopped and joined in. "How are y'all folks doing?"

I said, "We're doing as alrighty as... er... alrighty things, thank you."

And he said, "Hey, miss, are you from Ireland? Well, begorrah you are real pretty and you have a sparkling personality. Now you all take care and have a nice day."

Mum practically choked on her pig's leg.

Half an hour of alrighty time later

After our "snack" we staggered to the elevator and a complete stranger in tartan slacks and matching hat said, as he got out, "Now you enjoy Memphis, you hear?"

On the way up to our room I said to Jas, "What do they want from us?"

Inside

Mum went off with Libby into the "family" room and Jas and me went into our room. I heard Libby saying to Mum, "When is the kittykat plane landing, Mummmmmeeeee?"

Oh dear.

Our room

Wow and wowzee wow! It was HUGE! And it had its own private bathroom. No more chance sightings of my parents in the nuddy-pants.

When we got to our room the bellhop was putting our bags on one of the ginormous beds.

I said, "Oh, thank you very much."

And he slapped his thigh and said, "Now where are you all from?"

I said, "Erm, we're all from England."

And he did a bit of a dance and said, "Say something in British."

I looked at Jas, but she was busy walking in and out of the walk-in wardrobe.

It was really making me nervy having an ogling person ogling me from about an inch away from my head. Especially one who thinks that I speak British. Anyway, I said, "Do you know if there's a bus that goes to Manhattan, please?"

And he started hooting with laugher. I was just looking at him. Eventually he managed to wipe his eyes and calm down and went cackling off out of the room.

Jas said, "Georgie, look, there's like a cupboard thing with drinks and snacks in."

I said, "Oh thank God!"

But I was being ironic because I am so full of piglet I can barely move.

We lay on our ginormous beds and made a plan.

I said, "OK, the first thing is... we phone up directory enquiries and... zzzzzzzzzzzzzzzzzz."

Monday May 23rd

8:30 a.m.

What in the name of arse happened? I remember putting on the TV and Mum and Dad coming in and saying, "We are just going to have a little zizz." I thought, *Hahahaha, now is my chance. I will just lie on my ginormous bed and have a little rest to perk me up for my phone call to the Luuurve God.* And then it was now. If you see what I mean.

But hey hey hey, this is our official first morning in Hamburger-a-gogo land!

Jas was awake, looking at me, in her giant sleeping knicker ensemble and giant bed.

I said, "Howdy," and she said, "Alrighty," and I said, "Goddamn rootin' tootin' I'm alrighty."

And we laughed like loons in Loonland, which we are.

9:00 a.m. Hamburgertimewise

Jas was looking out of our two-hundred-millionth floor window, and I said, "Any sign of cowboys?"

She said, "No, but I can see some bloke doing nuddy-pants gardening on a roof."

Wowzee wow!! I leaped out of bed and went to the

window, and there was Mr Rudey Dudey Nudey on the roof of another hotel!

I said, "Boo, he's wearing tiny swimming knickers, or swimming 'panties', as we must say to get along with people here. I'm going to use our phone to call up Masimo in Manhattan."

Jas said, "Good luck. Hey, I wonder if I could phone Tom in Kiwi-a-gogo."

It was really groovy having our own phone for once.

I said to Jas, "What is the codey-type thing for Manhattan?"

Typically, Jas didn't know. I don't know what the point of coming top in history is if you don't even know the simplest thing, but I didn't say that because I am vair nearly in Luuurve Heaven City.

I phoned reception and an alarmingly cheerful person said, "Gayleen speaking, how can I help you, ma'am?"

"Oh... er... I would like to make a call to Manhattan please."

"You got it. Now you just wait, ma'am while I connect you to the appropriate party."

This was more like it. I said to Jas, "This is why I luuurve

the American-type people. They DO stuff for you. Also, they are very truthful – you know, like last night that bloke said I was beautiful and had a sparkling personality. That is why I like them, because they are full of sinceriosity!"

...And that is when Dad answered the phone.

"Dad!"

"Oh, yes. I wondered how long it would be before you were on the phone to your mates, telling them what you're having for breakfast and what colour lipstick you might wear."

Donner and Blitzen!

And *merde*!!

And also DARN!!!

Even on holiday, Dad is so mad and unreasonable. He has told the hotel to put all our calls through to him!

I said to him, "What if I needed to call the emergency services?"

"I could call them."

"But what if you had, er... fallen over your shorts and—"

"Georgia, shut up and just accept that you are not calling your mates on the hotel phone. You can use your own money in a phone box." Then he hung up.

Sacré bleu.

The phone rang. It was Vati again.

"And don't even think about eating anything out of the room bar or using room service without my permission."

What was this? A holiday or Stalag 14 on tour?

Through the Fat Controller (Dad), Jas and I ordered the "healthy option" breakfast.

Fifteen minutes later

Jas and me were sitting in the bath watching the mini TV on the shelf by the sink. It's like on a stem thing and you can twist it around so you can watch it from any angle, even on the loo. (By the way, we were sitting in the bath not in a lezzie way, just in a in-our-jimjams-way.)

There was a knock at the door, and our "healthy option" breakfasts arrived.

I don't know whose idea of a healthy option it was, but in my book twenty-five tons of porridge, four eggs and forty pounds of fried potatoes plus toast doesn't suggest health to me – it suggests death.

The smiling person (Dolly) who brought us the brekkie tray said, "Now you all have a nice day, you hear?"

And I didn't even say, "No, YOU all have a nice day."

I have never been smiled at by a waitress in my life until I got here.

Creepy.

I said to Jas, "What is it these people want?"

11:30 a.m.

We all climbed into the Loonmobile to go and explore Memphis. Uncle Eddie and Vati were wearing baseball hats backwards with their false Elvis quiffs sticking out of the front. There was no need for it. I said to Dad, "Dad, we are representing Her Maj the Queen, and quite frankly you two are doing a really crap job."

Uncle Eddie, once again at the "controls", accelerated away so suddenly that we were forced back in our seats – like that G-force thing. Only in our case it was the Uncle Baldy force.

As we careered along, there were signs all over saying, "Elvis the King dared to rock!" and so on. Every time they saw one, Dad and Uncle Eddie would start singing another Elvis song and moving their shoulders about and saying "Uh-huh".

I must find a phone box and set off to Manhattan as soon as I can.

Out of the Loonmobile and amazingly still alive

Memphis is blindingly hot and sort of groovy in a really loony groovy way. Everywhere you go there are Elvis songs blasting out of cafés and bars and shops, and people dressed up as him. I never thought the day would come when I would say this, but Dad and Uncle Eddie were almost sane-looking in comparison to some. Is it normal for old ladies who are fifty-eight stone to dress in rhinestone jumpsuits and false black sidies? "No", I think, is the answer you are searching for.

The grown-ups were all keen on going to look at Robinmobile Headquarters on the outskirts of town. I said to mum, "Please, please don't make me and Jas go. Please, we're only young, we have our whole lives ahead of us. Please, please."

Eventually they agreed that we could have a look round town and they would go "check the scene", as Dad pathetically put it, wiggling his dark glasses. Dear God.

As they went off he said, "Be back here, outside Elvis's

Rock Emporium, in two hours or say goodbye to ever going out by yourselves again."

Cheers.

But at least we were free!!!

As they went off and got back into the car, we waved and looked full of maturiosity. Then, when Uncle Eddie had careered round the corner in the Thunderbird thing, we did thumbsie upsies and a swift disco inferno.

I yelled, "Yes and three times yes!!! Goodbye, porky ones! We are off on the Luuurve Train! Or Luuurve Greyhound!!!"

Jas said, "I am not getting on a bus to Manhattan with you. And that is final."

I put my arm around her. "Come on, my bestest little pally, one for all and all for one and all for me."

"No."

"Jas—"

"No."

I resisted the temptation to kick her stupid legs, and decided to use my famous charmosity. "Jas, let us just go and find a phone box. I can phone Masimo and say, "Ciao Masimo, your dreamboat has landed." and you can phone Hunky and ask him how many boring... er, I mean how many fascinating bits of wombat poo he has found in Kiwi-a-gogo and so on."

Jas perked up then. "Oh yeah, I could... unless you think it's sort of... well, you know, keen... but I am keen, aren't I? And I have got his phone number – well, at least I've got the number of the farm he's staying on."

Good Lord. She is soooo, you know, pathetico.

And I say that with deep loveosity.

We had to wait to cross the road with the other Memphis-type people. One enormously friendly person, who clearly had "eaten all the pies", said there was a phone box in the "drugstore". Can you imagine it being called that in Shakespeare-a-gogo land? Anyway, as we waited at the lights they changed, and instead of the "Beep beep beep" thing, it had a woman talking in a Memphis accent. Honestly! She said, "Now you all are safe to cross the road."

A shop next to the drugstore had a notice on its door that said, "No drinking, eating or firearms in the shop."

Wow!

In the drugstore

We asked the drugstore man how to use his telephone thing. He gave us loads of quarters or something. I couldn't quite make out what he was saying, as he was eating a hamburger at the time. I did hear him say, "Are you going to phone Her Majesty at BuckingHAM Palace?"

What was he talking about?

Telephone box

The telephone was a bit low. Are there a lot of tiny people in Memphis? I was a bit phased about asking the operator for numbers in Manhattan on my first go at the phoney thing, so I thought I would try phoning Rosie.

Jas was looning about being an unhelp. I said, "Are they five hours ahead?"

And she said, "Well, if it's yesterday tomorrow in Kiwi-a-gogo, well, that makes it... er..."

As she was rambling on I picked up the receiver and it made a really funny dialling noise, and then I had to shove in tons of quarters. Then it made a funny ringing-type noise. It was almost like I was in a foreign country.

Perhaps no one was in.

Then Rosie answered the phone.

Yesssssss and three times yessssss!!! Contact!

England! England! A person who spoke my own language at last!

Rosie said, "Bonsoir."

"Ro Ro, it's me and Jas!"

Jas was trying to get the receiver off me and yelling, "Let me say hello. Let me."

Vair annoying.

I let her have a go, though, because I wanted her to do stuff for me. She was ludicrously excited, like we had been away for years in the Antarctic and had just found a phone on an ice floe.

"Rosie, it's me, Jas, in Hamburger-a-gogo!"

She rambled on for ages, saying stuff like, "What is the weather like there? Oh, is it? Raining? Is it that light rain that soaks you right through? Yeah? Right. Not really raining, more like spitting? It still wets you right through, though, doesn't it? It's boiling here. The money is different." Really really boring stuff. For ages.

I said, "Give me a go, Jas, before the money runs out."

She handed the phone over to me. I said, "Ro Ro, guess

how many people over here have said they love me?"

And Rosie said, "None?"

Happy days. Back to normality.

I luuurve my friends. Rosie is growing dreadlocks and Sven has had his thumb pierced.

After we had said goodbye to Rosie, Jas went off into another booth to speak to Hunky.

I took a deep breath got my coins ready and got through to the operator.

Fifteen minutes later

Do you know how many Scarlottis there are in Manhattan?

A million.

I could spend the rest of my life phoning them.

Jas came out of her tiny-person's booth to get more change, and I said, "It's bloody hopeless. There are about a billion people called Scarlotti in Manhattan."

She said, "Why don't you use sort of psychic luuurve bonding and just telepathically think of where he will be and choose that number?"

Fifteen minutes later

I have made many many new Hamburgese friends, all called Scarlotti. One of them seemed a bit on the Chinese side and I think I may have ordered egg fried rice to go, but that is life. Oh, I have laughed, I have cried with my new mates, I have talked about central heating and so on, but I have not spoken to anyone who knows Masimo. And I have spent almost all my money.

Jas was still on the phone, nodding like a nodding thing.

Huh, she was probably doing pretend snogging on the phone to Hunky.

I was exhausted.

I went up to the counter and ordered myself a milkshake.

The young chap wanted to talk. Oh dear. He said, "Now, where are you all from?"

I said, "England."

He said, "Oh wow... awesome."

He was just looking at me drinking my milkshake.

Then he said, "Do you know Prince Charles?"

Oh dear God.

I said, "Yes, I play table tennis with him."

Fortunately, or unfortunately, depending how you look at

it, Jas came and sat down beside me.

I said, "I have spoken to loads of people, pretty much all of them mad, and spent all my money and I have no idea where Masimo is. What about you? How was Hunky?"

"I don't know. I've just been told off for about a million years."

It turns out that when Jas eventually got through to the farm it was 1:00 a.m timewise and the Kiwi-a-gogo farmer who eventually answered wasn't pleased.

Jas said, "When he answered the phone he said, 'Are you there?' You know, with that funny accent that goes up at the end."

"Why did he say 'Are you there?' when you had just phoned him?"

"I don't know, it's the Kiwi-a-gogo way."

"Then what happened?"

"I said, 'Yes, I am here, are you there?' and he lost his rag for no reason and said, 'Don't go playing the bloody smartarse with me.' and started giving me a lecture about how hard they worked on the farm and what time they all had to be up. I said, 'Er, I'm in Memphis,' and he said, 'I don't care if you're in the bloody body of a whale, don't phone up in the middle of the bloody night.'" And he put the phone down on her.

Crikey.

I never intended to go to Kiwi-a-gogo, and now I know I made the right decision. Do you know why? Because they are all mad.

And they think that just gone midnight is late.

I rest my case.

Jas was all miffed, but she agreed to just have a look at the bus station. We shuffled off to find it. Hot as billio. I think I am getting a bit brown though. Everyone is soooo friendly, it's vair vair tiring. And all the men wear either Elvis costumes or dungarees.

I said to Jas to cheer her up, "I have never seen grown men wear dungarees."

She said, "They're not called dungarees in Hamburger-a-gogo land, they're called overalls."

I looked at her.

"How come you know so much about it? Have you got some?"

She went a bit Jasish. "Well, yes, I, er... use them for, you know, er... gardening and so on. They have many useful pockets."

Yes, I bet.

I had a sudden image of her and Tom cavorting around in her bedroom in their dungarees...

Bus station

Do you know when buses go to Manhattan? Never, that's when. Also, if they did go, it would take five weeks to get there and back.

Sacré bleu.

Jas said, "Look, be reasonable. We are not going to track him down, let's just try and enjoy ourselves through our love pain."

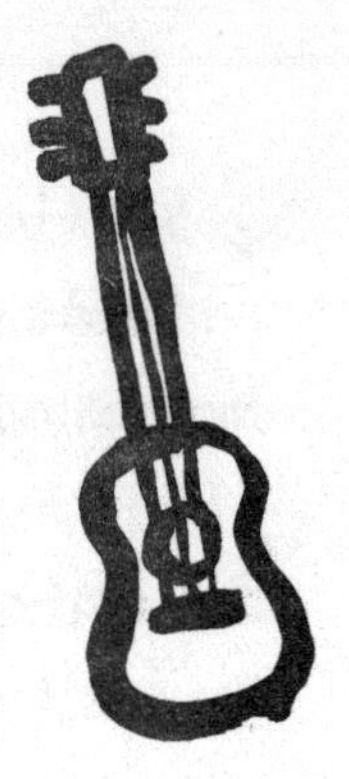

Let the nuddy-pants bison disco inferno dance commence!

Tuesday May 24th

Poolside

1:00 p.m.

The olds are all in their swimming cozzies drinking cocktails. Libby has made Our Lord Sandra a sarong. She seems to have forgotten about the cat-plane fandango because she is so spoiled by everyone she meets. If she eats any more I fear an explosion in the knicker department.

Vati is still being ridiculous about my gun.

When I asked him to get me one like in *Thelma and Louise*, he said, "What part of 'not a hope in hell' don't you understand, Georgia?"

"I only want a small one, just for the comedy value of it falling out of my handbag in a café or something. It could even be one of those cigarette lighter things."

But oh no, he is just too busy chatting bollocks to Uncle Eddie about clown cars and beards. Apparently there are more clown cars at the convention than anywhere else in the world.

Vati said, "What a sight: Robin Reliants for as far as the eye could see."

I said, "Hurrah" in an ironic way, but he didn't get it.

Uncle Eddie is allowed to wear his comedy-arrow-through-the-head hat when we go out to dinner.

It is soooo unfair.

Evening

When we were in the Live to Rock diner this huge bloke came over, also wearing a comedy arrow through the head. I thought he was one of Uncle Eddie's sad clown-car mates, but he turned out to be the waiter.

I said, "Could I have a glass of Coca Cola please?"

He said, "Coming right up, ma'am."

I said to Jas, "I could get used to this ma'am business; it makes me feel like Her Maj."

As we were leaving the diner the same bloke brought me this mag called *Dallas Monthly*.

He said, "I thought you would like it because of the cover, ma'am." And the cover was of some heavily-bearded bloke dressed as Her Maj smoking a cigar.

I just said, "Thank you. What a lovely gift."

Wednesday May 25th

Midday

I tried one more time in the phone booth of love, but after speaking to a petrol pump attendant and the mother of twins called Apple and Spaceboy, I decided enough is enough.

On the plus side, we did have a hoot and a half at Graceland, where Elvis the Pelvis lived. And died as it turns out – of a hamburger overdose.

We saw his bedroom and everything, and even his grave. Bought some marvy gifts in the gift emporium for the chums: a lovely Elvis mug, which I am sure some fool (Grandad) will cherish; hilarious wigs, and just to show that we can all live in peace and harmony, I bought the Prat Poodles two Elvis dog outfits. One was a little lurex all-in-one suit from Elvis's Las Vegas days – it even had a doggy-size quiff. The other suit was based on this film called

Jailhouse Rock and was a doggy prisoner outfit with a striped hat. I would have bought Angus and Gordy one each too, but they would have eaten them in minutes. Oh, and I also bought a very elderly man's CD. That was a bit of a mistake actually. This old bloke was sitting in the shop dressed entirely in blue Lurex and humming. I thought he was another elderly Elvis impersonator, but then his "assistant" informed me he was a blues legend.

Jas thought the man said "blue" not "blues". "Why is he a blue legend – does he always wear blue?"

She can be incredibly dim. He was called Moaning Clyde or Wailing Clyde or something – anyway, some kind of complaining was going on namewise. Sadly, Moaning Clyde took a shine to me and kept patting my head, so in desperation I had to buy his CD. And then he made us get a photo taken with him. He was quite a tiny chap and his head was practically resting on one of my nunga-nungas.

Jas whispered to me, "Moaning Clyde is your new boyfriend. He luuurves you."

She might be right, for all I know. I couldn't make out what he was saying; we may be married, for all I know. Still, as I said to Jas, "I don't think a hundred-year age difference is necessarily a barrier to our happiness. The fact that I will never see him again probably is though."

In our hotel

8:00 p.m.

Alone!!!

Dad and Uncle Eddie and Mum and Libby are all at the clown-car evening do with their incredibly sad new mates.

There are twenty-two stations on the TV, which is in a chest of drawers. There isn't a TV in the wardrobe, which is a bit of a blow. But ho hum, pig's bum.

Tuning into the local stations. Mostly it's fools plucking away on banjos and singing "I am the son of a preacher man". Or something about God or grits etc. But then we found a programme with a sort of agony-aunt person. She is called Delilah and is supposed to be cheering people up when they phone in with "luuurve trouble".

She wouldn't have cheered me up, I can tell you that. She was an alarming shade of orange and dressed entirely in pink. There was a suggestion of the criminally insane around the pigtails area. Some poor sod phoned in about her second marriage. She said, "Good evening, Delilah, I'm getting remarried and my son from my first marriage is having a little trouble coming to terms with my wedding. In fact, he is refusing to come. How can I persuade him to enjoy my lovely day?"

Delilah (looking intently into the camera with a mad/concerned look on her face) said, "So what you are saying is that your son is DEVASTATED by your new marriage?"

"Well, I wouldn't say devastated, I would—"

Delilah hadn't finished. "He is MORTIFIED that you have taken another man to YOUR BED who is not his father."

"Well, he hasn't mentioned the bed, it was just that he—"

"He CANNOT BELIEVE his own MOTHER would deceive him and LET HIM DOWN SOOOOO BADLY. He is in TORMENT!"

After having reduced the caller practically to suicide, Delilah then said, "But as you all know, music soothes the troubled breast, and here's a little tune for you to heal the wounds."

The tune was called, "You are a drunk and an unfit mother".

I wanted to ring the helpline number to complain about my mutti and vati, but then I would have only got through to Dad, and he's not even in.

Thursday May 26th
only three days till we go back to England
Poolside

Even if I can't find Masimo I can concentrate on becoming brown as a bee in a bikini. Jas and I had just settled down to heavy sunbathing duties when Vati tried to make us go to the clown-car convention with them.

He said, "What is the point in coming to a new country and then just lolling about by the pool. You could do that anywhere. You should get out and experience the culture."

I said, "Dad, how many hamburgers can one person eat? And anyway, Jas and I are soaking up the culture conversationwise poolsidewise. So get real and cut me some slack here because I am sooooo OVER you."

"Why are you talking rubbish?"

"Well hellOOOO, Dad, do not even GO there – that is

not rubbish, that is Hamburgese."

He went raving and grumbling on, but at last they left me and Jas in peace for a few hours.

3:00 p.m.

I said to Jas, "Have I got strap marks?"

"Let's see... yes, you have."

Excellent!

Evening

In the old Laughter Wagon again on our way to a hotel that everyone has been rambling on about. It's called Gaylords, which says it all in my book.

I said meaningfully to Uncle Eddie and Vati, "You two are certainly in the right place then."

Gaylords is "the Wild West experience under one roof". Apparently people can't be arsed to go to the real West, so they just come to this hotel. We went in through the "saloon door".

Inside Gaylords

Oh, this is so much worse than you can possibly imagine.

There are canyons and waterfalls and deserts all inside a hotel, and everyone is dressed in cowboy outfits, or shorts with high heels and gold belts for the ladeez. (Didn't you know that in the Wild West the ladies wore shorts and high heels?)

I said to Dad, "Now can I have a gun?"

But he and Uncle Eddie were too busy yelling, "Yee-hah" and staggering around in tight leather jeans. Yes, they were wearing tight leather jeans. I will just leave that image with you. Jas and I tried at all times not to be behind them, because then we would have to look at their bottoms bursting out of tight leather jeans.

Erlack.

By the Dodge City cinema there is actually a shop that sells "overalls".

I am not kidding.

Five minutes later

Oh good, Dad and Uncle Eddie have bought some and they have slipped off to the "rest rooms" or "bucks' room" (I know, I know) and come back wearing them.

This is a nightmare scenario.

In the bar area comfort zone they have bucking broncos as bar stools.

Nothing will make me go on one.

Two minutes later

I am sitting on a bucking-bronco stool, I have a pair of horns in between my legs... so has everyone. We are all sitting at the bar on bucking-bronco stools. My dad and Uncle Eddie are wearing overalls. The bar staff are all dressed like Wyatt Earp and crack a whip when you order a drink.

Nothing could be worse.

Wrong. Oh, so very wrongey wrong wrong.

The bucking-bronco bar stools actually buck. I found this out when "Rawhide" came on the speaker system. I was too late getting off, and before I knew it I was being thrown backwards and forwards and round and round. I was clinging on to the horns for dear life. Jas had fallen half off hers and was nearly upside down. Libby was absolutely hooting with laughter and yelling, "Giddyup!!!"

God I feel sick.

The stools eventually stopped bucking when "Rawhide"

finished, and Jas and me scrambled off and had a rest on a rock.

Four minutes later

"Rawhide" came on again, and Libby and Mum, Dad and Uncle Eddie, and everyone else at the bar started bucking about like loonies. It is sooooo sad.

Dad fell off.

Good.

Two minutes later

Dad and Uncle Eddie have made loads of new fat overally mates.

Hoorah.

The fun just goes on and on. From the safety of our rock we were watching a boy with alarmingly big white teeth and those leather things that cowboys wear over their jeans. They are called "chaps" for some reason. Cowboys wear them when they're rounding up cattle. White-teeth Boy wasn't rounding up cattle, he was line dancing like a fool.

I said to Jas, "He makes Sven seem normal."

Then he caught me staring at him, winked and came over.

"Do you mind if I take a little rest beside you, ma'am? I'm a bit saddle sore."

I said, "Sadly, it's a free country."

He sat down and said, "Hi, you all. Whereabouts in Australia are you all from?"

I said, "I'm English."

And he whistled and said, "Awesome!"

Is it?

Then he tipped his hat back and said, "Honey, I bet you are a real good kisser."

What a cheek!

I said with haughtiology and glaciosity, "I'm afraid I don't do snogging with strangers."

Jas almost choked on her mega-size Coca Cola (i.e., Coke in a bucket).

White-teeth Boy said, "What is snoggling?"

Snoggling?

It turned out that Mr Goofy knew next to nothing about the British language. For instance, when I asked politely, "Were you always an arse and a prat, or were you once just a prat?" he didn't understand what I meant.

Fortunately we were interrupted in our interesting

cross-cultural chat by Libby. She came over singing, "Head 'em cup, knead 'em in. Soooooorrreee hide!" and sat on my lap.

She was looking at my new "friend" and then looking at his trousers.

"Georgeee, why is that man so bulgy?"

Then she slipped down from my knee, and before I could stop her she went and stood looking and looking at his pouch trousers. He just had time to say, "Well, how are you all doing, little miss?" Before she thumped him in the trouser-snake area.

Happy days.

And lovely holiday moments.

Friday May 27th

only two more days to go

We were driving to the clown-car convention when we saw a big four-wheel-drive car thing, and in the rear window it had a sticker that said, "Honk if you see the twins fall out," which I though was vair vair *amusant*.

I said to Vati, "We could have one that says, "Don't honk if Uncle Eddie falls out."

Mum said, "Don't be so rude." But she needn't have bothered, as Uncle Eddie had his headphones on and was singing along (badly) to "I am proud to be a redneck". Which I think is spookily karmic, as his whole head is practically now a red neck, if you see what I mean.

At the clown-car convention

In Davy Crockett's diner we were all given fur hats to wear as we ate. Which is nice (ish).

Our alarmingly cheerful waitress came bounding up to us to tell us about the "special".

"Hi there, folks! Todays special has fresh 'erbs, including BAYzil , oRRRREgano, and fresh VEG-a-tables in it."

I said, "Does it come in alUUUUminum foil?"

And me and Jas laughed like drains.

But the waitress didn't get it.

2:00 p.m.

Jas and I slipped off by ourselves to get away from the overall-wearing fools. And do more sunbathing.

Libby came with us to the ice-cream stall and she started her usual shouting. "Me want a big big one pleeeeeeease!"

The elderly man and woman behind us, both dressed from top to toe in gingham, said, "Isn't she the cute one?"

I looked around, but amazingly they were talking about Libby.

"Hey now, let us get you a treat, little lady."

And they paid for her ice cream.

She said, "Fank oo ladies."

They were keen as mustard to know us, and Gingham Man said to me, "How are you all enjoying your day?"

I said, "Oh, fab, I haven't enjoyed myself this much since I injured my ankle playing hockey." But I said it with a charming and light smile.

Mrs Gingham said, "Oh, that is a cute accent you've got there. Whereabouts in Ireland are you from?"

Then Libby, in between mouthfuls of ice cream, said, "I can sing my song."

Oh no. I tried to gag her but she bit my hand and went on really loudly and with gusto. "Poo pooo bum bum. Poo bummy bum bum, arse."

Oh good.

The Ginghams clapped and laughed.

"Oh, soooo cute. But what is "arse"? That is not a word I

know. Is it an Oirish word?"

Libby started smacking her behind, singing, "Bum bum, arse arse." And the Ginghams clapped along. I hope they weren't escapees from the circus-clown-car mental home.

Then Mrs Gingham said, "Oh, I see, honey. You mean your *derrière*! You say arse in Oireland, but in the United States we would say FANNY. Can you say that word, dear? Fanny? Let me pat your little fanny."

I dragged Libby away quickly. With a bit of luck she would forget all about the fanny business.

As we went off, Mrs Gingham yelled, "Now you all come back and visit us from Oireland again, begorrah!"

Good grief.

But God bless them – if you can't beat them, join them, I say.

Jas and I shouted back, "Top of the morning to you!"

Saturday May 28th
Last whole day

The week has whizzed by, even though I didn't have any luck finding Masimo. What I like most about here is that everyone likes us. A LOT. It has made me and Jazzy Spazzy in such a good mood that we even went to watch a clown-car race.

Actually, it has to said that seeing a lot of clown cars roaring around a race track is very hilarious. It's like watching very old people with ponytails skating or something. At least my dad doesn't do that.

Dad and Mum and Uncle Eddie have made loads of new mates, and we all went out to a takeaway hamburger place for the last lunch. You drive up to some clown-head thing and then you shout your order at it and it talks back to you and then you go and get your order. Now that is what I call culture. Why can't we have something like that in England? I think I'll suggest it to Hawkeye when I get back to Stalag 14. It would make lunchtime a whole new experience clown-head thingwise.

Nuddy-pants bison-horn photo session

As the olds went off to get last-minute pressies and Libby went to get something for the kitties, Jas and I made our small but meaningful tribute to our visit to Hamburger-a-gogo land.

The only good thing about the nightmare trip to Gaylords was that me and Jas got to buy some souvenir bison-horn hats. So we were able to wear them for our farewell nuddy-pants photo session in the hotel room.

It was vair vair amusing. Jas in the nuddy-pants and bison horns reading a book on the ginormous bed. Me adjusting the TV in the bathroom in my bison horns and nuddy-pants. Packing suitcases, applying lippy, etc. Vair vair amusing indeed. I was nearly dead with laughing.

Sunday May 29th

Farewell Hamburger-a-gogo

Loreen and Jolene and Noelene and Gaylene and all the other "lenes" at the hotel actually cried when we left... honestly. They were hugging us and so on, saying, "Now, you all come back to us, soon as you can, missing you already."

Still, as I said to Jas, they are only human.

Adios amigos, as you say in Hamburger-a-gogo land. I love you all. But I must go as I have a Luuurve God to find.

Bum bum bum bum oley bum bum, and good afternoon officer

Still Sunday May 29th

Circling over England

7:45 p.m.

Blimey it looks like toytown.

Heathrow Airport

Home again, home again, jiggity jig!

Rain rain, lovely rain.

Vati's ludicrous van mate has come to pick us up. His van has a big sticker on it that says, "If you are looking for love, have a look at the driver's horn."

Still, no one knows me at Heathrow.

8:30 p.m.

As we were trying to get all our stuff in the van, a policeman came to tell us to move along because we were blocking the road.

I beamed at him. "Good morrow, constable, and how are you on this fine English eve?"

He looked at me as rain bounced off his helmet. "I'm as well as can be expected under the circumstances, madam."

"We've just come back from Hamburger-a-gogo land and the police over there have guns. Do you have a gun concealed about your person, officer?"

"I very often wish I did, madam. Can you pop into your van now so that we can sort out the twelve-mile tailback you're causing?"

Mum said, "I honestly am doing my best, sergeant, but my husband's comedy cowboy hat is a bit difficult to fit in anywhere without..."

I could see that the officer was on the point of violently shoving Mum and the hat in the back of the van, when Libby piped up. "I know a song, Mr Bobbyman."

Even I have to admit that Bibs can look like an ordinary charming child sometimes, and she had her fairy crown on and a pink dress, so you could be forgiven for the mistake.

The officer sighed and bent down to her. "OK, just sing me a little verse before your mummy and daddy quickly get in the van and GO HOME."

You never know what toddlers will remember. Libby sang her botty song to the officer. But worse, much worse than that, she sang the American version. She put her hands on her hips and gave her all to the constable.

"Bum oley, bum oley, fanny fanny bum bum."

I thought he was going to faint. He tried to stop her – God knows we all did – but on it went, even when Dad put her under his arm and shoved her in the back of the van.

"Poo poo and bummy bum bum FANNY! Pat my little fanny!!!"

9:00 p.m.

Dropped Jazzy Spazzy off at her house. She said, "It'll be weird not being together, won't it? Call me as soon as you get home."

I very nearly hugged her. But then I remembered we are back in Stiff Upper Lip land and I don't want any rumours of lesbianism to spread; you never know who might be watching.

On the way home to our house we sang "I was born under a wandering star". Vati is in a remarkably good mood. I can't believe that looking at clown cars can cheer you up, but it has.

Mum is still full of herself because all the men across "the pond" called her "ma'am".

Still, it was nice of them to take me and Jas to Hamburger-a-gogo, even if I didn't manage to find the Luuurve God.

Of course, the plus side is that now we are back, I don't need to see anything of them. I will be out all night and all day with my boyfriend.

If I've got a boyfriend.

I don't even know if he's back yet.

Oh, hello... Welcome back to the rack of love.

We arrived at our gate and unpacked all our luggage. The van man and Uncle Eddie drove off with a squeal of tyres. Uncle Eddie, still wearing his comedy arrow through the head, yelled, "Head 'em up, ride 'em out, RAWHIIIIIDE. Yeee-haaah!"

I saw Mr Next Door bob down underneath his window so that we couldn't see him. I also noticed that the anti-cat fence has been taken down. He will be thrilled with our Prat outfits. I may take them round later when he thinks we've gone to bed.

9:15 p.m.

Home! Our lovely house, surprisingly not a burned-out wreck.

Happy days.

I even found myself hugging Grandad.

No sign of his girlfriend.

In the loo

Ermmm... wrong about there being no sign of Maisie.

I am not being ungrateful, but why would anyone normal knit a toilet-seat cover?

In the Kitchen

Or knit covers for the door handles?

No sign of the kittykats.

Mum and Dad and Libby have taken Grandvati home, so it's just me in the same bat place.

I am going to think about all my experiences and what I

have learned on my great adventure about life, love and the universe.

I am simply going to enjoy my own mind.

In the peace and tranquility of my own room.

The simple joy of just being alone with my own deep inner thoughts.

In my bedroom

Please tell me it's not true that I am now the proud owner of knitted slippers.

9:20 p.m.

Rang Jas.

"Jas."

"Howdy."

"Howdy, how are you all doing?"

"Just fine and how are you all?"

"Have you heard anything from anyone?"

"There were about ten messages from Tom. He's having a nice time and everything, but he really misses me, and oh, he mentioned—"

"Jas, pleased though I am for your news about wombats

and so on, what I want to know is have you heard anything, you know, from the gang or anything?"

"Georgia, I have only been in the house for twenty minutes."

9:22 p.m.

Phoned Rosie.

Rosie's mum answered the phone.

I said, "Is Rosie in?"

"I'm afraid not, dear. She's gone to homework club."

Homework club?

Oh, yes, the old homework-club scenario – it's the Ace Gang code for going somewhere you're not allowed to. In Ro Ro's case it will be Sven's snogging emporium.

Tried Jools.

Out at homework club.

Ditto Ellen and Mabs.

Crikey! I hope they've not formed a lesbian coven.

Phoned Jas back.

"The Ace Gang are all out at homework club. What does that mean?"

"Perhaps they are, you know, doing their homework."

"Jas, are you mad?"

Hummmph.

Back from a million years abroad and the Ace Gang can't even be bothered to say "welcome home".

Back to Stalag 14 tomorrow.

I feel a bit sheer desperadoes because nothing has changed. No one has got in touch so I don't know where Masimo is. Is he back? Perhaps he has decided to stay over in Hamburger-a-gogo.

Oh *merde*.

Even the kittykats are all out – no sign of them anywhere. Once again I have dropped anchor in Poo Bay.

9:30 p.m.

Went round to Mr and Mrs Next Door's. I am sure they saw me coming up their drive and pretended to be out; I heard a muffled bark from inside the house. They are vair vair nervous people. Still, live and let die, I say, and I posted the Prat brothers' Elvis outfits through the letterbox.

I am sure they will love them a lot.

Really I am too good for this world.

Oscar, Mr and Mrs Across the Road's prepubescent, sex-maniac son, was on perve duty on the wall as I went back into my house. He looked across at me as I passed and said, "Cracking tits."

Oh, lovely.

10:00 p.m.

You always hear people moaning on about jet lag, don't you? "Oooh, I had to go straight to bed, I didn't feel right for three weeks." Namby-pambies. It's just another form of trave... zzzzzzzzzzzzzz.

Monday May 30th

7:30 a.m.

What happened? Did someone creep into my room with a mallet? I feel appalling. No one could expect me to go to school. I'll just snuggle down and... Hang on a minute! How will I find out about Masimo if I don't go out? I must be brave for my love.

Still no sign of the kittykats. I know they've been around, though, because all the plants are just stumps.

8:30 a.m.

Met Jas. She looked like death warmed up. She said, "God, I'm tired. Are you?"

I said, "Not many, Benny. Still, we can have an afternoon nap during German."

Stalag 14

When Jas and me got to the school gates the Ace Gang were waiting for us. We had a celebratory Klingon greeting and a quick burst of disco inferno. I felt quite emotional and came over all American. I hugged Rosie, I was so pleased to see her. She shoved me off and said, "Get off me, you appalling tart. And I mean that in a loving way."

Oh, it's so good to get back to normal.

Behind the fives court

Break time

Rosie said, "So what happened? Did you find Masimo?"

I said, "Well, in the end I thought, you know, it was a bit, like, uncool to get in touch, so I—"

Jas said, "So she phoned up all these complete strangers and made an idiot of herself instead."

Oh, thank you, Mrs What a Great Pal. NOT.

Actually, the gang were really nice about it. Jools said, "Well, he doesn't know you tried to find him, so he can go on thinking you are full of glaciosity."

And Ellen, for once, said something quite sensible. "And you are quite brown."

Good point, actually.

They wanted to hear everything about our trip, so we treated them to a quick chorus from Delilah's song "You are a drunk and unfit mother" and then told them all about Hamburger-a-gogo. You know – all about the different culture and the chance to communicate with foreign people in their own language.

Rosie said, "Let me get this right. You went to a place that was actually called Gaylords? And you rode a bucking-bronco bar stool?"

"Yes."

"With horns?"

"Yes."

"Please say you took photos."

Jas said, "Better than that. We brought you all special replica horns to wear. Look."

She got the gift horns out of her rukky and the Ace Gang tried them on.

They were thrilled, going "Oh wow!!!" and "Fabarooney!!!"

They looked *magnifique*.

Jools said, "We should form a band called the Bisons."

11:15 a.m.

The American disco inferno bison dance is born.

It is: foot stomp, foot stomp, arse wiggle.

Horns to the right, horns to the left, and clap.

Foot stomp, foot stomp, arse wiggle.

Horns to the right, horns to the left, and clap!

Ellen said, "It's like good and everything, but bisons don't clap, do they?"

Good grief. If it was up to people like Ellen, *The Simpsons* might never exist. She'd be saying, "No one has blue hair two feet high" and other gibberish.

I said, "That is where you are vair vair wrong, Ellen. Out on the range, when a travelling circus pulls in, the bison and the rest of the prairie folk go to see it, and the biggest clappers are always the bison."

Ellen looked even more confused than normal. I said,

"Ellen, of course they don't clap, but neither do they do disco dancing. It's poetic whatsit, you steaming ninny."

As we loped into Stalag 14 past the prison warders, Wet Lindsay and Hawkeye, and their guard dog, Astonishingly Dim Monica, Mabs said, "So you don't know where Masimo is?"

I said, "No, I don't know whether he's back or what's happening."

Wet Lindsay glared at me as we went in. I think she may have lost weight while I've been away. It's not a good look unless you like looking like a vair vair thin twit.

4:30 p.m.

Bloody *sacré bleu*. We've had our bison horns confiscated! How are we supposed to form a band now?

I was grumbling to Jas as we slouched off home. "Honestly, how petty is this place? I KNEW Wet Lindsay would try something. She's got it in for me."

Jas said, "We should have taken them off after German."

"Where is the law that says bison horns shall not be worn in the school corridors? Tell me that. Where is that law written down?"

"You said that to Wet Lindsay."

"I know I did, Jas. I was there."

"She said, 'Don't be ridiculous, there is no law written down that says don't poo in the corridors, but we know not to do it.'"

"I know she did and I think it's disgusting that we have to put up with that sort of language – poo talk – from supposed Head Girls."

"You said that to her as well."

"JAS, I KNOW I said that to her. I was there!!!"

"That's when she gave us all bad conduct marks."

"Yes, well, that is typico."

Home

I HATE Stalag 14. They treat us like bloody children. I wanted to practise my bison dance.

6:00 p.m.

Mabs phoned. "Gee, I bumped into Dom and he asked if we're going to the Stiff Dylans gig next weekend."

"Wowzee wow! Did you ask him about Masimo?"

"Er, no, I thought that would be uncool."

"Good thinking, Batwoman."

It is good thinking, but annoying, too, as I don't know anything about the Luuurve God.

On the brighter side, there is a Stiff Dylans gig, so if nothing else it means that Masimo will be back by then.

Tuesday May 31st

English

Still no news of Masimo. I was asking the Ace Gang what I should do but Miss Wilson kept interrupting our chat with her so-called "love of Shakespeare". For goodness' sake. Hers is not the love that dares not speak its name – hers is the love that bangs on and on about Billy. It's all "What ho, my lord" and "Oh look, here comes Macbeth talking total bollocks." On the plus side, she reminded us that the Foxwood lads are coming to help us backstage (oo-er) when we rehearse.

Wednesday June 1st

8:15 a.m.

Something really really freaky-deaky and weird happened. The doorbell rang and everyone had already gone out so I answered it and it was the postman. He said to me, "I have

a registered parcel for Miss Georgia Nicolson. Is she in?"

I said, "Oh, come on, you know I'm in, you're talking to me."

He's a surly old bugger. He shouldn't really have a job with the public, unless it's the public that lives in a prison. He said in his surly, officious way, "Well, you say that, Miss, but have you any way of identifying yourself?"

Now he was really getting on my nerves. I was just about to rip the parcel out of his hands when I had a vair vair amusing idea. I said, "A way of identifying myself? Yes, I believe I have. Would you just wait a moment?"

I came back a minute later with a mirror, looked into it and said, "Yep, it is definitely me."

8:30 a.m.

In the end he handed over the parcel.

Hmmm, what was the postmark?

Oh. New Zealand. If Tom has sent me a copy of "You're the only fish in my sea" or some photos of wombat snot, I may go mad.

It wasn't from Tom.

It was a letter from the Sex God. Robbie.

Blimey O'Reilly's panties.

I had a really queasy feeling as I began to read what it said.

Dear Georgia,

It's been a while since I wrote. I suppose I thought that you would reply and then I would write again. But you didn't, so... Tom arrived last week and it was brilliant to see him. We've been out in the bush...

I was thinking, *Oh here we go – back to hugging wombats and plucking guitars in the river*, but no...

...talking about home, and talking about you actually.

Tom told me about the boy-entrancer episode and your excellent dancing to "Three little boys". I thought I would never stop laughing. But it made me sad, too, because you like someone else and also because I'm quite a serious person and you are, in the nicest possible way, quite possibly clinically insane, and at the very least, a handful. I can just hear you saying oo-er to that last bit.

I don't know why I am writing, really. I suppose I wanted

you to have a picture of me out here, which I have enclosed, and I would really like one of you sometime.

You are always in my heart and often in my dreams.

Robbie

xxxxx

Oh God.

The photo was of him in jeans and a T-shirt sitting by a river. He was looking straight into the camera with those deep blue-black eyes that I thought I would never ever be able to look at again. He was just so... oh, I don't know.

8:45 a.m.

Got to Jas in a state of shock.

She was rambling on as usual. "Come on, come on, we'll be late. What's wrong with you? You look like you've seen a ghost. Anyway, Tom phoned last night, he said they found this amazing mushroom that was about two feet across. It's apparently delicious if you—"

"Jas, I... I..."

"And he said, do you know what, the Maoris eat the

larvae of the Hu Hu bug, they are big fat white grubs, and they roast them and then they eat them. Tom went to a hangi out there, he has a new Maori friend and his traditional Maori name is Brian and—"

"Jas, look at this."

Jas took the letter as we jogged along. And even she was silent.

She finished it and then looked at me.

"Bugger my giddy aunt."

For once Jas is not exaggerating.

I just don't know what to think. I had given up on the Sex God. I really had.

French

I kept looking at his photo.

He was bloody gorgey. And I mean that most sincerely.

But what in the name of Jas's commodious botty huggers was I supposed to do or think? He hadn't said, "Come to Kiwi-a-gogo and be mine." Nor had he said, "I am coming home to get you." In fact, to be frank, what he had said really was, "I still like you and think about you a bit."

Oh, why hadn't he written this last month? Why had he

written it after another Luuurve God had come along?

It's too much.

Break

I consulted with the Ace Gang.

They listened while Jas read the letter out loud. I don't know why I let her because she read it soooo badly, with a really crap New Zealand accent for some reason. I can safely say I am not optimistic that her performance of Lady Macbeth is going to bring the house down.

Then they all started the insane nodding-dog extravaganza.

I said, "So what do you think?"

Rosie said, "Dump him from your mind. He is yesterday's snoggee; move on, move up. We've gone European now, we are Euro citizens and it is our duty to kop off with as many European types as we can. Within reason."

Jools said, "On the other hand he is very very groovy-looking."

Mabs said, "And it would be quite nice to be Jas's sister-in-law, wouldn't it?"

Blimey O'Reilly's knob, I hadn't thought of that nightmare scenario.

Jas almost choked on her nibbly niblets.

It was, as ever, left to Ellen to completely and utterly confuse humanity. She said, "Well, I suppose... like really, you are, like, well... not really anyone's girlfriend."

Home

6:30 p.m.

I'd ask Mum for advice but you might as well ask Angus, for all the sense she makes. And also, she has gone out with Dad and Libby to the O'Shaunesseys' to show them our holiday photos.

8:00 p.m.

I wish I could talk to someone normal. Or even in.

Even the kittykats are out. Gordy is worse than his dad. He sleeps all day, wakes up, eats anything he sees, destroys a bit of furniture or some tights and then buggers off out. They both treat this house like a furry hotel.

10:30 p.m.

I can't believe this. Mum and Dad have come back Irish. We are being forced to be an Irish family. Vati says he has

rediscovered his Irish roots.

I said, "Yes, after six pints of Guinness."

He wouldn't shut up, though, and put on a Dubliners record. Libby is doing her version of Irish dancing. I don't remember the knickerless part, but...

In between slapping his thighs and shouting, "Come on there, girl, get them pegs moving!!" he said, "You see, there is a story in my family that my great-great-grandfather was an O'Dwyer from Killarney, but they changed the family name to protect them against the villainous English."

I said, "Dad, when you say villainous English, do you mean us?"

But he wouldn't be stopped. "They changed the name to Nicolson."

I said, "What, that grand old English name? NOT. Why would they change their name from an Irish one to a Scottish one? The English, i.e., us, hated the Och Aye landers just as much as the Leprechaun-a-gogo folk. More. That is why we built Hadrian's wall at the top of England – to keep the Ginger beardey folk out."

Dad was still rambling on like Paddy O'Mad. "And another thing: we look Irish. That man in Memphis spotted it – he asked you if you were Irish. He asked you that because you have the look of the Emerald Isle about you."

"No, he didn't, Dad. He was an American – he doesn't know where anyone comes from unless it's Texas. He was wearing gingham."

I slammed up to my bedroom.

Bed of pain

Ohgodohgodohgod.

I lay on my bed with a pillow over my head.

I am in a ditherosity of love and I have now become Oirish.

Thursday June 2nd

Jas got top marks again in history. She went all red and girlish.

As we walked home I said to her, "You are vair clever, Jazzy. You are as clever as Professor Clever at the University of Oxford department of Cleverosity."

I feel a bit better about the whole Robbie thing. If I don't mention his name, then I won't think about him. It's like voodoo, isn't it?

It is definitely beyond the Valley of Deffo and entering the Vale of Very Nearly Quite Sure that I luuurve Masimo.

Bathroom

4:45 p.m.

I checked the orang-utan situation. You can practically comb my legs.

4:48 p.m.

I can't be bothered with using Immac. Actually, what I mean is that Mum has run out.

4:50 p.m.

Dad has got one of those razors that leaves your skin smoothy smooth and attractive to women. So it says on the TV ad. I do want smoothy-smooth skin but I don't want to be attractive to women.

5:00 p.m.

I could risk it on my legs. What sensible lesbian is going to be at knee level with me?

5:01 p.m.

I won't think about the possibility of midget lesbians that are only one foot high.

5:45 p.m.

Actually, Dad's razor is really tip-top. I have no open gashes at all and my legs are like the advert says – smoothy smooth.

Mmmmmmmmm.

Washed the soap off Dad's razor and put it back where it was.

In my room

7:00 p.m.

Now then, the age-old question of what to wear for the Stiff Dylans gig. I must of course wear a short skirt to show off the smoothy smoothness of my legs. I would be a fool to waste the smoothy smoothnosity.

7:30 p.m.

I think if I'm wearing a really short skirt, I should wear a more covery-up top so that the nungas are not on display. I want to hint at sophisticosity, not prostitutenosity.

8:00 p.m.

I was just trying things on when my father went mad – yelling and barging about downstairs. I think I might tell him that swearing is an indication of lack of vocabulary. But not just now.

8:10 p.m.

He barged into my room, his face covered in bits of loo paper. Is this his new Irish look? He yelled, "Did you use my bloody razor?"

I looked hurt and puzzled.

"Your razor? I know this is your first shot at fatherhood, but perhaps you have noticed I am a girl. I am beardless. Mostly."

He said, "Don't be so bloody cheeky, you know damn well what I mean. HAVE you been using my razor?"

"Well, only a bit, just for my, you know, legs."

Why do I have to discuss my body with my father? I am sure there's a law about it.

Fifty years later, after his famous lecture about not using his stupid razor ever again, he went off.

8:30 p.m.

Shame about his face being all cut.

8:40 p.m.

Still... nice smoothy-smooth legs.

Friday June 3rd

8:15 a.m.

There is a certain amount of tensionosity about not knowing whether the Luuurve God is back in the country. I had relaxed my make-up regime because he was not around, and now I have to be on high alert all the time just in case. Also, and I know this is even for me bordering on the Universe of Madnosity, now that I have heard from Robbie, I sort of have to wear make-up all the time because I've got a letter from him, which has put him in my head and that might mean he can see me. From my head. Or from his letter. I told you I have entered the Valley of the Unwell. Get out of my head, ex Sex God!!!

I am going to try a bit of nostril breathing even at the risk of expanded nostrils.

Aaaaahhhhhh.

Four minutes later

I am a xxxxxx-free zone and I think you know that the xxxxxx starts with an R.

Donner and Blitzen and also *schiessenhausen*!!! I've thought of him again.

Make-up plan

My routine is a bit of lippy and gloss with a hint of mascara and just a really tiny bit of eyeliner. The difficulty is getting past sniffer-dog Hawkeye. Today I will be returning to that old favourite of putting my head as far into my bag as it will go and saying as I go past Hawkeye, "Oh, now where did I put my French homework? *Mon Dieu* and *Au secours,* it must be in here somewhere."

Ambling up the hill to Stalag 14

Jas said, "Did you reply to Robbie?"

Oh God.

"Er... no."

"Are you going to?"

"I don't know, Jas."

"Well, you used to really like him and he has written to

you, so are you going to reply or not?"

I didn't say anything so she just went on. "And if you do reply what will you say?"

I still didn't reply.

"I mean, are you going to talk to Tom about it when he gets back and ask his advice? He's back next week, you know, so will you wait until then and reply, or what?"

Eventually I was driven to having to reply to her. "Jas, shouldn't you be wearing a doublet and a false moustache and burning me at a stake? You are quite literally the Spanish Inquisition."

"Well, I am just saying..."

"Well, don't."

"Usually you want to go on and on about Robbie and Masimo, your so-called boyfriends."

"Jas, don't start... and anyway, you're having a laugh, aren't you? If I go on about MY boyfriends all the time, how come I know all the words to 'You are the only fish in my sea'? How come?"

Jas got the hump. "Oh, well, I'm sorry to bother you with MY life! Of course YOUR life is the only important thing, isn't it? Yes, yes, Georgia Nicolson is the only person in the universe. Not."

And she stalked off like a stalking stalker at a stalking contest.

Blimey, she could get huffy.

Ah well, I might try my Oirish charm on her, when I can be bothered.

Geoggers

Jas kept up her cold shoulders all morning, even when I sent her a little gift of two pieces of chocolate. She ate them and then went on *ignorez-vous*ing me!

Break

Jools was telling us the latest about her and Rollo. They have been to an all-nighter and spent the whole night together. She has snogged so much that she's got a cold sore coming on her lip. She showed us all.

Erlack.

Apparently sixteen of them stayed round at this mate of Rollo's while his parents were abroad and snogged the night away.

Ellen, as usual, was a bit baffled. "Did you all, you know, snog at the same time, or... er, was there dancing?"

Mabs said, "So, is Rollo like your bloke now?"

Jools said, "Well, I think so, but I never know when he's going to see me or ring me."

I said, "Blimey! So it's a sort of full-time s'later situation."

Jools said, "Yes, I suppose it is. Like on Saturday, I don't know if he's going to the gig with me or whether he'll turn up there and be with me or..."

Jas said, "I wouldn't stand for that. I need to know where I am."

I said, "You're here, Jas." and I gave her my bestest smile.

She didn't smile back. But she did say, quite nastily, "And who will you be seeing at the gig, Georgia? Or will you be just having a LAUGH, if you know what I mean and I think you do."

Oh God, she is playing dirty now, with this Dave the Laugh thing. She knows that I still haven't told Ellen anything about me and Dave.

School gates
4:20 p.m.

We were all ambling out of the playground when I saw him. Masimo on his scooter. Parked outside the school gates!

Ohmygiddygodspyjamas!!! I couldn't believe it was him. But it was!

He is absolutely gorgey. He has a tan as well. His hair is so black and wavy and he's got long legs and a fit body and everything.

He was just sitting on his scooter with his helmet in his lap, leaning back on one arm. He had shades on.

He is sooooo sexy. You could feel like a beam of sexicosity coming off him.

What was he doing here? Was he waiting for me?

The Ace Gang were doing their marvellous impression of walking goldfish.

Rosie said, "My God, he's fit."

Jools said, "Blimey. Did you know he was going to be here?"

Jas said, "He's brown, isn't he? He's browner than you."

I couldn't speak. All the girls streaming out of the gates were looking at him and doing that silly flicky-hair thing and smiling. Shutup smiling, you smiling minxes. I didn't know what to do. Should I just walk casually by him and *ignorez-vous* him, carrying on with my Mystery Woman scenario? Or should I be friendly and nice and smiley? Oh, I don't know.

I dithered around and made the Ace Gang walk really really slowly.

Had I got enough lippy on?

Was I wearing clothes?

I was just saying, "Oh my God ohmygod. What shall I do?" when I was saved from any decision making because Lindsay appeared at the gates. She wasn't wearing her uniform. She had a short white suit on and a headscarf. She went straight up to Masimo, doing a sort of ridiculous little run thing, and kissed him on the cheek!

He was smiling at her, and they were chatting. God, he has a nice smile. He has a really generous, big mouth – not like Mark Big Gob, just normal big. I couldn't help looking and watching like a sort of horror film. Even Jas stopped *ignorez-vous*ing me and linked arms with me because she knew how horrible it was.

We were very near to the gate now and I couldn't avoid going through it and passing by Masimo. The gang sort of shielded me and I kept my head down, but I still saw Lindsay putting on the spare helmet. It was awful. I was so miserable and trudged off with the gang.

I heard the scooter rev up and roar off behind me.

Rosie said, "That was a bit intense."

Everyone was really nice to me. Which sort of made it worse. They kept saying, "Are you all right? Do you want some chuddie?"

But nothing helped.

4:30 p.m.

After they had all peeled off home, it was just me and Jas.

She said, "Blimey O'Reilly, that is a turn up for *le livre*."

I said, "I must be jinxed in love. What have I done in a past life to deserve this?"

Jas said, "Perhaps you were, you know, like a wasp or something."

"A wasp?"

Jas is what is known in the business as an unhelp. But she can't help being a tiny dim pal. At least she's not me, though.

As she went off into her house she gave me a little squeeze on the arm and said, "I don't care what anyone else says about you – I like you."

I MUSTN'T cry. I must not cry until I get into my bedroom.

High Street

4:45 p.m.

Tosser Thompson and his mates passed me and said something, but I didn't know what. I felt like a ghost in the world.

I got to my gate and I could feel the tears welling up in my eyes. No one would be home yet, so at least I could get into bed and just wail.

What a hopeless fool I was.

I had even phoned up people with the same name as him in Manhattan.

One of them was a Chinese takeaway.

That is how pathetic I am.

5:00 p.m.

I was opening the gate when I heard the roar of a scooter coming up my road. I didn't turn around. Even if Dad had got an even more embarrassing vehicle than the clown car, nothing mattered any more.

But then the scooter stopped behind me. And he spoke. Him. In person. Himself. Not a facsimile of a sham. Him. The person I had been dreaming of for so long.

"Georgia, *ciao*, how are you? *Come sta?*"

I couldn't speak. I turned round. And looked at him. I looked straight into his eyes. I had forgotten how amber they were, sort of soft-and-hard-looking at the same time. He half smiled at me, and he has gorgey teeth – let's face it, he's gorgey all over.

"I just stop to say *ciao*. I have been away."

I still couldn't speak. Maybe nodding was all right? I nodded. Oh good, I was being a budgie in a school uniform. Eggscellent. Shutup, brain. You haven't joined in so far, don't start now.

He revved up his engine and said, "I too must go. We are rehearsing. Are you coming to the gig? I hope to see you there. *Ciao*."

Oh dear *Gott* in *Himmel*!!!

6:30 p.m.

Lying on my bed

I think I might be in a coma.

I have to speak to someone normal about this.

7:00 p.m.

Can't think of anyone.

7:30 p.m.

Still can't think of anyone.

7:45 p.m.

Gave up on talking to someone normal and called an Ace Gang emergency meeting at Luigi's.

9:30 p.m.

In between slurping coffee, the Ace Gang gave me the pep talk to end all pep talks. I have to go out and get my man!!! Yee-hah!

Rosie even sang the national anthem and said, "Gird your loins and adjust your nungas for battle."

Midnight

I mean, why would he come round to my house to say *ciao* if he didn't like me a bit?

1:00 a.m.

What is it with boys? Just when I thought I'd forgotten about my heartbreakosity *vis à vis* Robbie (*Merde* I've thought of his name again. I am going to have to call him something else so as not to attract the voodoo thing. I will call him... er... the Guitar Plucker.)... Anyway, where was I before I so rudely interrupted myself? Oh yes. Just when I thought I had forgotten about my heartbreakosity *vis à vis* the Guitar Plucker, he sends me a really nice letter. Then Masimo pops by.

Oh, I don't know!!!

Saturday June 4th

Churchill Square

11:00 a.m.

Rosie said, "In this sort of situation, she who dares shops." So in preparation for the Battle of the Chicks I am going to get a fabby and marvy pair of shoes.

Ravel

11:30 a.m.

I saw these cool shoes in the window, with a bit of a kitten heel and some groovy strappy bits round the toes and the heel.

In the shoe shop

We all trooped in and I asked for my size. The woman said the biggest they had was a size four until next week.

Next week! Is she mad? I have to go the gig, like, tonight!

I said to her, "OK, please bring me them."

Jas said, "What's the point of that, you take a size seven?"

"Sometimes."

Rosie, who was trying on some ludicrous furry boots that made her look like a yeti, said, "So do your feet change size then?"

I said, "Well, you know, it *says* a size seven, but then if they are made in Japan where they have very tiny feet, size seven is like a size fifteen over here."

They all looked at me.

Then the lady with the shoes came back. They were groovy as anything. Masimo would love them because, as every fool knows, Italians are the mistresses of footwear.

Five minutes later

Blimey. I couldn't get my heels in. I said politely to the lady,

"Have you got a horn?"

And that set the gang off into hysterics.

She looked at us like we were loons, but went off to get the shoehorn.

Five minutes later

Got them on! Yesss!!

The lady in the shop said, "Are you sure they fit? Walk around in them."

The gang were all slouched about waiting for me not to be able to walk. I got up. Ouch ouch and double *merde* and ouch. They were bloody aggers. I looked in the mirror. They looked fab. I must have them; I must go through the pain for him. I smiled like a loon. "Do you know, it's amazing, they are sooooo comfy as well as being groovy. It's almost like wearing slippers."

Bedroom

1:00 p.m.

I have stuffed my new shoes with newspapers to try and stretch them.

1:30 p.m.

Mum came snuffling around. "Give us a look at your new shoes."

I said, "Oh, I'll show you later when I'm all dressed up."

5:30 p.m.

Dad said he didn't know anyone who stayed in the bathroom for four hours. It's a great pity that he doesn't spend a lot more time on his appearance.

In my room

5:45 p.m.

I have two mirrors arranged so that I can see back and front. I am so smoothy everywhere that I am like a human billiard ball – there is not one single lurking rogue hair on my entire body. I am a lurker-free zone, and I have at least got my base coat of make-up on.

6:00 p.m.

I've got a couple of jumbo rollers in my hair, which I will take out at the last moment when I've done everything else so that I have max bounceabililty.

6:30 p.m.

Calm, ohm. Save myself and my energy for the battle. Better check the weather. Hmmm, a bit cloudy.

Phoned Jas. "Jas, do you think it will rain?"

Jas said, "Just a min."

I heard her scampering around, and then she came back to the phone.

"No, I think dry spells with just a tiny possibility of precipitation."

Blimey. I had to ask – I knew I shouldn't, but I had to. "Jas, can I ask how you found that out?"

"Oh, yes, well, the snails in the jar that Tom and I placed in the—"

"Jas, I really must dash. Libby is watching *The Sound of Music* again and I need to yodel along. See you at eight."

7:00 p.m.

Just about ready. I am not going to risk the boy entrancers, even though they are fab and entrance boys like billio. I don't want to take any risks gluewise. I've put eight coats of mascara on, so that should do the trick. I put on one coat and then put talcum powder over it and then another coat and so on. I can hardly lift my top lids up, but I like to think that gives me a mysterious sexualosity.

7:15 p.m.

My little blue skirt looks vair fab and I have put fake tan on my legs to top up my Hamburger-a-gogo browniness. I don't think you can really see the streaky bits unless you're at floor level, and who is going to be there? Apart from the midget lesbians I was worrying about before. I have got my strict bra on, the one that takes no nonsense from my basoomas, and a fabby blue and black top, which has got a really small pair of lips on it down at the bottom. You don't notice it, but if you did, it would imply I liked snogging without implying I am a tart.

7:25 p.m.

Mum called up: "Can I come and see what you're wearing?"

Oh God.

I put my shoes on.

OH my God!!! Ag city Arizona! They were made for a child! I pushed my feet in and managed to get them on. And stood up. If I walked about I would probably get used to them.

Mum came in. "Wow. You look really groovy! Is this for the Italian Stallion?"

Shut up. Please shut up.

Then she noticed my shoes. "Are they your new shoes? They are gorge, aren't they? Aren't they a bit too small for you?"

I said, smiling widely, "Gosh no, if anything they are a bit slack."

She was still looking at them. "What size are they?"

I looked at my watch and said, "Crikey O'Reilly, is that the time? I promised to meet the gang at seven thirty. S'later."

I dashed off down the stairs. Ouch ouch, aggers aggers. Bugger bugger bum.

on the way to Jas's

My God, these shoes hurt. On the plus side I think they're cutting off the blood supply to my feet, so with a bit of luck my feet will be numb soon.

I had to sit up on a wall for a resties just round the corner from Jas's house.

7:45 p.m.

As we walked along Jas said, "Do you want to go to the loo? You're walking funny."

Clock tower

8:00 p.m.

Met up with the Usual Suspects. Rosie had actually bought the furry yeti boots. Maybe they are to match Sven's. He has the most unusual dress sense I have come across in someone who is not actually working in a circus. I wouldn't have thought you could buy shiny purple suits with scarlet inserts, but you can. Also, if I could bear to think about it, I would say that he was wearing lipstick. He lifted me up and kissed me on both cheeks. "Hi, girly girls, let's hit it!!"

I looked into my compact. Yep, he was wearing lipstick.

We all trailed after him.

Jools is in a state of near madnosity about whether she is going out with Rollo or not. Jas is in one of her philosophical moods, so she said to Jools, "If it is meant to be, then it will be. Did I show you my song from Tom called 'You are the only fish in my sea'?"

As Jas got it out (oo-er) to read to Jools, I walked on

quickly with the rest of the gang. Ouch ouch ouchey ouch. Still got feeling in my feet.

Ellen said, "I think I am going to, like, make Dave the Laugh jealous."

I laughed and said, "Oh yeah, good luck."

And she looked at me.

"How do you mean?"

I said, "Well, he, you know he's not, erm... he doesn't really seem like the jealous type, does he?"

Ellen said, "Well, I'm going to, you know, dance and flick my hair about with that friend of Rollo's. I'm going to try all those tricks and stuff."

I said, "Promise me you won't try the infectious laugh."

By this time we were outside the Buddha Lounge.

In the tarts' wardrobe

8:40 p.m.

We had a last-minute Ace Gang conference.

Well, Rosie, Jas and I did. Mabs and Ellen and Jools were so eager for boy action that they did a quick lippy check, visit to the piddly-diddly department and off out on to the disco dance inferno emporium.

Rosie said, "Go through the check list."

I sat on the edge of a sink. (Oh, the relief the relief in the tootsies department.)

I began, "Mascara?"

We looked at my mascara. "Check."

"Lippy and lurker situation." Jas and Rosie looked and said together, "Check."

I said, "Attractive smile full of Eastern promise?" And I smiled.

Rosie said, "Phwoar, give us a snog, I've come over all lesbian."

I like to think she was joking.

I am ready to take on Lindsay. Flicky flicky. Hip wiggle hip wiggle. Smiley smile.

Left the tarts' wardrobe.

Just as we were about to hit the dance floor Jas said, "What about knickers?"

I looked at her. "Yes, what about them?"

"Have you got any on?"

Is she truly mad? But then I couldn't actually remember putting them on. When did I put them on? I remember putting the skirt on and my bra and top, but knickers?

Which ones were they? Oh God. Perhaps I had forgotten and then I would fall over and reveal my front and back bottoms to the world.

Or Sven would pick me up like he very often did when he was doing his frenzied *Saturday Night Fever* routine.

I dashed back into the loos.

Knicker alert over. I blame Jas entirely – she is so obsessed with underwear.

9:00 p.m.

Vair vair dark in the club – and rammed. We edged around to the bar; it took a while to get used to the dark. Especially if your eyes were weighed down with one pound of mascara and talcum powder. Dave the Laugh was about an inch away from my nose before I saw him. "Hello, Kittykat, you're back."

I smiled at him and then Rachel popped her head over his shoulder. "Hi Georgie, cool to see you."

She is always so alarmingly pleased to see me. Why? There's nothing wrong with her, but I'm Dave's friend, not hers. She pulled on Dave's arm and said, "Come and dance, babe."

He looked at me and I for once had the upper whatsit. I said, "Yeah, babe, go dance."

He gave me a cross-eyed look and went off to dance.

Rollo and his mates were all there at the bar with Jools, Mabs and Ellen hanging on their every word. Pathetico. I would never do that. Everyone was there.

I said to Jas, "Jas, just nod your head up and down wisely. You don't have to talk. In fact, I'd rather you didn't. I want you to be my decoy duck while I look around for any sign of Masimo."

Jas tried to have a strop, but I stopped her by saying, "You know I am only asking you to do this because you are my vair vair bestest pallsie in the whole world. Also, if you help me with this I will let you sing Tom's song to me."

Jas perked up then. "Yip yip, he's back in five days. I only came out to help you with all your boy troubles, you know."

I was going to give her a friendly dead arm for being so annoying, when some bulky girl trod on my toe as she was going by with her lardy mates. I shouted out, "Bloody hell in a hand basket, ouch ouch! Bollocking bugger bugger bum!!!"

Jas said, "Are you sure your shoes are OK?"

I said, "Jas, some complete imbecile of gigantic proportions has just trodden on my foot. That is why I am leaping like a loon."

I might actually have to slip off for a quick lie down in the loos and put my feet up on the loo seat.

But then "all pain dropped away from my tootsies forsooth", as Billy so eloquently put it in his famous sonnet "Ode to my feet". Masimo came up to the bar.

He looked mega-cool (and a half). He doesn't look like English boys. He's more sophis. He was wearing a cool, pale blue Italian suit with a T-shirt. Like me, he was wearing fabby shoes. (Although his didn't have kitten heels and he didn't look like he was going to wet himself.)

I put my shoulders back to give a bit of nunga emphasis (looking round first to make sure I didn't knock anyone over). Also, I let my mouth drop open a bit and put my tongue behind my bottom teeth. Like Britney Spears but without the big tongue piercing.

I was deliberately not acknowledging Masimo. I was absolutely tip-top full of glaciosity.

Jas, Ellen, and Mabs were, however, full of stupidosity. They all came crowding round me going, "Have you seen him?

Have you seen him? He's at the bar, over there – look, can you see him?" And so on. Soooo annoying and uncool.

I was still doing my tongue behind the teeth thing, so I said, "Thlear off, tho away, thleave me ayown."

I pretended to wave at someone in Masimo's direction, and the Luuurve God caught my eye and smiled. I slightly smiled, and he began to come across to me. Oh I love him I love him. But no! Remember the plan. I smiled again and then I forced myself to walk away.

And not look back. Cor, how difficult was this? It was like walking with my feet facing in one direction and my body facing in the opposite direction trying to snog him. Like a really crap mime artist. But I must do it. I must keep up my glaciosity.

Also, I was trying to make a good impression from the back. I was concentrating so much on crap mime-walking, hip-wiggling, hair-flicking and eschewing the Luuurve God with a firm hand that I went nunga-nunga-first into Dave the Laugh. Again.

He said, "Settle down, lads," straight to my basoomas. Cheeky cat.

However, he was the Hornmeister and there was no sign

of Rachel, so I told him what I'd just done. I said, "You would have been proud. Masimo came over to me and I walked away with glaciosity at all times. What do you think tacticwise?"

He looked a bit funny. If I didn't know that he was a callous Hornmeister, I would have said he looked a bit sad, but I must have been wrong, because he said, "Excellent work. Keep it up. What handbag has he got tonight?"

Then Rachel came bounding up like a friendly red setter. Dave was nice to her, but he looked a bit cornered. If I were her I would give him a bit more space. Blimey, I am suddenly full of wisdomosity about relationships. I have become an expert in the oven of love.

9:30 p.m.

No sign of my rival in love, the incredibly useless stick insect of the universe and back. Good. Oh, maybe she's dead. How sad. Never mind.

The Stiff Dylans are coming on in a minute.

9:40 p.m.

Wow, the place has gone hog wild!!! Girls were shrieking

when Masimo came to the microphone and said "*Ciao.* We are back."

10:15 p.m.

I am quite literally in a dance inferno. Hit it, lads! The whole club is kicking. All the boys are fit and cool and Masimo is a brilliant singer and sooooo sexy on stage.

10:35 p.m.

Girls were even trying to get up on the stage to get to the Stiff Dylans! One got up and managed to kiss Masimo on the cheek before she was pulled away by a bouncer. Vair vair embarrassing. The final straw was when Nauseating P. Green tried to get up on stage. No danger of her managing that. She got one knee on and then just jumped up about a foot and came back down again. She would have been stuck there for eternity going up and down, but a bouncer came and pulled her away. Her new enormous glasses were on sideways.

Attractive.

10:40 p.m.

I'm sweating a bit so I had better go and cool myself down

in the loos; the last thing a Luuurve God wants is a slippery girlfriend. I have been doing some of my best moves in front of him. Just subtly, you know, nothing flash, although I did have to shove Jas quite hard once or twice to get her to let me in. Now and again I have glanced at him and then looked away. Wet Lindsay has been dancing in front of him with her eyes fixed on him like she was trying to hypnotise him.

I said to Ro Ro, "As the Swan of Avon said in his famous snogging comedy *Midsummer Night's Snog*, 'When you wanteth to snog a Luuurve God, do not prithee danceth about like a prat with stick-insect legs.'"

Rosie said, "Ye are wiseth in the extremeth, my palleth. Billy also saideth, 'Forsooth and lack a day, do not have ye a tiny forehead, otherwise you are simply askething for a duffing-up scenario... eth.'"

Then we laughed like the proverbial draineth.

10:50 p.m.

As I went to the loos I saw Rollo and Jools snogging for England on the steps. And then in the corridor by the loos I found Mabs snogging someone – I couldn't tell who it was boywise as I didn't recognise the back of his head. As I went by, Mabs opened her eyes and winked at me. What was she on about? Then she pointed at her wristwatch, with the other hand she held up three fingers, then she did the thumbsies up. Still snogging. What in the name of arse? I went into the loos.

In the tarts' enclosure

Blimey! Good job I did a make-up check; I looked like a red-faced loon.

Then I got it! Mabs was saying that she had got up to number six on the snogging scale – a kiss lasting over three minutes without a break!

Yes! She'll be thrilled as a thrilled thing on a thrilling holiday.

Unless it was Spotty Norman.

They were all at it. Apart from me. It was so long since I'd snogged anyone, I couldn't even remember what it felt like to snog. Perhaps I had lost my technique. I tried a quick snog on the back of my arm, but it was very difficult to tell the difference between arm and lipsies.

I must take my shoes off for a moment. I went into a piddly-diddly kiosk and sat down on the loo seat. Hmmm, my

feet looked a bit red and swollen; maybe I should take my shoes off. But if I got them off I might never get them back on.

Perhaps if I just lay down on the floor and put my feet above my head on the loo they would go down a bit.

I got down on the floor and put my feet up. Ohhh, that was a bit better. I heard a door open and Wet Lindsay said, "What's going on?"

This really weedy voice answered, "Well, it looks like they're going to be having a break any time."

It was Astonishingly Dim Monica, the missing link between human beings and frogs.

Wet Lindsay said, "OK, I'd better get in there."

ADM said, "Treat 'em mean, keep 'em keen!"

And Lindsay said, "I don't think I have any worries about keenness if Thursday is anything to go by. They are very passionate, the Italians."

And she laughed.

God I hate her.

I lay on the floor for a moment feeling really really bad and miz, but then I remembered that I was not a facsimile of a sham. I was following my dream, I was living the dream! I struggled up to my feet. Owwww... *Sacré* bloody *bleu.*

Back in the club

The band were having a break – no sign of them. I could see Wet Lindsay hovering around near the dressing-room door. Appalling tart. The Ace Gang were all off grooving.

Rosie shouted over, "Come and dance, we're having a groovathon."

I said, "I think I'll sit this one out and just, you know, absorb the vibes."

Rosie said, "You mean your feet are hurting because you are wearing baby's shoes."

I gave her my cross-eyed Klingon look and she nutcased off.

Sitting down, I was doing a bit of shoulder dancing to the music when an arm appeared in front of me and handed me a drink. It was a brown arm, it had a gold ring on the third finger. I looked up, and it was Masimo's arm. And he was attached to it.

He smiled down at me. "*Ciao,* you are having tired from dancing?"

I went red – thank God it was dark. I took a big gulp from the drink and practically choked myself, but I managed to

say, "Yes, I mean, *sí*. I am indeed having a tired from dancing, yes indeedy."

He said, "It is long since I have seen you. I am glad you came. I would like, if you would like, to have your telephone number."

Oh now, what was the right response to that? Glaciosity requires that I say something like, "Maybe some other time." But he is a Luuurve God. He is bending over me, his gorgey lips are only inches away from mine.

Anyway, I was saved the trouble of doing anything because Dom came over. "Hi, Georgia, long time no dig. How are you?"

Before I could say anything he went on to Masimo. "Listen, mate, sorry to drag you away, but some bloke wants to talk to us about a tour in the North. Can you come over?"

Masimo looked at me with those amazing amber eyes. "I will see you later."

And he touched my shoulder and squeezed it very gently.

Oh no, he had said it. He had said the famous "See you later".

Donner and bloody Blitzen. Absobloodylutely typico.

I have got such bad snog withdrawal!!!

Merde and merdy *merde merde merde*. And a half.

I hobbled over to the groovathon and bobbed around trying to talk to Rosie as Sven flung her about like a deflated balloon.

Pant pant, groove groove.

"He's asked me for my phone number!"

Rosie yelled, "Result! Or Resultio, as we must say!"

I looked across and I could see the Stiff Dylans talking to some bloke at a table. Masimo leaned back in his chair and balanced on one leg. The chair leg, I mean, you fools!! Not his leg. He looked across at me and just looked and locked eyes with me. He was doing sticky eyes with me. It was a moment of incredibilosity. However, it began to feel like a staring competition because the mascara on my eyes was vair heavy. Eventually he looked away because someone handed him a drink, so I could blink.

11:30 p.m.

Band back on.

I am sooo excited. I said to Jas, "Do you think I should accidentally hang around as he comes off stage at the next break?"

Jas looked like she was thinking, *Oh dear.*

I can't rely on her opinion. I must consult with the gang. I rounded them up eventually for a gang meeting in the tarts' wardrobe. I was going to ask the Hornmeister but he was slow dancing with Rachel and she had her head on his shoulder. He was stroking her hair, but as I passed he looked, I don't know, not like Dave the Laugh. So I thought I wouldn't ask about Masimo.

When Mabs emerged from her snogathon it turned out to be one of the trainee tossers she was snogging. I said, "Mabs, you have vair little pridenosity, that is one of Tosser Thompson's mates."

Mabs was a bit surly and covered in her own lippy. She looked like she had been attacked by a ferret. She said, "Well, I'm only practising on him."

Fair enough.

It was a moment or two before I realised that Sven was in the loos with us.

Rosie managed to persuade him to wait outside. I don't like to think what she promised him as a reward, but she did mention herrings...

I said, "Masimo wanted my phone number and I was

just about to give it to him."

Rosie said, "Oo-er, missus."

But I just looked at her and went on. "I was just about to give him my number, when Dom called him away. So now the thing is, should I hang around at the end of the set and give it to him?"

Rosie was just about to say oo-er again until I kicked her.

Ellen said, "Well, if, you know... if he asked you, and well, he asked you... that means, doesn't it, that he, you know... wants it."

We all looked at Ellen.

I said, "Anyway, what do you think I should do?"

Jas said, "I would hang around. I mean, it's ridiculous playing silly games, isn't it?"

Rosie said, "Yes, I think cut to the action – go up and give him the phone number and then leave."

Hmmmm. Yes, that sounded good. Everyone else was nodding. And when all of the Ace Gang nod, you know that... er... you know that a nod is as good as a wink to a blind badger.

We did the Klingon salute and make-up duties and then went out of the loos together. The others careered back on to

the dance floor, apart from Mabs, because the trainee tosser was hanging around outside the door. I lurked at the back of the club near the tarts' wardrobes for a moment to sit down on the stairs. My tootsies were soooooo sore. I tried to ease my feet in my shoes but they wouldn't move. I must save my tootsies for a last walk across to give Masimo my telephone number.

12:30 a.m.

Outside the cloakroom getting our coats out. The band must be going to come out soon. I put my coat on slowly.

Dave the Laugh was with Rachel and she was linking up with him. He said, "S'later, Georgia."

And Rachel gave me a big hug goodbye. "Great to see you, Gee."

After they had gone I said to Jas, "Is it? Why? Why is she hugging me? We don't do hugging, do we? And we are very nearly mates."

Jas said, "I think it's nice that she's so friendly."

I didn't. It was weird. I went on. "Is she on the turn? Or perhaps there's a touch of the Froggy in her family? I must warn Dave."

I was so distracted by Rachel that at first I didn't sense the Luuurve presence. He was just coming out of the dressing room, putting his jacket on. How come even putting his jacket on was sexy?

I had the Particular and Cosmic Horn and a heavy dose of red-bottomosity.

He turned round to say something to one of the others, and Wet Lindsay appeared like the Bride of Dracula. She just appeared from nowhere. She was playing with her hair and she trailed her hand across Masimo's arm. He looked round and saw her and smiled. She kissed his cheek and said something in his ear. He said something back and then she whispered something else. He looked at her and sort of shrugged his shoulders. She smiled and then linked arms with him and they went off together.

Oh God.

1:00 a.m.

And we had to walk all the way home because we had done the usual "Jas's dad is picking us up" to my dad and "Georgia's dad is picking us up" to Jas's. In a fit of

desperation I thought about phoning Vati and telling him we were stuck, but then I would have to talk to him, and I didn't want to talk ever again.

1:30 a.m.

I managed to sneak in. Actually, I didn't really need to sneak because Dad was snoring so loudly in his bedroom. And Gordy was snoring in the lavatory. And, oh good, Libby was snoring in my bed.

Lying quite literally in my bed of pain

2:30 a.m.

I have tried to get my shoes off but I am so tired and upset I can't be bothered to struggle with them. So I've left them on and put my jimmyjams on over them. My feet hurt like billio, but not as much as my heart.

2:35 a.m.

What is it with boys and Wet Lindsay?

I dither about for hours thinking, *Shall I have glaciosity or shall I have boldnosity? What botty huggers shall I wear? Is the orang-utan gene making a surprise appearance?* and so on, for hours and hours. And she just goes up to him and says, "Come with me," and off he goes.

Unbelievable.

2:40 a.m.

I am not going to give up this time, though, I have had my heart burned in the oven too many times.

I am going to think of a cunning plan.

2:45 a.m.

Oh brilliant, Angus and Gordy are playing the mouse game with my shoefeet.

Owwwwwwwww.

2:46 a.m.

Libby woke up from her snoring extravaganza and sat up with her arms crossed. She said, "Bad Georgia. Sshhhhhhh!"

I tried to cuddle her but she got the hump and stomped off with Gordy under one arm to go to her own bed.

Rejected by my sister as well.

And she didn't even leave Sandra behind.

Sunday June 5th

10:00 a.m.

I woke up and I saw my shoefeet looking at me from the bottom of the bed.

Then I felt the pain… but I am going to have to bear it and take them off.

10:15 a.m.

Oh please. My shoes are embedded in my feet. My skin has been cut by the straps and then in the night everything has all swollen up. You can't even see the straps because the flesh has covered them up. Oh brilliant. Now I will have to have my feet cut off.

10:30 a.m.

Worse than that, I am going to have to ask Mum for help because I can't walk. I will never never laugh at Slim's feet again, because I have got them.

11:00 a.m.

Mum bustled into my room. When I heard her I put my shoefeet under the blankets. She said, "Come on and have

some breakfast. Dad's taken Libbs round to Josh's, so it's just you and me. We can do something nice if you like."

I said, "It will have to be something that doesn't involve walking about."

She said, "Don't tell me you are tired. Honestly, I had so much energy at your age – I'd go to parties and then play tennis the next day."

I said, "Well, I would like to play tennis, believe me, but Parky Elvis would never let me play in high heels – it would ruin his courts."

Mum said, "What are you talking about?"

I had to tell her about the shoes. Then I showed her my feet. She went ballisticisimus. "You STUPID stupid girl. Honestly, you have done some stupid stupid things in your time, but this takes the biscuit of stupidity. How could you do this to yourself? I told you about those shoes! Look at your lovely feet – ruined!!!"

And so on for about four centuries.

Mum had a go at getting them off herself, but I couldn't bear the pain, and in the end she said, "I'm going to have to phone for the doctor. On a Sunday."

Oh nooooo. I am so humiliated.

Midday

I heard Mum phoning the doctor. She said, "I am so sorry to disturb you, doctor, but it's Georgia..."

There was a pause.

"No, no the elbows are, you know, quite stable, it's... well, she has got her shoes embedded in her feet."

1:00 p.m.

I saw Dr Clooney's car arrive in the driveway and he got out. I hobbled back into bed – ouch ouch and double ouch.

Thank goodness Vati was out.

I heard giggling from downstairs.

1:25 p.m.

Oh yes, that's right, Mutti, just chat and flirt with Dr Clooney while I lie up here with my dancing days over.

Honestly.

Eventually Mum and Dr Clooney came up. My mum had changed into her short black dress and done her hair and make-up. Vair vair sad.

Dr Clooney gave me his crinkly smile. "Well, well, this is a first for me."

He is nice, though, very reassuring and funny. He didn't ramble on at me. He just looked at my feet and pulled a bit and I went "Owwwwww."

Then he said, "Hmmm, I'm going to have to give you a local anaesthetic and cut them off."

And I said, "Oh, doctor, can't you save them?"

And he started saying that he meant the shoes, not my feet, and I said, "I know. Can't you save them?"

Mum gave me her worst look, but Dr Clooney thought it was vair *amusant*.

2:00 p.m.

This is quite nice, actually, in a painful way. Dr Clooney cut off the straps and pulled the bits out with tweezers. He even had to put some stitches in the deep cuts in my feet. It hurt A LOT but I was brave as a bee on army manoeuvres. They are all bandaged up. Mum is bringing me snacks.

She sat down on my bed and I let her, I don't know why, I am probably weak.

She said, "So, Stumpy, did you have a nice time last night at least?"

I blurted out, "Well, it was megafab at first because Masimo asked me for my phone number, but then at the end Wet Lindsay made him go home with her."

Mum said, "I used to know a girl like Wet Lindsay. She got married to a boy I really liked."

I said, "Oh thanks, Mum, you're really cheering me up."

And she said, "Well, every cloud has a silver lining, because she is really really unhappily married. So all's well that ends well."

Sometimes my mum, and I don't want to get carried away by this, but sometimes she can be almost like a real person.

4:00 p.m.

It's quite cosy just me and Mum together. I was asking her stuff about how to make any twit fall in love with you (without actually mentioning that I had read her book, otherwise she would know that I had been rifling through her drawers and unreasonably lose her rag).

As we slurped our fifth hot choccy, Mum had a quick touch of wisdomosity. She said, "I think you should just relax and be yourself. What is the point of being a callous sophisticate, or tricking a boy into liking you? He's bound to find out eventually. It's the only real advice I can give you. Be your own natural self."

I said, "Like when you put that black dress on and loads of make-up when Dr Clooney came round?"

She stood up. "Well, be yourself within reason. At least get the right size shoes next time."

We have decided not to bother Vati with the shoefoot incident and settled for "girl trouble" until Wednesday, when I should be able to walk again.

I said, "You mean I get time off from Stalag 14 for good behaviour? Oh, thank you, thank you, Mutti, you know how much I love you."

I have agreed to be very nice to Vati and Libby and Mutti for the next couple of days in recognition of Mum's act of charity.

Midnight

I wonder what Masimo did when they left the gig?

I wonder what number they got up to?

Erlack. Shutup, mind, shutup.

Monday June 6th

8:30 a.m.

Well, I may get pretend-ill a lot. Dad brought me a cup of tea, and Mum phoned Jas and told her I'd be off school with a tummy bug for a couple of days.

Mmmm snuggle snuggle.

Ouch ouchy ouch.

10:00 a.m.

This is the life (ish). I am lolling in bed and everyone is out. I think I'll just hobble downstairs for a snack.

10:30 a.m.

I haven't been in the house on my own on a weekday for ages. It is an unknown world of peace and quiet and… cats. So this is what happens when we, the baldy folk, are out – the house turns into Kittykat Heaven.

Naomi is stretched out comfortably on the front-room sofa. I hope she has enough cushions. She sleepily opened one eye when I put my head round the door, but seeing I had no snacks she went back to sleep. Make yourself at home, Ms Minx.

Gordy is snoozing on the telephone table, probably

expecting an urgent call. And Angus seems to be covered in jam and lolling about on Mum's silk blouse that she left on the ironing board. She will go ballisticisimus.

I would move them, but I can't be expected to because of my condition.

10:40 a.m.

I opened the fridge for snacksies and took out the butter. It has a small paw mark in it. Surely the furry maniacs haven't learned how to open the fridge door? Freaky-deaky. They'll be dressing up in our clothes soon and driving the clown car off for a cat picnic.

Good.

12:00 p.m.

Fed up now. I wonder what the Ace Gang are doing? I bet they're talking about the gig. I bet they're talking about me and Masimo. They had better not say anything bad.

What is there to say that is bad?

I hope they're keeping up the staring campaign against Wet Lindsay. I'm glad I am not in today because she can't show off in front of me.

2:00 p.m.

I have shared two boyfriends with her.

2:10 p.m.

But Robbie, er, I mean the Guitar Plucker only went out with her because she was so upset when he tried to dump her. And she said she was engaged to him when she wasn't. I think she must be a bit unhinged.

She should be.

Actually, the Guitar Plucker acted very nicely about her and me. What I mean is, he dumped her. If anyone is asking for a good dumping, it's her. If he hadn't gone to Kiwi-a-gogo land, all of this wouldn't have happened.

I wonder what would have happened.

3:00 p.m.

I got out his letter and photo, which I had hidden at the back of my drawer. I took them back into bed. What does he say?

"I think about you a lot."

Huh.

He didn't think about me enough to not go to the other side of the world.

He was my first proper love. They say you never forget that.

I looked at the photo. He was vair good-looking, and he was very nice to me.

Even in front of his mates he would always put his arm round me and didn't try to hide me away.

3:45 p.m.

I thought about all the good times.

Maybe I should write to him?

4:00 p.m.

I think I will write.

And maybe send a photo.

I could send him one of when we were in Hamburger-a-gogo. It would remind him of the plans we had to go there with the band.

Ha.

I won't send him the one of me riding the bucking-bronco stool.

4:10 p.m.

Nor the one with that very very old bloke in the Elvis outfit.

4:25 p.m.

Or me at Davy Crockett's diner in the furry beaver hat.

5:00 p.m.

Or one of the ones me and Jas took in private with the bison horns.

No one must ever see those. No one. Not another living soul.

I must remind Jas.

I'll do it now.

5:15 p.m.

Phoned Jas.

"Jas, it's me."

"Hellooooo, how are your feet?"

"Bandaged up. Listen, you must never show anyone our bison-horn pictures."

"Oh, blimey. Hahahahaha. I'd forgotten about them. What a hoot and a half that was."

"Yes, I know that we thought it was very *amusant* at the time, Jas, but pictures of us in the nuddy-pants wearing just bison horns might, well you know, if they fell into the wrong hands."

She was chewing and thinking.

"Oh yeah, I see what you mean. Well, yes, I will only show them to Tom when he gets back. Do you know how many minutes it is until he's back? It's two hundred thousand—"

"Jas, shut up about minutes – you are not a Time Lord, more's the pity. Tell me everything that happened at Stalag 14 today."

6:00 p.m.

Well, that was a very interesting conversation. Not. I will tell you what happened at Stalag 14. Nothing.

I said to Jas, "Were people worried about me, that I had this tummy bug and so on?"

She said, "No, because we all knew it was because your shoes were too small. We said they were too small for your huge feet."

"Jas, I haven't got huge feet."

"You have now! Hahahahahaha!"

Oh charming. I said, "Oh yes, very funny, Jas. If you want a really good laugh why don't you just pop down to casualty."

6:35 p.m.

Anyway, the short and short of it is that no one said anything interesting, and even Wet Lindsay wasn't there because she was doing home study.

6:45 p.m.

Ohmygod. I've just had a horrible thought. Home study – that could mean home study with Masimo.

Surely he can't like her that much.

Surely.

Tuesday June 7th

I'm sick of being an invalid now.

I am sooooo bored and I am, it has to be said, completely hairless – I have spent hours plucking.

6:30 p.m.

Phoned Jas.

She isn't home. They have all gone off to the pictures.

Boo.

I'm even looking forward to my family coming home – that should give you some idea of how desperate I am.

6:50 p.m.

Mum and Dad and Libbs came in.

"Gingee, Gingee, it's meeeeeeeeeeee!!!"

I could hear her panting up the stairs to my room. She kicked open my bedroom door and ran from the door and leaped on to the bed, covering me with kisses.

"I LOBE you, my big big sister."

I couldn't get her off me. "Libby, just let me—"

"Kissy kissy kiss, snoggy snog."

"That's enough, now let me—"

"Mmmmmm, groovy baby."

What is she talking about? She is supposed to be going to nursery school to learn how to grow up, not turn into an even madder person.

Then she stood up on the bed and started thrusting her hips out and singing her favourite: "Sex bum, sex bum, I'm a sex bum."

Quite spectacularly mad.

7:30 p.m.

Mmmmm, quite nice supper of shepherd's pie. On a tray in bed. Mum didn't make it herself, of course, but at least she bothered to buy it. I think it may have given me the strength to go downstairs and watch TV to try and forget my sorrows.

7:33 p.m.

Oh no, I can't, otherwise Dad will spot the shopping bags I have on the end of my feet.

Maybe I can ask him to bring the TV up to my room. It's the least you can do when there's a sick person in the house.

7:35 p.m.

Just about to suggest this when I heard the roar of an engine.

Knowing my life, it would be Grandad on a motorbike in a leather all-in-one suit. And Maisie on the back in a knitted bikini.

I peeped out of my window – and practically fell out of it.

It was Masimo!!! Honestly. On his scooter. He was under my window and just switching the engine off.

I must run run like the wind to... oh no, I couldn't run. I must hobble, hobble like the wind to... no, no, what I must do is – I must remain calm. Calm calm. While all around you everyone is losing their minds you must, you must... put some bloody make-up on immediately, you complete arse!!

7:38 p.m.

Scrabble, scrabble, mascara... lippy and gloss... eyeshadow... please please don't do shaky hand now – I don't want to be a panda with huge feet!!!

Fluffy hair fluffy hair...

What was going on now? What? What???

Mid mascara, did a hobble-trot to the window and looked out.

There was just his scooter there. Like the Vespa Celeste. Had Angus eaten him?

Then I heard the doorbell ring.

Ohgoddygod.

Put something on. Disguise the feet!

Easier said than done.

I must have something.

Scrabbled through my wardrobe.

What about my extra-long jeans? Yes, yes, good thinking. Extra-long jeans, bit of a crouchy leg and… I looked in the full-length mirror. Yes, yes, that would do, you couldn't see my feet at all. I must remember to crouch though, and not hobble.

Right, right, I am ready for when Dad starts his ludicrous shouting up the stairs. It's OK though, because he will just say tummy bug, not shoes cut off.

I must not mention shoes cut off. No one should.

Good, good, that is good.

Excellent.

7:40 p.m.

What was going on?

Couldn't they understand what Masimo was saying? His English wasn't that bad.

8:00 p.m.

What *was* going on? Surely Masimo hadn't come round to see my mum and dad, had he? With my life, I wouldn't be surprised by anything. Perhaps like Dave the Laugh, Masimo fancies my mum.

I crept and shuffled to the top of the stairs. They were in the living room, so I could just hear the muffled sound of voices. Then Libby came bustling along the hall and opened the door to the front room. She waddled into the lounge, saying, "Gordy has done a big poo in his din dins."

Dear Lord.

8:10 p.m.

I had to rush back into my bedroom because Mum suddenly came out of the room to the kitchen and shouted up to me, "Georgia, I know you're at the top of the stairs. Come down – you have a visitor and your father wants to speak to you."

My father?

Wants to speak to me?

I have a visitor?

It's like *Blithering Heights.* If Masimo is dressed in tight breeches and a cravat, I will truly go mad.

I felt really really sick.

I went into the kitchen first.

Mum was making filter coffee. Blimey. I said to her, "What is going on?"

She said, "Oh, we were just having a chat with Masimo. He's lovely, isn't he?"

"Having a chat? Having a CHAT? You have left Vati having a CHAT with someone I never ever want him to talk to about anything. Having a chat about what?"

"Well, he has come to ask us, and in particular your father, if it's all right for him to take you out to dinner next week."

I was quite literally speechless.

8:15 p.m.

Mum made me go into the front room.

Masimo was sitting on the sofa with Libby on his knee. He stood up with her in his arms when I walked in and then he smiled. And when he did that my heart sang. Despite the fresh hell that was about to occur, he was soooooo gorgey.

Vati was standing up in front of the fireplace with his hands behind his back. Then I realised he was smoking a cigar. He never smoked cigars except at Christmas, and then he was sick. What the hell was going on?

He said, "Ah, hello, Georgia. Masimo and I have just been having a chat."

Oh dear God he was using that word again.

Masimo said, "*Ciao*, Georgia."

My vati said, "Do sit down, Georgia. Connie."

It was like being in a cross between a horror film and *My Fair Lady*.

I didn't know what else to do, so I sat down and so did Mum. As soon as we did, Vati and Masimo sat down as well. I fought an overwhelming desire to stand up again to see if they would stand up too.

Dad said, "Masimo has come round to ask if it is all right for him to take you out, and I think after careful thought and a few ground rules that... it would be... acceptable to your mother and myself."

Has he really snapped? He works for the Waterboard, drowning people and driving them out of their homes, but he is not in the Mafia.

He went rambling on about curfews and behaviour. Like the Godfather. He will probably expect us to call him Il Ministrone. Complete and utter bollocks about honour and his family reputation and so on. I was so so embarrassed. And Masimo just said stuff like, "Of course, I will, how you say, take *molto – mi dispiace*, I am sorry for my English, I will take great care of your daughter."

He smiled at me. "She will even have her own helmet."

And Mum laughed like a crazy person, like "helmet" was the funniest word she had ever heard.

9:00 p.m.

I only got a chance to speak to Masimo right at the end of the nightmare scenario. When he went out to go off on his bike I went out to the gate with him. I said, "Masimo, I am so sorry about my parents. I am dispiaggio times a million about them."

He smiled and said, "I thought it was the only way I will get your attention. Now I have your attention, no?"

"Oh yes, you have sure as sure as... eggs... have my attention, matey."

He laughed.

"I like it when you speak, it is like..."

"Rubbish?"

He laughed again and handed me a piece of paper.

"Here, this is for you. Phone me, *cara*, and let me know if you still would like to see me on Tuesday. *Ciao*."

He looked at me with that unwavering look he has. Oh

dear God, I had crumbly knees and jelloid knickers and I sooo wanted to go to the piddly-diddly department.

Then he roared off.

9:05 p.m.

Went back into the house. With a bit of luck I could get in without being seen by the seeing-eye dogs. But oh no, no such luck. Vati came out of the front room.

"He seems like a nice young chap. Keen on sports and so on. Good family, healthy lifestyle."

I said, "Shiny nose, glossy coat, that sort of thing."

He said, "I said to your mum that you're not old enough for boys, you should be concentrating on your studies."

Oh, blimey, I had wandered into the twilight world of Daddom. I wandered off as quickly as I could hobble, saying, "Oooh, do you know, Dad, I've come over all queasy. I must go back to bed."

In my bedroom

Yessssss! Double yesss and wow! I had a date with the Luuurve God. I looked at the piece of paper he had given me. It said, "Masimo 766739. Phone me. Please."

I had his phone number. No waiting around for him to call me. No more s'later for me! I am a s'later-free zone!

10:00 p.m.

God, I'm happy.

The photo of the Guitar Plucker was on the bed looking at me.

Maybe I will write to him.

As a friend.

A loving old friend.

A loving friend who has gone on to more Italian-Stallion-type things!

I wish I could ring everyone and tell them. I am deffo going to school tomorrow, even if Jas has to carry me there.

10:30 p.m.

I will never sleep with excitemondo!

What shall I wear? Are we really going to go out to dinner or is that just a snogging ploy?

I've never been out to dinner with a boy before.

11:00 p.m.

I tell you this, I am not having cappuccino and the foam-beard experience. If we are going to dinner I'd better plan what I'm having in advance because I don't want the attractive dribbly tomato sauce effect on my snogging arena (mouth).

"What PANTS through yonder window breaks?"

Wednesday June 8th

Stalag 14

Feet miraculously better. I am down to light bandages now!!

But even if I had no feet, I would be walking on air… Hahahahahaha, that's quite a good joke.

I said that to Jas, "It's a good joke, isn't it, Jazzy Spazzy?"

She said, "What is?"

In the corridor

9:00 a.m.

Saw Wet Lindsay, hahahaha. She glared at me and told me to hurry up to class. Hurry up yourself, old dumpee thong.

Fives court emergency tactical meeting

Rosie said, "'Be prepared' is always my motto."

Ellen said, "I didn't know you were a Girl Guide."

Rosie said, "Didn't you? Oh yes, me and Sven are keen Girl Guides, dib dib dib and so forth."

The whole thing would have disintegrated into madnosity, so I quickly said, "So what do you think I should do? How shall I handle it? Do you think he is really going to take me out to dinner?"

After much consultation and nodding, the gang have decided that we should have a mock date to prepare me for my date.

We are all going to meet round Ro Ro's place on Saturday when her parents are at the cricket. We're going to practise for my hot date. There will be snacks. But no Sven.

I had to beg and plead with Rosie. She said, "He would be vair vair useful, he could give us the boy point of view."

I said, "Couldn't he give you the boy point of view and then you pass it on to me, or you will just snog all day in front of us. Also, he is bound to smash something to smithereens."

Rosie has reluctantly agreed to ban him.

At home

6:00 p.m.

I am dying to tell Dave the Laugh.

Phoned him when the olds went out to a parents evening for Libby at the local school. Surely no school is going to take her on. She has been forbidden to sing the "Bum arse song" and not allowed to take Gordy. I still think it was a mistake to let her wear her leopard outfit, because a) it is for a child half her size and b) she becomes a leopard in it. But you can't tell people.

Anyway, where was I? Oh yes, Dave the Laugh.

I called him. I hoped my best friend Rachel was not there.

Dave answered. "Hello, Sensation Seeker."

"Dave, it's me. Something vair vair great and *bon* has happened. I am going on a date with Masimo. He came round on his scooter and asked my dad if he could take me to dinner. He asked my dad if he could take me to dinner!!!"

Dave said, "What an amazing bunch of crawlers the Italians are."

"Dave!!! Don't you get it? He has asked me out! I am going out with him!"

Dave said, "Well, I'm glad for you, Sex Kitty, but

remember what I said; he may be playing the field. He may just be blowing his Cosmic Horn."

He sounded a bit funny.

"You sound a bit funny, Dave. Are you all right?"

Dave said, "Well, not really, I had to finish with Rachel."

Finish with Rachel? I said, "Why? I mean, she's so... Well, she is so, you know... isn't she?"

Blimey, I've turned into Ellen.

Dave said, "It just wasn't right. But anyway, she's very upset. She's just gone actually. She came round and cried and I feel pretty bad."

I said, "Oh, I'm sorry."

But actually I'm not sorry at all. After I'd rung off I told Jas that, because she was my next phone call. It's not often I get a telephone window of opportunity in my house, so I am packing all my calls in.

Jas said, "Why are you bothered who Dave goes out with? He is not in your harem or anything. And another thing: Rachel was nice – not like you."

God, she can be annoying. I wish I hadn't called her now, especially as she did that "Guess how many minutes it is until Tom gets home?" thing again.

Saturday June 11th

2:00 p.m.

All the gang gathered at Rosie's for my practice date.

Rosie said she would be Masimo, and the rest of them would watch and be the judges, like in a sort of snogging *Come Dancing*.

Come Snogging, in fact.

2:10 p.m.

Rosie went off to her bedroom. She said, "I'm going to be Masimo, so I have to get in the mood for luuurve."

She came back five minutes later wearing a false beard, with a banana down her jeans.

I said, "Why have you got a banana down your jeans?"

Rosie said, "It was Sven's suggestion. He said it is representative of the pant python."

Ellen said, "I, er... do you mean like a boy's, er, well..."

Rosie said, "Exactomondo, my little pally." Which was a bit off-putting, actually.

Jas said, "OK, let's get on, because I have to get home earlyish. It's only ninety-nine hours till Tom gets home and I must prepare myself. What will you do when you first see him?" She pointed to Rosie, who was walking in a very peculiar way and waggling her beard. "There he is – tall, tanned Italian, sophisticated. So what do you do?"

I said, "Er, leap on him and snog him within an inch of his life? Taking care not to strangle myself on his false beard, or disturb his banana."

Jools said, "What does it say in the *How to Make Any Twit Fall in Love with You* book?"

Mabs was officially in charge of the book, so she looked up "first impressions".

3:00 p.m.

I have to hip wiggle up to him, look at him, look away, fiddle with my hair and do a bit of flicking. If I have any spare time I need to lick my lips a bit.

Mabs said, "The book says you should say something light and interesting to start the conversation. Also, if he says anything funny, you have to laugh like the proverbial drain."

I did hip wiggle, flicky, licky over to Rosie, while the rest of them sat looking and chewing. Rosie said (in what she imagines is an Italian accent but actually sounds like a fool), "*Ciao.*"

I said, "*Ciao*. Er, *prego*."

"*Ciao*."

All the gang were ogling me.

I said, "Masimo, did you know that the Spartans... you know in the old days of Sparta, which is quite nearish to Italy..."

Rosie had pretended to fall asleep. She said, "Get on with it."

I said, "Well, they used to keep teenage boys half-starved so that they had to go out and steal food, and if they got caught they would beat them to within an inch of their lives."

They all just looked at me.

Mabs said, "Do you call that light and interesting?"

I do actually. That is the deep sadnosity of my life; I find it vair difficult to be as superficial as others.

Jools said, "Think of something that he's interested in – think of something to do with Rome or something."

I tried again. "Did you know that the Pope has people who watch him poo to make sure he is a bloke and not a woman, because of Pope Joan?"

Rosie said, "You are not, as such, getting the hang of this, are you?"

An hour later

I am allowed to mention music, the weather, or something to do with him.

I said, "Yeah, but all I know about him is that I fancy the arse off him."

5:00 p.m.

After four packets of reviving Pringles we have managed to decide on, "*Ciao*, great to see you." and "What a fine evening."

Providing it is not tipping it down, which would make me a fool.

Now on to the meal.

Essentially, I have to pretend to eat a lot, but not really eat anything in case I choke to death.

Jas said, "You could have a nourishing soup, but don't do that slurping thing that you do."

I said, "What slurping thing?"

Jas said, "Oh, I can't go in to it now, I have to be off. I'm just saying don't do it."

And she went off.

How annoying is she?

6:00 p.m.

I have to listen to him a LOT.

Jools said, "And when you laugh, don't do your ad hoc laughing and let your nose spread all over your face."

6:30 p.m.

Then we got on to the snogging bit.

I said, "Do you think Italians snog the same as English boys?"

Rosie said, "I don't know if they do anything different with their tongues or what their ear work is like. You will have to give us a complete and full report. What number will you let him go up to on the first date?"

"I thought number six. A kiss lasting over three minutes without a break suggests deep sensuality without going that little bit too far into acting like a tart."

Then Rosie said, "Finally, as you haven't had any snogging practice for a while, try an experimental snog on the back of my leg."

What???

Absolutely not, not a snowball's chance in hell.

No and three times NO.

6:45 p.m.

On my knees snogging the back of Rosie's leg while the Ace Gang watch me.

Why am I doing this?

Rosie was shouting instructions. "Yes, yes, that's good. Good. And breathe. Too much teeth!! Too much teeth!!! A bit more sucky. Flicky tongue and... finish."

Good grief.

Have you ever snogged the back of someone's leg? Someone who is one of your mates and is wearing a false beard? Well, I hope you never have to, that is all I'm saying.

7:00 p.m.

I said as I was leaving, "Do you think I should ask him what his intentions are *vis à vis* Old Thongy?"

Mabs said, "I think you should act as if she doesn't exist and just find a way to subtly undermine her."

Hmmm. Good advice.

We are indeedy the Wise Women of the Forest of Snog.

Monday June 13th
English
2:00 p.m.

I have never laughed so much in my entire life. Today we had our first full rehearsal of *MacUseless.*

And what is even more vair vair amusing is that the Foxwood boys came to the rehearsal and Dave the Laugh was one of them.

The whole production is bound for the history books of life.

Dave and the lads were bussed in to the school and it was absolute pandemonium. Every girl in the school got up from their desk and started waving and screeching out the windows as the lads trooped across the playground. Hawkeye and her special storm troopers threatened us with embalming, beheading, etc., but no one paid any attention.

Those of us in the play went down to the main hall for our usual tongue-lashing from the enormous bee woman (Slim). The boys were all together at the back when we came in. As I passed by, Hawkeye said, "Georgia Nicolson, are you wearing mascara?"

I said, "It's for the bright lights, Miss Heaton. If you don't wear eye make-up the audience can't see the expression, and that actually detracts from the emotional impact of—"

She said, "Shut up."

Then she picked on Ellen. "Ellen, why are you wearing lip gloss?"

"It's for the play, Miss Heaton."

"Oh, yes, and what part are you playing?"

When Ellen said she was a witch, she was made to go to the loos and take off her lip gloss.

When Slim took to the stage, the lads started softly singing, "Who ate all the pies, who ate all the pies?"

Slim was shaking like a loon on shaking tablets.

"That's enough. Quieten down. I expect grown-up behaviour from all of you. You are being given the opportunity to show us that our trust in you is not misplaced. I know that I can rely on you all to act with decorum and maturity."

And that's when the first stink bomb went off.

Backstage

Mr Attwood, our part-time caretaker and full-time loon, is having a spaz attack to end all spaz attacks. He was up near

the roof fixing some lights to the lighting bar, and one of the lads removed his ladder.

Dave seems to have cheered up, even though he has broken Rachel's heart – allegedly. I said kindly, "She'll get over it."

Dave said, "As I have said many many times, Georgia, you are all heart. Are you going to be wearing a skimpy skirt and tights for your part as Macduff?"

And I said, "Why, was Macduff a transvestite?"

And Dave said, "Yes."

He is on "lights", which essentially means he hangs about backstage flirting and causing mayhem, and then switches a light on at the beginning. And he even did that at the wrong time.

Hanging around backstage with the lads and Dave the Laugh
3:15 p.m.

I have laughed so much that I almost forgot about Masimo. I told Dave about the fact that the Hamburgese, bless them, call knickers "panties", and it has entranced Dave beyond measure. He doesn't seem as heartbroken as he should be considering he has callously dumped his girlfriend.

3:20 p.m.

Dave has started this "pants" business, which he won't stop, and has given me an awful stitch. I cannot stop laughing. Miss Wilson is clearly going to kill me soon, but I can't stop. Essentially, he substitutes "pants" for everything, and it is vair vair *amusant* indeed. For instance, when everyone was on stage doing the battle scene, he started singing "Onward Christian Soldiers", but he introduced "pants" as a subtheme. So the lyrics in his Pants land are, "Onward Christian soldiers, marching as to war, with the PANTS of Jesus going on before." Although, as I pointed out, the American version would be "with the PANTIES of Jesus going on before."

3:30 p.m.

"The hills are alive with the sound of PANTS."

3:33 p.m.

Nauseating P. Green is doubling up her roles. She is my wife and also in charge of munitions.

3:35 p.m.

Well, when I say in charge of munitions, she has got a starting pistol thing that's going to be used for sound effects for the battle scenes. Also she has some bangers that she'll be letting off backstage with Spotty Norman as her co-idiot.

Miss Wilson told us that the first production of a Shakespants play in 1613 ended when a cannon used in the production set the thatched roof on fire and the theatre burned to the ground. So we can always hope for the best.

3:37 p.m.

Mr Attwood has got his fire buckets at the ready, so there is every chance of a conflagration. It would be a fitting end to his school career to be present when it burned down.

3:50 p.m.

Does anyone remember the world-renowned orange-juggling scene in *MacUseless*? No? Well, there is one in our production. Miss Wilson says it adds colour to the play. Hmmmm. How mad is she? It's during the banquet scene when MacUseless is planning to kill the other MacScottish person. She has got Melanie Griffiths and Mabs (who are trees in the later scene) to do the juggling.

They are vair vair useless at it but she has promised them they can wear false moustaches.

I said to Dave, "I am worried about Melanies nungas, I hope there is no unfortunate mix-up in the juggling bits."

You should see Spotty Norman and the other youth hanging around every time she's on stage, pretending to coil up electric cable and so on just so they can ogle her nungas.

Even Dave was watching her as oranges flew everywhere. He said, "That girl certainly has got a couple of areas of outstanding natural beauty. I hope they are adequately protected."

4:30 p.m.

As we left school Dave the Laugh walked along with us. He had his arm round me. It felt really, erm, friendly. Although, as it was Dave, his hand did sort of casually drift on to my nunga. I had to give him a yellow card and a stern warning. It obviously affected him because as he went off to his house he gave me a kiss on the mouth (!) and said, "S'later."

Hmmmmmm.

Home

Mum and Vati and Libbs and the furry freaks, have gone out on a clown-car expedition. Excellent.

Time to phone Masimo.

Put on my lippy gloss and a bit of mascara.

Right, here goes.

Better change out of my school uniform and put something gorgey but casual on.

Right, here goes.

Are boy entrancers going a bit far?

Right, here goes.

One minute later

"Jas."

"What?"

"I'm going to phone Masimo ."

"Good. Goodbye."

"Jas."

"What? Look, it's only twenty-four hours until Tom gets back and I—"

"OK, chocks away, Jas, I'm going in."

Two minutes later

Right, this is it. He has asked me out, so that must mean he wants me to go out with him. Unless the number he gave me was a safety-deposit-box number or his idea for a lottery number. Uh-oh, my brain has wandered off to Madland. Better get a grip.

Light, cheerful, with a hint of Eastern promise – that is what I must be.

Should I break the ice with a joke?

Yes, yes, that's a good idea. I'll just say, "*Ciao,* Masimo. It's me, Georgia. Hey, what is black and lies on top of the water shouting knickers? He will say in his lovely accent, "*Non capisco,* Georgia. What is black and lies on top of the *acqua* shouting knickers?" And I will say "crude oil". And he will laugh and I will laugh and it will be... er... a laughathon.

Good, good, excellent. And I will leave Sparta and Pope Joan out of it completely.

And pants.

Two minutes later

Phoned the number.

Oh noooooo, it was ringing. He might answer it. Ohhhhnoooo.

I slammed the phone down.

Calm calm calmy calm calm.

I was just about to try again, when the phone rang.

I picked it up and said, "Look, can you get off the phone? I am just about to make a very important phone call."

And Masimo said, "Georgia? Have you call me?"

Ohbloodyblimey.

I forgot about telling him the joke and made up some ludicrous story about me just having rung him when the doorbell rang and it was people collecting for Overseas Pants. I don't know why I said that, I just had pants on the brain from Dave the Laugh.

Anyway, I don't think he understood me because he still wants to go out with me.

It was gorgey and fabby to speak to him.

He has got a lovely voice on the phone.

He is going to meet me tomorrow at 7:30 at a little Italian restaurant that he knows.

Buennissimo!!!

Tuesday June 14th

The day dragged by. I started my make-up in double French. I could only risk nail varnish because if Madame Slack saw a hint of cover-up it would be off to the guillotine for me.

Ran home.

Operation Go on a Date with a Luuurve God and Not Make a Complete and Utter Prat of Myself

5:00 p.m.

My feet, thankfully, seem to be their normal selves again.

Dithering around in my room.

The phone has rung about forty million times from the Ace Gang asking me what I'm wearing. "Not much" is the answer, because I am too busy answering the phone.

6:30 p.m.

I can't dither around for much longer. For once my hair is quite nearly not useless, and I think my boots and skirt look good together. My feet fit into the boots as well, which is a plus.

I went downstairs as quietly as I could, but the Mad Committee were all there to see me off. All lined up by the

door. Even Angus had come in from his canoodling with Naomi. He was in the kitchen coughing and choking and looking like he was being sick. Then I noticed that was because he had a frog in his mouth that he was trying to eat. How disgusting and mad is that? It was still alive as well. Mum got into her usual position on the table and screamed at Dad to chase him out. Gordy tried to snack on it and Angus just biffed him over the head. I took the opportunity to sneak out.

7:30 p.m.

I was sooooo nervy as I arrived at the restaurant. He was outside waiting for me. He is the best-looking person I have ever seen. Why would he like me? Maybe he feels sorry for me?

Maybe he's a Christian and he thinks I'm a bit mentally subnormal.

Yes, that might be it. He might be an Italian Lady Cliff Richard.

He smiled at me when he saw me and suddenly I felt like the most beautiful girl in the world. He said, "You came. I am so glad and happy."

He held the door open for me. It was very like what I imagine a grown-up feels like. The owner of the restaurant came over and said, "Good evening, Masimo, *come sta*?"

And they chatted in Italian. Then we went to our table. I sat down without smashing the chair to smithereens, which is a good start.

Ten minutes later

We have ordered our food and I think I very nearly haven't said anything too mad. Or maybe it's because Masimo doesn't speak English well enough to know that I am being a fule.

Twenty minutes later

Then I inadvertently started the pants scenario again. I am going to have to kill Dave the Laugh. The Pantsmeister. Stopit stopit.

Masimo said, "My home, my family, is Verona. So beautiful. I would like you to see it one day. It is where *Romeo and Juliet* was set."

I was chomping on pizza as he was talking. I was doing quite well, cutting it up very small so that I didn't have any

bits falling out of my mouth, but then I momentarily broke my vow of sanity and quoted from *Romeo and Juliet*. I said, "Oh I love Rom and Jul, especially that bit when he compares her to the moon – you know, when he sees her and says, "But soft, what PANTS through yonder window breaks."

And then I started honking and snorting with laughter. Oh nooooooo.

Fortunately Masimo laughed as well. Not in a "quickly I'll get to the phone and someone keep her talking" sort of way. In a nice way. Like he really likes me.

An hour later

The meal was amazingly all right. I find him really easy to talk to. He is sort of in between Dave and the Guitar Plucker. I don't tell as many jokes and do stupidnosity with him as I do with Dave, but I don't get all tongue-tied and full of ludicrosity like I did with the Guitar Plucker.

I realised I was having a lovely time. I said a little inward thank-you prayer to Our Lord Sandra.

Then the snoggosity tension began to build. He touched my hand and looked into my eyes. His amber eyes have got little flecky bits of deeper yellow in them. Oh blimey, we were doing sticky eyes. I could feel my brain trickling out of my head.

He said, "Your eyes, they are like a pussy cat that has drunk *vino rosso*."

So is that a good or bad thing?

I took it as good and tried to keep any image of cross-eyed Gordy out of my mind.

He paid for our pizzas and then he said, "Would you like to walk? It is a nice night. We could look at the stars together."

I resisted saying, "Twinkle twinkle little PANTS."

We walked along to the edge of town and on to the back fields. It was a lovely soft evening, and as we walked he said, "Are you *freddo*?"

Oh dear God! He wasn't going to talk about elves and hobbits, like boys did, was he?

But then he said, "I am sorry, I mean are you, er, in English... cold?"

I said, "Well, I..."

And he put his arm around me.

I was almost fainting with anticipation. My whole body

was on high snog alert. I wondered what he would do next.

He said, "Look, *cara*, a shooting star."

And we saw a shooting star. I wished very hard in my head for world peace, and to get to number six.

And it happened!!!

Not world peace, obviously, although you never know.

When I looked up at the shooting star he put his hand on my chin and gently turned my head towards his. Then he kissed me like he did the first time we saw each other. Just a little soft kiss. Like Jas's lezzie aunt's kiss.

I thought, *Oh no, here we go again on to the rack of love.* But then he kissed me again. A bit harder this time. It was soooo fab and groovy and gorge. I accidentally began singing that famous song from *The Sound of Music* in my brain. "The hills are alive with the sound of PANTS!" Shutup brain. And get out of my brain, Julie Andrews. You snog people in leather shorts if you like.

As my brain was burbling on to itself, Masimo changed his snogging technique. He began kissing my neck with little soft kisses. From the bit near my earlobes right down to near my collar bone and then back to my mouth. Wow and wowzee wowow! I turned into Melted-neck Girl.

I don't know how long we were out there in the field. And for one of the first times in my life my brain froze. I actually stopped thinking and just felt things. Oo-er. You see now I have started thinking again, but I didn't while he was kissing me.

He ran his hands through my hair. His lips were really soft and sort of firm at the same time. He was talking softly in Italian to me. And every now and again he would look me in the eyes. It was a bit like being hypnotised, but in a nice way.

We should put sticky eyes on the snogging scale I think because it's vair vair nice and groovy and full of the spirit of red-bottomosity.

I felt like all the blood had drained out of my body and I would have stayed there all night attached to his mouth. Then he nip libbled!! He could do nip libbling!!! Dave wasn't the only one who could do it. It was so nice and felt so good that I even had the courage to nip libble him, just a little mousey nibble but a nibble nonetheless. And he liked it. He did that moaney thing. Officially in my *How to Make Any Twit Fall in Love with You* it is the girl who is supposed to do the moaney stuff, but live and let snog I say.

We didn't bang teeth or anything. It was like a mouth dance. And I was Missvairgoodatmouthdancing!!!

And then it happened... number six!

He put just the tip of his tongue in my mouth. It was really sweet. I felt so full of luuurve for him that I put my tongue in his mouth a little bit. And our tongues touched!!! They were snogging as well!!! When you describe it it doesn't sound like it would be very nice, but it is. Perhaps that is why Angus and Gordy put the tips of their tongues out, because they know how sexy tongue touching can be.

No, on second thoughts, I know that they put their tongues out because they are idiot cats.

I was liking the kissing so much that I didn't even think about breathing. I had acquired David Blaineness – I could very possibly not breathe for weeks if the Luuurve God was kissing me.

But then he stopped. Boooooo, stop stopping!!! He said, "Come, Georgia, I must take you home. Your father will like it."

Bollocks to my vati. I wanted more snogging!!

I said, "What time is it? Er, I mean, *Che ora per favore?*"

Masimo gave me a big kiss on my cheek.

"*Mille grazie* for speaking my language. *Sono le dieci.*"

I said, "Ah. Good. Er, *buono*. Yes, marveloso all round."

He said, "You don't know what that is in time, do you?"

"No."

"It is ten o'clock."

Phwoar, we had been snogging for almost two hours. Yesss!!! I bet we had even out-snogged Rosie and Sven.

I said, "Vati said I didn't really have to be in especially at any time tonight. In fact, he said if I wanted to stay out all night that was fine by him."

Masimo put his arm round me. It felt fabby to be held by his lovely armio. "Georgia, I don't think that you are a fibber but maybe... just maybe you are insane."

Then he laughed. "Come on, bad girl. I take you home, your papa is pleased, he thinks I am the good guy, then we go out lots more, no?"

We walked home, stopping every few steps for more snogging. Unfortunately we didn't bump into anyone that I knew. Drat!!! Mind you, every girl that we passed gawped at Masimo. Shutup, gawpers, he is mine all mine mineio. I think.

I hadn't mentioned the Wet Lindsay scenario. In fact I

hadn't really asked him anything about girlfriends, even though I am dying to know.

He asked me about the Guitar Plucker though. He said, "And how do you feel about Robbie now? Do you still like him?"

Hmm. This called for diplomosity with just a hint of caringosity. Under no circumstances did I want him to think I was a minx who just picked up boys and tossed them aside... oo-er.

I said, "I like him as a friend now. He plays the guitar in streams."

Masimo looked at me and said, "I understand."

Which is a plus. And a surprise, actually, as I certainly don't make any sense to myself.

He kissed me at the gate, and he did that varying pressure thingy, and a quick kiss under my earlug... phwoar... and then he sort of shook his shoulders and sighed and said, "OK, *cara*, now we are sensible and good. Sad for me."

He took my hand and led me to my door and rang the bell. Vati came and answered the door. Oh blimey, he was Il Ministrone again. He NEVER smokes cigars, but he happens to be smoking one now. AGAIN. Also he has semi-proper trousers on, not his joggerbums, which make him look like Porkman.

He said, "Well, good, fine. Well, did you have a pleasant evening?"

I was about to say, "What in the name of arse has it got to do with you?"

But Masimo shook his hand!! And he said, "*Buona notte*, Mr Nicolson. Here is your lovely daughter home safe."

He turned to me and kissed my hand and said, "Thank you for a lovely evening. *Arrivederci* till the next time."

Vati went back indoors, shouting out, "*Arrivederci* then." He really does think we are in *The Sopranos.* He'll start having his mates "rubbed out" soon.

As I went through the door I looked after Mr Gorgeous. He turned round and winked at me and blew me a kiss. And he said, "*Subito.*"

In bed, the bed of the Luuurve Goddess

He said "Subito" to me.

How fab is that?

Later

Actually, I don't know how fab it is, as I don't know what it means.

Ten minutes later

Something to do with submarines? I'll have to look it up in my *Idiots Guide to Italian*.

Fifteen minutes later

It means "soon".

That's a bit like "s'later", isn't it?

Oh dear God.

Wednesday June 15th

Walking along with Jas, trying to get a word in edgeways with Mrs Mad.

Tom is back on a flight at 6:15 p.m. That is 6:15 p.m. Do you get it? Not 6:00 p.m. but 6:15 p.m. And do you know how many minutes that is? I do. I have also become a Time Lord.

Jas was actually SKIPPING as we went along to Stalag 14. Dear *Gott in Himmel* I have got a lamb as a mate. She was saying, "OOOooooohhh, I am soooooo excited."

"Yes, I know you are. Look, can I just tell you about Masimo?"

"Do you think he will go home first and drop his bag off or come straight round to mine? I wonder what kind of pressies he has brought me from Kiwi-a-gogo land."

Hopeless trying to talk to her.

Break

Ace Gang meeting.

They all (apart from Jas who has gone off to the woods to "think"... I laughed at first when she said that, but then I realised she was serious)... anyway, what was I saying before... Oh yes, the whole Ace Gang wanted to know about my date.

Rosie said, "So dish the goss. What are our Pizza-a-gogo friends like in the snogging department?"

"Absobloodylutely fabby fab and marv."

Mabs said, "Really?"

"Yep, he did nip libbling, neck nuzzling, tongues, etc."

Ellen said, "Did he, you know, I mean did he..."

I said, "Yep."

Which seemed to satisfy her.

As the bell went Rosie said, "So when are you seeing him again? I mean is he the official boyfriend now?"

Hmmmmm. Good point, well made.

Last period

The Foxwood lads over again for *MacUseless.* Dave smiled at me when he ambled in. Ellen immediatedly dashed off to the loos to apply more lippy.

I wanted to tell him about Masimo, but before I could go and chat to him, Miss Wilson came in to give us her official loon on loon tablets address.

Ellen came in all tarted up and red and sat down near Dave.

Miss Wilson said, "Now then, let us get on with the production in the professional manner that I know you are all capable of."

3:30 p.m.

The witches were making so much racket doing their improvised dance round the fire bit that Hawkeye was attracted into rehearsals. She shouted at them from the door.

"Stop that idiotic prancing around immediately."

Rosie said, "It's our improvised witches' dance, Miss Heaton."

"I don't care what it is, I can hear it in the science lab."

I said to Miss Wilson after she had stormed off, "I don't think Miss Heaton quite appreciates the beauty of the Swan of Avon, Miss Wilson."

Rosie said, "You should tell her that you used to go out with him in the olden days."

Miss Wilson started getting all flustered. "Now, don't be silly, Rosie. Of course I did not go out with William Shakespeare..."

Dave joined in. "Why? Didn't he want to go out with you? Was he too busy or something? The Devil makes work for idle PANTS."

Then it was quite literally all pants from then on.

Miss Wilson finally called it a day when I said, "Macduff was from his mother's PANTS untimely ripped."

As we got our stuff from the cloakroom, Mabs said, "I saw Rachel in town and she is really really upset about her and Dave breaking up."

Ellen has been mooning around him in rehearsal. He's

been quite nice to her actually. I wonder if I would mind if he went out with her. I should, as a great mate, be really pleased if he did go out with her but... anyway.

Ellen and Dave were by the gates as we ambled out to go home. I am in such a good mood. Maybe Dave and she *should* go out again.

As I watched them Dave gave her a little kiss on her cheek and she went bright red. You could tell even from about two hundred yards away, and then Ellen tripped off home. Dave looked after her and then turned round and leaned on the gate. He was chatting to girls as they filed past him. He is a big flirt.

It was just Jas and me walking home because Rosie was off to see Sven for a quick four hour snog in the woods, and Mabs and Jools were going shopping.

Dave came with us as we walked along. I said to him, "Pantsmaster, can I tell you about Masimo?"

Dave looked at me. "Am I going to be able to stop you?"

As we were walking along Jas was saying, "Stop walking so slowly, you lot. Oh, I can't stand this." And she started running. She yelled at us, "I've only got two hours to do my make-up for Tom, coz he likes me just natural."

What was she talking about? As we watched her bottom disappear into the dusk, Dave said, "It's nice, really, isn't it, to be that simple?"

"What? You would like to be as stupid as Jas?"

"No, I mean Jas and Tom. They just like each other and that's it, no sign of the Cosmic Horn or red-bottomosity."

I could feel things getting a bit philosophical and I wanted to talk about snogging. "Dave, I was going to ask you about Mas—"

Dave said, "What if you were really meant to be with someone? But you kept messing about and having the Horn and so on and you lost them."

Oh, brilliant, Dave the Laugh was having one of his unlaugh moments.

Bugger, he had gone all girly. I was going to have to talk about his stuff before I was allowed to get on to the interesting stuff about me and the Italian Stallion.

I said really quickly, "Look, I'm sure that if you went back to Rachel she would forgive you, she is remarkably stup... er... stupendously nice."

Dave looked at me and said, "You just don't get it, do you?"

"Oh, you mean Ellen. She would have you back tomorrow; she has no pridenosity."

He said, "You great kittykat loonie. I am talking about you and me."

"Don't be daft."

Dave didn't say anything, and then he said, "The bigger the PANTS the harder they fall."

What?

The Big Furry Paw of Fate

In my room
5:30 p.m.
What was Dave the Laugh talking about? Besides the pants, I mean. Him and me? Losing the person meant for you. Has he snapped?

6:15 p.m.
Tom will just be landing now – Jas will have gone mad.

6:16 p.m.
Phone rang. It was Jas. I was right.

"Gee, he's here – he is in the same land as me."

Yeah, well, its debatable whether anyone normal is in the same land as Jas, but I let it go.

Amazingly she was prepared to talk about me.

She said, "I'm all ready so I'm going to talk to you and let you talk to me so that I don't go mad, because I reckon it will take about half an hour through customs, he may have brought back some interesting specimens of nature and that might hold him up, and then it will be another hour from the airport and then he might go to his house so that is about 8:30 p.m."

It is truly like talking to the speaking clock.

After we had been through the minutes business again Jas rather unexpectedly remembered that I was alive. "Georgia, you know Masimo?"

"Er... YES!"

"Well, I think you should be, you know, brave with him. I think you should just tell him how you feel and not do glaciosity or anything."

"Really?"

"Yes, I do, because then you would, you know, be like real and not a facsimile of a sham. I mean, even if you convinced him that you were normal, sooner or later you would forget and go back to being you."

"Er, Jas, this is not exactly—"

"It's like your nose, isn't it?"

"My nose?"

"Yes, I mean, say you wore like a nose disguiser."

A nose disguiser?

The strain has finally sent her over the edge.

I said, "You mean from the 'nose-disguiser' shop?"

"Whatever. Well, sooner or later he would discover that you had a big nose."

"It's a generous nose."

"You don't have to tell any of us that, Georgie. Anyway, what I'm saying is, I think you should be you because actually you are quite nice."

She put the phone down then because she decided to change her skirt and wear jeans because Tom might want to go on a ramble when he arrived home.

A ramble?

Be myself?

Not use glaciosity or visit the nose-disguiser shop?

I was feeling a bit unusual.

7:00 p.m.

I went downstairs and Mutti and Libbs were in the kitchen.

They both gave me big smiles when I came in. Mum said, "Hello, darling, you are getting so leggy and pretty and grown-up. Isn't your big sister gorgeous, Bibbity?"

Libbs was in the middle of putting Gordy's slippers on, but she looked up and said, "Hello my Gingey, I lobe you. Kiss Gordy."

I kissed a cat!

I really am losing my grip.

Mum said I was gorgey.

She looked at me as if she was going to cry.

8:30 p.m.

Blimey life is full of confusiosity. Suddenly everyone luuurves me. Dave the Laugh rambling on about what if we were meant to be together, the Guitar Plucker says he misses me... I've kissed Gordy. What next? Hawkeye apologising for confiscating my bison horns?

The phone rang.

Oh God!!! It can't be Hawkeye about the horns, surely!

I yelled downstairs, "Phone!!!"

Mum must be having the usual communal bath with Libby and Angus and Gordy because there was a massive amount of giggling and splashing and shrieking going on. Hang on a minute, there was a man's voice as well. Was Libby doing impressions?

Mum yelled, "Georgia, can you get that?"

I said, "I'm upstairs. Why can't Vati get it?"

Then Vati yelled up, "I'm all wet. You get it; it will be for you anyway."

Oh bloody hell.

As I went to get the phone I had to pass the bathroom and I saw something that may mean counselling for many many years. It was my father with no strides on!! I mean it! He was standing up in the bath, and Mum was in there and Libby, and they were all in the nuddy-pants!!! I almost choked.

I had seen my own father in the nuddy-pants.

With my mum in the nuddy-pants.

Together.

In the nudey-dudeys.

How horrific and unnatural was that?

Still in a state of shock, I answered the phone.

"Hello."

"*Ciao*, Georgia."

Masimo!!!

"I have been thinking about you. I will look forward to seeing you. Can you see me on Saturday?"

I said, "Well, yes that would be. I mean yes, erm..."

"If you can't wait to see me, you could, how you say... come tomorrow night. There is a gang of us going to Late and Live, you know, with Lindsay, like before. Can you come?"

I don't really remember what I said to him.

9:00 p.m.

Phoned Jas. Her mum said, "Hello, love, she's gone out with Tom for a bit of a ramble."

Good grief.

Phoned Rosie. "Rosie."

"Hubble bubble toil and pants."

"Rosie, this is serious. I just spoke to Masimo and you know you were asking me about the is-he-my-boyfriend scenario?"

"*Sí.*"

"Well he asked me out on Saturday, and then he said that if I wanted to see him before then he is going to Late and Live with the gang and Lindsay."

"Crikey."

9:30 p.m.

Phoned all of the gang and now I am really really teetering on the brink of bewildermentosity. I may be driven to talk to my mum again.

9:40 p.m.

I can't get the picture of her in the nuddy-pants out of my head.

I have managed to superimpose a pair of all-encompassing overalls on the mental image of my vati *vis à vis* the bathroom scenario. But I can't do it with Mum because bits of her basoomas keep re-emerging from anything I camouflage her with. Very like in real life.

10:30 p.m.

As it happened, she came up to my bedroom to say good night anyway.

As she was at the door I said, "Mum, if I tell you something, will you promise not to come over all mumish?"

She said, "I'll try. What's going on?"

I told her about the snogging – well, a bit, I skated over the details – well, in fact, I said, "it was a really nice night

and he kissed me good night." I didn't go into the tongues and so on.

Then I told her about him phoning me and asking me out again and then the Lindsay bit.

She sat down on the bed. "Hmm. That is tricky, isn't it? I mean she could be just another mate. He doesn't know a lot of people yet, does he? Or maybe he doesn't want you to get the wrong idea about him being a serious boyfriend."

Oh buggery bum.

Then she thought a bit and said, "Do you know what I think? You have to decide what you want. Ask for it and either get it or, if he doesn't want the same thing as you, you have to accept it. Life is for the brave."

After she had gone I lay in the dark and thought about what she had said.

It was sort of what Jazzy Spazzy had said, even though she went on about the nose-disguiser shop. Even Dave the Laugh had said more or less the same thing.

Yes, well that was it. Ask for what I want and Devil take the hindmost. Good.

Midnight

Yes, but what do I want?

Thursday June 16th

Stalag 14

Love hell

Wet Lindsay seems to be everywhere I look today, adjusting her thong. I am sure she's looking at me as well. I wonder if she knows about me and Masimo? He must be in contact with her, otherwise how would he know that she's going to Late and Live? Also he gave her a lift home the other day. And how do I know how often he sees her anyway?

German

Even Herr Kamyer sitting on his glasses and then not being able to find them because they were stuck on his bottom couldn't cheer me up.

I have to make a decision. I can't go on like this.

Break

Jas is quite literally on Cloud Nine. On and on about Tom. I

wanted to spoil it for her somehow. When she started skipping again (I am not joking, I wish I was) and going "Oh I am soooooo happy", I said, "So are you going to MARRY Hunky and never go out with anyone ever again? For the next fifty years?"

Jas said, "Well, if you found the right person what would be the point of going out with anyone else?"

I said, "Because he might not BE the right person; you might only THINK he was the right person."

"I do think Tom is the right person."

"Yeah, but he might not be."

"Yeah, but he is."

"Yes, but he might not be."

"But he is."

We could have done that for several hours.

7:30 p.m.

Anyway, I am not going to go to Late and Live tonight. The fact is that I am not really brave and sophisticated and a glacial minxy. If I saw Masimo getting off with Lindsay, or anyone else for that matter, I wouldn't like it A LOT. And that is a fact. I am a bit of a jelloid person and I want someone to like me as much as I like them.

And I do like Masimo.

9:00 p.m.

Mooning around. They will be all at Late and Live now. Ooohhhh. I can't stand this.

9:30 p.m.

I can't even speak to Hornmeister Dave, because he said that odd thing the other day on the way home. Surely he isn't serious about me and him. I mean I really really like him. A LOT, and he does make me laugh but... ooohhhh God! It is all quite literally giving me the Cosmic droop.

9:40 p.m.

Went down into the front room. Angus and Gordy were grooming each other. They were both licking each other's heads with their tongues. Aaaah how vair sweet. They loved each other despite everything. Love conquers all. Look at Katheeeee and Heathcliff in *Wuthering Pants* and Jane Eyre and Rochester in *Jane's Pants* and so on.

Just then Gordy licked Angus's fur the wrong way and

Angus biffed him so hard he flew straight off the sofa and into the wastepaper basket.

Vati is out with his lads' army. They have taken up roller skating now and go to this roller dome place where other complete prats career around injuring themselves.

I said to Mum, "I am convinced there is a book called *How to be the Most Embarrassing Dad in History* and it has hints like "Grow an amusing novelty moustache", "Wear leather trousers", "Talk bollocks in front of your teenage daughter's friends", "Pretend to be Il Ministrone", "Adopt a hobby – roller skating or clown-car racing are particularly good".

Anyway, I slumped down on the sofa and Angus got on my knee and started doing that kneading thing they do to make you all comfy. For them. I am like a human bean bag to him. Mum came and sat next to me. She even touched my arm. I let her though because I am too tired to do anything about it.

She said, "You know what you were asking me last night? Well, this is what I think... I think you are not a two-timey sort of person really, it makes you anxious and upset and hell to be with, frankly. Soooo... even though you might be with a person only for a bit, I think you should take that bit seriously so that you act nicely and get the best out of it. And if you have to say goodbye or they have to say goodbye some time, well that is life, and good training for you both for when the right person comes along."

Blimey.

That was almost full of wisdomosity. If I could figure out what in the name of arse she was on about.

I said, "Let me get this, you think I should tell Masimo that I want to be like a girlfriend and boyfriend, and if he doesn't want to then I should probably not see him?"

She nodded.

Crikey, this was all a bit radical.

I liked it when I was led around by the Horn.

When did this acting with maturiosity happen?

Friday June 17th
School

Wet Lindsay was unbearable today. I am sure she is stalking me. Everywhere I went, there she was. I went into the canteen and was sitting there minding my own business, looking through my *MacUseless* script, when she came in

with ADM and another complete loser called Rowena. There were loads of spare chairs to sit on but, oh no, they had to come and sit on the table next to me. Lindsay looked at me like I was a snot creature having my snot lunch. Then they started talking.

Lindsay said, "It was groovy last night, wasn't it? I think it is such a cool venue, and there is an older crowd so you don't get all the crap dancing and useless behaviour. I'm tired again though, it's such a late night midweek and Mas is, you know, well, you know what he is like. Italians, eh?"

And she laughed sort of knowingly and they all joined in.

I couldn't stand this. I got up and walked off.

I wonder if I could just kill her accidentally.

4:10 p.m.

I was waiting at the gate for Jas. she was still dithering around in the loos doing her lippy.

Tom came to meet Jas after school and it was really really nice to see him. He does look a lot like his brother.

He hugged me.

"Georgie how are you? Beyond groovy to see you."

He snogged Jas when she came puffing up. She must have

spent the last class doing her fringe because it looked very nearly normal.

We walked along together. Jas was all over him like a rash. It was vair nice to have him back. He told us all about Kiwi-a-gogo land.

"When you leave they don't say 'goodbye', they say 'hurrah'."

I said, "That seems a bit rude."

Tom said, "I rest my case. I did have a great time though. We did loads of water sports. Surfing and white-water rafting. There is an amazing range of flora and fauna there."

I looked at him. He laughed. "No, perhaps I won't tell you about the wombats. Robbie sends you his love. He said he hadn't heard from you. And he would really like it if you would write back."

Jas looked at me in a "I told you so" way. I hope she is not going to be even more of a Wise Woman of the Forest now that Hunky is back; it is the last thing I need.

There was a bit of an awkward pause. Then Tom said, "Look, Georgia, Robbie is my brother and I love him."

(Hang on, what is going on with blokes? Mincing on about their feelings. There is none of this stuff in *Men are from Knob land Women are from Pink Frilly land* book.)

Tom saw my face and said, "No, Georgia, I am not on the turn. What I mean is, he left you and you can do anything you like. All I am doing is passing on a message. Anyway, I hear there have been developments on the Italian Stallion front."

Radio Jas pretended to be checking her bag.

5:00 p.m.

Jas and Tom left me at Jas's gate and walked up her path with their arms around each other. I felt a bit lonely for my pal. Now that Tom was back I wouldn't have her to myself any more, and I thought about the times in Hamburger-a-gogo land and the nuddy-pants scenario.

Rosie had Sven. Mabs seems to be keen on Tosser's mate, Jools sort of has Rollo, and even Ellen is keen on one of the backstage *MacUseless* people. I was beginning to be a spinster of the parish.

5:10 p.m.

I wandered off lonely as a clud once more and as I walked along I got my mirror out of my rucky and looked in it. OK,

I wasn't the most beautiful girl in the world but I had a nice face (ish) and Masimo had said he liked my eyes. Mind you, who knows what he had said to Lindsay. Surely not "Oh, *cara*, you have the *bueníssimo* tiny forehead."

I put on a bit of lippy and mascara and eyeliner. I would do a bit of hip waggling and flicky hair to cheer myself up. Amazingly, almost immediately a boy leaned out of a car window and went, "Niiiiiice."

Crikey, a bit of lippy and hip waggling and you could rule boyworld. How vair vair superficial they were. On the other hand I liked a good-looking boy myself, and I liked nice hair and I liked Masimo's clothes and scooter. I wouldn't like him just for that though.

Everything is vair vair confusing.

5:20 p.m.

I was crossing the road for home when Masimo sped round the corner on his scooter and came to a halt next to me. He got off and took his helmet off quickly. He didn't say anything, he just came over to me and snogged me. A proper number five. There in the middle of the street.

Oscar and his mates were slouching along trailing their

ruckies on the ground, walking backwards and shouting, the usual boy stuff. When they saw Masimo snog me they all went, "Come on, my son, get in there!!"

And so on. Sensationally mad.

Masimo didn't even notice them. He stopped kissing me and held me at arms' length. "You didn't come last night. I missed you."

I felt all flustered and red and before I could think I blurted out, "Did you? Why? Wasn't Lindsay enough for you?"

Masimo sat down on his scooter seat.

"Georgia, tell me what is all this?"

So I blabbed everything out. Things I didn't even know I was going to say. In other words rubbish probably. Anyway, I told him that I wasn't cut out for callous sophisticosity.

"I know that Dave the Laugh says that we are young and we hear the call of the Horn, and it is true, but I would give up the Horn to see how I felt properly."

Masimo looked a bit puzzled. "The Horn?"

"You know, like red-bottomsity."

"Red-bottomosity."

"You know, when you said you had been burned in the

oven of life and you just wanted to live in Fun City. But I don't want to live in Fun City. Well I do. But not with anyone, just with... anyway. That's what I mean."

Masimo laughed. Crikey, he had a nice laugh.

"Oh, now I see, Signorina Georgia. You are saying you would like me to be your boyfriend."

Blimey.

Now he had said it.

I went all red and stupid.

"Well. I suppose, yes I am. I'm sorry."

He was just looking down at the ground.

Oh God, what had I done?

I tell you what I had done, I had listened to my stupid mother, who hadn't spoken a word of sense since Henry VII was alive. I had listened to someone who couldn't control her breasts. Ohgodohgodohgoddygod. I was a fool.

I had to say something because Masimo was so quiet. I said, "Look, look forget it. I am sorry, *mi dispiace*. I well... it's just me, and you were not even thinking about... oh look, please forget what I said. I just can't do casualosity. It must be something in my genes."

Masimo did look up then.

"You have something in your jeans?"

"No. Look, oh, blimey I had better go. I have a bath to fill and a bottle of gin to buy."

I was about to start crying, I knew it, so I started to cross the road. And Masimo was just sitting there not saying anything.

I got into my house and just leaned against the door shaking. What had I done?

Angus and Gordy were sitting on the top of the bedroom stairs looking at me. Angus was biffing something around with his paw. Some poor little woodland creature, or a spider or something. I knew what it felt like to be biffed around by the big furry paw of fate.

In my room

Oh Goddy God's panties.

The letter from SG was still on my dressing table where I had left it. Another reminder of someone else I had lost. Why did he have to write to me now? I looked at his picture. Did he have to be so gorgey, even when I was eschewing him with a firm hand and had put him in the basket of yesterday? Why was I even bothered? I suppose it was because he was my first true love.

Ohhh booo.

I will NOT cry.

Why did all this happen to me? Had I really been a wasp in a former life, like Jas said?

Five minutes later

They say you always remember your first snog. And that is what he was. I was a snogging virgin until he came along with his guitar plucking.

Two minutes later

Well, he was my first PROPER snog. No one could be expected to count Whelk Boy, unless you were some kind of pervert who liked molluscs.

One minute later

I wonder where the SG's tape is that he made for me when I came back from Froggy land.

I think I put it at the back of my top drawer out of Libby's reach, with my boy entrancers and special-occasion knickers.

Two minutes later

I've found the tape, but where are my boy entrancers and special-occasion knickers? Dad's probably borrowed them.

One minute later

Put Robbie's tape on. I am full of nervosity because I do not want to be on the rack of love for him again. I am already on one rack.

Three minutes later

"Oh no, it's me again" about Vincent Van Gogh remains the most depressing song ever written. SG was not tip-top on the hilariosity front.

Gorgey though.

How full of confusiosity life is.

Two minutes later

Looking out of my window at the empty streets of life. Why does nothing ever go right for me? I could see Mr Next Door gardening in his enormous shorts. He could have a small African nation in them and you would never know. But he has Mrs Next Door to love him, shorts and all. And does he ever go looking for another Mrs Next Door? No he does not. He has big enough shorts to accomodate big red-bottomosity, but he does not use them.

Then I saw Mark Big Gob coming up the street with his lardy mates and with his arm around yet another tiny girl. Why does he like tee tiny girls? More to the point, why do they like him? How could anyone in their right mind snog him?

one minute later

Hang on a minute! Erlack, I'd managed to forget about him resting his hand on my basooma. Get out of my brain!!!

Four minutes later

Oh, Masimo, what have I done? Why did I listen to my stupid mother? I never normally do. She may have ruined my future happiness with her "just be yourself" bollocks. Dave the Laugh warned me, he said that you had just come out of a serious relationship and only wanted to have fun. Why can't I just live in Fun City and not be bothered about Being Really Me City?

What does Dave the sodding Laugh know about it

anyway? He has just finished with Rachel and before that he dumped Ellen. He is a serial heartbreaker.

Although he hasn't broken my heart yet.

In fact he has only ever been a bit mean to me when I used him as my red herring to attract the Sex God.

How many times have I accidentally snogged him? He is a good snogger, it has to be said.

Three minutes later

What did he mean about me and him? He's just my mate. And occasional snog buddy.

Ohhhh. I will never be happy again.

Or eat again.

One minute later

Not that there is ever anything to eat in this place anyway.

In the kitchen

Oh joy unbounded, there is a bit of leftover cold sausage.

What did Dave the Laugh say that really made me laugh when we were doing the battle scene in *MacUseless*? Oh, I know. He was waving a sword around (very nearly cutting off Melanie Griffiths' nungas) and shouting "Pants, pants! My kingdom for some pants!!!"

He is a vair funny person.

In my room

Well, why couldn't I just like Dave?

But then I thought of my night with Masimo when we had looked at the stars together, and I felt like crying.

If only I had had a chance to get to know him, I could have found out all about a different culture. I could have found out about neck snogging and everything. But I had well and truly blown it now. Wet Lindsay will be dancing about on her stick-insect legs when she finds out. Which she is bound to because of Radio Jas.

I wonder if I should phone Jas up and see what she thinks?

Am I mad? I might just as well phone Mrs Mad in Maddingtonshire.

Then I heard the familiar roar of a scooter engine below my window.

The doorbell rang.

I knew I should go and answer the door, but I couldn't

move my legs. Oh, marvellous, I was paralysed! Come on, come on legs, be brave, don't let me down now.

Hahahahahha, I was telling myself really crap inward jokes. Hurrah!

I eventually managed to stagger downstairs.

Oh, *mon Dieu,* I hope I don't inadvertantly go to the poo parlour division.

For confidence I picked up cross-eyed Gordy. He was busily chewing something so he didn't attack me.

I opened the door.

Masimo was there.

Oh God.

He looked at me and his eyes looked so soft and sad.

"Georgia. This is a big thing. Give me a little time. I will see you in a week and I will say yes or no. I will not, how you say. I will not mess about with you. I will say yes or no. *Ciao, cara.*"

And he blew me a kiss and got on his scooter and accelerated off.

I shut the door and stood there holding on to Gordy.

What had I done?

Gordy looked up at me, eye to eyes, and I looked down at

him. He looked at me as if he could see deep into my soul and understood. He even stopped chewing the spider thing he had in his mouth.

And suddenly I understood as well.

It wasn't a spider he was eating...

...And then he ate my boy entrancers.

Georgia's Glossary

boy entrancers · Ah yes. The re-emergence of the boy entrancers. Hmmm... well... boy entrancers are false eyelashes. They are known as boy entrancers because they entrance boys. Normally. However, I have had some non-entrancing moments with them. For instance, the time I used too much glue to stick them on with. It was when I was at a Stiff Dylans gig trying to entrance Masimo. I was intending to do that looking up at him and then looking down and then looking up again, and possibly a bit of flicky hair (as suggested in *How to Make Any Twit Fall in Love with You*). I did the looking-at-him-and-looking-down thing, but when I tried to look up again I couldn't, because my boy entrancers had stuck to my bottom lashes. So my eyes stayed shut. I tried raising my eyebrows (that must have looked good) and humming, but in the end, out of sheer desperadoes, I said, "Oooh, I love this one..." and went off doing blind disco-dancing to Rolf Harris's "Two Little Boys". So, in conclusion, boy entrancers are good, but be alert for glue extravaganzas.

chokey · A prison cell. Also known as pokey. Maybe because they are quite small cells.

chuddie · Chewing gum. This is another "i" word. We have a lot of them in English due to our very busy lives, explaining stuff to other people not so fortunate as ourselves.

David Blaine · For Heaven's sake, don't you know who he is? He's from New York, New York. He stands in blocks of ice for a year without food, and steals peoples watches. He came to England and hung around in a glass cage over Tower Bridge for a month. No one knows why.

fule · Fool. This is a more pleasant way of saying it (ish). It sounds more Christmassy, somehow... "Let's all go sing, a hey nonny no, and bring in the Christmastide fule for the fire", and so on.

hangi · in Kiwi-a-gogo land when Maoris have a picnic, they don't bother lugging sandwiches, flasks and so on; they get some beer and drink it, then they dig a big hole and put hot coals in it, then they chuck in six hundred pounds of sausages, eight sheep, hu hu bugs, etc. Then they fill in the hole with earth and leave it to cook all afternoon. The Maoris chat and play poi poi, then they dig up the food and tuck in. Yum yum. (Unless you get a hu hu bug, in which case erlack a pongo.)

Immac · A cream you use to remove evidence of the orang-utan gene. Hair remover.

Land of the Big White Clots · Now I am glad you asked me this, because it is a hilarious play on words. (It is, believe me.) Anyway, this is it. Kiwi-a-gogo land is called something in Maori that translates as "Land of the

Big White Clouds". But I have changed "clouds" to "clots" to hilarious effect, because it implies that Kiwi-a-gogo land is full of clots. Hahahahahahahhaha!

Oh dear God, you don't know what clots are, do you? I can feel my life ebbing away. But as it's you and I love you so much, I'll go on. Clots is an olde Englishe worde for "fool" i.e., a person who is in between a twit and a tosser.

laters · plural of s'later. Really, if I was being a nit-picking swotty-knickers (i.e., Jas) I would always say "laters" when I said s'later to the Ace Gang because they are plural. However, I am not Jas (hurrah!), so I say what I like.

O.A.P. card - stands for Old Age Pensioner card. This is a card to identify the elderly mad in our midst. It's supposed to mean that they show their card and get on buses for free and get cheap tickets at the cinema and so on, but really it's to alert people to their presence so that they can be ejected when they start causing trouble. You know the sort of thing – rattling their sticks and clacking their boiled sweets against their false teeth in the quiet bits of the film.

oeuvre · Now this means... er... hang on a minute, maybe it IS the french plural for eggs? Now you've got me all confused. *Un oeuf*, two *oeufs*... it's not two *oeuvre,* is it? Any fool would know that. Yes, I am pretty sure that it means "work", as in work of art. And not egg. Look, just leave it.

phased · A bit put out by something. Full of confusiosity and redness, and inward mayhem.

Pizza-a-gogo land · Masimoland. Land of wine, sun, olives and vair vair groovy Luuurve Gods. Italy. The only bad point about Pizza-a-gogo land is their football players, who are so vain that if it rains they all run off the pitch so that their hair doesn't get ruined.

quiff · You put some gel on your hair and make the front bit stick up in a wave. Elvis had one.

red-bottomosity · Having the big red bottom. This is vair vair interesting *vis à vis* nature. When a lady baboon is "in the mood" for luuurve, she displays her big red bottom to the male baboon. (Apparently he wouldn't have a clue otherwise, but that is boys for you!) Anyway, if you hear the call of the Horn, you are said to be displaying red-bottomosity.

score · Twenty pounds. (You are obsessed with money.) Score is a numbering system from Henry VIII's times. "Three score year and ten" meaning 70 years. The Hamburger-a-gogo types have no idea of the amount of words we have to remember in our land. They are very lucky that they made up their own language and can miss letters out – like aluminum and 'erbs instead of aluminium and herbs and so on.

sidies · Bits of face hair that men grow down the sides of their ears to their chins. If you are asking me why, try asking the Hamburger-a-gogo people, as I believe you will find George Washington started it.

slag · Slag is a lovely, complimentary word for girls, meaning madam. No it's not, it's a word that means "you are a rough, common, tarty girl with very low moral standards".

spangelfurkel · A kind of German sausage. I know. You couldn't make it up, could you? The German language is full of this kind of thing, like *lederhosen* and so on. And *Goosegot.* Vair vair good value.

squid · In English currency a pound is called a quid. (I don't know why, to be frank with you, but what I do know is that it is nothing to do with Harry Potter and quidditch, so don't even go there.) Squid is the plural of quid, and I do know why that is. A bloke owed another bloke six pounds or six quid and he goes up to him with an octopus with one of its tentacles bandaged up, and he says, "Hello, mate, here's the sick squid I owe you." Do you see? Do you see?? Sick squid – six quid??? The marvellous juxtaposition of... Look, we just call pounds squids. Leave it at that. Try and get on with people.

strop · A strop is number three on the famous "losing it" scale. This is as follows:

1. minor tizz
2. complete tizz and to do
3. strop
4. a visit to Strop Central
5. FT (funny turn)
6. spazattack
7. complete ditherspaz
8. nervy b (nervous breakdown)
9. complete nervy b
10. ballisiticisimus

truncheon · A fat piece of wood for policemen to bop criminals on the head with, or twirl about for a laugh. I have been told (by Jas so I am not relying on it), that the Hamburgese say "baton". But why their policemen have the time to conduct orchestras at work, I do not know.

updated snogging scale · Jas had a nervy b when I suggested adding "sticky eyes" as number one on the snogging scale. She said that would mean that everything else had the wrong number and that we would not know whether we had done number six or not, and so on. I said, "You speak for yourself, Jas. If someone sticks their tongue in my mouth, I will be the first to know." But, anyway, as she went sensationally red I came up with my expected stroke of geniosity. "Sticky eyes" is number a half on the snogging scale and "neck nuzzling" (mmmmm – dreamy) slips in (oo-er) at six and three quarters.

Turn the page for a sneaky peek at my next book...

www.georgianicolson.com

Friday June 17th

on the rack of romance

And also in the oven of luuurve.

And possibly on my way to the bakery of pain.

And maybe even going to stop along the way to get a little cake at the cakeshop of agony.

Shutup brain shutup.

9:01 p.m.

In my bedroom looking out of my window at the stars.

It says in my *Meditation for Fools* book that it is very soothing looking at the universe and stars and everything.

Ommmm.

9:03 p.m.

God stars are annoying. Winking and blinking like twinkly idiots. No wonder they are so cheerful: they know nothing of the call of the Horn and snogging. They don't know what it is like to be me. Does anyone tell them to get into their PE knickers and rush about getting red? No. Do Luuurve Gods say, "I will let you know in a week's time if I want to go out with you or not."? No.

9:03 and a half p.m.

Anyway what are they actually for? You can't even read by them. They just hang about. Like dim torches.

9:07 p.m.

Oh brilliant! Every grey cloud has an even greyer lining; I can hear the powerful sound of a battery-driven Loonmobile. Hurrah the Swiss Family Mad are back! Still, my door is shut and it is quite obvious that I want a bit of privacy. That is what a closed door implies.

9:08 p.m.

That and the notice on it that reads KEEP OUT EVERYONE AND THAT MEANS YOU VATI.

9:10 p.m.

Oh good. My darling little sister has kicked open my door and flung Angus at me.

"HEGGOOOO Gingey!!! We is back. Heggo!! Watch my panties dance. Sex bum, sex bum, am a sex bum!!!"

Oh dear *Gott* in *Himmel*. Angus was livid at being thrown and once he'd stopped doing that cat sneezing and shaking thing he dug his claws into my ankle. Owwwwwww. Now I'm on the way to the cakeshop of aggers with a gammy leg. Hurray!!!

Libby put her frock over her head and waggled her botty around like a pole dancer. Where does she see people doing these things?

Then Mum came mumming in and scooped up Bibbs.

"Time for Boboland young lady."

Libby carried on singing and wiggling around in Mum's arms, and then Mum noticed me. Being in my bedroom.

"What are you up to, Georgia? Why are you in here?"

I said, "Not that anyone notices but this is actually my room. You know, for ME being in. I was in bed as it happens."

Mum said as she went out, "Oh you must be sooo tired,

all that lip gloss and mascara to carry round all day."

Vair vair amusing. Not.

9:25 p.m.

I've been in my bedroom for two hours since Masimo left me at my door saying he would let me know if I was his girlfriend or not. Why did I admit I wanted him to be like my proper boyfriend? Why why?

9:26 p.m.

And also thrice why? Whywhywhy? Why couldn't I have just been a callous sophisticate? Why? I could for once have just shut up and been all full of casualosity and *savoir* whatsit.

9:30 p.m.

If I'd played my cards right I could have had loads of boyfriends. All at the same time. Masimo the Italian Stallion for a weekendy boyfriend, with a touch of Dave the Laugh for a rainy weekday. And also maybe even have the former Sex God (whose name I wasn't going to mention even beyond the grave) as a sort of Kiwi-a-gogo airmail boyfriend. But oh no I had to moan on about wanting to be Masimo's one and only.

9:40 p.m.

I was so happy snogging Masimo under the stars on our date. Stars didn't get on my nerves then. Nothing did.

Saturday June 18th

11:40 p.m.

I'm going mad. In fact things are so sheer desperadoes that I am going to have to phone the Big Knickered One and hope she doesn't ramble on about bat droppings.

Phoned Jas.

"Jas?"

"Sorry I'm out at the moment."

"Jas, please don't try and be amusing. Just be yourself. I have something *sehr schiessenhausen* to tell you."

"What have you done now? Stuck your toe up the bath tap?"

"Jas, I—"

"Thought it would be funny to paint a false moustache on your face but did it with indelible ink?"

"Jas I—"

"Shaved one side of your hair off?"

"Jas, shut up!!! Have you finally and completely snapped? Why would anyone paint a false moustache on their face with indelible ink?"

"I don't know. Why would anyone shave off their eyebrows?"

"Well, that was different, as you know I was using Vati's razor and—"

"Why would anyone go to a party dressed as a stuffed olive and paint their head and neck red as the stuffed pimento bit?"

"Actually, Jas, that was your idea – the stuffed bit. I was only thinking of being an olive, it was you that—"

"Why would anyone stick their false eyelashes together so that they couldn't open their eyes and then go dancing off to Rolf Harris's 'Two Little Boys'?"

"Jas, I really hate you when Tom gets back, you are so full of yourself."

I was absolutely full of lividosity, but she was so much in Jas 'n' Tom land that she didn't even notice I was going to kill her when I saw her. She just went on rambling for Europe.

"Oooh it's so groovy that he's back! I only saw him briefly yesterday. Only eight short hours but he is going to bring around his flora collection from Kiwi-a-gogo land in a bit and that will be sooo... oh..."

"Indescribably dull?" I said.

She said, "I have to go now."

"Jassy Wassy, can I come and see you? I need your help."

"No."

Jas's bedroom

3:00 p.m.

I am lying amongst Jas's sad collection of stuffed toys, mostly owls, while she ponces around in front of a mirror. What is she doing?

I said, "Jas it's very distracting trying to tell you stuff, important stuff full of tragicosity about me, your very bestest pally, when you keep pouting like a goldfish. What are you doing?"

"I'm practising puckering."

"What?"

"Puckering. I had, well, a bit of a problem *vis à vis* snogging with Tom last night."

Despite my world coming apart at the seams I am always interested in snogging tales.

"Tell me."

"Well, I was quite nervy at first when I was waiting for him."

"Were you doing your annoying flicky fringe thing?"

"I don't know... anyway, when he came in I was sort of jelloid. But then it was all right because he got his whatsits out."

"Pardon?"

"His, you know, snapshots from Kiwi-a-gogo land. As we were looking at them Tom got closer to me and put his arm around me. Then we... well... we, you know, started snogging and so on."

"And so on? What number did you get to?"

"Er... five and a bit of six. It was really groovy, I felt like I was all melting in to him and then... well... then I had sort of a lip spasm."

"A LIP SPASM???"

"Well I got cramp in my lips and they sort of seized up?"

"What does that look like?"

And she showed me. Blimey. You know when you put food in a baby's mouth and they don't like it and their eyes go all goggly and then their whole face goes into a spasm and the food comes shooting out of their mouth? Well even if you don't know, believe me I do. Libby could make rice pudding reach the other side of the room.

While Jas was showing me her spazzy face I said, "If you don't mind me saying, Jas, that is not very attractive."

She said, "I expect it was snogging withdrawal. I hadn't puckered up for ages so, you know, I was out of practice. But it won't happen again."

"Good."

"Because I have an exercise regime now. Shall I show you?"

"No."

"OK. It goes pucker, relax, pucker, relax, pucker, relax. Do you see?"

I didn't say anything, I just lay there staring at her with big starey eyes like the rest of the owls as she pouted her lips and then relaxed them. She looked like a mixture of Mick Jagger and an idiot. Not necessarily in that order.

She was in full ramble mode now.

"And then for the pièce de résistance it's darty tongue, darty tongue."

God it was horrible sitting there while her little tongue went in and out like a mad vole. Fortunately I was able to shove a Midget Gem in her gob so that I could continue with the sad tale of my Italian Stallion.

10 minutes later

She said (chewy chew), "So you said that he had to be your one and only boyfriend scenario or else that was it? *Arrivederci* Masimo?"

I said, "Yes, but—"

"Well, what in the name of Slim's outsize pyjamas were you thinking of? Are you mad?"

"No I'm not mad, Jas, I just happen to have a friend who looks a lot like you who said, 'Just be yourself.'"

"What?"

"You said being yourself and genuine was like having a generous nose. Like I have got. The exact words used were, 'Just because you have a generous nose, don't go to the nose-disguiser shop, let your own nose run free and wild.'"

"What complete fool said that?"

"YOU did, Jas."

"Did I? Well yeah, but I didn't mean it, did I? Clearly.

That was in the sanctity of our own brains, wasn't it? I mean we were going to the PRETEND nose-disguiser shop. I didn't actually mean you should BE yourself. That is just stupid."

I really really could kill her. In fact if I just attacked her stupid fringe suddenly she might choke on her stupid Midget Gem and that would be good.

Sadly Jas had got interested now. She said, "So let me get this right – he's choosing between you and Wet Lindsay? Blimey, does she know that? Because if she does you are dead as a doughnut. Deader."

Cheers.

Back in my bedroom of pain
9:30 p.m.

I had better plan what I am going to wear the day he comes round to see me. It may be the deciding factor between happiness and sadnosity.

I must make sure he doesn't see me in my school uniform: it will only remind him that I go to school.

9:40 p.m.

Oh what larks, I think I may be developing a lurker on my chin. Perfect, it should just be nicely ripening into a massive red puss-filled second chin by this time next week. I must take evasive action.

Five minutes later

I think you are supposed to draw lurkers out with ye olde poulticey thingy so that they come to a head quickly. What can I use as a poulticey type thingy?

In the bathroom

I have just looked in the "medical chest" and it has got some mouldy old oranges, a leg from Libby's Pantalitzer doll and some dried cat poo in it. How disgusting.

Mutti and Vati's bedroom

I've found some corn plasters in a drawer. Maybe they would do. I'll stick one over the top of the lurker.

Before I do I'll just squeeze it a bit to see if I can get anything out.

Five minutes later

Bloody hell now it really does hurt. And it's redder than Jas's head when she gets her enormous knickers in a twist. And that is very very red believe me. What can I do to calm it down. Maybe it needs something to dry it up – something with alcohol in it...

Sherry. Would that be good?

Two minutes later

Oh that is disgusting and sticky.

One minute later

Vati's aftershave has got alcohol in it. I'll try a dab.

Owwwwww buggering hells biscuits!!! Ow and owwy ow ow!

Ow.

Two minutes later

I'll put the corn plaster on now.

Well that is attractive. Not.

But who said that love was painless?

11:00 p.m.

God the lurker is throbbing. I hope the corn plaster isn't drawing anything else out. I don't want to wake up with no chin.

One minute later

Loony alert.

Bang bang crash. Why can no one in my family open a door normally. Crashing around when starving people with two chins are trying to sleep!

I heard Dad say, "Good grief! What is that smell?"

Mum said, "It's coming from Georgia's room."

Oh please leave me alone.

Dad yelled up the stairs, "I know that smell, it's my expensive aftershave. GEORGIA, WHAT THE HELL HAVE YOU BEEN UP TO NOW?"

Oh dear Lord. Rave on...